The Carpathian Assignment

The True History of the Apprehension and Death of Dracula Vlad Tepes, Count and Voivode of the Principality of Transylvania

Chip Wagar

Copyright © 2014 by Chip Wagar

All rights reserved. This book or any portion thereof may not be reproduced or used in any manner whatsoever without the express written permission of the publisher except for the use of brief quotations in a book review.

ISBN: 1495498905
ISBN 13: 9781495498909
Library of Congress Control Number: 2014902888
CreateSpace Independent Publishing Platform
North Charleston, South Carolina

Printed in the United States of America
First Printing, 2014

"I shall not wholly die, and a great part of me will escape the grave."

– Quintus Horatius Flaccus,
The Odes of Horace

Preface

In the old Empire of Austria-Hungary, the honorary title of 'knight' was the first order of aristocracy. My grandfather was a knight, termed a "Ritter" in the German language of Austria he spoke as a young man from Budapest. The same designation in his native Magyar tongue was a "Lovag." There were many knightly orders commonly used during the centuries when knighthood fluourished in Europe. Some were honorary. Some were hereditary. The Order of the Golden Fleece, for example, was the Order of the Kaiser of Austria and King of Hungary. At the end of the 19th century, nearly all of its members were of the ruling Habsburg dynasty or other royal houses of Europe. Other orders were created for warriors who had earned the honor for deeds of heroism or bravery in battle. My grandfather's title was of the latter. His name was Kálváry Istvan and he was a member of the Order of St. Stephan, the patron saint of Hungary and its most famous king.

I write my grandfather's name the way he wrote it: in the Magyar style with the last name first. Hungary is still the only country in Europe to invert names and is the land of the Magyars, one of the last invading tribes sweeping into Europe from Central Asia in the Dark Ages. The term "Magyar" describes both the people and the peculiar language they speak, unlike any other in Europe.

My grandfather was, above all, a Hungarian in his heart and temperament. Proud, stoic, and with immense personal courage, he was typical of the gentry of Hungary who, through the ages, often exhibited a reckless disregard of their own safety in the pursuit of a sacred cause. He did not, however, share the rebellious spirit of the Hungarians who chafed and bridled at authority, as they insisted on their rights and dignity to a fault. This was, no doubt, due to his military training and career. His loyalty to the Crown as a military officer and a knight was unquestioning and absolute while at the same time, he had a discerning mind and temperament. His proud bearing never interfered with listening to the opinions and advice of others but once convinced of a correct course of action, he plunged in with the élan of a Hungarian hussar at the head of a cavalry charge.

This is, in part, the story of my grandfather, Kálváry Istvan, and his battle against an extraordinary adversary, known in these times as Count Dracula of Transylvania and, in other times, by other names. In part, it is also the story of confrontation between good and evil, between science and religion, logic and superstition and between the ancient and the modern. My grandfather was fully aware of the history of the death of Count Dracula, published at the end of the last century by Abraham Stoker. Details of that account came most prominently from the English solicitor, Jonathan Harker. His narrative was known in detail by my grandfather for more than a decade. As he reached the end of his life, he confided in me the "rest of the story."

My grandfather never wanted to embarrass Mr. Harker, with whom he corresponded for many years after the events told here. Yet the Transylvanian part, as told by Mr. Stoker, omitted many integral details. Whether this was at the request of Mr. Harker or, perhaps his friend and patron, Arthur Lord Godalming, we never knew. In part, it must have been because much of the background of the monster with whom Mr. Harker became acquainted, Bram Stoker could not have known. Yet, at least in part, it must also have been because the truth regarding many details would have scandalized Mr. Harker for reasons that will become clear in the telling of this tale.

Omitting the context, background, and many pertinent details would have, in time, robbed humanity of knowing extraordinary persons and fascinating aspects of this great story that deserve to be told. Hence, this "unabridged" account you are about to read. With Mr. Harker's untimely death during the Great War, which succeeded my grandfather's by three years, I have been free to publish this account and honor my grandfather's request not to publish it in his or Jonathan Harker's lifetime.

This book is based upon a number of contemporary sources. They include my grandfather's diary from his days in Bistritz, a scrapbook containing many things he collected such as telegraphs, letters, and photographs. It includes conversations I myself had with my grandfather late in his life when he visited me in Vienna, as well as from conversations with his second wife, his colleagues in the police forces of the former Royal Kingdom of Hungary, and other witnesses of less importance who confirmed many of the details.

The central events of this story occurred in the mountainous country near the city of Bistritz, then within the kingdom of Hungary, and, in turn, within the late Austro-Hungarian Empire. The Principality of Transylvania, which is today within the Kingdom of Romania, is one of the most starkly beautiful places you could ever see in Europe. Its violent, tumultuous history is unquestionably due to its location at one of those crossroads of Europe that perpetually provoke invasion and conquest. Too Balkan for Hungary, too Christian for Turkey, too Magyar for Austria, the people of Transylvania were a heterogeneous admixture of races and religions united in their fear and suspicion of outsiders who invariably and consistently sought to oppress them.

My grandfather, Kálváry Istvan, began as a common soldier in the Austrian army at the age of sixteen in 1856, the eldest son of a silversmith. He was born and raised in Old Buda, now part of the Hungarian capital of Budapest. At nineteen, he served in the war with Piedmont in 1859 and had risen to the rank of sergeant by the time of the war with Denmark in 1861. His cool, professional leadership and intelligence was noticed by a superior officer. He was offered and accepted study at the Military College in Mödling in Lower Austria to become an officer in the Imperial Army in 1862. There he learned the German language essential to high command in those days.

In the War of 1866 with Prussia and Italy, my grandfather had by then achieved the rank of captain in the cavalry and served under the Archduke Albrecht in Italy. He distinguished himself again at Custoza, where the Italian army was defeated. He was wounded in the leg during that battle while capturing an artillery battery. For heroic bravery in action, he was knighted and enrolled into the Order of St. Stephan by Kaiser Franz Joseph himself, after the war. Thereafter, he was entitled to be addressed as Gnädiger Herr, by the Austrians, or Úr by the Hungarians, both of which were honorifics and the equivalent of "Sir" in England.

My grandfather married my grandmother, Julia, an Austrian innkeeper's daughter, while attending the Military College in Mödling. My mother, Renata, was the oldest child and her brother, Matthias, the younger. At the time of the events in this book, I was about four years old, living in Vienna with my mother and father, Max Dietrich, who was a university professor.

My grandfather's spectacular military career had just ended in 1896 when this story begins. He was a widower, having lost my grandmother Julia to an influenza epidemic two years earlier. After forty years of service to the crown at the age of 56, now with the rank of colonel, my grandfather contemplated a lonely retirement on half-pay. Given his experience and prominence in his later years as Chief of Detectives in the Royal Military Police, friends at Court in Budapest obtained for him a Carpathian assignment upon his retirement as Chief of Police of the Bistritz district in Transylvania. Here my widower grandfather arrived to take up his appointment in the early spring of 1896 with all his personal belongs. It is here where this remarkable story begins.

Stefan Dietrich
Vienna, 1924

Chapter 1

The young woman hurrying down a dark street was lost in thought, remembering the consuming passion of the afternoon's tryst that had extended on into the early evening and kept her from hearth and husband. Her lover was young and strong and their secret meetings had been going on for two months, ever since she had met him at a Christmas party. The woman had already thought of the excuse she would use for her husband for being late, but she still hoped to get to their house before he arrived and the need arose. She had set out late though, and would have to walk very fast to have a chance to precede his arrival home. As her mind flitted between the erotic and the anxious, she heard the sound of horses' hooves and the crack of a groom's whip close behind her. She turned to see the source of the audible interruption.

Coming toward her out of the darkness, she saw a beautiful *calèche*. Its gleaming black enamel gilded in gold leaf reflected the moon, the stars, and the hissing, sputtering gas lamps on its mirror-like surface. The spokes of the carriage wheels slowly spun bright yellow in contrast to the shining black veneer of the coach as it approached. The silhouette of the driver's high, top hat; two black stallions, steam shooting from their nostrils, blinders on their eyes; gold sconce lanterns glowed on each side ahead of the doors. The coachman wore a heavy cloak and scarf drawn up over his chin obscuring his face.

She kept glancing backward as she hurried along. As the carriage neared, she realized it was slowing and easing closer, toward her side of the street. She continued walking but could not help herself and looked back again as the coach drew closer. The clip-clopping of the horses' hooves was the only sound she heard. Nobody else was in sight as the carriage pulled even with her. It had now slowed to a walking pace. The coachman called down from his seat.

"Madame. It is cold. My carriage is empty. May I offer you a ride?"

The voice was deep and she looked up. His face was pale under the black hat. As the flame from the lamp flickered momentarily, she could see his dark eyes and thin, pursed lips as he waited for her reply. Despite the hard look of the man in the cold night air, she felt increasingly tempted to accept his invitation. She glanced into the window of the *calèche*. Indeed, it was empty. But as soon as she looked away from the coachman, a feeling of dread welled up inside her mind. She didn't know where it came from, but it was like the feeling of being tracked by a wolf determined to kill her unless someone or something intervened to stop it. The feeling of deepest fear and dread increased as she saw no one and nothing nearby to help her.

She looked back up at the driver. Immediately, her panic subsided. He nodded toward her genially, never taking his eyes off hers. As she looked, she noticed the sclera of both his eyes were completely bloodshot and red, but the more she looked into his eyes as the flame in the sconce danced, the more kindly she felt toward the man. He seemed to respond with a faint smile. Then silently, smoothly, somehow he was down out of his seat, next to her, as if by magic. Somehow he had descended from his seat to the pavement and now he reached for the handle of the door. His long fingers were encased in black leather gloves. Slowly the door opened. In gold, centered in the middle of the door's window frame was engraved the letter "D".

The door swung open to reveal a plush, red-cushioned interior. Again, she felt a dread in her heart surge throughout her body. She thought she smelled the odor of dirt from within the carriage: a wet, earthy smell making her slightly nauseous. She backed away from the door. The coachman bowed to her from the waist, removing his top hat as he did so in a sweeping gesture of deference and respect. At that precise moment, a cold gust of wind suddenly kicked up, blowing snow flurries into her face and sending a chill down her spine.

"Please, Madame. There is no reason to suffer so. Where are you going, Madame?"

It was too late. As the coachman had bowed and taken his eyes from hers, a nameless, mindless terror came over her. Something was wrong. Something was terribly wrong. She knew it as certainly as she had ever known anything, and yet the source of the danger was still obscured. She knew it was there, though. Her only thought now was flight. *Flee from this carriage and this coachman,* she thought. *Flee although you don't know the reason. Just go.*

And she went. She turned her back on the coachman and practically ran away from him down the street. She didn't look back, but before long faintly, ever so faintly, she could hear in the distance the clip-clop of the horses as they started up. There was a small alley between the backs of two rows of houses and she quickly darted into it. There were deep shadows there. The alley was lit only by occasional chinks of light from a couple of shuttered windows in the walls of the adjoining houses on the badly cobbled street. She hurried down the alley, hoping to be more deeply hidden by the darkness when the carriage would overtake her and the coachman, perhaps, might peer down from his seat into the dark alley.

As the woman hurried into the protective darkness, she could see the street at the other end of the alley. It was a lighter shade of grey and she could make out objects on the other side of it. *A low fence, perhaps?* Something scurried across her path, something alive with tiny claws clicking on the stones. The carriage was about to come into view at the end of the alley behind her. She pressed herself up against the closest wall in the darkness. In her periphery, she watched first the black stallions, then the yellow wheel, then the coachman, high up on his seat. She saw his profile. His top hat. His whole head turned as the carriage rolled to a stop. She held her breath and felt her heart pounding in her chest. The white tatting trimming her bodice trembled rhythmically and she was afraid he could see it in the dark. The seconds ticked past. She listened, straining to hear whether the coachman got down from his seat and stepped into the alley after her, but no. The carriage started up again and, in a moment, the clip-clopping began to fade away.

She felt sick with nameless terror. She ran toward the far end of the alley. As she neared the far street, she suddenly heard it. The distinct sound of horses hooves and she knew before she saw it that it was the same calèche and coachman. She was still in the dark alley a few paces from the end where it met the street when the black carriage pulled up in front of her not three meters away.

The face of the coachman, pale and hard. The dark eyes. The red lips and a faint, mocking smile. She felt herself go weak. She turned to run away, but as she turned around, there was another figure there. Behind her. It was the coachman again, standing there. He stretched his arms out on either side, his dark cloak opening, as if beckoning her to embrace him.

Not possible, she thought. *Impossible!* She turned to run away from him, but there he was again. Now hunched forward in the seat, tipping his top hat toward her in greeting. Snickering. Back again. He was right behind her again. She felt herself blacking out. Falling. Falling. Then she realized the coachman was carrying her into the carriage. And she was blacking out again. Vaguely, she heard the crack of his whip and the horses. Then she passed out for good.

The lamplighter watched as the calèche pulled away slowly with the woman that had been walking on the street a moment earlier now inside, where she was tossed. As the coachman cracked his whip over the horses, he turned for a moment and looked at the lamplighter. Burning red eyes met his with a look of hate and contempt. The lamplighter had seen that look before. He had seen that carriage before. The carriage rattled down the cobblestoned street with what, he knew, was its doomed passenger. He knew she would never be seen again. But what could he do? The poor woman, he thought. The poor woman.

Chapter 2

Kálváry Istvan left Budapest on the Transcarpathian line on March 24, 1896. After watching his luggage loaded, Istvan had settled into one of the coach compartments and waited to see who would join him, if anyone. Passengers looking through the window into his car saw a distinguished looking, retired officer of His Majesty's Royal Cavalry wearing a light grey, military tunic with brass buttons and a high, round collar embroidered in gold. Above the collar was a handsome head with thinning black hair parted in the middle with a touch of gray at the sideburns ending at the base of his ears. Long, still-dark eyebrows arched over large, brown eyes and continued laterally, down to the junction of his upper and lower eyelids. He had a masculine, pointed nose and a bushy, salt and pepper military moustache, but otherwise was clean shaven. Istvan was tall, slender and quite fit for his fifty-six years due in large part to the physical demands of his long and active military career, but also to his passion for horseback riding.

A cold, late winter wind had blown across the Hungarian plains from the mountains, after his departure from Budapest bringing snow and ice in its wake. Since Margitta, the rolling Hungarian plain had given way to the ever-rising Carpathian mountain chain curving in an arc from northwest to the southeast as a sort of backbone to the Kingdom of Hungary. For centuries these mountains had protected Hungary and Budapest from invasions by barbaric hordes from the East. Istvan lit his pipe and watched the smoke curl upward and then out the window he had left cracked open at the top.

The mountains also formed an informal, physical border between the old kingdom of Royal Hungary and Transylvania, the vast province captured by the ancient Hungarian king Stephen in 1003 and incorporated into his kingdom.

The train had been delayed at several stations after entering Transylvania and its mountain passes. Parts of the track had to be cleared of snow. They had stopped for hours at *bahnhofs* further along the line while still more track and mountain passes had to be dug out from the blizzard. At Klausenberg-Cluj, the train had stopped again. The conductor had advised Istvan they would be waiting for several more hours. Istvan got off the train to stretch his legs and had dinner alone in the station's restaurant as snow flurries continued to fall outside.

It was after midnight when the train started chugging out of the station with a whistle-hoot and clouds of steam. Istvan dozed off soon thereafter, vaguely aware the train stopped several times during the night either at small country stations or in mountain passes where once again, snow had made the tracks impassable. In the morning, he was awakened by the conductor pushing a trolley of hot biscuits and coffee. Istvan gladly purchased a small pot with some rolls and watched the stunning scenery pass by his window as he ate and drank. The windows were ice cold and the morning had dawned with a bright sun and dark blue sky. Rocky crags of high mountain peaks passed as the train rolled on.

It was a new day, Istvan thought. Perhaps it would give him some reason for living. He was lost without Julia. It had been nearly two years since she had died, shattering his dream of retiring with her to a country home and traveling to long-postponed places he still wanted to see. He had stayed with his daughter and her family after the funeral but eventually, he had to return home. The apartment in Budapest was silent and empty without her to the point where he almost could not bear it. He gladly accepted investigations outside of Budapest to get away from the nothingness that enveloped him when he locked the door behind him at night or spent the hours wandering the streets and parks of Budapest or sitting alone at a café, miserable.

The prospect of his impending retirement had filled him with dread. He envisioned days, weeks and months of purposeless existence and contemplated suicide. He confided in one of his colleagues his melancholy vision of life after retirement from the Army as the day grew ever nearer. Istvan sipped at his coffee. He heard the chuff-chuff of the train laboring up another steep incline through the mountains. A dark tunnel and then bright sunshine again as the train emerged on the other side of another mountain. Then began the process again. He looked at his pocket watch. He estimated it would be late in the afternoon when they arrived in Bistritz, assuming there were no further delays.

A letter had arrived one day from the chancellery in Budapest. Word of his situation had reached the King's ear, who had been reminded of his valor and wounds at Custoza and the knighthood he had bestowed after the war was over. Yes, of course. His Majesty would be pleased to appoint his retiring, loyal subject, *der Oberst* Kálváry Istvan, to the post of *Chef der Politzei* of the Bistritz District in his Majesty's Crownland of Transylvania. A Royal Patent and Commission was duly delivered by an equerry from the Palace and, as was the custom in those days, he personally thanked the King and Kaiser, Franz Joseph, at a levee a month later. Over a hundred recently appointed ministers, governors, mayors, and generals made their way to the receiving line to greet and thank the sixty-six year old monarch for one appointment or another. He spoke to each of them in turn for a few moments before they excused themselves with a bow.

"Ah, yes, Kálváry! It pleases us to see you again, especially when we hear your long and loyal service to our Army is coming to an end," the king said with restrained but still obvious pleasure, coming forward and taking Istvan's arm with his white, gloved hand, a gesture of signal honor. The King remained true to ancient monarchical protocols and never shook hands with anyone outside his immediate family. He did not do so now, but his penetrating blue eyes gazed intently at Istvan as he continued. "It is so very comforting nowadays to see comrades from the War. So many of them have already passed on, you know."

"Where did the time go, your Majesty?" Istvan returned. "I was just a boy when I began and look at me now ..."

"You? Look at me. I have ten years on you, Colonel. I, too, was just a boy when I started. If I had only known then what I know now." The king smiled, indulgently. His fondness and gratitude toward members of his Army was well known, especially officers of high rank who had reached their position through merit, as he knew Istvan had.

"Indeed. I often think the same. I want to express my thanks for this position you have seen fit to ..."

"Yes, yes ..." the king interrupted. "But it is our people who will benefit from this assignment, we are very sure," the king said with a suddenly serious look. "You have ever served us and our House all your adult life. We follow our officers' fortunes more closely than you might expect. We heard of your sad loss. I was meeting the Tsar in Poland when someone told me the news. It is a heavy blow, Istvan." Again, the king reached out and placed his hand on Istvan's shoulder as a gesture of belated sympathy.

"Our condolences. Perhaps you will meet a woman there, sir. If you're able now. . . Someone to grow old with. We shouldn't grow old alone, now, should we?" The king ever so lightly raised an eyebrow with this last remark and smiled. The interview was over. "*Grüss Gott, Oberst.*" A flick of a military salute with his hand and he turned away.

It was night again as the train approached the Bistritz *Vasútállomás* or railway station. Istvan dimmed the electric light in his compartment and watched as the sun's rays played behind the mountains rolling by in the long dusk and twilight that now prevailed with the coming of early spring out here in the wilderness. Shades of brilliant reds roasted the undersides of the clouds. Then came the ever-softening pinks and purples playing against the mounds of cumulus nimbus clouds floating in the sky. Snow flurries began again as they descended from the mountains and forests into farmland that surely marked the approach to Bistritz.

It was 7:15 on the clock as the Budapest train hissed into the Bistritz station with its new district chief of police aboard. Bistritz was the end of the line for the train. There were no more tracks north, east, or south of Bistritz, a dead end last stop in the foothills of the Carpathians.

A welcoming committee consisting of the Lord Mayor and several provincial aldermen had been waiting for two hours in the heated lobby. The gaslights were already lit at the station as Istvan alighted from one of the coaches on to the platform. The sun had been down for over an hour. He carried a suitcase and a valise.

"*Gnädiger Herr*, Kálváry Istvan?" one of the men inquired in Magyar accented but official German used by high imperial officials of the old Empire.

"*Ja, Herr Bürgermeister*," Istvan replied. "Sorry you have had to wait for me for so long."

"No matter, *Uram*," replied the Mayor, switching to their common Magyar tongue now that the formal greetings were over. "We are pleased to meet you in any event. I am Mazaly Kula, Lord Mayor of Bistritz."

Further introductions were made to the aldermen. Then followed the usual polite inquiries. Would he join them for supper? What was the weather like in Budapest? Would his wife be joining him soon? Alas, a widower? So sorry, but there are quite a few eligible ladies here who will be very happy to meet you. . .

A porter was summoned, a Wallachian peasant, who gathered Istvan's few articles of furniture and personal effects from the baggage car. A carriage was waiting and summoned. Soon the little party clattered off to a nearby tavern in *Die Golden Krone* Hotel where Istvan would be staying for a few days until his new lodgings in town were secured. Given their status, the little group was seated promptly at a large round table. Small glasses were placed at the table in front of each guest by the innkeeper himself.

"*Schnapps* or *Slivovitz*, Gnädiger Herr?" the innkeeper inquired. Istvan indicated the schnapps.

The innkeeper, a burly man called Oszkár, poured schnapps for Istvan from a dark green bottle of *Rumple Minze* and moved around the table. There were only a few patrons in the dining room that evening. Istvan noticed it was paneled in dark wood with old gaslight sconces on the wall rather than electric lamps, as was the fashion now in hotels in Budapest. A picture of the King was on the wall over the mantle of the fireplace. Polite chatter at the table largely emanated from the portly mayor while the other county officials seemed to be taking the measure of their new Chef der Politzei.

A toast greeting Istvan was duly made by the mayor, and then it was bottoms up. Another round was quickly poured by the innkeeper standing at the table's edge waiting for Istvan to reciprocate. Then a chalkboard with the menu written in Magyar was brought to the table. Istvan ordered the lamb.

"And so, Istvan, I suppose you were briefed on our last chief?" The mayor tasted the *Vorspeise* of goulash soup and fresh bread.

"No, not really. What about him?" Istvan replied, in a friendly tone of voice.

"Nobody is entirely sure," the mayor continued, speaking cautiously. "He left a note, resigning his office suddenly and without any warning at all. Very strange. He simply disappeared! His note indicated he was required to leave suddenly due to a family emergency in Bucharest. None of us knew he had any family there, let alone someone so close and important to cause him to leave his house and all his belongings behind. We tried to contact him in Romania but he left no forwarding address and evidently has not made himself known to the authorities there. Our telegrams have gone undelivered and unanswered."

"Very strange indeed," added one of the aldermen, "but then, he began acting strangely for a few months before he left. Most unlike himself."

It was quite unusual for a civil servant to desert his post in those days without the King's permission, which Istvan knew. He was surprised by this revelation. It was almost equivalent to desertion in the army.

"Was he married? Did he have children?" Istvan was curious.

"His first wife died many years ago. He married another much younger woman. She had left him a few months earlier," the mayor said softly, deliberately trying not to be overheard by the diners at nearby tables. "Disappeared. It was a bit of a scandal here. Evidently she must have been having an affair and one day, she was gone. Ran off with her lover, it seems. The chief was quite disconcerted, of course. Nobody knew what to say or do. He said little about it himself. I suppose he was embarrassed. Who wouldn't be?"

"And his children?"

The second alderman, a dark-skinned older man named Fodor, spoke up. "In Galicia, somewhere. We were not sure. I thought he mentioned once having a son in Kraków, but we hardly knew what to do. . ." The man paused, shaking his head with bewilderment. "So far, nobody has come forward. Evidently, they were not close. Perhaps the younger second wife, you know …"

This was all very curious, Istvan thought, but for the moment, there was nothing more to be said. As the evening went on, he began to try to perceive the nature of what was, in effect, the local government here in Bistritz. The mayor impressed him as a pompous, self-important type, fat with the reddening face of an alcoholic. The man frequently interrupted the others in conversation, an irritating habit but one that suited Istvan who, as a detective by trade, was attuned to listening more than speaking.

The three alderman were all gentlemen, by dress and appearance. Fodor, it soon turned out, was landowner gentry with several large farms and a country home between Bistritz and the next town to the north, called Dumitra. His face was sun-darkened after years of overseeing his lands. Istvan estimated Fodor was in his sixties. Courteous but taciturn, he conveyed an air of quiet dignity.

The second alderman, Nagy Ferenc, was much younger with sandy blond hair. He was the head of the local branch of the ÖNB, the Österreichische Nationalbank. With his pince-nez glasses, carefully combed hair and pin-striped suit, one could easily guess his profession. He was likely to be the financial brains behind the scenes in Bistritz. Few business transactions of any significance would likely escape the hawk-like attention of this young man, Istvan suspected.

The last alderman was the token Wallachian, Andrei Patrascu. The Wallachians put their surnames last, instead of following the Magyar custom of announcing surnames first. Even more reserved than his colleagues, no doubt due to his social inferiority, Andrei's conversation was unctuous to a fault. Nonetheless, he was the owner of the largest retail dry goods store in Bistritz, as well as numerous other smaller stores. Istvan wondered if beneath the servile veneer, he might be the wealthiest of the four of them, in spite of his Wallachian birth.

The conversation veered off into other political and police issues. It was a quiet district, Istvan learned. Theft was a problem of course, largely due to the presence of the Roma people in the forest who had to be watched, especially when they broke camp and wandered about the district, but nothing too challenging for someone of Istvan's talents, they assured him.

Jewish and Slovakian peasants drifted through the district from the nearby crownland of Bukovina or the adjoining Empire of Russia, leaving destitute farms behind and, in the case of the Jews, pogroms and persecution. They were looking for work on the local estates or in the towns in the case of artisans and tradesmen such as tanners, smiths and the like. Harvests had been good the past few years and many of the noble families hired these itinerants and the Roma to plant, cultivate, and harvest their crops, sometimes granting them tiny cottages for shelter with plots to farm vegetables on their own.

The dinner broke up amicably with best wishes from everyone to the Chief on his new assignment. The innkeeper bowed low to the mayor and alderman as they stepped out into the snowy night and then showed Istvan to his room upstairs.

Chapter 3

The next morning, the weather was even colder and it continued to snow on and off during the day. Istvan took a walk around the town while the porters moved his belongings into an apartment he had rented, at least for the first few months until something more suitable could be found. Istvan noticed the details of the Bistritz neighborhoods as he walked and concluded it seemed quite a handsome town. The streets were either cobbled or well paved. Many of the townhomes were quite impressive in size and the architecture was inviting and tasteful. The Lutheran Church in the city center had been erected a century ago by the Saxon settlers from the time of Empress Maria Theresa and was imposingly beautiful with an enormous clock tower dominating the town. Eventually, he found the *Polizeipräsidium* and decided to visit his new office.

When Istvan entered the building, he noticed it appeared in disrepair, dirty, and unkempt. Pale green paint was peeling off the walls leaving blotches of white plaster. The floors seemed not to have been swept in quite a while. A duty officer behind a window was reading a newspaper in his chair, which was tilted back against a wall. The duty officer looked up from his reading, annoyed at the interruption. There was a smell of stale tobacco smoke in the air. From somewhere there were muffled sounds of people talking.

"I am Kálváry Istvan, the new Chef der Politzei," Istvan said to the officer in formal German. The officer's chair tipped forward with a thud and the officer abruptly stood up. He groped for his cap on the nearby table without breaking his stare at Istvan and managed to put it on his head, albeit crookedly.

"*Jawohl*, Gnädiger Herr! My name is Radu Popescu," the young man fairly shouted out. He was obviously a Wallachian. Istvan asked who was in charge and was escorted to an interior office, down a dimly lit corridor smelling even more strongly of stale tobacco smoke to which was added the distinct odor of cooked food. They entered another office and Istvan came face to face with the Acting Chief, Gábor Kasza, who had apparently been laboring over some papers. A cigarette was smoking in an ashtray. He took off his glasses, and rose to his feet at Popescu's introduction, and extended his hand, a questioning look on his face.

"Uram," Kasza said quietly in Magyar, nodding his head. Istvan's first impression was disappointment. The man was disheveled, his hair in disarray; long and falling from his head in loose, greasy curls. A rumpled, wrinkled white shirt rolled up to his elbows. A frock coat hung loosely on the back of his chair. He had a milky white complexion and watery blue eyes. All in all, it looked as if the Acting Chief stayed indoors too much, but then again, winters were long and cold in this part of Transylvania.

Istvan knew this man would be his most senior assistant, at least at first, and so it would be expedient for him to take the time to make his acquaintance. He dismissed Popescu who bowed his way out of the room and went back to his desk. Istvan sat down and began with some general inquiries about Kasza's family, his upbringing, education and his ongoing career in the police department. At first wary, Kasza slowly warmed up to the older man's gentle questions and encouraging nods as the details began to emerge. Istvan asked his permission to smoke and when Kasza readily assented, took out his pipe and meticulously began to pack it as he listened.

It turned out that Kasza was not a native of this area either, but came from Balatonfüred, a summer resort town on the north shore of the great Hungarian freshwater lake, Balaton. He was thirty-nine years old and had received his primary and secondary education in his native Veszprém county. He had been recruited into the local police, showed promise and received further police training at the academy in nearby Pápa, a pretty baroque city Istvan had passed through years earlier.

Kasza's interest in science and its application to solving crimes helped establish him as a top detective in the constabulary of Vezprém county and attracted the notice of officials in Budapest. Before long, he was summoned to the capital to attend the Ludovika Academy. Not long after he graduated, by luck, he participated in the discovery and arrest of the notorious serial killer, Béla Kiss. It was Kasza's use of plaster casts to match one of Béla's boots to the footprints of the killer that solved the case against the so-called "Kiss of Death". The footprints had been found under the window of one of his victim's houses. He was promoted thereafter to become one of the youngest Inspectors in the Royal Hungarian Gendarmerie (RHG). Istvan noted in his face Kasza's quiet pride in his accomplishments as he re-lit his pipe.

"And so, Kasza, what brought you to this distant outpost, then? A man of such talents seems a bit wasted in this quiet backwater."

"Not at all, Uram," Kasza replied. He insisted on using the Magyar honorific which Istvan now waved away with his hand, dispelling the smoke rising from his pipe in the other. He disliked formalities. "No need for that," Istvan said softly.

"What shall I call you, then? How about Vezér?" This Magyar word loosely translated to "boss" or "chief".

Istvan smiled. "All right then, that would be fine. But why were you sent here?"

"The section chief, Franz Török. He was transferred to the Transylvanian branch. I worked with him in Budapest on the Kiss case. When he established himself in Klausenberg, he requested I be sent here from Budapest. I was brought here to head the investigation into the unsolved murders and kidnappings here in the Bistritz district."

Istvan felt his heart skip a beat. "What are you saying?" Istvan asked slowly, lowering his pipe now and gazing intently at Kasza.

"We aren't sure, but we think there is a serial killer at large here. Didn't they tell you about this in Budapest?"

Istvan felt a rising annoyance because the young Inspector was bringing something of this magnitude to his attention for the first time. It was embarrassing not to have known this beforehand.

"Perhaps they did, Kasza, but there were many other things discussed, as you can imagine."

"Of course, Vezér. But the magnitude of this one ..."

"What do you mean?"

"It may be hundreds. Nobody can be sure, of course. We have only just started, but it might be bigger than Báthory Erzebet."

Istvan knew he was speaking of the 16th century Hungarian "Blood Countess" who had been convicted of some eighty murders of young girls in her castle. She was accused of having killed more than 600 by the year 1610 when she was imprisoned and bricked up in *Csejte Vára*, her residence and later prison, where she died a few years later.

Now Istvan was truly stunned. "What?" he gasped incredulously.

"Yes!" Kasza replied eagerly. It was becoming clear that Gábor Kasza relished his work and this Carpathian assignment. For Istvan, however, the prospect of a mass murderer on this scale disturbed him deeply. He had assumed from time to time, of course, there would be random, unpleasant crimes to be resolved, but he had envisioned a largely quiet and bucolic life in this wild and beautiful country until he was able to retire. Within a single day, his conception of how he would spend the twilight of his career was rapidly disintegrating.

"How can you be certain?" Istvan probed, still nurturing the hope that it could all be a mistake.

"It's difficult to be sure at the moment, but it has all the telltale signs. Since the Kiss of Death case, I have studied this subject as much as I could. The Whitechapel murders in London. The case of Dr. Holmes in Chicago. I think so. Yes."

"And Török Ferenc?" Istvan asked, inverting the name of the Transylvanian Constabulary (TC) chief, Hungarian style.

"He's not so sure, but suspicious enough to have brought me here. And then, your predecessor disappeared ..."

Another little detail the authorities in Budapest had omitted when they had awarded him the post, Istvan recalled. "A vacancy has just arisen ..."

"What do you know about that?" Istvan fingered his pipe.

"A mystery unto itself," Kasza replied. "It was very strange. He was a troubled man, of course. I didn't know him well. He kept to himself and left me on my own. Occasionally he inquired about the investigation, but we had just started. Didn't seem too concerned or interested until his wife left him. Then he changed. He wanted details. What we were thinking? What we were doing? Who did we suspect? Things like that."

"Do you really think he just left?"

"I don't know. Perhaps suicide, but if so, he was very careful how he did it. So far, no body. No trace."

A clock chimed the hour from somewhere down the hall. Istvan took out his pocket watch. It was already four o'clock in the afternoon.

"This has all been very enlightening, Kasza," Istvan said, rising from his chair. "I look forward to further discussion with you tomorrow when I will visit again. I suppose there are quite a few other things I should know about this office."

"Not too much, Vezér. It's a pretty quiet place, except for what I'm doing. But I'll be glad to get back to working on this project alone now that you're here. There are so many things to do."

"Really?" Istvan asked.

"Oh yes. So many clues."

As Istvan walked down the steps of the building after his visit, he felt the familiar pangs of his loneliness rising in him. His own children were far away, in Vienna and Budapest. He had no family here and no friends. He hated dining alone, but there was no alternative. And after that? There was not much to do in this small town, he could see. There would be no concerts, no opera, no interesting cafés or society. He would have to content himself with a book in front of the fireplace tonight at the Golden Krone, he thought. Plenty of time to consider Kasza's revelations. He looked up into the grey sky. Snow flurries were falling again.

Chapter 4

Natália, daughter of Béla and niece of Nikola, leader or *Hetman* of the *Sinti Estraxarja* tribe who lived in the forest near Bistritz, was thinking about the gathering soon to take place in a few hours, after sunset. Only some of the men were allowed to go. That was the way it had always been when the Lord and Master summoned the Sinti.

They were Roma, shunned by the Magyars and Saxons and Wallachians and everyone else who lived in the other world, beyond the forest, in places like Bistritz and on their farms. Natália, dark haired, slender and beautiful, was not allowed to leave the forest without her family for fear she would be raped or killed by the outsiders. The Sinti men went out to find work occasionally but most of the time they stayed in the forest.

One afternoon, Natália was churning butter just outside the squalid shanty where she and her father slept and took cover from the cold and snow. A small fire burned in a pit outside the door, providing some light and warmth as the temperature grew colder and colder. In another hour or so it would be dark, and then the men would go. They would meet their Master. The one who let them live in his forest, under his protection from the cruel people beyond the forest. They would listen to the Master and they would do what he asked.

That had been the way things had been done for as long as Natália could remember. She was now about twenty years old, but she couldn't know for sure. There were no records for the Sinti Estraxarja. Not when they were born. Not when they died. Not anytime. And when the government came to count them and tax them, they gave them other names to confuse and fool them. The Sinti were an invisible people never to be truly seen or known by the outsiders beyond the forest. They could not be trusted, those people in the towns and on the farms. They would always try to hurt the Sinti in the end.

When Natália had been a little girl, they kept moving in their caravans across the countryside of Transylvania, from town to town, before the townspeople started to chase them, accusing them of crimes and even killing them. But then they came here where they found a lost settlement of the Sinti who had lived here in the forest for generations; as long as anyone could remember. They had been given refuge by the great Lord who lived in the castle and who owned the farms and forests around the Borgo Pass. He was Master of the knightly Order of the Dragon and a Magyar lord. A count; Drakula Gróf, in his native Magyar tongue. Drakula, Son of the Dragon. The Dracula were descendants of princes and voivode of Wallachia who had taken the oath of allegience to the Hungarian kings long ago. This she had learned from the elders when she was a child.

Natália had never seen the Master. Most of the Sinti had never seen him. Only the men and only the most important men could approach him in his castle when he called and only when he called them. Otherwise, they could never go near his home, his castle in the mountains. Sometimes the other men would be called to the castle to work. The castle had largely fallen to ruins, she knew. Once she had seen it from a distance when taking food to some of the men who were working there, but her uncle had quickly led her away and scolded her father for letting her get so close to danger.

Now as the cream turned to butter, her uncle approached and sat down on a little three-legged stool near where she was sitting and warmed his hard, callused hands on the little fire. He smiled at her, and threw another log on the fire. Then he took out his knife and began to whittle a piece of wood he had been working on for the last few days; a bird of some kind. The fire blazed higher as the new piece of wood began to burn. The shadows of the forest were growing long as the sun went down.

"Why do you go at night to see the Master?" Natália asked. "If he has some business with us, why doesn't he meet you during the day?"

"I don't know, my sweet," Nikolai replied. "It's always this way. He meets us in his great hall and then we talk." Nikolai continued to whittle the piece of wood as he spoke, carefully turning the knife this way and that as he carved.

"What is he like, Uncle?" Nikolai paused and she could tell he was formulating his answer carefully.

"He is not like us. He is a great Lord from an old and great family that has ruled here for centuries, Natália. He is not Roma. An outsider, you know. He is different from us, but this is to be expected. We do not question him. We obey him and he protects us from the outsiders. He lets us live here in the forest."

"Do you like him, father? Is he a kind man?"

Nikolai paused again. "He is not kind or unkind. He ..."

Natália noticed her uncle shudder out of the corner of her eye.

"He is polite. He is good enough to us. But he is a Lord. He has always been obeyed. He's not like us, Natália."

"What is the castle like inside?"

"I have only seen some parts of it, my sweet. It is big and old. There are many rooms, I suppose. I have only seen the courtyard and the great hall where he summons us. There is a chapel in ruins. The Dracula family crypts ..."

Nikolai's voice trailed away as he said this. Natália could tell in her uncle's mind's eye he was reliving some moment and seemed preoccupied and distracted. Then he seemed to come back to himself.

"What things does he have you do?"

"Different things. We repair things. We maintain things."

"We dig. That's what we do more than anything," said Béla, who emerged suddenly from behind the shanty. "We dig and throw the dirt in boxes and then we take them away to God knows where."

Natália watched her uncle rise and glare at his younger brother. "Never mind that now, Béla... She doesn't need to know all about that."

"About what, Father?" Béla and Nikolai exchanged looks and then her father turned to her.

"Never mind, Natália. Just mind your churning, now girl. And remember what I've told you. Never go near the castle and stay indoors at night."

"But why?"

"Because I said so!" Béla suddenly said in a loud voice that frightened her. "There's evil things that go about in the world at night. Things you're too young to know or understand. Keep the Evil Eye from seeing you, Natália! Keep your head down and quiet. The less you know about the Master and our dealings with him, the better." Then Béla turned back on his brother.

"You don't need to tell me to be quiet about him. You're the one that started talking to her about him. Why did you do it?"

"I was just answering some questions she had. You're right. I shouldn't have said anything," Nikolai said softly. "She's your daughter, not mine. You have to protect her as you see fit." And with that, he rose and walked away.

Chapter 5

Istvan had been in Bistritz for two weeks when he met the Baroness Ribanszky Julianna at the Golden Krone one evening after dinner. He was lounging in the lobby, actually, packing some excellent Tabac Turc in his pipe when he noticed a very well attired woman in her 50s advancing on him, her eyes intently meeting his.

"Are you the new Chief of the District Police?" she asked.

Istvan hated to delay tamping his tobacco for smoking but this was not a time to be distracted, he realized. He rose to his feet chivalrously, and bowed slightly.

"Do I know you, Madame?"

"You do not, Sir. I am Ribanszky Julianna"

"Baroness of Jelna?" Istvan had come to know a few names of notables in the district over the past few weeks.

"The same."

She extended her hand. Istvan held her cool fingers gently, bowed from the waist and kissed the back of her hand like a gentleman. He rose and looked at her. She was a handsome woman, no doubt, with a strong nose, distinct lips and penetrating blue eyes that captured his own and held them. She was dressed and moved in a manner that would have attested to her aristocracy in Budapest. Here in provincial Bistritz, she stood out like a diamond. Istvan was impressed.

"Won't you sit down, Highness?" motioning toward a comfortable divan across from the leather tufted chair in which he had been sitting.

She sat down gracefully and took a deep breath. Clearly, she had something on her mind; probably some official business. It was well to make a good impression with the local gentry, Istvan had always maintained. They could be a great help. Or a hindrance. He preferred to seek out and maintain good relationships with them and the sudden appearance of a Baroness offered the opportunity to form one early in his stay here.

"Would you care for some tea or coffee?" Istvan inquired.

"Coffee. Thank you." Istvan summoned a porter who after taking the order withdrew to bring the service to them. Istvan sat down. Some introductory chatter followed until the porter reappeared with a silver tea set which he set down on the low table between them and began to pour. Eventually, the preliminaries over and etiquette satisfied, Istvan opened in his most personable manner.

"What can I do for you?"

"I would like to know where the investigation into the disappearance of my daughter stands? I knew they would eventually assign a new Chief to replace Novotny Janos," she said. "I waited until you came. I have waited now for you to get settled. Do you know about my daughter's case?"

Of course Istvan had heard about it. Novotny Janos was his predecessor as chief. After having been assigned to the Bistritz district for a little more than a year, Istvan had learned Janos had met the Baroness' daughter, Ema. It was Ema who had left Janos weeks before Janos had suddenly "disappeared" as well, the mayor had suggested the night Istvan had arrived. Now Istvan was facing the mother of the wife of the man he had just succeeded as Chief.

"They had been married for several years and had no children," the Baroness continued. She certainly minced no words, Istvan observed. "He was too old for her. I knew it when she first told me about him. She wanted children. He was too old and didn't. I knew she was unhappy. After she went missing, I found out she was having an affair."

"How?" Istvan asked, now eyeing the pipe settled in the ashtray, laden with soft, pungent Turkish tobacco. He couldn't resist. He picked up the pipe, but did not light it.

"Go ahead," the Baroness nodded, glancing at the pipe in his hand.

"Do you mind, Highness?"

"Not at all. Please suit yourself. I am imposing on you, sir. But I trust you can spare me just a few minutes of your time?"

Istvan lit the pipe and savored the rich, warm aroma of the tobacco. He looked again at the Baroness.

"As much time as you need, Highness. I am your servant," Istvan replied in the courteous idiom cultivated by the very highest strata of society and those, like himself, who aspired to befriend it. Again he nodded his head in deference to her, bidding her continue.

"How did he know?" Istvan spoke softly in a voice meant to coax more information out of someone he was interrogating. Istvan sought root causes and sources of information.

"He knew. There was evidence. He missed it for quite some time, of course. The unexplained absences he didn't pursue at first. Fearful where it might lead, no doubt. But then the time comes. You have to know for sure. He found out. He had her followed. I don't know who did it. One of your informers or police here, I'm sure. He never said and it didn't really matter to me. He told me he was devastated. She didn't deny it. And still, he stayed with her."

Istvan's professional instincts were now aroused. These were details he had not been told about by the mayor and the others. This was quite a different story. Perhaps a scandal.

"Go on," Istvan encouraged. "Do you think your son-in-law murdered her and then fled? Or did she run off with her lover with Janos in pursuit?"

The Baroness gazed at him with a look of annoyance. "I would have thought that was a question the police would have answered by now. Don't you know?"

"Madame, in the first place, I have only begun to assume my duties here ..."

"Yes, yes, I already mentioned that," the Baroness interrupted. "But you have been here now for a couple of weeks."

"But my duties do not necessarily include becoming involved in any particular case."

"Yes, I know. That is why I have come to you. I would like you to become involved in this one."

"Madame?"

"What do you know about Novotny Janos and his sudden disappearance? Isn't that worthy of your time? After all, he is your predecessor. Shouldn't you know what happened to him? How do we know he simply resigned and left the country? And then my daughter, his wife? What about her? Where did she go? She would have written to me. Not a word. Can you understand?"

Istvan thought for a moment. He had learned little about his predecessor aside from what had been told to him by the mayor and the aldermen. Since there was no pending complaint from anyone, there had apparently been little or no investigation. And yet, it was all very odd. He had thought it odd from the beginning, but Istvan had been so preoccupied with relocating and familiarizing himself with his staff and position, it had simply escaped his attention. Now, hearing the Baroness, he felt drawn to instigate some action.

"Highness, your concern is very understandable. Your daughter. Yes, very understandable. I will promise you I will look into this case personally." The Baroness' face relaxed for the first time into a faint smile of, was it pleasure? Or relief?

"Thank you," the Baroness said softly as she arose from the divan. "I understand you are a stranger here in our land. Would you come to tea at my house next Tuesday, Gnädiger Herr? You can tell me then what progress you have made."

Istvan arose as well. "It would be my pleasure, Madame."

She nodded. Another kiss of the hand and she was gone. Her perfume faintly scented the air around him where she had been and mingled with the traces of pipe smoke in the lobby as he resumed his seat. It had not been an entirely unpleasant interruption of his evening smoke and reading, he thought. His mind drifted to Julia.

Dear Julia. There would never be anyone for him like Julia, he thought sadly for the ten thousandth time. Never. But she was gone now, he knew. Until they met again in Heaven, he would have to soldier on. Istvan thought he still believed in Heaven. He had been raised a Catholic, but was not particularly observant. He had lost his faith somewhere along the way. He couldn't remember exactly when or where. Then again, it had probably slipped away little by little over a long period of time. He remembered when he had it. Like before the Battle of Custoza. But that had been a long time ago.

Bistritz was a mix of religions complying with the ethnic fault lines of the city and the nation. The Saxons in Bistritz were mainly Lutheran and their church, built in the main square of the city in the fifteenth century, was the most prominent. The outlying Wallachians were mostly Eastern Orthodox believers. All had their churches and parishes throughout the district and Istvan was certain he would slowly come to know them all.

As he resumed his smoking in the wake of the Baroness' departure, he began to think about the conversation he had had with Gábor Kasza in those first days after his arrival in Bistritz. Relieved of his administrative duties over the entire Polizeipräsidium, Kasza had returned to his detective work with a single track mind. To tell the truth, Istvan had been preoccupied settling into the new job, learning the names of the staff in the headquarters building, the sub-district police officials and constabulary, the finances of the whole district, personnel issues, interactions with the Royal Hungarian Gendarmerie in Budapest and the Transylvanian Constabulary in Klausenberg. As a result, his conversations with Kasza had mainly been brief ones about who was who and what was what in the district police organization; not about his ongoing investigation into the myriad kidnappings, missing persons and murders that had attracted the attention of Török Ferenc and the TC and been responsible for bringing Kasza here.

This business with Novotny Janos and the Baroness' daughter seemed to fit right into the strange business Kasza was about. It was then Istvan remembered that Török Ferenc was about to visit the District in the next few days and concluded it was high time he became a little more familiar with this investigation. If there really was a demented, mass killer about, it wouldn't do for him to know nothing about it. Yes, first thing in the morning he would summon Kasza to his office and start getting to the bottom of this.

Chapter 6

"Good morning, Vezér," Kasza said amiably as he entered Istvan's private office within the Polizeipräsidium. Istvan waved him to the chair in front of his desk. Kasza opened a pack of *Admiral* cigarettes and offered one to his chief.

"No, thanks, Kasza," he said, noting again the somewhat disheveled appearance of the RHG Inspector. Kasza worked well after the normal quitting time and was often back in his office at the crack of dawn, poring over papers, reports and so forth. His pale complexion and long hair may have been the result of his lack of exercise and outdoor activities, Istvan assumed. He didn't ride and seemed to have no hobbies or interests at all beyond his police work. Even women. For a young man, Istvan never saw him about the small town socializing or enjoying the company of the local ladies his age.

Istvan began the conversation by inquiring into the disappearances of Ema and Janos Novotny.

"Are they part of your larger investigation?" Istvan inquired.

"Actually, yes, Vezér."

"Well, what can you tell me about them?"

Kasza methodically ticked off the known facts. Novotny Ema had been having an affair with a cavalry officer who had recently settled in Bistritz; a Hungarian by the name of Györky András. It had been going on for some time. Janos had learned of the affair from an informer and had confirmed it himself. This much had been clear. Then she had disappeared. Györky had been confronted as the prime suspect, but it became obvious he was also distraught by her sudden disappearance and knew little of any consequence. He had last seen the woman in the afternoon and early evening hours of January 25, he admitted under questioning. She was returning home at nightfall. She left cheerfully but hastily to her home, given the circumstances. After a few days, Györky made inquiries and learned she had been missing. He was obviously in an awkward position and had not known what to do. All this had been established by Kasza himself through interrogation. Györky had been eliminated as a suspect; at least for now.

A manhunt had been organized but it went nowhere. Janos had become more and more agitated as the days went by, according to the staff here. Understandably, of course. Then he was gone too. There was his note. Written in his own hand. Gone to Bucharest. The authorities there had never seen him or heard of him when inquiries were made later.

"I remember when I first heard about this from the *Bürgermeister*," Istvan said when Kasza paused. "I remember thinking how strange it all sounded. A member of His Majesty's Civil Service does not simply disappear like that. It's not credible. Something obviously happened to his wife. Something untoward. And something likely happened to him, too. Don't you think?"

"Yes. And this is the pattern one sees with a serial killer, Vezér. People just disappear. Years go by and it keeps happening. Sometimes in bunches. Sometimes in isolated ones and twos. And all the while, the killer is right in the midst of his victims. Waiting and watching until the moment comes, often after careful study of the next victim. Then he pounces."

"Perhaps he had been watching Ema's affair with Györky and ambushed her on the way home?"

"If it is a serial killer, that is definitely possible. Something about her attracted his attention. He watched her. And then he made his move." Kasza stubbed out his *Admiral* in a brass ash tray on Istvan's desk. "May I show you something?"

Istvan followed Kasza back to his office. He had tacked to the wall a large map with many colored pins stuck into it and threads leading to pictures and names of individuals missing or found murdered. Notwithstanding the piles of paper heaped on chairs and tables, overflowing ashtrays and other debris, Kasza had assembled a filing system of dossiers with meticulous diligence; one for each victim. Everything known about the victim and his or her disappearance was in their dossier. Istvan was impressed with his organization.

"It's very good, Kasza, but is it helping?"

"I think so. There are some interesting facts when you start to look at it this way."

Istvan turned to look at the map again, putting on his reading glasses and moving closer. There were dozens of pins; perhaps fifty or more he guessed without counting them. There were clusters of pins in some of the cities like Bistritz. A number of pins were also in Vatra Dornei, the nearest major town on the other side of the Carpathians in the next province of Bukovina. The remaining pins were scattered about the countryside, some in little villages and hamlets, others on farms and estates located in the hills.

"What do you see, Kasza?"

Kasza moved closer to the map, staring intently.

"Look at the pins and then this."

His hand traced an imaginary line between Bistritz and Vatra Dornei along the highway between them that passed through the Carpathians.

"This ancient road that leads east from Bistritz is a virtual cart path as it goes into the mountains through what the Wallachians call *'Tihuta'* and we Hungarians call the 'Borgo' Pass. As the road passes down again into the Bukovina, mainly northeast but then almost due east, there is a forest known as *Tinovul Mohos.*" Kasza paused and lit another cigarette.

"What of it?" Istvan inquired.

Kasza shrugged his shoulders. "Roma live there."

Istvan grunted. So, that was it? Istvan shared the usual Hungarian suspicion about the Roma. They were dark-skinned and strange. As a policeman, he knew there were many petty thieves and horse rustlers among them, no matter what they said. They were close knit and kept to themselves, moving from one place to another.

"How long have they been there?" Istvan asked.

"A long time. Nobody knows exactly, but for many years."

"What? That is unusual for them isn't it," Istvan said.

"Yes, it is. They are nomadic for the most part. This tribe is Sinti. They have been in Europe for a long time, especially in this part of the world. These have stopped roaming and live in a little hamlet not far off the road. You can see their camp as you pass by. They sometimes come out of the forest and do day labor for the farmers and on the big estates, especially at harvest time. Some of them tinker in the towns and villages. They keep to themselves, for the most part."

"Is this forest on crownland or an estate?"

"An estate, Vezér."

"Whose estate?"

"The Count Dracula."

"Who is he?"

"Old family; well-known name: Dracula. They go back to the thirteenth or fourteenth century. Something like that. One of the old Transylvanian *voivode* that fought the Turks."

Istvan made a mental note of it. Another aristocrat he would probably do well to meet and cultivate.

"Where does he live?"

"We're not sure. In Budapest or Bucharest. But for some reason, he has given permission for these Roma to squat on his land, in his forest, and there they stay."

"I see. And do you think the serial killer is among these Roma?"

"It is my working hypothesis at the moment, Vezér, but there are some problems with it."

"Such as?"

"They are close knit. Tribal, really. For one of them to stray from their camp for long, on his own … That would be unusual. It would be noticed. Kidnapping victims and bringing them back to their camp would be noticed. There is no place to hide the victims or their bodies. These killers are pariahs, even in the world of the Roma. They strike in the dark. In secret. The Chicago killer, Holmes, for example, built an elaborate fake hotel where he imprisoned his victims, tortured and killed them, out of sight. In secret. He was a loner. The Whitechapel murderer had the anonymity of the slums of London where he could mutilate his victims in the darkness of their fog and narrow alleys, unseen. Again, secrecy. I don't see how this could work with the Roma. For a pure killer, yes, but not for the kidnapping type. Where would he hide the victims in a Gypsy camp?"

"I see. Interesting, Kasza. When Török Ferenc arrives, I would like to meet him and pursue this further."

"Of course, Vezér."

Istvan told him about his encounter with the Baroness.

"I'm sure Ferenc would like to meet you," Kasza said. There is a lot more to this that I haven't told you."

"Indeed?"

"Yes. How much time do you have?"

"I tell you what, Kasza. This is all very interesting and important, but it would be good for me to learn more about the basics. For example, I have never been to the Borgo Pass or this Forest. I think I will take a ride."

Istvan moved near the map again and peered at its details, particularly the winding road leading east from Bistritz that, to the Hungarians was known as the *Közúti Moldvában*, or the Moldavian Road. Within the city limits, it was a major boulevard, cobbled and busy during the day and lined with stately homes and buildings in the commercial center.

Near the road, a few kilometers south of the peak of the Pass, was a tiny Wallachian hamlet by the name of *Piatra Fantanele*, Istvan saw as he used his glasses to read the very small print denoting the tiny population of the place. Next to the dot on the map was a pin and a thread.

"What happened here?" Istvan asked. Kasza followed the thread to its end. There was a name on a slip of paper. Stela. Lucescu. Kasza went to the files and found her dossier.

"Wallachian female. Peasant's daughter. About sixteen when she disappeared. Last seen by her parents feeding livestock just before sunset. She was missed for dinner. This was in '95. Never seen again."

Istvan felt his heart sink as Kasza related more details. He had visited the parents of comrades killed in the wars. Many of them he had seen years after their sons had died. Grief from that could destroy you, he knew. A part of your soul is lost forever when a child dies.

"Good, Kasza. I think I will take a look around there."

"May I go with you, sir?"

Istvan thought about it for a moment. "Why not? Do you have a horse, Kasza?"

"Well no, actually. But I have a friend and can borrow one."

Istvan had his horse from Budapest and had arranged for it to be kept by a Saxon farmer at his stable just outside of town.

"How far is it to the Borgo pass?"

"It's about 50 kilometers, Vezér".

Istvan calculated it would take a day to ride there, especially on a road that eventually reached an elevation of over 1100 meters at the pass. There would be no inn or lodging in such a small town. Guessing his thoughts, Kasza continued. "There is a monastery in Piatra Fantanele. I would imagine they take in travelers for a small amount of coin. From there, we could also see the Forest of Tinovul Mohos. I've been wanting to do this since I got here, but I just haven't had the time and with Török Ferenc coming, well, it's embarrassing really."

"You need to get outdoors more, Kasza," said Istvan reprovingly. "Get some fresh air and sunshine. I've heard these parts are quite beautiful. Yes, we'll go together. I'll check with the Abbot here in Bistritz about the monastery just to be sure. See if they can put us up for a couple of nights, eh?"

Kasza nodded vigorously.

It was the first time Istvan had noticed a sparkle in his eyes and a wide smile of enthusiasm. *A bookworm*, Istvan thought. That was the trouble with these young intellectuals. They had never done any soldiering. Just stayed in schools and office buildings. *They lost touch with the people*, Istvan thought. Istvan needed to see things with his own eyes. Get his fingernails dirty, as his father used to say.

As he left Kasza's cluttered office, Istvan took a last look at the map. So many pins. Could these all be the work of one man? If there was just one man, a single killer, he must be caught and hanged. They would have a look around the Borgo Pass. Yes, they certainly would. All this second hand book investigation was good, but Istvan wanted to talk to the people. Another thought entered his mind. He stopped, turned on his heel and walked back to Kasza's office.

"Kasza, with regard to the Baroness' daughter, Ema. You say nobody came forward?"

"No, Vezér."

"This morning, post a police bulletin on all of the kiosks in Bistritz. Offer a 100 *Karona* reward for any information regarding the disappearance of the *Edle Herrin* Ema von Jelna on the evening of 25 January 1896 that leads to the arrest and conviction of those responsible. Make clear that any information and the identity of any person coming forward will be kept completely confidential."

"Yes, Vezér!" Kasza smiled and smartly clicked his heels together with another broad smile. It was clear he was glad to have gained a comrade in his lonely investigation. Istvan smiled also and gave a casual salute with his hand to his forehead as he turned again to leave. In spite of his bookish, intellectual tendencies, Istvan realized he did like this young man and was looking forward to their little trip.

Chapter 7

As usual, the Master was nowhere to be seen Nikolai thought as he watched several of the young men lift a large square wooden box into a wagon that had already been loaded with several boxes of dirt from a sort of quarry located near the ruined chapel and crypts. He wondered what was in this box. It was not nearly as heavy as the boxes filled with dirt. When they had picked the box up from inside the chapel, whatever was packed inside seemed to be loose and move around when the box tilted one way or another. It was not hard because it made no noise when it struck the inside surfaces of the box. It was too heavy to be clothing. What in the world was it, he wondered?

This particular shipment was bound for the port of Constanta in the nearby kingdom of Romania and from there, who knew? What could anyone want with piles of dirt and God knows what else from this place, Nikolai wondered again for the hundredth time. The lighter box was not to be opened under any circumstances, the Master had said. Any circumstances?

The Roma were to bring the wagon to Vatra Dornei in the Bukovina where the boxes would be transferred to a rail car and then to the seaport of Constanta. It was about a day's ride to Vatra Dornei, largely downhill on the eastern slopes of the Carpathians. The boxes were to be tightly guarded by a dozen Roma, armed with rifles that he, as hetman of the Sinti tribe of Tinovul Mohos, would lead. His brother Béla always accompanied him on these trips and would do so again this day.

With the work finished, two of the younger Sinti swung shut the door at the rear of the cart and bolted it tightly. A canvas cover was draped over a half dozen bowed arches and tied down on the sides. A young lad, who went by Petrov and had worked as a teamster, climbed up into the seat, released the brake and cracked a long whip, starting the quartet of horses forward with the cargo. Béla and Nikolai spurred their horses forward and took their positions ahead of the *leiter-wagon*. The rest fell in pairs behind and they were off.

It was a beautiful, clear day in March with the air crisp and bracing. Snow still covered most of the peaks and mountaintops as they made their way along the rutted mountain trail down into the Bukovina. Small roadside shrines with images of various saints, dead flowers or spent candles appeared every few kilometers, placed there by who knew? Nikolai did not, of course, believe in the Christian saints. He worshipped Kali. The Black One. Goddess of time and change and the patroness of the Roma for all time. Around his neck he wore a necklace and amulet with an image of The Black One to protect himself from evil.

The first few kilometers were panoramic with wide, sweeping vistas of the mountains and valleys, but then, after a time, they passed into forested areas that almost encroached the road and wound this way and that. Then there were the terrifying parts with steep drop offs and cliffs to their right and sheer rock to the left that had to be carefully navigated. At mid-day, they had come down quite a bit and pulled over near an apple orchard by the side of the road near a farm.

The Roma dismounted and scattered about to eat their lunches, packed by their wives or mothers back at the settlement in the forest. Béla and Nikolai spread a blanket on the grass near the wagon and sat down. The temperature was a bit warmer now as the sun had climbed in the sky. They sat in silence, eating their chicken dumplings and black bread with jars of strong, honey-sweetened tea. Then Béla spoke.

"I would like to know what is in that box." Nikolai stared at him for a moment. Before he could respond, Béla continued. "Why do boxes of dirt need to be escorted by armed guards to town? They don't, of course. Dirt is worthless. So it stands to reason that whatever is so valuable we have to guard it is contained in the last box. And what could it be?"

"It doesn't matter," Nikolai responded. "The Master said it was to be kept closed. It's his business whatever it is." Nikolai gave him a hard look before resuming his lunch.

"I'm not going to take anything," Béla said quietly. "You can watch me. I just want to know. I just want to open it and look inside. See what it is." Nikolai stopped eating and lowered his chicken to his lap.

"The Master said not to open it. There must be a good reason for that. Forget about it."

"How many years now have we done this, Nikolai? How many years? Let's just look. Just this once. Just for peace of mind. We'll close it back up tight and nice. Nobody will ever know."

This conversation went on in this way throughout their lunch with Béla arguing with his older brother, just as he had done when they were children. Slowly, he began to persuade him. Nikolai couldn't deny that he too was curious. They would never take anything, no matter how valuable it was. What harm could it do? Finally, as the other Roma were lighting their pipes and cigarettes after finishing their lunches, the two brothers climbed into the wagon and located a crow bar that was lying on the wagon bed. It would just be a peek. A quick look and then they would knock it back tight again.

It was Béla who took the flat end of the crow bar and wedged it into the crack between the sides and the top. He pushed it down and slowly the corner of the top opened a couple of centimeters. Nikolai thought he heard something move inside as Béla moved the crow bar a few centimeters further and pushed again. He could see the entire length of one of the nails near the corner as it pulled out of the wood on the side. And then he did it again and again. Little by little the top was coming up and off, but it wasn't until he got around the next corner that enough of the top had been detached to where he could insert the crow bar deep into the box, stand up inside the wagon and pull up on the crowbar, pulling almost the entire side of nails out at once.

There was a terrible sound from within the box. Something was alive inside. Nikolai looked at Béla. His brother was moving to look into the wide crack that had now opened. The sunlight shining into the crack was not yet enough to illuminate anything but the topmost part of the inside of the box. There was certainly something alive in there. A smell of dirt and decay was emanating from the box. Nikolai gestured.

"Open it! Hurry!"

Béla took the crowbar around the third corner and wedged it into the crack. Another huge lift and the top nearly came off, attached only on the last side. Béla now dropped the crowbar and both he and Nikolai grabbed the top of the box with their hands, pulling it wide open.

Inside was a woman, sitting in a crouched position. Her head moved. She gazed at Nikolai with a fierce look of hate, opened her mouth and then there was a terrible scream. It was so loud the force of it knocked both brothers backward. The woman stood up in the box suddenly. Her hands went to her head and she ran her fingers into her long black hair as her scream continued. It was a scream of both rage and agony that paralyzed them both as they watched her. Suddenly, her body burst into flames and she began writhing in pain.

The heat of the fire within the wagon was so intense that Nikolai scrabbled backwards, toward the rear of the wagon. He felt someone's hands grabbing him under his armpits and pulling him out of the wagon. In a language Nikolai could not understand, the flaming woman pointed at him and shrieked. A curse, no doubt. Nikolai pointed two fingers at her to deflect the Evil Eye and then she went silent. Slowly she collapsed into the box again from whence she had come.

She burned for another half hour until Nikolai summoned up the courage to get into the wagon again and look in the box. A pile of grey and white cinders and ashes resting upon the mass of black soil in the bottom of the box was all that could be seen. She had burned so hot and so completely that not even bones were left. She was gone. She had disintegrated into ashes.

Chapter 8

Istvan thought of the discussion he and Kasza had with Török Ferenc the preceding day as their horses trotted along the coach road to the Bukovina, now a few hours out of Bistritz. The snow-capped mountains were far from the road in the distance, but from his study of the map in Kasza's office, he knew the closer they got to the monastery in Piatra Fantanele, the mountains would close in and then they would begin to climb up and up into the stony embrace of the western slope of the Carpathians. They passed farms, some near the coach road and others that could be seen far off in the distance. Twice a day a diligence left Bistritz for the Bukovina and twice a day the Bukovina replied with a diligence of its own.

Istvan and Kasza watched as one approached now, coming toward them from the Bukovina. It bore the imperial Habsburg colors of yellow and black with yellow spoke wheels and a black top. The driver waved to them as he passed and Istvan could see that he had a half dozen passengers in the coach, a couple of whom looked out the yellow framed windows at them. Kasza was a better rider than Istvan had thought he would be, seeming to be quite comfortable with the gelded stallion he had leased from the farmer where Istvan kept his *Kisbér Felver* stallion named Balazs. A formerly spirited cavalry horse that was now reaching middle age, he was still strong with great stamina.

"An excellent idea, the reward," Török had exclaimed after Kasza had given him a detailed account of his investigation and organization to date. "It is still not clear whether or not all these disappearances and presumptive murders are the work of a single man. We have now inquired with our stations in the Bukovina, in the Banat and in Royal Hungary itself. We have compiled a list of hundreds more missing persons and kidnappings around this district that seem to go back as far as recorded records were kept. It's extraordinary, really, what our inquiries have dug up. For comparison sake, Kasza, I asked for similar information from your old homeland in Veszprém county. We counted sixty-three missing persons in the ten-year period between 1886-96. By contrast, Bistritz-Nasaud County had over six hundred."

"Extraordinary, indeed," Istvan murmured.

"And that's not all," Török continued. "Of the sixty-three missing persons in Veszprém, over fifty were closed by the police. Murdered. Kidnapped and returned or kidnapped and murdered. The point being something like ninety percent of these events were solved one way or the other. Here in this district, by contrast, of the 600 or so missing persons, only forty-seven were closed. The opposite situation. When people go missing in this part of the world, they stay missing."

"Where do they go?" Kasza wondered aloud.

"Where indeed," said Török. "And why has this never come to the attention of the RHG or the TC before?"

"Of course, it is very remote and rural here," Istvan speculated. "I have been discovering this is not, as they say, Budapest."

"Right, but surely there must be some understanding among the people in this area something out there is terribly wrong," Török ventured.

◎ ◎ ◎

He would see about that, Istvan thought as they continued on the coach road. By afternoon, the horses were going steadily uphill, into the mountains. At times the path was steep and just a rutted, rocky cart path for the most part.

The two men were cheered when as evening approached they discovered a battered sign for the Monastery, now only five more kilometers.

Mountain cabins and cottages were few and far between in the high country but still occasionally lined the road in some flatter runs. The men and women who lived there invariably stopped to watch Istvan and Kasza pass. Istvan had purposely worn his royal uniform complete with sword and scabbard to encourage the people he saw along the way to get to know him and secure their loyalty. He wanted these country folk in the Borgo Pass to know he cared about them and was looking out for them against any dangers afflicting them. Istvan waved at the hearty mountain folk as they watched. Some of them waved back. Others watched quietly as he passed by. A few crossed themselves and pointed at him with two fingers, the customary sign to protect against the Evil Eye.

The sun was setting behind the mountains now, in a glow of red and orange. The forest was close by the road here and already it was becoming difficult to see much beyond the edge of the road into the woods. It was dark looking into the woods and would soon be black as pitch with only the moon and the stars shedding light. Istvan spurred Balazs into a canter in hopes of reaching the Monastery at Piatra Fantanele with a few rays of the sun still in the sky. Kasza did the same. The temperature had dropped steadily with the rising altitude and now did so even more dramatically as the sky tended to purple with flecks of red and gold. The Borgo Pass was another ten kilometers or so to the east.

As the horses came around a bend in the road, it straightened out for three or four hundred meters, Istvan reckoned, and there they were. A pack of wolves darted across the road about halfway down the straightaway. They had heard the horses' hooves and most shot quick glances at them as they leaped from the road up into the rocks and forest, but one exceptionally large wolf trotted out into the road and glared at them as he stood there. He seemed fearless, with large yellow eyes Istvan could see, even from a distance. His red tongue lolled out of his mouth as he panted, framed with large white teeth. He was in no hurry, as younger, smaller wolves skittered across the Coach Road behind him, and now the horses caught sight of him.

Kasza's gelding murmured an initial worried protest while Balazs continued to plunge forward but as he neared the animal, he suddenly shied and skittered sideways so as to get a better look at the wolf. There was a momentary standoff as each side warily regarded the other. Istvan suddenly realized the wolf was the source of a deep rumbling he could hear. He started to lean back in his saddle and reach for his cavalry rifle but then the wolf suddenly turned and bolted into the same dark wood as his companions, leaving them the road.

"I've been in worse situations," Istvan called to Kasza in a voice more confident than he really felt. Kasza, the city boy, thought Istvan, was looking a bit shaken and stared at Istvan from his mount. Then he nodded and flashed a wan smile of thanks.

"Come on ... let's find this Monastery," Istvan called out again and they were off. The horses seemed to have found renewed strength and took off at a proper pace down the road as it continued to roll and wind through a fairly level part through some woods. Soon they were out in a mountain valley momentarily revealing a scattering of houses and a great hill atop which was the white brick Monastery of Piatra Fantanele. Istvan could see the road switched back a couple of more times and that yellow lanterns and lights within the Monastery were being lit, as well as in a few of the cottages. Istvan looked back at the dark green and black forest that was now receding behind them and could not repress a shudder for some reason. He had to admit to himself he was relieved to be in more open country with his destination in sight as twilight set in.

Once through the heavy, wrought iron gates, the sisters at the Monastery took care of their horses, bid them inside and fed them a hearty meal of *Paprika Hendl* with wine. The Abbess joined them afterwards in the Great Room where a pleasant, robust fire burned. She offered them some of the plum brandy distilled at the monastery and for which it was locally famous. A conversation among the three of them began with the usual exchange of pleasantries: the thanks of the guests to the hostess for her hospitality, the dismissive acknowledgement of the hostess for the trifling favors afforded and apologies more could not be offered. In due course, however, each side began gently to sally forth to gather information that could be useful.

"You said you have come to us from Budapest?" the Abbess inquired of Istvan.

"I did, Your Grace," Istvan admitted. "I am a son of a silversmith from Old Buda, but that was a number of years ago. And you? Where are you from originally?"

Her Grace revealed she was also from Budapest and discovered Kasza's home was Balatonfüred which engendered a number of inquiries directed his way about the state of Lake Balaton these days; a place the Abbess had visited often as a young girl.

"And so what brings you to these parts, Gnädiger Herr Kálváry Istvan? It isn't every day we are blessed to receive Royal dignitaries from Budapest or even Bistritz. The diligences pass us every day going this way and that, but few stop here unless one of our people wants to be picked up. Where are you bound, Uram?"

"I am learning my geography in your beautiful mountainous country that is the envy of the Magyars of the flat plains and cities, Blessed Mother, wouldn't you agree?" The Holy Mother nodded with a faint smile.

"Of course, it is beautiful country in the daytime," the Abbess replied.

"In truth, we are interested in some developments concerning this district. This area has experienced quite a number of missing persons. Are you aware of that?

"There have been quite a few disappearances over the years," the Abbess said, cautiously. "Very sad cases, of course. Some of the missing over the past few years happened only a few kilometers from here."

"Is that so?" Istvan replied, leaning forward in his chair deliberately to signal his interest.

"Yes. There was a whole family of tenant farmers, lost one by one until they were all gone. Just a house left. Empty."

"Really?" Istvan replied. Kasza quietly took out a little notebook from his jacket and a pencil to make notes. The Abbess noticed his movement.

"Are you sincerely here to investigate missing persons out here in the mountains? There have been others, you know. They came and left us here, never to return."

"Who?" Istvan inquired.

"Novotny for one. He was out here once. Asked some questions and left. Nothing was ever done. Nobody ever arrested. More people have gone missing since then. The ones who talked to him, particularly. They all went missing too. This is common knowledge around these parts and may, shall we say, inhibit your investigation."

"Are you saying the people out here are afraid of some kind of retaliation if they talk to us?"

"I'm afraid so," the Abbess replied. "This hasn't been handled very well in the past."

"What do you know about prior investigations into missing persons out here?" Kasza spoke up for the first time. The Abbess turned to him.

"I know they didn't last long, they didn't get far and it did no good. I know the police themselves have gone missing at times. The police station up here has been vacant for quite some time, hasn't it?" Istvan looked at Kasza who nodded, affirming her statement.

"We are concerned, of course, and worried this may be the work of a serial killer," Istvan stated in a quiet voice. "We are here to find what clues we can, if that is the case."

"I wish you the best of luck in your inquires, then," said the Abbess, rising now from her chair to leave. "It has long been an affliction in these parts."

"Madame, have you no thoughts of your own about the cause of so many people in this area going missing?" Kasza asked.

"Me? I have no opinions. I have no idea why it has happened to us or if indeed it is a single person. It is God's will, and I leave it at that. It is for you and your people to have opinions about things like this."

"Have you heard any rumors or speculation from anyone?" Istvan persisted, rising from his chair as the Abbess neared him on her way out the door. She paused and turned to face him.

"Of course. One hears rumors all the time. The local peasants come here to mass and confession. We talk to some of them"

"Can you tell us what they say?"

"They are very superstitious. They worry an evil eye is upon us and think it comes down from the Castle."

"What castle?"

"You will find it a few kilometers north of the Coach Road at the end of a path that meets the Borgo Pass. An old ruin of a castle. It is owned by the Count Dracula Vlad. The country folk around here think he is a vampire and is the source of all the evil and mischief in these parts."

"A vampire?" Kasza exclaimed.

"As I said, I have no opinions."

"But surely …" Istvan had not finished before the Abbess swept out of the room and he found himself looking at Kasza.

"What do you make of that, Kasza?"

"Superstition explains things that ignorant minds cannot understand or comprehend."

"I wonder, does the Count Dracula actually live at this ruined castle, or somewhere else?" Istvan replied.

"Nobody lives there," Kasza replied. The immediacy of his answer and tone of voice conveyed the fact he had already thought about this and had done some background checking. "At least not most of the time."

"So the castle is inhabitable, at least in part?"

"Perhaps, Vezér. That is what they have told me."

"I would like to see this castle and meet the Count," Istvan said. "And I am anxious to see the Roma in the Forest. This seems to be interesting country here indeed. We may have to stay an extra day, Kasza." With that they went to their beds for the night.

As Istvan gazed out the windows of the Monastery into the night before climbing into bed, he could see a broad shallow mountain valley in the country below the hill upon which the building perched. A couple of dozen cottages lay scattered about the meandering path leaading to the coach road from which they had arrived. Beyond, several kilometers away, on the horizon was the forest where the wolves had been encountered and the quickly steepening peaks and hills around and beyond it. Moonlight revealed the dense, tall pine trees that obscured the Coach Road and bristled like a spine along the crest of the nearest range. Like a mass of soldiers marching upward, the forest of pines seamlessly covered and obscured the rocks and crags that lay in the woods.

Istvan heard wolves softly baying. It was a far away noise, at times obscured by a breeze. At times the dogs abruptly stopped, but they were out there. Perhaps it was the pack he and Kasza had encountered, or perhaps it was another one. At times it was only one or two he heard, but other times, there were many more voices. He listened to them, curious now. They were out in the wild, Istvan thought.

When was the last time he had been in an area so populated with wolves? Bohemia. He had been stationed there after the War with Prussia as a young officer. He saw them all the time in the woods and mountains there. In packs they were a fearsome animal to confront. They always had a cunning leader. They had a plan and discipline. The collective intelligence of a wolf pack was not to be underestimated, he came to know. They were out there tonight, he thought, as he pulled a heavy Eiderdown over his shoulder and his head nestled into a pillow. They were out there on a mission and who knew what? This was wild country, he thought. Beautiful, but wild.

Chapter 9

Nikolai, Béla and the Sinti had carefully repaired and restored the box that whoever or whatever had been placed in and delivered the whole cargo to the stationmaster at Vatra Dornei without saying a word to anyone about what had happened. Everyone knew if the Master knew what had happened and who was responsible, his wrath would know no bounds. No bounds. Each man had time to think to himself what he would do if someday, somehow, he came face to face with the Master and he demanded to know what had happened. Some of them harbored the illusion for a few hours they would have the courage to defy him, or lie to him, but in the end, each one knew that they would betray Nikolai and Béla rather than risk the unthinkable consequences with Lord Dracula.

"We bought some time, Béla," said Nikolai as the day wore on and the troupe of Roma headed back home. "He will find out. He will desire to mete out vengeance when he finds out. He will demand from us how this could happen and why we said nothing. When that conversation happens ..."

"If that conversation happens, we will be dead soon after," Béla interrupted. "We can never go to him again because we will never know when the day will come and when we find out ..."

"It will be the day we die."

"Perhaps death would not be so bad. It could be worse. Why don't we kill him?" Béla said quietly. "We've thought about it before. What choice do we have? What about our children? My Natália? We are at his mercy and, as you and I both know, mercy is not a quality in large supply with the Master."

They rode for a while as Nikolai thought about the question in his mind. Of course, if they could kill the Count, the retribution surely to come would be avoided. And if they failed to kill him, he would kill them in a slow and grisly fashion, to be sure. Nikolai had seen evidence of the Count's penchant for cruelty over the years and knew only too well of the depths to which he could sink.

"How do you kill something that is not alive?" Nikolai responded at last.

"They say you must cut off its head. Stake his heart. Expose it to sunlight and let it burn to ashes like what we saw today."

"Where does he lie, though?" said Nikolai. "How can we be sure to find him in the daylight hours. It would take days to search the castle and we haven't got days, brother. If we don't find him tomorrow or the next day, I think we're doomed. Maybe it would be best to gather up our families and flee tonight, while we have the chance, before he knows."

"What about our people?" Béla asked. "What will happen to those we leave behind? What will he do to them? He will know we have gone and he will look for us. These men and even the people in the camp will betray us to him if we breathe a word of our destination. He will hunt us down. We will have to give up our Romani life and live in a city to hide. And what city?"

"We know where he has sent his boxes of dirt. Bucharest. Budapest and Belgrade, Constantinople. There are Roma all over Europe. We can join them."

"What about them?" Béla flicked his head indicating the four Roma following behind the leiter-wagon and the driver. "You can bet they are all talking about how they should tell the Master what we did to save their own skins." Nikolai turned around in his saddle and was met by a baleful glare from the oldest of the Roma guards. Another averted his eyes and gazed off into the distance, pretending not to notice. The wagon driver simply stared straight ahead, not making any eye contact at all.

A mutinous crew in all probability, Nikolai thought. He turned back to Béla.

"We'll have to kill them before we get to the Borgo Pass, then."

"Are you crazy? There are five of them and only two of us. They're all armed. We'll be killed."

"We will have to surprise them." Béla turned in his saddle to look back for a moment and then looked over at his brother.

"There will be no surprise with them," Béla said in a low voice. "They may do it to us first."

The brothers continued like this for a couple of more hours, pondering what they would do next. By the afternoon, they had persuaded themselves there was no good way out of their dilemma and they were approaching the mountain village of Poiana Stampei, the last town before the forest of Tinovul Mohos and the Roma camp. They were soon approaching the point of no return when they decided. Turning his horse, Nikolai commanded the troupe to halt.

"Brothers," he began with a soft but firm voice. "Béla and I have been discussing what to do about our problem ..."

"Our problem?" spoke up the oldest one. "It is not our problem. It is your problem."

Nikolai had anticipated this. "Yes, Lajos," he said, calling the man by name. "But don't think for a moment the Master will content himself with our heads. Everyone was guarding the boxes. Everyone will be to blame from the Master's point of view. We must stick together on this or ..." He didn't have to finish.

"What do you suggest?" asked one of the younger escorts, trying to defuse the situation. The seven Roma were now clustered in a circle as their horses snorted and pissed on the ground.

"In the first place, we go home and say nothing to anyone. You understand? Not a word. It was a routine job. We brought the boxes to the station and we left. By the time the box is opened and found to be empty, it will be in some far off place. When the Master finds out, of course, he will want to know what happened. He will call for us and question us. We will say nothing happened. How can he know when the box was opened between the castle and wherever it was going? It was opened by someone for some reason, but not by us."

"But the ship's crew, they will say they stowed it. The longshoremen who receive the boxes will say they just picked it up and put it on some other carts. He will suspect us," argued the older one, Lajos.

"Suspect us he may, but he won't know. He won't know unless one of us tells him. I propose we swear a blood oath to Kali to keep this secret. We must all trust one another. What do you say? Are you all in?" Béla had quietly circled his horse behind the others. The brothers had agreed, if anyone balked at the pact, they would be killed. If necessary, they would kill all of them or die themselves. They had agreed it would be better to die out here at the hands of their countrymen than whatever dire fate the Master would have for them.

Lajos looked at Béla from his mount out of the corner of his eye. Béla decided right then that Lajos would have to be killed, if not now, soon. The younger ones, out of respect for the hetman or confusion about what to do each affirmed they would keep the secret. Lajos was last and did so petulantly. They all cut the palms of their hands to draw blood, then one by one they shook hands on it. Finally, they turned their horses toward home and the Forest of Tinovul Mohos.

They entered the camp at sunset. Dozens of campfires with dozens of boiling, sizzling pots and their heavy scent could be smelled for nearly a kilometer as the troupe approached. The anxiety Nikolai had felt all day along the trail lightened a bit as they neared. Then Béla learned toward him.

"The one, Lajos. I will have to …" Nikolai nodded firmly, repulsed by the deed and waved his brother to do what needed to be done as he spurred his horse off to his own cottage and his wife. Béla parted company with the others and rode to his little shanty where Nátalia was stirring a pot of rabbit stew for him. He thought of his wife who should have been there to meet him, may Kali preserve her soul. But at least he had his daughter.

◎ ◎ ◎

The Carpathian Assignment

It was about midnight when Béla crept from his bed and with bare feet, quietly padded across the floor with his clothes in his hand, enveloping a large knife that would quietly do the night's dirty work for him. He had considered everything carefully as he lay awake, waiting for Nátalia to fall asleep; exactly how he would approach Lajos' cabin and softly call him outside. Lajos was so disagreeable, he lived alone, Béla knew. Once Lajos came out to see what was the matter, Béla would slit his throat before he could make a sound and then stab him to death. The steel knife was big and sharp as a razor and Béla had sharpened it again that night before he went to bed to be doubly sure. Lajos would be sleepy and Béla was strong and quick with a knife, as everybody knew.

Béla dressed outside the door of his hut while listening carefully. He did not hear Nátalia stir inside. There was a half-moon up in the night sky which, together with the stars on this clear night in the mountain air, gave him just enough light to navigate through the little village he knew so well. He felt his heart beating in his chest as he crouched near the corner of Lajos' door for a moment to gather himself for the deed and to make sure nobody was awake or saw him.

It was eerily quiet as he crouched for a minute or two, gathering his nerve and his strength. Slowly, it occurred to him that Lajos' horse was not tied to the rail outside his door. His horse was gone! Fear and panic now welled up inside him. He sprang up and tapped on the door.

"Lajos?" he rasped in an audible but coarse whisper at the door. "Lajos!" he repeated, tapping again. Nothing. He tapped again and then again. Nothing. He put his ear to the door, but could hear nothing stirring inside. A comforting thought sprang into his head. Perhaps Lajos was drunk. Living alone, Lajos was often known to drink too much. That was probably it, Béla thought. With that, he slowly turned the crude handle on the door and gently opened it a few centimeters. Again he put his ear to the crack, but heard nothing. Not even heavy breathing. Panic again. Was he gone? Had he broken their vow and ridden to the Master? He had to know.

Béla softly opened the door wide enough to admit him and closed it behind him to hide whatever happened or was going to be said from the nearby cottages of Lajos' neighbors. It was pitch black inside. He fumbled in his pocket for a match. There it was. He pulled a match stick out and groped around in the dark to find something to strike it on. With his left hand, he pulled the dagger out of his cloak, just to be ready. He struck the match and the phosphoric flash dimmed in an instant to a tiny flame. Lajos' bed was empty! Damn him, thought Béla, but no sooner had this thought flashed into his mind than he realized he was not alone. There in the corner of the one room cabin, sitting in a rocking chair, gazing at him with the huge pupils of his eyes flashing red as they reflected the flame that would soon go out, was the Master himself.

Chapter 10

As Istvan opened one eye to look out the window, he saw that it was snowing. The room was freezing cold, Istvan realized, which made getting out from under the warm Eiderdown unappealing but inevitable. As he listened, he could hear distant but audible sounds from somewhere down stairs and corridors; no doubt the nuns getting ready for breakfast. He had been awakened at dawn by a little bell sounded in the yard of the monastery signaling the morning prayers or Matins, but had decided to ignore it and went back to sleep.

Istvan reached for his glasses on the night table by the bed and then for his gold pocketwatch that he had received upon his retirement from the army. He popped open the cover and once again, as he did every morning, marveled at the opal-like white face of the TAG Heuer watch with its black Roman numerals and gold hands. On the inside cover was inscribed the Habsburg Doppeladler or "double headed eagle" and below that the Latin inscription *"Fidus Corona Et Patriae"* or "For Loyalty to Crown and Country". It was 8:12 and snowing outside.

Slowly Istvan swung his feet out of bed on to the hardwood floor and grabbed his trousers and shirt, which he had laid on the small table at the foot of the bed. He quickly pulled them on, went to the door, looked down the whitewashed hall to the toilet. He saw that the door was open and brought his military toilet kit with him; the same one he had used for over twenty years with its shaving powder, brush and razor. In a short time, he had finished, dressed and walked downstairs to the public dining room.

A long wooden table was set for breakfast. He could smell sausages being sizzled on the stovetop of the nearby kitchen and suspected, in that case, a Hungarian Villásreggeli or "breakfast with a fork" had evidently been ordered by the Abbess in their honor. Pancakes and compote were already on the table and Istvan realized his mouth was watering in anticipation of it.

As preparations were obviously not complete and Kasza had not yet arrived, Istvan decided to casually explore the monastery a bit more while he waited. He left the dining room and passed the stairs to the second floor, down a long corridor with windows looking out over the village below. Wall sconces with fresh wax candles lined the walls. Dark oil paintings of the Madonna or other biblical scenes. Chairs rested against the walls. Then there was an archway leading to a small foyer like room. A library with many books lining the walls. Polished tables and chairs and a large chandelier hovering over them.

There was a quiet air of austerity here, Istvan thought. Silence and contemplation hung in the air. Several nuns were reading at the table and nodded silent greetings to him as he surveyed the room. Not wanting to disturb them, he quickly turned and left. As soon as he did so, he came abruptly face to face with none other than the Abbess again, who nodded to him in greeting.

"My lord," she said formally.

"Holy Mother," he responded with equal formality, but as warmly as he could manage. The denouement of the previous evening had not been entirely satisfactory and he welcomed resuming a conversation with her in the light of day.

"We have breakfast for you and your companion," she said, as she resumed her walk down the long hallway back in the direction of the dining room.

"You are very kind."

"Did you sleep well?"

"Like the dead." As soon as he said this, the Abbess shot him a sharp glance and crossed herself.

"That is not an expression to use lightly in these parts."

"Madame?" It seemed like he could not keep from making mistakes with this woman.

"The people around here are superstitious and it would be better not to allude to things like that."

"Ah, yes, indeed."

They sat down at the table, just the two of them. The Abbess served herself a pancake and some blackberry compote.

"We will be back this evening after we visit the Forest where the Roma reside and a few of the farms along the way. We will go as far as Poiana Stampei and then back."

"Quite a beautiful ride in the daylight, as I remember," the Abbess remarked.

"We will pass through the Borgo Pass. Where is that castle of Count Dracula, if we have time?"

"Take care with the time and don't tarry. Make sure you are at least at the Coach Road when the sun sets, if not back inside our walls. You will find the road to it off the Coach Road just after the peak of the Pass. There are no other roads up there. You will find it." Istvan could sense some uneasiness in the Abbess' face and pointed tone.

"Surely, Madame ..."

"I don't know what you believe, my Lord ..." Her voice was soft but now completely serious and grave. "Of course, we are the Holy Mother Church. We believe in God, but there is also Satan. He is also something we believe in, do you understand?"

Istvan nodded silently, encouraging her to go on.

"I have a personal belief. It is not Catholic doctrine, but based on my own experience here in Transylvania. I believe when there is great good, something that shines brightly on the hillside of our lives, it is also seen by the Evil One. The greater the good, the more brightly it shines, the more he is attracted to it; to extinguish it. Our monastery ministers to the poor, the helpless, the despairing and downcast. We have been here for more than two centuries. Do you understand what I am saying?" Istvan had stopped eating now, fascinated by this impromptu discourse and where it was leading them.

"All around us, as you said, people have disappeared over the years. Many are oppressed by a daily fear something dark and mysterious is near them, but cannot be seen. It's just outside their grasp, but it's there nevertheless. Its icy fingers have touched the backs of their necks, but when they turned around it was gone. That's what it's like to live here, in the Borgo Pass, my Lord. A day's ride from Bistritz. A day's ride from anywhere. We are out here alone, in cold and darkness. Too poor to flee, the people come here to seek the safety of the cross within our walls."

Istvan leaned back away from the table and sipped his cup of Turkish coffee as she spoke. He did not believe anymore. The certainty of a God and an afterlife that had buoyed him in his early life, that had fortified him before a battle, that he had accepted without question from his teachers, his parents, and his culture as a young man had withered in his middle age. It was now reduced to doubt and even hostility to the dogmas of the Church. He hoped he was wrong, of course, because he wanted to be with Julia again, but hope was not belief or even faith. It was just hope.

Istvan suddenly realized the Abbess had stopped speaking and was looking at him.

"So there is a balance in this little universe here, is that it?" Istvan replied.

"Yes, I believe there is."

"Offsetting the Christianity and good works here at the Monastery, there is an equal and opposite force in play?"

"I am afraid there may be, my Lord." Istvan could see the Abbess was quite serious. There was no denying the sincerity of the woman's strong belief. He envied her. He envied her certain faith he did not, could not share.

"And this warning to be back by sunset, does that have to do with this evil, as opposed to highwaymen who might rob us?"

"We haven't had many of those since the Turks retreated from here for good," the Abbess said matter-of-factly. "It seems like things happen after dark here. That's all. Especially near the Borgo Pass. Do not linger at the castle and whatever you do, do not allow yourself or your companion to be found there after sunset." As she uttered this last statement, with the utmost conviction, Istvan realized the Abbess knew more than she had revealed so far. For some reason, she was holding back yet, in her sincere concern for their safety, he decided he would not confront her just yet.

Kasza had quietly joined them a few minutes earlier, but had been listening in silence. He and Istvan now traded looks. It was time to leave.

"Madame, we will most definitely plan to return before sunset if for no reason than to enjoy some more of the delicious cuisine you serve here." The Abbess responded with a faint smile and the conversation became lighter at that point.

"May God bless you and keep you," the Abbess said, making the sign of the cross in the air between them. Istvan nodded gratefully.

"And with you, Holy Mother," Istvan replied.

Chapter 11

Natália was sleeping soundly when she felt a hand on her shoulder shaking her awake. It was her uncle, Nikolai. He had a candle in his hand that lit his face in the darkness. Something was wrong. She knew it instinctively. His face was lined and haggard.

"Get up! Hurry! Get dressed and pack a few things in a blanket that you might need. We are leaving here."

"What? Where is Papa?" She had noticed her father's bed was empty. What was happening? Voices outside. She could see through the half-opened door that there was a crowd gathered in the central clearing of the camp. Torches had been lit. There was a buzzing and murmuring punctuated by an occasional raised voice.

"Never mind. He has had to leave. I will explain everything to you in a little while, but hurry now. You must come quickly." Natália got up quickly as her uncle left the little cottage so she could dress, closing the door behind him. She dressed in a simple smock and sandals. She bundled some other clothes into a blanket with a hairbrush and a few other possessions and then opened the door. There, her uncle took her roughly by the hand and pulled her toward his horse. She attempted to look back toward the clearing, but he turned her head away with his hand.

"Don't look over there!" Nikolai said sharply to her, but as he locked his hands together to boost her up on the horse, she could not repress a glance that made her heart stop. The torch lights being held by the Roma put in silhouette a horrifying sight of a man, impaled on a long spear that had been jammed into the ground. Several men were bent over the bottom of the pole, trying to pull it out of the ground while others, arms extended, prepared to catch the dead body. Many faces turned toward her to watch her, all with looks of fear or sadness, some with hands covering their mouths, others crossing themselves.

"I said, don't look over there!" Nicolai shouted, heaving himself up into the saddle. He wheeled the horse into the woods and kicked its flanks. Within moments, they were galloping through the dark woods with the flames of the torches quickly dimming and then disappearing into the background. Her uncle knew the trail through the woods well, Natália thought, because otherwise almost nothing could be seen in the darkness as they sped along. Slowly, disbelievingly, she began to put the images she had just seen in her mind together with her uncle's behavior and that of the crowd and her missing father and she began to cry.

Her uncle reached back and his hand fell on her leg which he seemed to pat as reassuringly as circumstances permitted, but it only confirmed her worst fears. She lay her head on her uncle's back and held on to him as best she could. Soon, they reached the Coach Road and her uncle turned west; up toward the Borgo Pass. Her grief began to change to disbelief and then quickening fear as the horse pounded toward the destination that had always been forbidden, especially at night.

"Where are you taking me? Where is my father? I'm frightened!"

Nikolai slowed the horse down to a canter as they neared the turn off to the castle from the Coach Road.

"I'm so sorry, Natália. Your father and I wanted to protect you from all of this but now there is no time to explain. I'm taking you to the Count's castle tonight as he has commanded me to do. I have no choice, my little dove. I cannot disobey him." Natália's eyes were wide with terror now. "It should be all right. You must do as he says. He wants you in his service now. He will take care of everything. I will visit you as soon as I can."

"But no! I can't ..." Natália could not get the words out before her uncle, clenching his teeth and eyes brimming turned away from her and kicked the horse forward again at breakneck speed down the forest road.

Rolling clouds unveiled and then covered the moon Natália could see overhead, between the lines of tree tops that crowded the narrow road. As they came to a clearing, she saw again for only the second time in her life, the castle brooding on a mountaintop. They were making for it as fast as her uncle could ride.

It was another twenty minutes or so by the time they reached the vast, arched gate into a courtyard; the entrance to the castle. In the gloom, at the far side of the courtyard, Natália could see some arched passageways leading into blackness. There was a pair of double doors with heavy iron nails, hinges and braces at the top of some stone steps. Nikolai dismounted, then reached up and helped Natália down off the horse and unstrapped her bundle of clothing and belongings from his saddle.

"What will happen now?" Natália asked in a whispered voice.

"Just wait. He will be here in a moment." Natália looked around the cobblestoned courtyard. There were a number of tall, empty windows that lined the stone walls of the residence that seemed to frown down upon them disapprovingly. The roofline appeared jagged and uneven with some parts crowned by a high sloping roof, while another was topped by a tower.

"Natália, there isn't time to explain everything but I give you this. It belonged to your mother. It is the sign of the Christian God, Natália." He placed a rosary with a silver cross around her neck. "They say that he ..."

At that moment, there was a sound behind the massive double doors of a bolt being pulled. Natália noticed that where all of the windows had been black, now the one closest to the door glowed yellow. Another bolt being shot, then the sound of a key turning in a lock and then the door opened.

Standing in the doorway, was a tall, slender man dressed in black from head to toe holding a gas lamp. He had a thick mane of white hair and a thick, white mustache that rested beneath an angular, aquiline white nose. He had a very pale complexion but strikingly full, red lips. The flame from the lamp reflected reddened eyes which were immediately fixed on her. Nikolai fell to one knee, head bowed in obeisance to the Count. Natália was so frightened that she forgot to do anything but gaze back at him. He motioned to her with his free hand to approach, his lips parting to expose vividly white teeth. He appeared to be a not unattractive but hard-looking older man, in Natália's youthful estimation. Once he had caught her gaze, she could not look away.

"Come in, my child. Come in," the Count invited with a gesture of his hand. His voice was the deep, smooth sound of a cello. She felt a gentle push from behind, guiding her into the castle even though her uncle was on his knees to her right and the Count was standing directly in front of her. He opened the door wide and stepped back away from the threshold. Natália was in no position to resist and stepped over the threshold into a dimly lit foyer.

As Nikolai rose and made to come in also, the Count's expression changed in a flash to irritation. "Thou mayest go, Nikolai."

The doors swung closed without any effort on the part of the Count who remained standing just inside the door with a small candelabra in his other hand. Natália looked back in terror at her uncle as the doors slowly began to close. For just one instant she caught his eyes. They were full of despair and helplessness. He bowed again gravely to the Count, turned and mounted his horse and in a moment her uncle had clattered out of the courtyard and the gate, leaving her behind.

"Come, come ..." the Count beckoned, again waving his hand to her. The heavy door finally shut behind her with a heavy boom that echoed off the walls of the castle interior and the process of re-bolting and locking began without any motion or effort on the part of the Count, she saw in amazement. So it was true, then. She had seen it with her own eyes. The Count had magical powers. She was lost. She was totally in his power. Strangely, the utter helplessness of her situation restored her to a state of fatalistic calm.

The room she was in was a vast foyer with a high vaulted ceiling and a large arch on the opposite wall, to the left side, leading down a dark passageway lit by torches in sconces. A wide stairwell that slowly spiraled from left to right, over the archway, and then continuing to climb in a slow spiral back to the left again where it ended on what seemed to be, in the dim light, a sort of balcony that overlooked the foyer..

"My dear, dost thee know who I am?"

"You are the Count Dracula, our Lord and Master," Natália replied softly, lowering her eyes and giving a shallow curtsey. He moved slowly toward her, his eyes fixed intently on hers. She heard a low buzzing sound in her ears, like the sound of bees. She began to feel slightly dizzy and light headed.

"Take thee off that detestable thing," he said as he raised his arm and pointed with a long, white finger that ended in a sharp pointed nail toward the crucifix hanging from her neck. "No good doth the thing if thou believe not in it," he said, the red lips pursing as if he smelled a disgusting odor. "And methinks thou dost not ..." He was speaking to her in the old Wallachian tongue from long ago. She could understand him with effort, but noticed the antique manner of his speech.

Natália felt her knees began to give way. She reached for the Christian cross, wrapping it in her hand softly. Strangely, it felt warm in her hand. It hung from a simple, fine chain from her neck. She lifted it from around her neck until she was just holding the cross in her hand, with the chain dangling in the air.

"That's it," the Count continued, his voice soothing. "Take off the thing and throw it on the floor."

It seemed to glow and sparkle as she regarded it, perhaps from the flickering torchlight. She held it up, between her and the Count who stepped back, his face transformed suddenly to a fury. He opened his mouth and roared so loudly she reached for her ears impulsively to stop the sound, dropping the crucifix on the floor. The sound of his voice was deafening and as soon as the cross hit the floor, she felt herself falling. The room began to darken to black. She felt the arms of the Count catching her. Then, there was nothing but blackness.

Chapter 12

Soon Kasza and Istvan took their leave and were on the Coach Road again. Within a quarter hour, they reached the peak of the Borgo Pass. In a few more minutes, they came to an intersecting cart path at a clearing that wound into a thick, mountain forest within 100 meters.

"That must be the road to Count Dracula's castle," Istvan said, seated on his horse as he gazed down the road. Kasza noticed there was a stone marker by the side of the road at the intersection. There was the number 33. It was thirty three kilometers to someplace, Istvan thought. Probably Vatra Dornei in the Bukovina. They would not be going nearly that far; perhaps eight or ten kilometers north and then east. It had stopped snowing, but the sky was grey and at times, as they resumed their progress to the Sinti encampment, a breeze kicked up that chilled. Istvan and Kasza were both wearing heavy cloaks with hoods and suede leather gloves.

"Someone has been here recently," Kasza said as he let his horse amble a few paces up the path. His black, gloved hand pointed down at the path which revealed both horse' hooves and the tell-tale lines of a wheeled conveyance of some sort. "Probably a landau or *calèche*, I would guess. The wheel marks are too thin for a wagon or cart and too deep."

Istvan allowed his horse to wander down the path also, looking at the markings and grunted affirmatively to Kasza's observations. The depth of the wheel markings suggested a fairly heavy vehicle whose weight rested on thin, elegant wheels rather than the broad rims of a cart or leiter-wagon.

Kasza had taken out a cigarette and lit it as they continued to survey the little intersection. It was quiet. Patches of melting snow here and there. Trees still leafless and bare. Kasza pointed up and Istvan followed his gaze until he saw an enormous white owl perched on a branch of a tree nearby. The bird was beautiful with large yellow eyes that occasionally blinked as it gazed down at them fearlessly, watching them.

"Come on, we should be going," Istvan said after a few moments observing the bird that stood almost motionless above them. As they returned to the Coach Road, and proceeded a short distance further north, Istvan noticed another roadside shrine by the side of the road. He had seen quite a few of them that morning. They were invariably built by local farmers to safeguard passers-by on the road. They often had inside their little frames small Madonnas, with or without the Christ child, or crucifixes or icons if they were Orthodox-built. This one was empty.

The landscape changed again as they approached the camp. Open, rocky landscape began to become thick woods on the southern or eastern side of the Coach Road with steep rocks on the other side. Then it became all forest.

It was about noon when they saw the first Roma, on horseback. A pair of them. The Roma darted away, presumably on a shortcut to their camp after they spotted them. Suspicious behavior, Istvan thought, but not surprising among these people. Istvan's dim views of the character of the Roma, or Gypsies as Istvan often regarded them, had been ingrained over nearly six decades of life and no matter how much he tried to ignore his instinctive prejudice, the Roma would do something that awakened it. In any event, Istvan surmised they were, essentially, sentries and were even now announcing their approach.

The Roma women and little children were the first people Istvan and Kasza encountered, as they reached the outskirts of their village in the woods. As the two figures from the outside world passed, they blatantly stared at them in wonder and suspicion. Uniformed people from the outside were rarely good news for Roma anywhere in Europe and were not welcome. Fearful of the punishment royal authorizes could bring down on them, the Roma tolerated, humored and eventually attempted to trick them whenever they appeared. So it would be here, Istvan thought.

By the time they reached the core of the village, a hetman approached from the opposite direction and called out to them in some dialect of the Wallachian tongue, signaling that it was to him that they should direct their attention. As he approached them, Istvan could see out of the corner of his eye a handful of younger men slowly emerged in empty doorways and from behind trees and carts. Some of them probably had pitchforks or rifles easily at hand, Istvan thought, but for the moment none of them demonstrated any overt hostility.

To show the slightest fear at this moment was out of the question, or one would lose control of the situation, but that was not in Istvan's mind. An imperial tone laced with official condescension was appropriate here and he readied himself to address the hetman, approaching slowly on horseback. It came naturally to his Magyar heritage anyway. After two and a half centuries of control the Austrians had taught the Magyars the language of power and command. The Magyars had learned their lessons well and when their independence from Austria was achieved in 1867, they used it in turn on the 'lesser' ethnic groups within their kingdom, especially the Slavs. Roma were even lower on the social order.

"I am Kálváry Istvan, Chief of His Majesty's District Police for the Bistritz District," Istvan began formally, in the Magyar tongue, still seated on his horse while the hetman stood on the ground looking up at him. "This is Gábor Kasza, Inspector of the Transylvanian Constabulary from Klausenberg."

"Would you care to sit down at my table, at my house?" inquired the hetman in heavily accented Magyar, bowing low and gesturing in the direction of where he lived. He identified himself as Nikolai. Istvan nodded and soon found himself seated across from a swarthy but ruggedly handsome Roma whose voluptuous wife was anxiously preparing her kitchen. A smell of garlic and strong earthy vegetables permeated the room, not unpleasantly. Nikolai offered tea, to which Istvan and Kasza accepted. Some pleasantries were exchanged as they waited for the tea to be served in some heavy earthenware cups, and then Nikolai's wife withdrew to let the men talk.

Kasza spoke first as Istvan removed his pipe from his cloak pocket and began to pack a bowl. "My Lord Istvan wanted to get to know his District better, and so he invited me to ride out with him to meet the people of the Borgo Pass. We have heard of you people and your settlement here in the Forest. We wanted to meet you." Nikolai appeared to listen warily to the Inspector from Klausenberg and Budapest. Kasza wasted no time in coming to the point.

"We have come to learn that this area seems to have a very unusual number of missing persons. Were you aware of that?" Kasza inquired directly.

"What is normal? What is unusual?" Nikolai parried the question without answering it. Istvan noted the evasive answer, but Kasza continued.

"Have your people here at this camp noticed or experienced any missing persons for the last five years or so?"

Nikolai seemed to give the matter some considerable thought, but eventually answered "not that I can think of".

"Have you ever heard this discussed much out here? This Borgo Pass area? Ever hear about missing persons from any of the farmers or villagers around here that you might have done some work for?"

Again, Nikolai seemed to need to give this a lot of thought. "I can't say as I have, Sir. There was a case some years ago. I vaguely recollect it, my Lord. But it didn't concern us and we don't get mixed up in other people's things, Sir. You understand, don't you?" With this his eye glinted with a look of sardonic humor. "We stay to ourselves around here, pretty much. We do some work for the farmers and smiths, it's true, but we stick to ourselves and mind our own business."

We're not going to get any information from him at this rate, Istvan thought as he puffed on his pipe now, exhaling a delightfully pungent cloud of smoke as he listened to the conversation between Kasza and the hetman continue along these lines. Kasza would thrust and the hetman would parry at each inquiry, becoming ever more evasive and vague as Kasza persisted. What farms around here did they work? What about the case you just mentioned?

Who was it? Where did they live? Did he not hear about the farm where every member of the family eventually went missing? At first, Kasza took notes of the man's responses in his usual fastidious way, but Istvan noticed he had stopped, probably because the man was saying nothing of importance. That was the way they were, Istvan thought. The only way to deal with a Roma was through fear or greed. Eventually, Istvan decided he had heard enough.

"Ever hear of a vampire living up in this area?" Istvan asked the hetman in a matter-of-fact manner, watching the bowl of the pipe while he re-lit and toked on it again. There was a pause and he looked up. The hetman's mouth was open, having been caught in mid-sentence playing his word games with Kasza. Now his eyes locked on Istvan's and the Chief noticed he had hit something. His face reflected a new concentration as color drained from it and for a moment, Istvan was certain, a look of deep and profound fear could be seen behind his eyes before he regained his composure. Istvan had triggered some mind vision, all right, and for an instant the hetman had been unable to hide it.

"Who told you that?" the Roma chief responded evasively, obviously playing for time, but Istvan would have none of it.

"I asked you a question. Do you remember what it was?" Another pause. Another look. This time inquiring. Kasza was watching intently as well. Whatever the man said next, Istvan thought, would be a lie.

"That's just a superstition, my Lord. People talk about such things but nobody has ever seen one. Know what I mean, Sir? A lot of talk. People around here in the mountains are what you might call superstitious. Believe in different Gods, Sir. You might be surprised, I imagine."

"Satan at work?"

"Satan, sir?"

"You heard me. You believe in Satan, don't you?"

"Nay, my Lord. Not Satan. I believe in the Christian God."

"Do you?" Istvan could barely repress laughing in the man's face, so obvious were the hetman's lies.

"There are no Christian signs in your house. I see not one cross. No image of our Lord and Savior Jesus Christ? No, young man, I doubt you are a

Christian. Now, back to my original question. You agree, the local people believe there is a vampire in these lands? And that it has something to do with the missing people? Is that what you are saying?"

Istvan could see that the hetman realized he had been caught out by the sly older man and was embarrassed. He had lowered his eyes like a cowardly dog that had been hit with a newspaper, ashamed of his inability to trick the older policemen.

"Yes, it is true," Nikolai responded carefully. "There are some that think so. I don't think it, Sir. I don't believe in such things, but many up here do."

"And who is this vampire, do the villagers and farmers think?"

"They ..."

"Have you ever heard anyone claim that the Count Dracula is a vampire?"

"I don't think so, Sir. I can't recall that, no Sir." Istvan could tell the hetman was genuinely nervous now, his demeanor was clear. The hetman looked away and would not meet his eyes. The man was an inveterate liar, Istvan had concluded. They were always this way with the police. He was not angry about it. It was just a fact. But in truth, Istvan knew the answer was the opposite of the hetman's response. He had confirmed in his own mind quite a few people in the area thought the Count was a vampire. Not that Istvan believed in such Balkan superstitions, but the fact aroused his suspicion regarding why it was this Transylvanian noble would be singled out. The more anxious the hetman became, the more Istvan inquired, persisted, insisted and even bullied.

"Who is he to you, anyway?"

"It is on his land that we live, my Lord. He has given us leave to settle on this part of his vast estate, in this forest."

"Ah, I see. He is your landlord, then?"

The hetman paused. "You could say that. Roma have very little money. We repay him in labor and in kind." Istvan nodded.

"I would like to meet him," said Istvan to the hetman. The pipe was drawing very nicely now, Istvan thought. He did not need to pay any attention to it for the moment, and could gaze directly into the dark, brown eyes of the hetman without blinking, looking for the slightest flicker of emotion he could recognize, categorize, analyze and extrapolate. This was perhaps Istvan's greatest talent as a detective: his ability to discern the slightest telling sign while posing questions that slowly led him to the truth. As he announced his intention to meet Count Dracula, the hetman looked away and said nothing.

"Would it be too impolite for me to visit his residence on my way back to Piatra Fantanele?" Istvan pressed, waiting for the hetman's reaction.

The hetman turned back toward him and for a moment, and Istvan read his face. It was the face of someone confronting a fool. "Of course, why not? If he is there, I am sure he would be very anxious to meet the new Chief ... and the Inspector," he said with a wan smile and a nod of his head. He wanted them to meet the Count, for some reason Istvan concluded. And so did Istvan. "But he doesn't live there now. Nobody lives there now. The castle has been abandoned for years." Another lie, thought Istvan.

Kasza nodded his head. It was time to go. Istvan rose. The hetman rose. Istvan thanked the man for the tea and his hospitality and asked him to convey his compliments to his wife. The hetman bowed in exaggerated submission to the departing policemen and they were soon mounting their horses and on the way out, subject to the same silent stares, but now many of the Sinti women pointed their two fingers at them, warding off the Evil Eye they feared might be with these outsiders.

"Not too friendly, are they?" A rhetorical question from Kasza.

"Let's get some lunch," Istvan replied and with that he kicked Balazs into a quick trot and headed back to the Coach Road.

◎ ◎ ◎

It was just after noon when they arrived in the town of Poiana Stampei. Fat conical hay ricks with long stakes projecting from the top nestled in the thin coat of snow still clinging to the ground near the road. Peasant cottages were scattered here and there. Many were built adjacent to the road and close together. All, without exception, had a crucifix with the body of Christ nailed to the frames of their doors. The solitary tavern in town, known as Vatră Ciobănesc, was the same. A cross by the door and a small statue of the Madonna in blue robe in front to boot. The two policemen ate a lunch of beer, cabbage stew and dark bread, served by a plump woman named Freda who turned out, not surprisingly, to be the tavern keeper's wife.

Dressed in a typical Wallachian grey smock with white apron and a babushka, Freda spoke some Saxon German Istvan and Kasza could barely understand as she cheerily dished out their lunch. She was quite happy to see the new Police Chief and to have them at her tavern. About midway through their lunch, however, the husband appeared from the kitchen and it quickly became apparent he was the source of his wife's thin knowledge of the German tongue, being a Saxon himself. Before long, Istvan had the man sitting at the table with him and Kasza, comparing the virtues of Turkish and Virginia pipe tobacco.

"As a matter of fact, I have some Virginia tobacco. Would you like to try it?" the owner asked.

"Really?" said Istvan in surprise. "Of course! I'd be delighted!" Before long, Dieter, as he was called, placed on the table a tin of T.J. Brown & Company tobacco. Istvan carefully examined the English words on the label and although he did not speak the language, gleaned that this tobacco actually came from a place called Winston in Carolina. He had only once before in his life smoked American tobacco and Dieter, regarding his expression, glowed with pride as he took out his own pipe, a long curved thin-stemmed pipe with a moderate bowl at the end with a silver band.

"Go ahead," Dieter beckoned with his hand, smiling. The cover was off now and Istvan could not resist. He picked up the tin and held it to his nose. The rich, pungent aroma was overwhelming and his mouth watered to try it. He pulled his own pipe out from his cloak and dipped it in the tin. "More, more ..." Dieter encouraged, smiling. Istvan filled the bowl of his pipe with a generous helping and then Dieter did the same.

Within a minute, both men were tilting back their chairs, drawing the thick smoke and blowing clouds into the rafters high above the room to Kasza's amusement.

"Fantastic," Istvan marveled. "So smooth! How do they do it?"

"Secret tobacco stolen from the Indians, I've heard," Dieter replied. "We have nothing like it."

"Where did you get it?"

"An Englishman came through here a week or so ago. A solicitor from London named Renfield. He had some business with ..." And then he stopped. A cloud passed over his face, Istvan noted.

"An Englishman?"

"Yes."

"Out here? In this country?"

"Actually, he had become a bit lost. He stopped to ask directions."

"Where was he going?"

"To the castle"

"What castle?" With that, Dieter's demeanor changed even further. He placed his pipe on the table, eyes narrowing now as he eyed the Chief with unconcealed suspicion.

"Where are you going, my Lord? Why are you here?"

Kasza leaned forward now and spoke in a low voice. "What's the matter, old man? Didn't you hear my Lord's question? What castle?"

"*Das Schloss von Dracula*," replied the tavern keeper, now in a low sullen voice that conveyed the distinct impression had this line of discussion been aired earlier, the Virginia tobacco would never have been offered.

"*Mein lieber*, Dieter," Istvan rejoined, in as soothing a voice and manner as he could muster. "What is the matter? We are here getting to know this country. We are newly arrived here, Kasza and I. We mean no harm. We are on our way to the monastery at Piatra Fantanele, do you know it?" Istvan saw no need at this point to mention where they had been or what interest they had in visiting this remote mountain hamlet. Then, in a gruff voice he turned to Kasza.

"There's no need for that tone, Kasza. This isn't a police interrogation!" He turned back to Dieter with a rueful smile, as if to say not to pay any mind to this brash youngster. The tavern keeper seemed somewhat mollified, picked up his pipe and re-lit it. After drawing on it a couple of times, he exhaled a long plume of smoke, and then spoke again.

"No. It is all right. I have no right to ask you what you're business is here. It is not my business."

"Quite all right, sir. Quite all right. Now, as you were saying, an Englishman named Renfield gave you this tobacco after asking directions to Schloss Dracula? Did you ever see him again?"

"No. He had actually come from Bistritz and gone too far."

"Yes, I think we will pass the road to that castle on our way to the Monastery, won't we?"

"Yes, you will. You should be going, my Lord, if you want to get to your destination before dark." With that comment, the tavern-keeper seemed to study the reaction in Istvan's face.

"Yes, I suppose we should. Kasza?"

"Yes, my Lord?"

"Pay our bill to *der nette Herr*, and I thank you again for the most excellent tobacco from America."

Dieter nodded and smiled faintly, acknowledging the Chef der Politzei as Istvan flung his heavy cloak around his shoulders, preparing to leave.

"By the way," Istvan ventured in an offhand way, "we were thinking of calling upon the Count Dracula on our return. Does he come here? Do you know him?" Kasza, who had taken a few steps toward the door turned and looked back at the tavern keeper who now gasped audibly and stepped back, crossing himself as he did so.

"You should not go there, my Lord. Especially at night. You are looking for *der Engländer*, aren't you?" Dieter was talking quickly now, clearly upset. "He didn't stay here for long, my Lord. And I warned him not to go there, but he said he had business. And that's all I know about it. Never saw him again."

Istvan was surprised at this outburst; this protestation of innocence when in fact, he had known nothing about the Englishman before walking into the tavern. Slowly he walked over to the man, who now looked at him almost pleadingly.

"What is it, Dieter? What is troubling you so?" Istvan placed his hand on the man's shoulder, as if to comfort him, coaxing the truth out of him. "Why should we not go to see the Count?"

Dieter crossed himself again. *"Er ist ein Vampir, mein Herr!"*

Istvan did not make light of Dieter's obviously earnest accusation and belief. Instead, he went on.

"I have heard that from others since we came to these parts," Istvan said. "Why do you think that?"

"My Lord, I am in mortal danger speaking about him. I am afraid. If he should know that I spoke to you in this way ..."

"Be calm, Dieter," Kasza said. "Nobody is going to know what you said to us but you. We will never tell. Answer the Chief's question, now, old man. We're here to help you and all the people who live up here."

"I can't, I can't ..." whimpered the owner. "There are some things worse than death. Him. He is the bringer of terrible evil and a fate worse than death." Istvan sat down at the table again and motioned to Dieter and Kasza to sit down with him.

"I have some tobacco with me that I would like to share with you, Dieter. It's a Turkish blend. Let me see that pipe of yours again." Istvan's soothing voice and calm demeanor had its effect. Dieter seemed to relax a little and handed his pipe to Istvan who dipped it into a pouch and handed it back to him. Istvan did the same and soon, once again, the pleasant smell of pipe tobacco filled the air.

"Something is wrong in these hills, Dieter," continued Istvan. "It's not Renfield. It's more than that. People are missing and we think they are dead. Quite a few people. But you know this already, don't you?" Dieter nodded slightly as Istvan paused and then continued. "It will go on and on unless someone puts a stop to it. That is why we are here and that is what we are doing. We need help to do our job, Dieter. People we can rely on.

People who will be our eyes and ears up here in the mountains, do you understand? Dieter nodded again.

"Good. Now tell me about this Count Dracula. What do people around here say about him? What do they know about him? Why do you and they think he is a vampire? Whatever you tell me will remain in strict confidence. It will go no further. We need your help, Dieter." The tavern-keeper toked on his pipe slowly as Istvan made his remarks and then seemed reluctantly to make a decision.

"God help and protect us," he began, making the sign of the cross. "He must never even know you were here. He will come here some night and question us. He will kill us. Do you understand?"

"Why? A nobleman?"

"A nobleman, yes. And a sorcerer. And a vampire. How do we know this? Because he is known here for generations. He is the same man as when my grandfather was a young boy, and his grandfather before that. It is the same man, you understand? How can that be? How can a man live so long unless he is one of the un-dead?"

"How do you know it is the same man as your family has known for 100 years? You were not alive 100 years ago or 200 years. So how can you know this, Dieter?"

Dieter shook his head and looked away as if thinking of how to explain a fantastical concept to someone essentially incapable of understanding it.

"My Lord, I can tell you are a sophisticated man. You are an educated man in the ways of science and the business of being a policeman. A detective. I can see you approach things in a logical way. And so what I would tell you is something you will never accept; never believe. You will dismiss what I tell you as superstition and backward ignorance of country people, no? Yes, you will. Don't deny it."

"Dieter, I am an open-minded man. I agree not everything can be explained by science. You see me as a skeptical cynic, but I see you too, Dieter. I see a man who has no trust in outsiders, even if they come in peace and are trying to help. You dismiss me as one who will not listen or place any weight on the truthful observations and knowledge of any man who is not an intellectual from Budapest or Vienna. You underestimate me, Dieter. I am interested in what you have to say. I rule out nothing at this point. As I said, we are the ones who need your help if we are ever to get to the bottom of this."

There was a pause after these comments. Dieter seemed to be considering carefully his next response. Making up his mind.

"All right. I will tell you some more, but I must have your word on some things."

"What are they?"

"First, you may never reveal to anyone from whom the information I will give you comes. Swear it!"

"I do swear it," Istvan replied solemnly.

"Second, we must be protected here. The last time we had someone who manned the district station here was years ago. We are alone up here, my Lord. Alone. With him and his Roma bandits." He crossed himself again. Istvan considered the question for a moment, and then responded.

"I agree. It is high time that we had a fully manned district station here. I cannot promise how soon it can be done, but you have my word."

"Then I will tell you what was told to me by my father, and by him from his father. That Dracula was in life a warrior prince of Wallachia at the time of our king, Matthias Corvinius. Facing the Turkish hordes of the Sultan, he was sent in his youth to the mountain school of *Scholomance*, where Lucifer himself taught the secrets of black magic, the language of the animals and all dominion of the weather to ten disciples at a time, claiming the tenth as his own. It was there that the son of Dracul learned his sorcery and where he lost his soul for all eternity."

Istvan looked at Kasza as Dieter now described the folklore of the Carpathians Istvan was sure had held sway here for a century or more. Kasza had taken out his pen and pad and was scribbling down the tavernkeeper's words as quickly as he could. As a military man, a man of learning and science, and as a detective, even though Istvan did not believe in these wild myths and legends, his experience had taught him to listen carefully and reserve judgment, no matter how far-fetched the evidence might be. And so, by gesture and disposition, Istvan encouraged the man to continue.

"They say he pretended to have been killed by his own bodyguards in an ambush in a forest near Bucharest, and he fooled the Sultan by arranging to deliver to him the head of a similar looking man preserved in honey. Then he returned to his stronghold, the castle we dare not even see. As a boy, I was told from my earliest memory never to go near the Castle and never to be in the Borgo Pass at night. This has always been the way, until these times of railroads and telegraphs and now the Coach Road is frequented by commerce and travelers as it never was in the old days. And yet, you will never find someone from these parts anywhere near the Pass or even outdoors alone at night."

Kasza looked up at Istvan at this and Istvan could not repress the urge to glance out the window and notice that it was now mid-afternoon. They could still make it to the Monastery by nightfall if they left soon.

"His powers as a sorcerer are great. He may change himself into an animal of the night, such as a wolf or bat and to summon and control wild and domestic animals alike. The weather near him is his servant and he can become so small as to pass through tiny cracks or crevices. He requires no other sustenance but fresh human blood. He is repulsed by garlic, the sign of the cross and holy bread. He is also unable to enter a place unless invited to do so but once invited, he can come and go at will. But most important of all, he may not see the direct light of the sun or he will be utterly destroyed and so he is never seen in the daylight.

"This is what I know, my Lord. As I told you, it is not something we share with city folk and outsiders because we fear revenge from the Count and because we have learned you people never believe us. Until it is too late. Have you ever asked what became of the ones the District Police sent to guard us up here?" Istvan realized he had no idea what had happened to them or why it had been left abandoned for so long. "Investigate it, my Lord. See if you can find out what happened to them, but I think you will find that they all disappeared. Abandoned their post. You'll see."

◎ ◎ ◎

As Kasza and Istvan rode their mounts west on the Coach Road back to the Monastery, they talked about the day's events and, indeed, of the events since they arrived in the Borgo Pass area. It was late in the afternoon when they reached milepost 33 and the lonely cart path that veered off into the woods. Istvan reined in his horse and looked at Kasza for a moment.

"Let's have a look, Kasza." Kasza glanced at the sky as if to gauge the position of the sun and how much daylight was left, but the grey, overcast sky gave no clue as to its location. Up here in the high peaks the air was crisp and cold and even a gentle breeze chilled the bones.

"Don't you think it would be a little rude to appear at the door without any warning at this time of day?"

"Let's just take a look at the place and see what's there," Istvan replied. "The hetman said nobody lives here now, didn't he?" And with that, he turned his horse into the road and urged it into a trot. Kasza followed.

The road was obviously little used, but Istvan observed again the distinct ruts of the carriage and myriad hoof prints that had pounded the path in the not too distant past. The woods were quite thick and near the road for about a kilometer as it wound this way and that, hewing to the shoulder of another peak to their left and the inevitable sloping down and drop off to their right as they pressed on.

As they rounded another bend in the trail, they emerged from the woods and were immediately confronted with the object of their curiosity. In the distance, about three kilometers away, was a stark castle dominating another peak. It sat like a crown atop the peak, its outer walls seeming to rise up from very steep slopes of the peak itself so as to give the impression that the castle and the mountain on which it rested were almost one and the same. Indeed, the stone from the castle may well have been quarried from this location because its color was virtually the same.

Istvan removed from his saddle pack a pair of military binoculars and put them to his eyes. The trail they were on obviously continued through another small wooded area, and would then rise steeply in zigzag fashion as it ascended the steep sides of the mountaintop. At some point, the rough trail had been paved with cobblestones because, in its final run to a great arched gate that probably led into a courtyard, Istvan could see it in this fashion.

"Do you see anyone?" Kasza asked after a few moments. Istvan passed the binoculars to Kasza, who gazed through them himself for a couple of minutes.

"I didn't see anyone, do you?" Istvan knew his eyes were not as sharp as his young colleague's.

"No. Nothing." As Kasza swung the binoculars here and there to inspect the castle and the countryside, Istvan became aware of some movement out of the corner of his eye. It had come from the edge of the woods not more than 500 meters ahead of them, where the road sloped down again into the small mountain valley between where they were and the castle. What was it? It was probably nothing. Another breeze shivered past them and there it was again. Istvan leaned forward in his saddle but couldn't see anything. There had definitely been some movement, though.

"Kasza, look over there." Kasza took the binoculars down from his eyes. Istvan was pointing toward the edge of the woods. "I saw something right at the edge. What is it?" Kasza put the binoculars up and looked over toward the woods. Istvan could see him sweeping the area, left to right and then suddenly he stopped.

"It's a wolf."

"Really?"

"Yes, actually, there are two of them. No, wait. Three." Kasza handed the binoculars back to Istvan. Now he looked. At first, he couldn't locate them, but at the edge of the field of vision, he saw one of them move again. It was a big one. Now it was trotting out of the wood into a field of high grass and rocks between them. In the binoculars, the wolf's face was visible. It was black and shaggy with distinct, yellow eyes. Now there was another one coming out. Yes, there was a pack of wolves in there, Istvan realized, and they were now starting to come out toward them.

"My God, there must be twenty of them," Kasza gasped. A whole cluster of them were now clearly visible. The large black one was watching them and moving directly toward them in a measured trot with the others behind. Now more wolves bounced and cantered out of the woods. There might have been thirty or more.

"I suppose we'd best be going," Istvan said, placing the binoculars in his pack and turning Balazs back in the direction they had come. Kasza did the same and they began to re-enter the woods when there was a loud wailing howl behind them. Istvan turned back to see. It was the black wolf, baying to his pack to attack. The dogs were at full speed now in pursuit. Istvan could hardly believe it. He kicked Balazs with his heels and urged him on. The horse needed little encouragement to break into a gallop now, and hell for leather the two horses flew with the wolves in pursuit.

After a couple of minutes of hard riding, Istvan slowed his horse and looked back. The wolves had fallen far enough behind he could no longer see them, the way the road twisted and turned through the woods, but he could hear them. Then there was a loud roar up and to his right. On a jagged piece of rock high up on the side of the mountain was the black wolf baying for his pack. He must have taken some short-cut, Istvan thought. The wolf could not get at them directly without taking a tremendous fall, but he paced and howled, his head tilted up toward the sky, regarding him all the time with one yellow eye.

"Come on!" Kasza yelled. He had continued up the trail a bit father and was clearly alarmed. Once again, Istvan spurred Balazs on and the horse responded. In another minute or so, they came to the straightaway where the trail would intersect with the Coach Road, but in the deepening gloom, Istvan could see that something was moving up ahead as well. Shapes. Dark shapes. Large dark shapes. What in the world? Then Istvan realized that there were men on horseback passing at a slow pace. There was a flash of brass, glinting in dusky light. It was a military unit. Cavalry. Istvan felt a flood of relief and continued to gallop up to the road.

As Istvan and Kasza came within a few meters of the milestone, they received a startled look from one of the troopers, who immediately placed his hand on the pommel of his saber and turned his horse toward them.

"War geht da?" the trooper called out to them.

"Politzei!" returned Istvan with a smile and a wave. The cavalryman quickly noted Istvan's cap and uniform and nodded in response, turning his horse in the direction the rest of his squadron was riding. Istvan watched them pass with relief. The wolves were nowhere to be seen or heard now, having no doubt heard and shied away from the pounding of dozens of cavalry horses passing through the Borgo Pass. They looked splendid in their dark blue uniforms with gold braid, their shako hats with the imperial and royal crest stamped in brass. Istvan and Kasza fell in behind them as the rear guard passed, heading west toward the Monastery and Bistritz.

"Well, at least we've had a look at the place," Istvan exclaimed over the dull thudding of the horses ahead of them.

"This is certainly a queer and bleak part of the world," Kasza replied. "Do you suppose this wolf pack is the same as the one we saw last night?"

"I don't know. I don't remember seeing a black wolf like the one we saw leading them on among the ones we saw before."

"Well, there are certainly quite a few of them in these hills around here," Kasza replied. "They seemed fearless, didn't they?"

"Yes, very aggressive, Kasza. You don't usually see that, but once a wolf pack gets together and in numbers, they can become an entirely different species of animal altogether.

Chapter 13

Richard, Baron von Krafft-Ebing had just finished his afternoon lecture at the University of Vienna School of Medicine. *Psychopathia Sexualis*, Krafft's seminal work on explaining sexual deviation, had made him overnight into one of the foremost authorities in the world on the emerging "talking cure" being called "psychoanalysis". The *métier* had sprung from the work of the young Sigmund Freud and his mentor, Josef Breuer in Vienna the previous year. Their publication, *Studies on Hysteria*, had been an equally great hit in medical circles one year prior to Krafft's work.

The Baron was actually on his way to meet Freud and Breuer at the Café Central to discuss a joint project in response to a government grant. The Austrian Ministry of the Interior was interested in the application of these breakthroughs to the field of crime and criminal behavior. The Café was busy, as it often was on a cool Spring day. It was a quintessential Viennese venue to discuss interesting theories and enjoy juicy conversation and gossip.

"Let's sit outside," Freud said, lighting a cigar at the door as Baron Krafft arrived on foot. Breuer was alighting from a fiacre, the door held open for him by the driver as a black stallion stood by patiently. Breuer, the oldest of the three, nodded indicating he would follow them in a moment and then turned to pay his driver.

"So you may have a case study, I heard?" asked Freud after Breuer joined them at the table.

"Perhaps," said Krafft. "The Minister has word from his counterpart in Budapest of a possible case in Transylvania; potentially dozens of victims."

The waiter brought water and then was given the orders for a *Phariseer*; a cappuccino mixed with brandy. Freud and Krafft each ordered one. Breuer had a Calypso, with rum. Evenings still came early and chilly in Vienna in the spring. Some discussions with these three could last well into the night and nearly all went on for several hours.

"And one murderer for all of them?" asked Breuer, taking his *Meerschaum* pipe out of a leather case in his jacket pocket.

"Right," Krafft replied. "They think so. Possibly an aristocrat. Like the Countess Bathory."

"Transylvania? Where is that, exactly?" Breuer asked, now beginning to pack the bowl of his pipe, carefully pushing the leaf in with a silver tamper attached to an elaborate onyx pocket knife.

"Northeast part of Hungary. Carpathians. Very wooded, mountainous and wild. Beautiful, I hear, like Bohemia," Freud said. "But what else do you know about this case?"

"It's an extraordinary statistical aberration that got the attention of the Royal Hungarian Gendarmerie. The RHG in Budapest calculated the ratio of missing persons to the per capita population of each county in Hungary."

"Now that's the kind of thing we're talking about," Breuer commented approvingly. "Using science to understand crime on a large scale."

"Exactly," Krafft continued. "Anyway, they determined an average figure per thousand people, per county each year. Sure enough, there was a district and a county where the numbers were exponentially higher than all the others."

"Marvelous," Freud sighed. "Fascinating. Go on."

"They actually have a department in Budapest created to discover and solve mass crimes," Krafft stated, now beginning to get excited himself as he described the situation to his colleagues. "One of their inspectors was sent to Bistritz, the county seat. He and their District Chief of Police believe there may be a serial murderer at large in their district. They have asked for help in the investigation."

"And in return?" Breuer inquired, sipping his drink, eyebrows raised.

"We can use the case in our work. We can publish it, if it works out, of course."

"What else do you know about the case?" Breuer asked.

"Nobody arrested, so far. No eyewitnesses have come forward or were willing to say they had seen anything. Nonetheless, many villagers in the areas in and around Bistritz were unaware so many of their neighbors were afflicted. The area as a whole has just become self-aware of their problem, so to speak. Now, apparently, some people have come forward, but most are ignorant, superstitious peasants or villagers who want to blame the disappearances on a local Count they claim is a vampire."

"A vampire?" chuckled Freud. "What do you think about that? Here we are, on the cusp of the 20th century, in a civilized country like this ..."

"Overly civilized, if you ask me," Breuer remarked.

"... and people still believe in ghosts and witches," Freud smiled.

"They would like us to help them," Krafft said with some seriousness. "There may be hundreds of dead girls and young women. Some men, but overwhelmingly, the victims are women."

"Psychopathia Sexualis," Freud said, smiling and nodding at Krafft who acknowledged his gesture with a slight smile.

"That's right," Krafft said. "This could be a classic case study of a sexual predator and psychotic killer on a massive scale that may not happen again in years. Decades even."

"I think these killers have been around forever," Breuer said quietly. "We're just waking up to their existence among us with the modern means of communication now at our disposal. The telegraph. The telephone. The typewriter. Word spreads fast now, and there is no limit to how far it goes. The Holmes murders in America. The Ripper murders in London."

"What have we learned, gentlemen?" Krafft asked rhetorically. "That is what the Royal Hungarian Gendarmerie wants to know. What can we do to help them?"

Chapter 14

Istvan and Kasza were riding back to Bistritz on the Coach Road. It was a cool, sunny afternoon and they had another couple of hours to ride. Istvan had been thinking about the events of the previous day for several hours. There was certainly something very queer about this country but whether it had anything to do with the disappearances of dozens and dozens of people over the past few years was another question altogether.

Istvan pulled out his pipe as he rode and scooped out a bowl full of tobacco as he considered the situation further. Kasza seemed deep in thought as well, gazing out over the passing countryside, saying little. The Abbess had approached them from a spiritual point of view, suggesting she and her abbey were in the vortex of a supreme battle between good and evil. The Roma were hiding something, as they always did when they were confronted by authority. The innkeeper's fear was palpable, but Dieter had been correct, in the end, convinced his superstitious explanation was not something Istvan could accept. Then there was the visit to the castle and the wolves. Yes, it was very queer. If he were not an educated man, he might well have succumbed to the superstitions of the mountain people. Istvan turned to Kasza, riding alongside.

"Kasza, what do you think about vampires and sorcery? Do you think they really exist?" Kasza looked abruptly at the Chef der Politzei, seemingly shaken out of a daydream. He hesitated for a moment, seeming to give the matter more thought than Istvan had expected.

"I don't think so, my Lord," he spoke thoughtfully. "I don't doubt the people who live here do, though, and I wonder if it might be something imaginary cultivated by the Count for his own purposes."

"What do you mean, Kasza?"

"Well, the gentry in these rural counties have ruled the peasants here with cruelty for years, in my opinion. There have been a few peasant uprisings out here in Transylvania. We heard about them at the RHG. Estate houses burned. Families murdered. Many of these nobles moved off their estates to Bistritz or Budapest leaving their overseers to squeeze the peasants while they sip champagne in the safety of the towns. I'm thinking this Count Dracula is one of them. Look at the poverty in this area. Except I think maybe he's found a way to keep his peasants in line. He has them all thinking he's a vampire."

"We must meet this Count Dracula, Kasza."

"I was thinking the same thing, my Lord."

Chapter 15

The residence of Ribanszky Julianna, Baroness of Jelna, was situated only a short distance from the center of Bistritz on a large, semi-wooded tract of land. The house itself was made of brick and mortar with a wide *porte cochere* for the carriages expected to arrive at such a splendid palais for balls and receptions. As Istvan dismounted his horse under its roof, a groom appeared to take Balazs to an unseen stable somewhere in the rear, no doubt. A butler waited for him at the door.

"The Baroness?" said Istvan, expectantly, handing the man his card.

"Is expecting you, my Lord," said the butler in heavily accented Magyar after glancing at the card. Probably Wallachian, Istvan thought. "May I take your coat?"

Istvan nodded as the butler helped him take it off and disappeared, momentarily. Istvan took the opportunity to inspect the room. He was in a foyer. The ceiling was quite high with a medallion in the center and a large chandelier of some kind. The room was quite empty of furniture, but there were a number of large paintings on the walls of the room. The landscapes were of African scenes and were accented by several marble plinths with black marble busts of what appeared to be Negro warriors. The effect was quite exotic and not at all what he had expected. The African motif continued as the butler escorted him through a gallery with more paintings, but now there were stuffed heads of African game and leopard skin fur covered furniture. Then he entered a large tropical Solarium where the Baroness stood waiting for him.

"Excellency ..."

"Your Highness," Istvan replied, taking her hand and giving it the light touch of lips her position required, but with pleasure.

"I am so very curious about your investigation, my Lord. I heard you recently embarked on an expedition to the Bukovina. Won't you sit down?" The Baroness motioned him to a chair, opposite of which was a low table and a large wicker settee in which she sat. The air within the greenhouse was slightly warm and carried with it an earthy smell. Large palms and ferns grew as tall as the ceiling where there were evidently small steam pipes Istvan could see.

"Thank you, my Lady," Istvan replied. "It was interesting, indeed. In fact, one of the reasons I asked to see you arose on the trip, but I will come to that in a minute. First I must offer my compliments on the remarkable décor of your home, my Lady ..."

"Thank you. You are too kind. Since my husband died several years ago, I haven't had the heart to change it. He was quite an avid sportsman and loved Africa, as you can see."

"A hunter, Madame?"

"Yes, he was, but we also found the tribal civilizations and customs to be fascinating as well."

"You accompanied him?"

"Oh, yes. On several trips I was with him. Sailed down the Nile and all. We were with the Kaiser's entourage in '69 when the Suez Canal was opened."

"When did your husband pass away, if you don't mind my asking?"

"It was three years ago. Cancer."

"So sorry." The butler arrived with a tea service and biscuits which he set on the low table. As the Baroness poured the tea, Istvan could not help but notice her fine hands and skin, her handsome face and arresting blue eyes. Although some grey hair was visible, she was still mainly blonde and the whole effect was very attractive. "I'm a widower myself."

"How terrible. When?"

"Two years ago. Influenza. She was there one day and gone the next, my Lady …"

"Call me Julianna," she said, touching his hand in sympathy. "I see we have something in common, then."

"It is a sad fate to be alone at this age. I had thought that we would live a long life if I weren't killed in some war. Once our children were born, I thought she would certainly outlive me, but it goes to show one never knows."

"No, I'm afraid not," the Baroness replied pensively, sipping her tea. Then she smiled warmly, as the invisible barrier of formality between them began to fade. "I'm so glad you came, actually. I was beginning to wonder if you would." She was alluding to the invitation she had given him more than a week earlier when they had first met. "Now, Excellency, please tell me some good news."

"Call me Istvan," he replied.

"Very well, then …"

"I'm not sure I have any good news to tell you, Julianna," Istvan began. He then shared with her the information he had gathered in the week or so since he had last seen her. The unusual number of disappearances. The kidnappings. Missing persons. And the suspicions surrounding Count Dracula he had gathered on his trip. "And so that has brought me to you. Do you know this Count Dracula? And would you be able to introduce me to him?"

The Baroness shook her head. "I have never met him," she started, slowly. "I have heard of the family, of course. I know of the property of which you speak on the Borgo Pass, but I had thought the castle had long been abandoned and was uninhabited. It's quite ancient, you know. I think it was built in the fifteenth century as a stronghold against the Turks. Some people say there is some rare marble or granite or something quarried there on the property, but as far as I know, nobody has lived there for a century or more."

"I see. The Roma nearby seem to think the Count owns the property but the hetman I spoke with also thought nobody lives there these days.

They work the property for him, though. The Roma. And the hetman says he repays them by allowing the tribe to live in a forest on his land. Did you know that?"

"No. I have never paid much attention to the lands outside Bistritz or who owns what."

"The folk out in the country seem very afraid of this Count. Many of them believe he is a sorcerer and a vampire."

The Baroness raised her eyebrows in surprise. "Really?"

"Yes."

"And what do you think of such things, Istvan?"

"Superstitious nonsense from the Dark Ages, Julianna, but even I have to admit there are many things that are unexplained. What does interest me is so many of the people out there direct their fears and suspicions toward this one man and this one place. I am, at the end of the day, a policeman. There must be a reason. My instincts tell me ..."

"I will tell you what I can do, Istvan," the Baroness interjected. "I will make some inquiries about him. As I have said, neither he nor his family have been active in society here for as long as I can remember. It is not entirely primitive out here," she said, smiling and extending her arm indicating the solarium.

"Yes," Istvan smiled in return. "I can see that."

"There are parties, social events, shootings, balls ... that kind of thing. Many families in society keep a residence here as their country home but live much of the time in Budapest or Vienna or somewhere else. Others have income from farms and estates they no longer inhabit but are worked by the local people out here. It sounds like Count Dracula may be one of those. It wouldn't be unusual for there to be some long-abandoned family home to exist on an estate, but I must admit, a castle like that is rare."

"I will appreciate any information you may find out about him," Istvan said, rising to leave.

"There is one more thing," the Baroness said, softly. "The Bürgermeister. He might know him. Official business, you know. Bürgermeisters don't get where they are in Hungary or anywhere without cultivating wealthy, powerful patrons. You know that, Istvan. If Count Dracula owns this immense property, he is a very wealthy man. And if he is a wealthy, landowning member of our class, in this district, any politician would have met him by now, seeking his patronage. I can't get rid of the man, myself. The Bürgermeister, I mean."

"An excellent point, Julianna. I will certainly follow up on that suggestion, to be sure. And now, I must not impose on you further ..."

"Not at all. Do come again, sir." She extended her hand once again. Istvan looked at her sparkling blue eyes, the beautiful white teeth and handsome face as he bowed slightly and gently kissed her hand. He felt something stir within him he had not felt since Julia died. He took in her perfume and her elegant figure as he backed away from her, standing in her tropical garden, and thought to himself that he would certainly enjoy having the pleasure of her company again.

"I would very much like to, Julianna. Perhaps you would do me the honor of dining with me on Friday evening? By then, I would hope to have some additional news to report."

She hesitated, then nodded, smiling."Of course. I would be delighted. And by then, perhaps I will have some information for you as well."

"Excellent," Istvan said, bowing more deeply now as he reached the door. "Shall we say, eight o'clock? At Die Golden Krone?"

"I will see you then ..."

Chapter 16

"It's a post from Dieter," Kasza explained when Istvan arrived at his office the following morning. Kasza was sipping coffee from the cracked teacup he let make rings on his desk and only occasionally cleaned, to Istvan's amazement. Kasza referred to a letter on Istvan's desk. He picked it up. It had been posted two days ago. He opened it.

My Lord –

It is my sad duty to report the news that has just yesterday been made known to me of a Roma hetman and his daughter from the encampment you visited. There has been a murder and perhaps more. Several members of their tribe passed my way making for the Bukovina this evening. Some mention was made of the wrath of their "master" for some transgression being visited on them. Your discretion, my Lord, I pray.

Dieter

"By the Grace of God, Kasza! What do you make of that?" Kasza had been reading the letter over Istvan's shoulder.

"I think we should summon the cavalry and have a look at that castle. You're a colonel, Vezér. And if we need to, we shoot every wolf in the forest to get to the door."

"Ah, that's what I like about you, Kasza. A man of action. But what legal right do we have to break open the door of a nobleman like the Count Dracula, if he is there? Have you thought of that? And what evidence do we really have against him?"

"Just rumor and hearsay, Uram."

"Exactly. Let's think again."

"What about that professor? The one from Vienna? Have you heard from him?"

"As a matter of fact, I have. He assures me he is very interested in this case. So interested, as a matter of fact, he offered to come and consult with us first-hand."

"And what did you say?"

"I accepted, of course. He is due on the train from Budapest tomorrow."

"Excellent news, my Lord. I have some news also. I have been informed by the RHG that the Kaiser will be here in Bistritz for military maneuvers in a few months. The cavalry troop we saw is just the start of an increase in concentration of the army here that will continue for many weeks."

"Well, that is interesting news. I wonder if some of my old comrades will be here?"

"There will be a number of preparations by RHG headquarters," Kasza continued. "They will be combing the countryside for agitators, anarchists and the like. Perhaps a call at the castle, as a courtesy, would not be out of line?" Istvan could see where Kasza was going with this idea. A pretext for having a close look at the Count's Borgo Pass estate.

`"Perhaps not, Kasza. Perhaps not. But I have another idea that I would like to explore. I have arranged to call on his Honor, the Bürgermeister, this afternoon. The Baroness suggested it."

"Mazaly Kula? That fat drunk? What could he possibly know?"

"Is he, Kasza? Well, let's suppose he is. Did you ever wonder how such people get to positions of high office? They don't do it themselves, do they?"

"I'm not sure I'm following you, Vezér."

"Perhaps somebody wants a fat drunk to be the mayor of this city. You know how these things go, Kasza. The local powers-that-be get together. They find someone who is willing to do their bidding and the council elects him."

"I see the logic now, my Lord."

"Exactly."

Chapter 17

The City Hall building in Bistritz was a grandiose affair, out of proportion to the population of the city. The basic construction was Habsburg yellow brick and plaster with white trim and columns designating it as an official, imperial building. An ornate clock tower graced one side of the building. An elegant, interior stairwell led up to the main floor where Istvan was met by a polite uniformed clerk at the top of the stairs sitting at a small desk. The clerk nodded, taking in Istvan's uniform. Yes, the Bürgermeister was expecting him. Would he be so kind as to take a chair? The Bürgermeister was attending to some personal business but would be with him in a few minutes.

To his irritation, the Bürgermeister kept him waiting for nearly half an hour, but was so effusively apologetic when he finally emerged there was little Istvan could say as he was escorted into the mayor's inner office. It was an enormous room with yellow and white damask-covered walls, columns, a red carpet, a Bohemian crystal chandelier and all the usual trappings of power to which Istvan had become accustomed over his long career. The mayor motioned him to a chair and then sat opposite him.

"I am so glad you have come, my Lord. It is high time we have a discussion of the police situation. I suppose you have heard the news of the summer maneuvers and the Kaiser's visit? We must ensure His Majesty's security while he is here, wouldn't you agree? And we will look to you to ensure that, of course …"

Istvan listened as Kula rattled on about this and that. The mayor alternated between obsequious flattery and self-importance as he lurched and swayed from subject to subject. A simple nod or a mumbled "quite so" was sufficient to fuel another lengthy ramble. What had this simpleton done to obtain his high rank, Istvan wondered? He would not have held a lieutenant's commission in His Majesty's army. Eventually, the Bürgermeister himself realized he had been talking for nearly a quarter hour without permitting the Chef der Politzei to get a word in edgewise.

".... But listen to me go on, my Lord. It was you who made an appointment to see me, after all. So what is it that I can do for you?"

Istvan composed his face into one of grave severity before beginning.

"Your Excellency is quite right to be concerned about the security situation in this district, but I wonder if you are acquainted with the unusual number of kidnappings and missing persons hereabouts over the past several years?"

"What do you mean, sir? Unusual? Unusual in what way?"

"In number, sir. In the number of them, as compared to elsewhere in the Kingdom. I wonder if no one has brought this to your attention before, is that correct?"

"No. No one has. This ... aberration has not been mentioned before to me. Your predecessor, of course ..."

"Is missing? Yes, it's true. His whereabouts have never been confirmed, Excellency. Nor that of his wife. Nor that of dozens ... I should say hundreds of others gone missing in the past several years."

"How do you know this?"

"Modern methods, Sir. We have a national police force now. The Royal Hungarian Gendarmerie. Perhaps you have heard of it? We have a provincial police force as well. The Transylvanian Constabulary. They keep records and statistics. Did you know we have a special Inspector working here in Bistritz with us on the likelihood that a serial killer has been and is still at large in this district?"

Kula was clearly shaken, removing his pince-nez and staring at Istvan with a blank look of incomprehension. Istvan continued.

"Questions are being raised, Excellency. Questions in Budapest and in Klausenberg. Questions about why this has persisted for so long? Questions about why nothing seems to have been done about it? Questions have been raised in the countryside and even by religious authorities there about the district government seemingly abandoning them to the random cruelties of this killer."

"Now I really must protest!" cried the mayor. "I cannot be held responsible for this! This is a police matter! How could I have known if I wasn't told?"

"I agree. It doesn't seem fair, Excellency. I have only traveled outside the city once to familiarize myself with the local conditions as I found them on my arrival. In speaking with the common folk, it wasn't long before this ... unpleasantness brought to my attention by my colleague with the Transylvanian Constabulary was confirmed. Would you agree with me this is an intolerable situation that must be immediately resolved?"

"Indeed! But what can I do?" Kula responded, now pacing the floor in anxiety.

"The Baroness of Jelna suggested I approach you with an issue we have. As you know, it was her daughter ..."

"Yes, yes ... I know who she is," Kula waved him off dismissively. "That little slut of a daughter was the wife of Novotny Janos. Ema." Istvan detected more than a trace of irritation in the mayor's voice and deduced the existence of some animosity between Kula and the Baroness, but he continued.

"The area where I visited was along the Bukovina Coach Road. You know the area?"

Kula stopped pacing and gazed at him intently, awaiting the next sentence with anticipation.

"There are quite a number of missing persons thereabouts. Many are suspicious that the Count Dracula, whose estates are located in and around the Borgo Pass, may have knowledge of facts crucial to our investigation."

Istvan bent the truth slightly, but only slightly in fabricating an excuse to meet the gentleman and size him up himself. The mayor's face was momentarily frozen with dread at the mention of the nobleman's name. It was only a fleeting moment, but Istvan caught it. He had been looking for it. The reaction had been there.

"I would like to interview the man, Excellency. Do you know him? Can you arrange it?"

There was a silence in the room as Istvan concluded his last request. For an uncomfortably long moment, Kula said nothing. He appeared to be thinking. Straining his substandard, weak mind to think of something to say, Istvan thought. Something contrived, Istvan expected. He would not get the truth from this man on this point.

"I have not seen him in many years," Kula began cautiously. He did not know him well, the Mayor asserted. They had known each other when they were young. In school a long time ago, he claimed. He thought he now lived in Budapest some of the time, but was often abroad.

"Police business. That's what you'll have to tell him. We will meet him at his residence, wherever that is. Otherwise, you may advise him that we will seek a court order to inspect the estate, the buildings and ruins of the Castle at the Borgo Pass and to compel him to attend a police interview at our request in Bistritz."

Istvan did not wait for an answer. Silently he rose and left the room. There would be no negotiating with the man. He was quite certain his message would be delivered, and delivered promptly.

Chapter 18

There was no express train from Budapest to Bistritz. It was a "milk run", thought Richard, Baron von Krafft-Ebing, as he gazed out the window at the passing countryside. The flat farmlands and plains of Royal Hungary had changed to rolling, forested hills and mountains of ever increasing size. Most were still snow-capped, Krafft noted. In Lower Austria, the snows had already receded, particularly in Vienna. He was sitting alone in his compartment and had opened the window to clear the smoky air from his cigar. When he had done so, he was treated to such a blast of cold air it reduced the temperature inside the car to nearly freezing in a matter of minutes. In the mountain passes, there were occasional snow flurries as the train chugged on to its destination.

How different this area was from the sophisticated, cosmopolitan world of Vienna, Krafft thought, or even Budapest. Out here, it was as if he had entered another country; another world. The wildness of the scenes that passed his window increasingly fascinated him. Steep gorges. Towering, craggy mountain tops. Vast, seemingly uninhabited forests with massive pines that marched like soldiers up the slopes of many of the lower lying hills and mountains until, as if from exhaustion, they stopped and left bare the grey rock protruding further to the skyline. Here and there one could see a farm or house, clinging to the side of a hill or squatting in a valley. Krafft could not imagine the loneliness of such an existence, so far from the intellectual stimulation of the city.

Krafft had dozed off in the late afternoon as the milk run rolled on interminably toward Bistritz, stopping occasionally at village stations, as the sun sank lower on the horizon. A knock on the door by the porter awoke him. A quarter hour to Bistritz station and the end of the line, the porter said, nodding to him and then sliding closed the door. It was night already. The Baron took out his pocket watch and saw it was 6:20 in the evening. He took his valise and suitcase down from the shelf above his seat in anticipation of the impending arrival at the station.

The train from Budapest roared into the station in Bistritz, grinding to a halt alongside a roofed platform where it punctuated its arrival with a blast and hiss of steam. Conductors stepped out first. Porters approached with carts and wheelbarrows. A general stir of activity in the station, Krafft observed, that must happen every other evening as this mighty train from the Hungarian capital arrived, only to leave again the following morning.

The Baron stepped off the train, his lungs filling with the cold night air of a provincial city in the midst of forests of pine. Gaslights flickered and glowed a warm yellow and orange that gave those under the station's thatched roof a mellow welcome. A tall man in a police uniform was approaching, his heavy cape fluttering slightly as he strode across the floor.

"Gnädiger Herr! Sind Sie der Baron Krafft-Ebing?" inquired the officer Krafft took to be the retired colonel Kálváry Istvan, his recent correspondent. He was a tall man, the Baron noted at once. Although he was a man clearly in his mid-50s, the Chef der Polizei appeared to be in excellent physical shape with dark, short cropped hair tinged with steel grey under his cap. His stern, questioning facial expression quickly transformed to one of sincere pleasure when Krafft confirmed his identity. "Let me help you with that," Istvan offered, reaching out to take the Baron's suitcase.

"Thank you, mein Herr, but perhaps this instead," Krafft said off-handedly, giving him the much lighter and smaller valise. "Much of what is in it I will give to you anyway," he said smiling.

Istvan nodded and motioned Krafft this way, out of the Bahnhof to a waiting landau being driven by what appeared to be a young, Wallachian policeman. The dark, gas-lit streets were fairly quiet as they proceeded to *Der Silberlöffel*, a tavern recommended by Herr Kálváry. The police chief had correctly assumed that Krafft spoke little Magyar and conversed with the Austrian doctor in the carriage in very good, if accented, high German.

"I will be introducing you to a young colleague in a moment, *Freiherr Doktor*," Istvan said as the carriage turned down a side street. "He is on assignment from the Royal Hungarian Gendarmerie and will be able to give you many details about the situation here. I can only relate to you, as I mentioned in my letter, my own first-hand observations which have become far more extensive recently after a trip into the countryside."

"Do you have any suspect at all?" the Baron inquired.

"Not really. Frankly, we are not sure exactly what kind of individual we should be looking for. Someone capable of so many crimes on this scale, one would think should be obvious but, of course, it is not. It seems logical to me that someone like this would be capable of great deception and anonymity. That he would be of above average intelligence to so cleverly conceal his crimes. He would have to have great patience and cunning to be able to strike and abduct his victims, unseen and unsuspected by anyone else. These are my thoughts, Freiherr Doktor Krafft. Am I on the right track?"

Before the Baron could answer, the landau rolled to a stop outside *Der Silberlöffel*. The driver opened the door and the two men stepped out and walked into the restaurant. It was a rustic tavern, Baron Krafft noticed, with exposed plaster and beams across the ceiling. A number of working men sat drinking large steins of beer at the bar, smoking pipes or cigars. Others sat at crude wooden tables. Young serving girls walked to and fro with food or drink. A young man sitting at a table near the back wall was waving at them. Istvan waved back and motioned Krafft to follow. Introductions were made to Gábor Kasza and the men sat down.

"I was just beginning to discuss with Freiherr Doktor Krafft the kind of man we think we are looking for ..." Kálváry began but was interrupted by his young colleague, Kasza.

"Sorry, Sir, but before we begin, I have some news."

"What is it?"

"Do you remember the reward we offered for information about the disappearance of the young woman, Ema? The wife of ..."

"Yes, yes. I remember. Go on ..."

"Well, a man came into the station this afternoon, after you left. Very nervous, he was, but he asked to see someone involved in the investigation. He is a lamp-lighter, my Lord. An elderly man. He was actually lighting lamps in the street the night of Novotny Ema's disappearance. He saw her walking on the street."

"What street?"

"*Király József II utca*. King Joseph II Street," Kasza translated from the Magyar. "He said he saw the young woman being driven away from his vantage point on the corner of the Coach Road where he was just lighting a lamp."

"Driven away? By whom? I thought you said she was walking?"

"Yes, my Lord. She had been walking when he first saw her. A black calèche approached her on the street as he watched. There was some conversation and then she continued walking away, down another side street. He lost sight of them at some point and continued his work until he reached the corner. Then the calèche appeared again, rolling down the Coach Road. He says he distinctly saw the woman in the carriage as it went past him, driving East."

"What kind of calèche?"

"It was very distinctive. Black varnished veneer. Brass lanterns. Yellow spoke wheels. A pair of black stallions. And here is the most interesting thing. The monogram on the carriage door was the letter 'D'."

Krafft observed with this last comment that Kálváry and Gábor exchanged a long, knowing look. Then Istvan nodded.

"This incident you described ..." Krafft ventured, "was this around the time that one of the victims went missing?"

Kasza turned to him. "Exactly. The same evening."

"Then I suppose you would be interested in speaking to the individual who was driving that calèche?" Krafft said, stating the obvious.

"I ... Yes, indeed," Istvan replied softly. "Let us have a meal, Freiherr Doktor, and give you a summary of our present situation before we discuss this latest news any further."

For the next hour and a half, the men talked. Krafft spoke least, taking it all in, his interest and excitement growing as the information was conveyed to him, mainly by Kasza but with significant observations by Istvan as well.

Kasza briefed him on the statistical background initiating the investigation, disclosing the locations of the various victims known to the police in the past decade, alluding to the map he had at police headquarters. Clues and statements obtained from the victims' spouses, parents or families he had pieced together. Then the recent venture into the countryside and the Borgo Pass, the rumors in the countryside about the Count. The breaking news about the *calèche* now made sense to Krafft and he could understand completely the heart-stopping significance of this clue to the two investigators.

"Well, it seems I have arrived to witness the conclusion of this case. It would seem to me you have all you need to arrest this Count Dracula and bring him to justice," Krafft said, lighting a cigar. "In which case, I would be most interested in interviewing the gentleman at some point to add to our body of knowledge, for which I must thank you." Kasza and Istvan exchanged another knowing look, and then Istvan spoke.

"Not so fast, with all due respect, Freiherr Doktor. We do not have a case. There has been no identification of the Count in all of this. There is no evidence even that the woman was taken against her will. We would have nothing, in a court of law, against this man. It should not escape your attention, Sir, that he is a member of our aristocracy. Charges such as murder are not lightly brought against persons of such rank in Hungary, without firm proof. No, Freiherr Doktor. This is an important clue, no doubt, but nothing more."

"It may show the Count is concealing information from the police, my Lord," Kasza offered. "Someone was driving that calèche who knows something about the whereabouts of this woman that evening and who has said nothing to us. The calèche presumably belongs to the Count. The driver had access to the calèche. Presumably he is or was in the service of the Count and has a name."

"Quite so, Kasza. Now that, my dear Baron, is how a policeman thinks," Istvan said as he removed a pipe from his pocket and a pouch of Turkish tobacco. "I haven't had time yet to tell you of my meeting with the Bürgermeister this afternoon, Kasza ..." With that, Istvan related the details of his meeting with Mazaly Kula. "We will hear from the mayor very soon, I suspect."

Chapter 19

Indeed, the following day, as the three men poured over the map on the wall with the pins and the dossiers Kasza had assembled, a courier from the mayor arrived with a note addressed to Istvan. The note was contained in a blank envelope, sealed in wax on the back with the crest of the mayor imprinted.

My Lord –

I am informed by His Highness, the Count Dracula, that it would be his pleasure to meet with you forthwith regarding the matters discussed with the undersigned yesterday but that he is at present abroad and consequently, not at liberty to do so. He has bid me inquire whether you would be so kind as to do him the honor of making his acquaintance at his residence in Budapest, as he has no plans to be in the district in the immediate future and, having heard the nature of your business he is, naturally, anxious to do anything in his power to assist in your investigation of the matters that brought you to me.

Would you be so good as to reply to me at your earliest convenience your disposition to accept His Highness' invitation and, if so, whether it would be convenient to attend him on the coming Tuesday, April 25, at eight o'clock in the evening?

With your favorable reply, further arrangements will be forthcoming.

Your humble servant and with best personal regards,

MAZALY

The sugary prose notwithstanding, Istvan concluded immediately from the alacrity of the Count's reply the suspicion of the Baroness of a connection between the two was beyond doubt. Wherever this Count was in the world, a telegram from the mayor must have reached him within hours of Istvan's meeting, describing in sufficient detail the context of their meeting so as to prompt such an extraordinary reply. That meant the mayor, despite his dissembling comments to Istvan at their meeting, knew exactly where the Count was and exactly how to reach him.

"Gentlemen, shall we accept?" Both Kasza and Baron Krafft burst out laughing at Istvan's sardonic quip which brought a smile to his face. He reached for some stationery and wrote his reply.

My dear Mayor:

Please allow me to convey our gratitude at the prompt assistance you have provided to us with respect to the investigation we are undertaking and your arranging our introduction to His Highness, the Count Dracula.

In reply to your note, would you be so kind as to convey to the gentleman our thanks for his invitation and our appreciation for his condescending to meet with us. We will be most honored to visit with him Tuesday next, in Budapest, at the hour designated in your note.

We look forward to your further advice as to the exact location of his residence there so as to make all necessary arrangements. Would you also please advise His Highness that I must further tax his kindness and hospitality by advising him I will be in the company of two other colleagues, who join me in expressing their eager anticipation at making his acquaintance.

With the utmost regard and thanks to Your Excellency, I remain, your obedient servant, etc., etc.

Kálváry

"Very good, my Lord," Kasza said as he read the reply.
"Yes, perfect …" Krafft agreed.
The courier was summoned and left with the note immediately.

Chapter 20

Kálváry Istvan had ordered Radu Popescu and a contingent of mounted police to investigate the murder and abduction at the Roma encampment. Popescu had been thrilled to receive this assignment. As a detective of five years' experience, this would be the first murder investigation to which he had ever been assigned lead investigator.

"I want you to make yourself seen and felt in the area," Kálváry Istvan had instructed him before they left. "The people up there have long felt abandoned by the police. You will probably find them fearful of speaking to you, especially the Roma who are always fearful of the police. Nonetheless, make yourself conspicuous. You may make arrangements to billet you and your men at the Monastery of Piatra Fantanele near the Borgo Pass. Make contact with the Abbess on your way to the encampment and billet there this evening. I want the Abbess, the country folk and even those Gypsies to know we are there to protect them. I have a mind to establish a new substation up there, Radu, and I have you in mind for the post."

Radu knew his great opportunity to rise in the ranks had arrived and there might never be another one like it for the son of poor Wallachian peasants like himself. Now thirty-two years old, he had educated himself in the German and Magyar languages, so useful in this polyglot enclave of the Habsburg Empire; itself an amalgamation of different nationalities and languages. He had apprenticed as a fledgling detective for years with the Bistritz District Police after having paid his dues as an ordinary policeman. He had toiled far longer than the Hungarian cadets who, after having served their time in this remote province, left for Budapest or Fiume or other more glamorous places to practice their craft. He had read books of chemistry, biology, anatomy and science and others on the art and craft of detection.

Radu Popescu had stayed in Bistritz and through sheer perseverance; talent and attention to detail had slowly gained the grudging respect and trust of his Hungarian superiors. Now as Radu's troop of mounted police picked their way along the trail that the Coach Road became in the high mountains, he was in charge of a largely Hungarian contingent, he realized with some satisfaction.

As the mounted troop entered the Roma camp, there was a scurry of activity that greeted their arrival. Women picked up their babies and brought them inside their huts and hovels. The men were nowhere to be seen. Smoking campfires were unattended. They proceeded to the middle of the camp where there was a large, open area. He signaled his men to stop.

"Hello! Hello there!" Radu shouted in each direction, in the Magyar language. Still nothing. "We're here to help you! Who is the leader here? Please! Come forward! We will not hurt you!"

Radu paused and waited. For a few moments, nothing happened. Then a face appeared from behind one of the thatched roof huts. It was a young Roma male, about 19 years old, Radu guessed. He met the gaze of the young man and slowly dismounted from his horse. The other troopers maintained their seats in silence.

"Come here, young man," Radu called in as friendly a tone as he could manage. Slowly, warily, the man emerged from behind the hut and began to approach him. "Do you understand me? Do you speak Magyar?" The young man nodded. "What happened here? We have heard that a man was murdered here and his daughter is missing, is that right?" The man nodded affirmatively again. "Do you know who did it?" The man lowered his gaze to the ground, standing silently. "I said, do you know who did it?"

The man looked up at him sullenly.

"No. Nobody saw what happened. It was the middle of the night. There were no sounds."

Radu began a litany of basic questions. Where had the body been found? Impaled on a long stake? When was it found? At daybreak? Who found it first? A woman going to get water for her kettle, then others when she raised the alarm. Where is the body? Being prepared for cremation in one of the huts. Where was the stake?

Over the course of the next two hours, Radu Popescu of the Bistritz District Police inspected the decedent's hut where the missing girl had lived with her now dead father. He examined the area where the victim had been impaled. More Roma were summoned and questioned, but the story was essentially the same. Nobody had seen or heard anything and had awakened to this horror. Their hetman, Nikolai, brother of the decedent was also missing.

The questioning continued. Had the hetman Béla quarreled with anyone? Was there any apparent motive for the murder? Why would the other brother have fled? Where had the brothers been the day before? Then it was learned they had been delivering some crates to a warehouse in Vatra Dornei that had been picked up at the Castle of their Lord, Dracula Gróf. The castle was at the end of another mountain trail off the Borgo Pass.

Radu obtained meticulous descriptions of the hetman Nikolai and the girl, Natália, and then dispatched two of his troopers to race down the Coach Road to Vatra Dornei in the Bukovina, to see if anyone had seen the pair. Radu also instructed them to call at the warehouse to determine the nature of the cargo that had been delivered and then ride back to the monastery as quickly as they could. If they were to find the hetman Nikolai or the girl, they were to be arrested immediately and returned here.

Given the unexplained, sudden departure of the hetman, Nikolai, Radu speculated some quarrel must have erupted between the two brothers. Nikolai had evidently killed Béla and then absconded with his daughter. It was a working hypothesis but the spectacular manner in which the murder had been carried out baffled him. He asked to see the body.

Kindling wood was piled up in a clearing near a mud hut in readiness for the body. Radu could smell incense coming from inside the cottage as he approached the door. A toothless old woman sat at a chair next to the door. Radu guessed she was the one who would prepare the body for cremation. The woman rose as he neared the door, mumbling something. He entered the open door. Several troopers crowded in behind him to watch quietly.

Béla, hetman of the Sinti of Tinovul Mohos, was laid out on a long, wood table under a white sheet. Radu gently pulled back the sheet over the head and folded it over the victim's chest. He immediately noticed two dark, purple holes on the man's neck, just above the common carotid artery. He bent over to examine it briefly, and then pulled the rest of the sheet off the naked body beneath. A ghastly wound was immediately obvious just beneath the sternum where the stake had evidently protruded from the man's belly outward. There was a murmur of disgust from the troopers behind him at the sight of it.

"Quiet!" he commanded. "There is not enough light in here and I can't work with all this smoke and incense. Pick up the table and move him outside where I can see." The troopers immediately surrounded the table, lifted and carried the table and the corpse outside. A fairly large crowd of Roma had gathered by now to watch as well.

Radu opened his leather kit and took out a large magnifying glass. He picked up first one hand, then the next, examining the fingernails meticulously. He removed a small pick and ran it underneath each fingernail, wiping the residue on a white cloth he had pulled from the bag and examined it carefully. There were no signs of dried blood that would have indicated a death struggle. Radu then carefully examined every inch of the body from scalp to toe. There were no bruises, except in the immediate area of the belly wound, the edges of which were dark purple and white. He opened each eye. The pupils were dilated, fixed and motionless. Using long, thin surgical tweezers, he forced cotton up into each nostril and swabbed the throat. No blood.

"Turn him over!" he commanded. Once again, the troopers came forward, took hold of the man's torso and legs and flipped him over on his stomach. The entry wound was just as obvious on the back as the front, located somewhat to the left side, superior to the kidneys, Radu noted.

Oddly, there was no livor mortis, the natural pooling of blood to the back or bottom of the body after death. In this crude village, no embalming or draining of the blood would have taken place. Once again, Radu bent over and meticulously examined the posterior body for bruises or other marks. There were none. It was puzzling.

The man was in his early 40s, Radu estimated. His body was muscular and he probably weighed around 85 kilograms. Assuming the man knew how to fight, he would have been a formidable opponent, yet there was no sign of a fight.

"Again, turn him over". Again, the process was repeated and the body was turned face up. Radu kneeled at the head and returned his attention to the two dark purple marks on the neck; the only visible signs of trauma other than the stake wound. Under the magnifying glass, he quickly concluded the two spots were clotted blood, as he had suspected. He prodded them with a curette.

The scabs were easily removed and Radu placed them in another sterile white cloth he removed from his kit and then placed the cloth in a small, sealed bottle for further microscopic examination. He then gently pushed his curette into the flesh at one of the still dark spots. There was no resistance. The instrument easily slid right into the common carotid, Radu noted, until it met resistance on what he was sure was the inner wall of the blood vessel. He repeated the process with the second dark spot with the same result. Odd, he thought. What were these holes and what had made them?

"Who prepared this body? And who took this body down from the stake in the morning?" Radu turned and asked the crowd. Again, there was a silence until Radu spotted the old woman who had been sitting by the door.

"You there," Radu said, pointing at the old lady. The woman immediately became very agitated, raising her hand and pointing at him with the two fingered sign to protect herself from Evil. There was a sullen murmur from the Roma. Then another very dark, middle-aged man stepped through the crowd.

"I was one of those who took him down," he said in a soft voice. "What do you want to know?"

"How was he removed and brought here?"

"We broke the stake that was in the ground and then pushed it through the body from back to front until it was removed. Then we carried him here to the woman. She will wash and prepare his body as is our custom. We will place him on this pyre at sunset."

"Was there any sign of a struggle in his house? Furniture knocked over? Dishes smashed? Anything like that?"

"No, Your Honor. Nothing like that. Just him on a stake in front of the house of Lajos."

"Was there any blood on the ground? Or on the floor of his house or the house of Lajos?"

"Nothing like that, Your Honor."

"Where is this Lajos?"

"He left this morning with some of the others of our tribe. He is gone."

"I see. What about the others who went on this errand transporting these crates to Vatra Dornei from the castle? Where are they now?"

"All gone, Your Honor. They have all left with their belongings."

"Where have they gone?"

"Into the forest," the man replied, indicating with his arm the woods at the edge of the camp.

Radu considered the situation carefully. The decedent had no signs of having engaged in a struggle at all. He could have been surprised and killed in his sleep, but how? Had someone dragged in a huge stake and impaled the man as he slept in his bed? It was absurd. Why would anyone with murder on his mind bother with such a cumbersome method? If they succeeded in surprising a strong, muscular man like this in his bed, they would have simply cut his throat, but there was no cut throat. How could he have been killed so silently that an entire village had slept through the whole affair, including his impaling, right outside the door of one of their tribesmen?

Then there was the absence of blood. No blood in his bed. No blood on the ground. No blood on the body, notwithstanding a huge wound. No livor mortis. There was just no blood anywhere.

And then there were the mysterious twin perforations of the neck. Logic compelled the conclusion in Radu's mind that somehow, these two holes had been the cause of death which must have occurred before the impaling. But where had the blood gone? And, after the killing, how could someone have dragged the body from the man's house to the front door of this Lajos' house, impaled him and planted the stake in the ground with the man on it? No one man could do that, Radu surmised. It had to be a group of men. Probably the ones who had fled the village this morning along with the hetman, Nikolai.

The disappearance of the other men involved in the transportation of the cargo from the nearby castle to Vatra Dornei along with the brother suggested a conspiracy, perhaps. A falling out between the dead man, on the one hand, and his brother and the rest of the company, on the other. What had been in those crates? The manner of the killing was an important clue. It was meant as a warning. It was meant to be seen and to shock. But the man had been dead by the time the stake had been rammed through his body, apparently by the neck wound.

"Come!" Radu commanded the four remaining troopers, gesturing to them to mount up. He looked at the sky and concluded that there were still a couple of hours of light. He turned to the Roma.

"Go ahead and burn the body, if that is your custom. I am sorry for this intrusion. We will find who did this terrible crime and they will be punished. My name is Radu Popescu. I am leading the investigation into these crimes. I will be at the Monastery of Piatra Fantanele for the next few days. If any of you have any information that will help us solve this crime, you can find me there."

There was another low murmur from the crowd as they began to come forward to wrap the body again in the sheet for cremation. Radu nodded at the young man and the older man who had spoken to him, conveying his gratitude. They nodded in return. Then Radu mounted his horse with the others and out of the village they rode, back to the monastery. That evening, after dinner, Radu prepared a report to the Chief that he would arrange to be posted to the diligence that would pass by on its way to Bistritz in the morning.

Excellency —

It is my duty to confirm the death of the hetman known to the police as Béla and the abduction of his daughter, Natália by unknown assailants. The victim Béla was murdered and then impaled on a large stake near his house during the night, in the midst of the camp, and discovered by villagers at first light. The whereabouts of his daughter, the Roma girl Natália is, at present, unknown. His brother, Nikolai and several other Roma have fled the encampment and so are, naturally, suspected. The villagers are reluctant to discuss the details of these events and claim no knowledge or understanding of how this could have occurred in such proximity to their lodgings without their knowledge.

I completed a crude post mortem as best I could under the circumstances here. The cause of death appears not to have been the actual impaling of the body, but the wounding of the decedent at the neck by some piercing instrument or pick. We were unable to locate the weapon, however. Further, no sign of struggle on the part of the decedent was apparent.

We have been acquainted with the fact that on the day prior to the murder, a band of these Sinti Roma, including the decedent and all those who have now fled the village, were engaged in escorting a cargo of some kind from the estate of a Count Dracula to a destination in Vatra Dornei in the Bukovina. The content of this cargo is at present unknown, but we are suspicious that the crimes here are somehow connected to this recent undertaking. It is our intention to visit the Count's estate tomorrow and inquire there about the transaction.

We await your further instructions and will maintain order here from the Abbey which your Excellency was so good as to have commended to us for lodging and meals before we left. We will continue to keep you advised of further developments here.

POPESCU

Chapter 21

Natália had been sleeping, she knew, but she had no idea for how long. There was a slow feeling of dread in her as she lay on her back, eyes closed. It was very quiet. Slowly, ever so slowly, she opened her eyes.

She was in a small, round room. As she looked up, she saw exposed beams made the ceiling of the room. Turning her head, she saw a tiny fireplace that was not lit. A small dresser, chamber pot, wooden chair and table with candles were against the wall. The door from the room was closed. She was alone. There was a small window across from her. Natália rose and slowly walked to the window.

She was in a high tower, overlooking the walls of the castle, and the fields and forest beyond, she surmised. She could see for miles. Steeply sloped rock descended away from the castle until it rolled out into a clearing with high, brown grass that continued for perhaps a kilometer to the edge of a forest. Several kilometers away rose some pine covered slopes and mountains. She stuck her head out the window and looked left and right.

To her far left, she could see a trail that led up to the castle from the woods. There were no signs of life anywhere she could see. Natália guessed that it was mid-day, from the look of the sun in the sky. She knew the door would be locked, but tried it anyway. No luck. Back to the window. The window was at least 100 meters from the ground below; a courtyard with what appeared to be grey, slabs of flagstone. To jump from the window would have meant instant death. This tower was meant to hold her as a prisoner, she knew, and without warning she felt herself begin to sob. She cried for awhile. Some of it was out of sadness. Some of it was out of terror. A little of it was out of bitterness that her life would end this way, although she had done nothing wrong to deserve this fate that she could think of. She wished her father were here with her and sobbed because deep in her heart, she somehow knew he was dead and she would never see him again.

Natália had placed her trust in her father and, after him, the Sinti tribe. She had felt sure that she was protected and safe in her village. Now, she was in this dreadful place. She thought back to her arrival at the castle the preceding evening and her introduction to the Master. He was down there somewhere, she knew. He had put her up here. She knew that too. She shuddered when she thought about what he had in store for her, and cried some more. The thought of throwing herself out the window to a quick death she found herself considering seriously. Some things were worse than death.

But nothing happened for hours. She found a pitcher of water and a glass had been left for her, but no food. She was not hungry. There was nothing to do but wait and watch. As hours passed, the sun went lower and lower on the horizon. The sky went pink, then purple and then twilight until the sun sank behind the mountains. Then there was a noise.

It was a faint nose like that of a heavy door opening and closing somewhere far below, inside the castle. It was the first sound of any activity at all. Minutes went by and nothing more happened but Natália knew that sooner or later, someone would come for her. Then she heard another noise. It was close by. It was the sound of a bolt on the outside of her door being pulled open. Then the sound of a key in the lock turning. Natália felt her heart pounding as she stared at the door. There was no knocker. No voice asking to come in. The door just swung open and there was a woman standing at the threshold.

"Here you are," the woman said, smiling, her voice mellifluous as she glided into the room. She had on a long gown that was quite strange, given the circumstances. She seemed to almost float into the little round room, moving about its circumference, never taking her eyes off Natália. She was pale, Natália noted, with long blonde hair, luminous blue eyes and red lips. When she smiled, Natália noted her small, perfectly set white teeth. "How pretty you are, my dear. No wonder the Master had you brought here." The last was said with a slight tone of jealousy.

"Who are you?" Natália asked, feeling very uncomfortable in her presence, tuning to face her as she circled the room.

"I am Narcisa," the woman smiled. "You are Natália, from the village in the forest, are you not?" As she said this, the woman began to approach Natália.

"Yes. I am. I was brought here ..."

"Yes, I know. By you-know-who!" Narcisa said playfully. Despite her seeming friendliness, there was something menacing about the woman, Natália thought. As she neared, Natália tried to back away from her, but it did no good. Narcisa continue to stalk her and there was very little space in the room. Natália looked at the open door and then back at Narcisa's face. Narcisa's tinkling laughter was punctuated by the door suddenly slamming shut and the bolt behind the door behind thrown, all by unseen hands.

"I thought we could get to know one another, Natália," the woman said. "You will be with us here for a while, isn't that right?"

"I don't know," Natália returned. "I don't know why I'm here, to be honest."

Narcisa's tinkling laughter now became peals.

"But it's for us!" Narcisa exclaimed. "You're here for us! To keep us company. To play with us. To protect us while we sleep. Let me touch you," Narcisa said, as she approached Natália again. Natália felt her resistance giving way at first fearfully and then with resignation. She surrendered herself to the advancing beauty whose eyes held hers in rapt attention as Narcisa's hands played over her, drawing her closer. Soon their faces were touching and she felt the woman's cold lips touching hers.

"You are so warm," Narcisa purred, pulling her tightly to her now. Natália could feel the coolness of Narcisa's skin and her almost desperate clinging. Kisses rained all over her face and neck. Little bites and licks too, as Narcisa gently bent Natália back onto the bed, into which she slowly fell.

Like a cat pouncing on a mouse, Narcisa was on her. Her hands roughly unbuttoned Natália's blouse and pulled the halves apart, exposing her breasts. Natália was a virgin and her breasts had never been touched by anyone, so she gasped with surprise as they were firmly but smoothly caressed in Narcisa's hands as she lay down beside her. Natália was too dumbstruck and frightened to say or do anything while Narcisa became more and more excited and insistent in her attentions. Her hands ranged far and wide, over Natália's breasts and stomach. They were soon down into her pants as Narcisa continued to kiss and fondle her. It seemed nothing was going to stop her when Natália dimly heard a fluttering sound, like the wings of a bird, above the panting woman beside her .

Narcisa must have suddenly noticed it too. She looked back toward the sound and as she did so, Natália saw that a huge, black bat had flown into the room and lit on the table by the wall. Never in her life had Natália seen a bat this size. Its rodent face and yellow eyes could distinctly be made out in the gloom. Natália's wonder turned to awe when, at this, Narcisa jumped off the bed and scampered back against a wall, cowering in terror.

The bat on the table grew in size into a fiendish beast, its black wings now spread out, the head expanding with the body growing legs as Natália watched it in the twilight. Soon it was the size of a large dog. Then, it was as big and tall as a man. Then it was a man. A man with his back to both of them. He was dressed in black with high, black leather boots. The man turned around to face them, his eyes ablaze in red fury. It was the Count.

"How darest thou come here!" the Count hissed.

"I just wanted to see her! To touch her!" Narcisa replied in the contrite voice of a little girl.

"Hath thou tasted of her? Hath thou?"

"No, my Lord. I was just ..."

"Begone, then! Get thee hither this instant! And never come ye back here again unless I tell ye! Dost thou hear?"

Narcisa now drew herself up to her full height and slinked toward the door, her face hurt and contemptuous.

"Are you going to make her one of us?"

"It is no concern of thine."

"Are we not enough for you?"

"Go thee to thy sisters and begone, I tell ye! Later will I will talk to ye." And with that, Narcisa was gone.

Dracula now turned to her. "She will not disturb thee again. None of them will."

The candelabra on the table now lit itself, of its own accord, as well as several sconces on the walls. The room blazed into light.

Natália had now more than enough evidence to understand she was in the presence of a supernatural being. A monster from hell of unknown and perhaps unlimited power over her. Why he had spared her life was her only remaining wonder.

"What do you want from me?" Natália was surprised at how calm her voice sounded.

"Dost thee like thy room?" There it was again. The strange, antique Wallachian tongue from centuries past.

"I would like to go home, my Lord."

"And so shall ye go home, Natália. Soon. But first, thou must do as I tell thee. Serve me in all things that I command, thou must. All things. Dost thou understand?"

"I understand, my Lord."

"Thou hath seen my power."

"Yes, my Lord."

"Come with me, then."

With that, Dracula took the candelabra and led her out the door and down a dark, spiral staircase that followed the outer diameter of the round tower where she had been. It took a number of minutes before they finally reached another room at the bottom and went out a door into another large room. In an instant, innumerable torches about the room blazed to life and the Count set the candelabra on a crude stone table where it extinguished itself.

"Now my dear, let me tell thee a few things thou shouldst know before we go any further. There is a young English solicitor who will be coming to visit me in a few days …"

Chapter 22

Traces of snow in the cold shadows could be seen at Budapest's Keleti Pályaudvar, the railway station handling east-bound traffic to Transylvania and the Balkans. It was definitely a bit warmer here than in Bistritz, Kálváry Istvan thought as he placed his cap firmly on his head. The snow on the streets had obviously melted some days ago. Gábor Kasza and Richard, Baron von Krafft-Ebing followed him to a rank of hansom cabs. The cabbie took them briskly to the Gellert Hotel where the three of them decamped for the afternoon. As arrangements were made by the hotel clerk to complete their registration and remove their luggage to their rooms, he ordered them complimentary *Zwack* which was served in the customary ice-cold manner by one of the porters. The dark, amber liqueur was warming and bracing.

"We'll rest and get ourselves together for the evening festivities," Istvan announced drily to the other two, who nodded in agreement. It would be four hours before they would need a carriage to take them to the urban residence of Count Dracula. "Let's meet for an early supper at six o'clock, and then we will leave after that." Having stayed here in the past when visiting the royal capital Istvan knew there was a very nice bar and dining room in the hotel.

After washing his face in the water closet of his room, Istvan felt too restless to nap and decided to take a walk. The Gellert was near the Danube, the great river that cut through the heart of Budapest and was its most iconic symbol, along with its famous bridges, its Parliament and the residences, palaces, and public buildings that gazed out over or into it.

Budapest was no longer the provincial, quaint capital city that it had been in his youth, Istvan thought as he set out for a brisk walk along the river. Since the Kingdom of Hungary had achieved its independence in 1867 and especially after the unification of the three cities of Buda, Old Buda and Pest in 1873, the city's optimism and energy knew no bounds.

The electrification of the city center had been completed in 1878. The entire city had been electrified by 1893. The underground railway system had opened this year. Only London had anything comparable. The king himself had been present at the opening of the Franz Josef Bridge this year; the third bridge over the Danube. It was estimated Budapest had nearly one million people now, making it the sixteenth largest city in the world. Where Vienna was melancholy and Prague was cranky with its never-ending quarrels between Czechs and Austrians, the Magyar capital was exuberant; certain its best times were yet to come.

Istvan turned up the *Verejték utca* and started the climb to the Citadella; the fortress at the top of Castle Hill built by the Habsburgs after the ill-fated Revolution of 1848. As he caught glimpses of the Danube below, he realized how much he missed this beautiful city. He really must come back to Budapest more often, he thought, and certainly he would return here when he retired. Then he was awash in doubt. What was the point? With whom? And for what? Without a companion, without a wife, at his age a visit to Budapest would be just re-tracing steps from years ago; sad nostalgia about what had been or could have been since Julia had gone.

Then he thought about Julianna. He had thought about her on and off for several days, if he were honest. Her striking blue eyes and blonde hair mixed with gray. Her voice. The curious mixture of a strong personality inside a feminine character. Yes, she might give him a reason to keep on living, he thought. Then again, could he do the same for her? He was not her social equal. It would be presumptuous to attempt to court her, he thought. Not without some sign from her.

Istvan walked as he thought, wandering through neighborhoods. He observed the people walking by. He window-shopped. While sipping an espresso at the New York Café in the Seventh District, Istvan read in a newspaper the Italian army had been routed in Africa by an Ethiopian army at Adwa. Istvan snickered on reading this news. Ever since '66 when he had fought in the Imperial army under Archduke Albrecht and they had defeated the Italian army at Custoza, Istvan had held a low opinion of Italy, Italians, and particularly the Italian Army. Serves them right, he thought.

There was a chill in the air as late afternoon began to fade, ever so gently, into early evening. The electric streetlights came on. Trolleys rumbled by, packed with workers, domestic servants and ordinary people on their way home. There was a smell of smoke in the air from the wood stoves that still warmed the hearths of Budapest on cold nights. Evening bells began to ring from the church towers and steeples and shortly, Istvan found himself striding into the hotel's bar, braced by the cool late-afternoon walk. It was nearly six o'clock. Krafft was already at the bar, looking at a newspaper while smoking a cigar and sipping a glass of *amontillado*.

"Have one," Krafft offered. "It's quite good. I found out about it when I was in Spain a few years ago. Sherry, really. *Del Duque*. A very nice brand." Istvan looked at the bottle on the bar and nodded to the bartender that he would have a glass. Before too long, Kasza joined them.

"Shall we eat?" Kasza inquired. As planned, they took an early evening meal, discussing among themselves how they thought the interview would go. Not knowing exactly what to expect, the men discussed the possibilities with Krafft leading the way.

"So, what are we looking for, Krafft?" Kasza inquired.

"Of course, these killers are experts at deception and concealment, given the nature of what they do. They seem quite ordinary and have cultivated the ability to blend in ... to mix with other members of society without notice," Krafft explained. "Most prefer to be alone. Some of them are completely insane. They hear voices telling them to kill people; a form of hysteria."

"Are there certain things I should ask him this evening?" Istvan queried.

"I can't really give you a question to ask. It will be important to get to know him. For example, it would be interesting to know how our subject mixes with society? Or does he tend to be alone most of the time; out of sight?"

"One type kills for money or valuables. Given the high social status of our subject and his apparent wealth, this seems to be out of the question in this case. My own favorite, however, is the lust killer. He obtains sexual gratification from the act of capturing and killing his victims, enjoying their terror and absolute power and control over their life and fate."

"A monster," Kasza volunteered.

"Yes, indeed," Krafft concurred. "These types are very devious because they know, of course, that conversations revealing their pleasure would be horrifying to the average person and lead to their capture. Thus, they are experts at subterfuge. They were the children who had a morbid interest in mistreating and even torturing to death helpless animals and other living things. Most of them are younger men. They are usually of above-average intelligence; some quite brilliant. They often come from dysfunctional families and were sexually or physically abused as a child, usually by family members."

The men agreed that Istvan should take the lead in questioning Count Dracula. Krafft and Kasza would try to remain in the background, but Istvan welcomed them to ask questions and follow up on issues they felt were important if he were distracted or failed to do so. Before long, they finished their supper and departed the dining room to begin the evening's mission.

Istvan noticed a cold wind had kicked up off the river as they walked out the door of the Gellert Hotel to the street. As they waited for a cab to pass, he noticed a large dog approach on the opposite side of the street. There was no mistaking its wolf-like appearance.

"Look! A *Sibirier-hund.*" Krafft exclaimed, pointing at it. Istvan knew the breed. It was a Russian sled dog from Siberia. The dog trotted to a stop and sat down, almost exactly across from them. Its blue eyes seemed to gaze at them intently, but the dog made no attempt to cross or move closer and ignored passing pedestrians whose heads turned in surprise at the unexpected sight of the big dog. A cab was hailed and pulled to the curb. They got in but as the cab pulled away, Istvan caught sight of the dog again, rising, watching them and then turning and trotting away, into the night.

They gave the cabbie the address of Count Dracula in the Rózsa Hill neighborhood of Buda. Istvan knew the area quite well. It was on a hill, not far from and overlooking the Danube. There were many leafy boulevards and avenues that wound around the hill with villas and mansions that vied for an undisturbed view of the passing river, discreetly situated behind tall hedges, stone walls and gates or on tree-lined avenues. The Ottoman Turkish aristocracy had built many of the beautiful houses here when they had ruled Hungary for 150 years in the sixteenth and seventeenth centuries.

The stone mansion where the cabbie stopped was what Istvan had expected. Large deciduous trees in the front and around the sides of the house. Gardens. Lawns. Gas-lit lanterns on either side of a polished double front door at the top of wide marble stairs. Electric lights blazed forth from the numerous windows. Istvan paid the cabbie and the three men walked to the door and pulled the bell which made a tinkling sound. In less than a minute, the door swung open and they were greeted by a butler, who bowed and motioned them inside.

"My Lord is expecting you. Please, this way," the butler gestured with manicured fingernails.

The house was brilliant with fine Bohemian Tomia glass chandeliers hanging from high ceilings, reflected in the dark green marble floors. Oil paintings and mirrors graced the walls, along with huge tapestries. The butler soon ushered them into what was clearly the Count's study. The interior walls were made up of bookshelves opposite huge floor-to-ceiling windows looking out over the back of the house. There was a stone pool with a fountain in the middle that could be seen even in the darkness, then the view of the Danube sweeping past. A large fireplace dominated one end of the room. A cluttered desk covered with papers comandeered the other. A globe rested on a side-table within reach of an arm chair. Wing tipped, tufted, dark leather chairs in one corner of the room by a window would be where the interview would obviously take place. The butler bade them sit down.

"May I offer you some refreshment, gentlemen? Coffee? Cognac?" Coffee was requested and as he retired, the butler advised that his Illustrious Highness would be with them momentarily. True to his word, a few moments later, the door opened and a portly man in his early 60s, Istvan guessed, walked briskly into the room.

"No, no ... keep your seats, gentlemen," the Count said in a pleasant voice as he approached to shake hands and join them. The man was slightly flushed, as if he enjoyed drinking wine just a bit too much. He had a well-kept, gray mustache that fashionably offset his pattern baldness and blue watery eyes. He was dressed in a dark blue frock coat with a yellow vest and dark blue cravat, slightly out of fashion for the mid '90s but, as an older man, quite acceptable.

"Dracula Radu, Excellency," he said as he shook hands with Istvan and then all around. Introductions were made and the Count bade them sit down. He had a firm grip and shook hands with both of his with what appeared to be genuine warmth and enthusiasm.

"Now then," the Count said as he sat down in one of the chairs facing his three inquisitors, "how can I help you? My old friend Kula said that it was very important I meet with you right away. Something about missing persons and goings-on near our estates in Transylvania?"

Istvan glanced at his colleagues who looked back at him blankly. This man did not look like a serial killer, although one never knew. For one thing, he was too old and a little too fat.

"Would you mind if we spoke in German, my Lord? My colleague here does not speak Magyar and it would save time ..."

"*Natürlich, meine Herren,*" Count Dracula replied in quite perfect accent, as far as Istvan's practiced ear could tell. It was *de rigueur* for most of the Hungarian aristocracy to speak German from an early age due to Hungary's centuries long association with the Austrian half of the Habsburg Empire.

"May I ask, Highness, about your property in Bistritz?" Istvan began.

"Of course. To what property are you referring, though? Our estates in Transylvania cover many tracts."

"Let us begin with the one near the Borgo Pass."

"Ah yes. With the ruins. Been in the family for generations. Built by one of our ancestors as a stronghold against the Turks in the fifteenth century. What of it?"

"You say 'ruin'. Is the castle inhabited?"

The Count smiled. "No. It's been abandoned for more than a century, as far as I know. It is, however, the oldest ancestral home in our family's possession. The orchards and farmland nearby are still profitable. So we keep it."

"I see. Is the castle itself used for any purpose?"

"No, indeed. We had problems with squatters when I was a child. My father had the place boarded up and secured. The place is completely uninhabited and abandoned as far as I know. Why? Do we have vagrants there again?"

"Perhaps, Highness. When was the last time you were there?"

"Gracious!" The Count paused to think. "It's been years. I think I was in Bistritz in '89. I remember we met with the hetman of the Roma tribe that lives nearby and works on many of our lands. I would think we must have at least passed through the area and seen the place, but to tell you the truth, I really can't remember."

"We, my Lord?"

"Yes. Me and my *Faktotum*. Is that the word in German? My estates manager. We had retained the hetman Nikolai to be our local manager after several managers from Bistritz resigned or ..."

"Yes?"

"... went missing, come to think of it. They just disappeared without notice."

"I see. But the hetman Nikolai has been working for you in the Borgo Pass area for these past seven years?"

"Yes. I really don't know him very well. As I said, I met him a number of years ago, but even now I can't really remember his face. My manager corresponds with him when necessary."

"I see. Do you maintain any conveyance at the castle or in Bistritz?"

"Whatever for?" the Count said with a look of bemusement.

"A calèche. Black with red interior. Yellow spoke wheels? With the letter 'D' on the doors?"

"No. It's not mine. Why?"

"There was a kidnapping. In Bistritz. A black calèche like the one I just described was involved and seen. A witness swore to us that it belonged to the Count Dracula who lived in the castle."

"Extraordinary!" the Count expostulated. "As I say, gentlemen, I haven't been to Bistritz in years and I do not own such a carriage. Is that why you're here? Do you suspect me in this kidnapping?"

"You must understand we have to follow up on all leads, Highness. Your assistance in the matter is already of much help. Can you explain why a number of individuals whom we have interviewed have insisted that you, my dear Count, have in fact lived in this castle continuously for many years?"

"That's impossible! Quite impossible! No, I cannot explain what these un-named people think," the Count replied, now somewhat heatedly. "That's preposterous. Why would anyone, such as myself, wish to live in a ruined castle with no electricity, no comforts of modern life, in such a desolate, isolated place? Why would anyone live there? What exactly have these people seen?"

"They are terrified of you, my Lord," Kasza spoke up for the first time. Count Dracula turned to look at him.

"Terrified? Why?"

"They think you are a vampire."

With that, Count Dracula stood up. "Really, gentlemen. I cannot imagine you would ask to meet me here to convey such superstitious drivel." The Count was now quite agitated and began to pace about the room, although he spoke in a low, contemptuous tone.

"What my young colleague has said is true enough," Istvan rejoined. "Quite a few of the peasants and townspeople in the area point to this ruin of a castle and the Evil Eye of a Count Dracula Vlad as the source of their misfortune. Murders. Kidnappings. Missing wives, daughters. Of course, we do not believe in their superstition, but it is an old saying that where there is smoke, there must be a fire. Perhaps now you can understand our interest in meeting you and also in seeing the castle itself."

Istvan's earnest tone seemed to calm the Count. He sat down again and, as Istvan watched, he stared at the Persian carpet at their feet, his eyes playing over the patterns. He was obviously thinking. The room was silent for almost a minute when the Count looked up and began to speak again in a quiet and solemn tone.

"These things that you have heard, I cannot explain. I am not Dracula Vlad. I am Dracula Radu, first of all. There are no members of our House with the name Vlad. There is a reason for this. Do you know anything of our house? Our history?"

All three of the men shook their heads no, without saying a word. The Count paused again, stood up, and slowly walked to the fireplace. He warmed his hands and began to speak to them again, with his back turned.

"It is all so long ago. Ancient history, really. Few people know the story nowadays, but it has been recorded in the history books. You can look it up, if you have a mind to. Nobody in our family is named Vlad because of our notorious ancestor, Vlad Tepes. The Impaler. Vlad III, Prince of Wallachia and Transylvania who died in 1476. Our family is descended from his brother, Radu, for whom I am named. Radu was the brother of Vlad and they were mortal enemies. It was in the time when the Ottoman Turks were conquering the world. Our family allied with the Ottomans. Vlad allied with the Hungarians and warred with his brother constantly. Their hatred spawned a civil war in Wallachia and Transylvania and went on for twenty years.

"In due course, Dracula Radu attained complete control over Wallachia and continued to raid and defeat his brother who fled first to Transylvania and then to Hungary to seek the help of the great king, Matthias Corvinius. Due to his brutality in his relations with the Hungarian gentry in Transylvania, however, he was arrested by the king and held for a long time in the royal dungeons until after the death of Radu. His captivity reduced his power to nothing but surprisingly, he lived, was released, and eventually mounted another rebellion against the Ottomans. He died in an ambush near Bucharest, or so they say. There is a legend that his head was preserved in honey and brought to the Sultan in a barrel, but who knows if it's true. Nobody knows where he was buried.

"Vlad was a vicious killer, even by the standards of his day. He spread terror everywhere when he was Prince. He impaled a whole army of 20,000 Turkish soldiers after one battle that gave him his name. He burned disloyal villages to the ground slaughtering everyone. He once burned a church after herding the entire population of a village into it, killing everyone inside. He was feared, despised, and cursed by the Muslims and Christians alike. We are not descended from him and to this day, no Dracula will be named Vlad due to his cursed memory.

"It was Vlad who built the castle at the Borgo Pass. It was his best and last stronghold. It was never taken by the Turks or anyone else while he was alive. After his death, the castle was abandoned. He had no children and the property eventually passed into the hands of my ancestors by law. Some attempts were made, as I recall, to restore the castle in later centuries, but the place was too isolated and difficult to supply. Nobody has lived there for more than a century. I am quite sure of that.

"That was over 400 years ago, gentlemen," said the Count as he turned toward them and walked again to his seat. "Nonetheless, in those regions of Transylvania, his horrifying legacy was the stuff of legends and myth. I remember tales that were told when I was a boy growing up in Bistritz that the castle was haunted. Yes, and when you say vampire, there were those who believed that, too. I was reminded of those stories when you said it just now. I hope this helps, gentlemen. It sounds to me as if you are looking for a monster, but I dare say, it's a human one and not a ghost or vampire."

There was a silence in the room after the Count finished as Istvan and the others took it all in. Kasza had been taking notes all along.

"Of course, Highness, we do not believe in the existence of ghosts or vampires," Istvan began after a time. "Nonetheless, we would be grateful for the opportunity to visit and inspect the castle itself. We would like to rule it out as the hiding place or refuge of the criminal who has perpetrated

Chip Wagar

these crimes for so long and, perhaps, cultivated in the minds of these simple country folk the fear that some supernatural inhabits it."

"Very well," the Count replied. "I understand. Of course, you are welcome to inspect it. I will have my manager deliver to you the keys. As I told you, my father had it secured decades ago. I am not sure the keys will still turn the locks. They're probably rusted, but regardless, I will have them delivered to you with my blessing."

With that the interview concluded and the party of investigators was shown out of the Count's Budapest mansion and into the night. The Count had offered the use of his carriage to take them back to their hotel and they waited outside the front entry for his driver to bring the landau around.

"Charming man," Krafft said. "Unlikely to be your killer, from a purely psychic point of view. No sign of neurosis or psychosis. No. I think he is not your man."

"As I said before, Vezér, someone out there is frightening these people and masquerading as a vampire to intimidate them to cover his crimes. These myths and legends, it's perfect. Those ignorant peasants up there in those mountains believe this stuff ..."

As Kasza went on, Istvan's attention was attracted to two small red discs in the trees at the edge of the estate. As he looked more closely while Kasza talked, his eyes adjusted to the darkness. He began to realize the red discs were the retinas of an animal, reflecting the light from the house. The animal, whatever it was, was crouching in a shadow, watching them intensely.

"Look over there," Istvan said to his two companions, pointing in the direction of the tree. They turned to look and then Istvan saw the silhouette of a large dog abruptly rise and disappear.

"What is it?" Kasza said. Krafft was squinting into the darkness, his hand shading his eyes from the bright lights of the house.

"I don't see anything," Krafft said.

Istvan knew what he had seen. It was a large canine. He had only seen the briefest glimpse of its coat as it turned away, but he was sure of it. It was the silver grey of a wolf or, perhaps, of a Siberian. And it had definitely been watching them.

Chapter 23

It was cold. It was dark. It was absolutely quiet as Natália became conscious. In boredom she had laid down for an afternoon nap that had now extended past dusk. She was hungry. She decided to go down into the kitchen to make something to eat.

There was no fear now, though. Only sadness and despair. And hunger. She felt weak as she put on her shoes. What was the point? She could see no future to her continued existence. A prisoner with an indefinite, never-ending sentence. It was so unfair. Why had this happened to her? What had she done to deserve this fate? Why had her own family betrayed her like this? As she thought about it all, she felt an anger welling up inside her.

She had been a prisoner all her life, she thought. She had been made to work in the camp by her father, cooking for him, cleaning their small hut and having no life of her own. Her every move had been subjected to the strict supervision of her father. When the young Roma men like Lajos had shown interest in her, Béla had run them off with dire threats. She had wondered then whether she would ever have a life of her own. She could not leave the village in the forest. She had been a prisoner in that way too. Imprisoned in a sylvan cage, away from the outside world and the people who occasionally strayed into or past their little enclave. She could not leave. They could not come in.

And yet, she had done everything asked of her. She had been a slave to her father, to her uncle, to her tribe. And this was the result. She had been brought to this lonely, terrible place and given over to a new jailer.

She was a slave to a new master. There was no explanation or reason. It had just happened. Her father had abandoned her. Her uncle had betrayed her. Her tribe had never done anything to help her and would not help her now. She was out of sight of the Sinti and, she imagined, out of their collective mind. She felt at one moment as though she would weep with despair, and at another, she felt a mounting rage.

A mist was still on the earth outdoors, Natália could see, as she reached the bottom of the stairs. In the Great Hall, she noticed a shower of tiny sparks that seemed to be suspended in air in the middle of the room. She came closer and the little sparks seemed to be tiny specs of dust that slowly began to spin in the air. As the specs thickened before her eyes, they continued to spin but take on the shape of a woman. Then a second woman. And then a third. The three companions slowly emerged from the swirling orange dust, cackling and laughing.

"How did you do that?" Natália asked them as they all came together in the middle of the courtyard.

"It's a magic spell, dear," said Anasztázia.

She had an unusually deep, sultry voice for a woman. Almost as deep as a man's but smooth and soft as a cat's purr. To a woman, the sound of her voice was hypnotic. To a man, Natália thought, it would be intoxicating. Anasztázia was the Hungarian mistress of the Master, Natália had quickly learned. She had long, dark hair with hazel, green eyes. The undead always had large, dilated, black pupils and pink or red sclera, depending on how much the craving was upon them. The craving for human blood. The better to see with at night, when they lived.

"A spell to come ..." Narcisa cooed to Anasztázia.

"And a spell to go ..." Anasztázia replied as she glided smoothly to Natália; her ball gown swishing the stone courtyard floor. "Perhaps someday you will learn these things ..." she continued, as she stroked Natália's chin with long, white fingers with long, darkly polished fingernails. Her green eyes seemed to peer down into Natália's very soul leaving Natália with an overpowering sensation of defenselessness at the same time enthralled as Anasztázia's presence enveloped her at such close range.

"... The Master can teach you," said Narcisa, dressed in a Wallachian native costume, finished Anasztázia's sentence. Her long, sharp fangs marred and hardened her feminine beauty when she was hungry. When she got the craving for blood, it was difficult to suppress. She had already come to know this. "The Master will teach you how it's done if you're good to him."

"How long have you been here?" Natália asked. Anasztázia and Narcisa looked at one another for a moment, and then smiled. The third wife, Sophia, shot a sly look at her.

"It doesn't matter, my love, how long we have been here," said Anasztázia. "That is a question of centuries, Natália. Why are we here? That is the question. I can only speak for myself. I'm here because I want to live ... as our Lord and Master lives. We will die someday too, Natália. Someday, something will happen. We will be exposed to the sun. Men will find us who know how to kill us, and they will. Or perhaps, one day, we will kill ourselves. Who knows? Whoever knows? We are not so different than mortal men, are we?"

"And women," Narcisa joined in. "You will see. Perhaps you will come with us and be with us in our world. There are not many like us."

Sophia now approached her with a serious face.

"Why are you here?" she asked. "Why do you live? What is the reason for your life? Do you have a purpose? We exist to indulge ourselves and the Master. There is no purpose, Natália. There is no purpose. No point. No reason for your life or for ours. Don't you see?"

"The Master will be back soon," Anasztázia said, backing away. "We're going to fly away now. Explore the castle some more. He will find you. There are many interesting rooms. Not much furniture, though, darling. Each room has a story. He will tell you. *Viszlát*, my dear."

As she spoke, Narcisa and Sophia had come near her again and placed their arms around Anasztázia's waist. They morphed into large black flakes that became a sort of black powder, swirling then contracting into three large, black bats that flew up over the walls of the courtyard and into the night.

Chapter 24

The Gellert Hotel was a blaze of lights when Istvan returned with his two colleagues. He almost winced at the brightness of the electrical chandeliers in the lobby as they entered. Greeting them were pink columns and plush furnishings with potted palms, low tables and the murmur of after-dinner conversation over cognacs and cigars or champagne, in the case of the ladies. One in particular caught his eye. Her blonde hair and shapely figure in a beige and black gown as she rose and came toward him was that of none other than the Baroness of Jelna, Ribanszky Julianna.

"Will you excuse me, gentlemen?" Istvan said quietly. "I see the Baroness of Jelna over there," he gestured. They looked and saw her. "I will see you both at breakfast tomorrow?" The two men nodded and smiled. Istvan could see in their faces that they understood. He would handle this himself.

"*Bonsoir, Vezér,*" said the Baroness as Istvan approached. Isn't that what Kasza calls you? Vezér? Such a charming word and so apt for you. The boss." She held out her hand. Istvan took it and kissed it. She smiled warmly as he did.

"What are you doing here?" Istvan said after greetings were exchanged.

"I came to see you."

"Really? I was not expecting this. Julianna."

"I know I have gotten you into this affair. Kasza told me right before he left what you were doing. I came to the Polizeipräsidium. You weren't in."

"I was going to meet you. Friday. At *Die Golden Krone*. Remember?" Istvan replied.

"Yes. You were going to bring me the news. And I told you I might have some news for you."

"Do you have news?"

"Nothing of any great interest. I came wondering if you did."

"I have met Count Dracula," Istvan said.

"I would like to hear all about it," Julianna said, holding out her hand again for him to take, which he did. He led her to a low table in a salon off the lobby. They were immediately attended by a waiter.

"Champagne, please," Istvan ordered for both of them. "A cheese plate also, I think …" The waiter was off. Istvan regarded her diagonally across the table. Once again he could not help but appreciate the smaller accents to her that only a wealthy aristocratic woman of uncommon beauty would have. There was, for example, a large diamond and ruby amulet suspended from a thin, roped gold braid necklace that lay delicately on her chest. Diamond earrings sparkled in the subdued, warm light of the room. Istvan could smell the slight, subtle scent of a perfume. As he looked again into her face, he saw a faint but encouraging smile.

"And what did you make of the Count?"

"A nobleman, certainly. If there is any devilish business going on around his estate in the Borgo Pass, I will be surprised if he knows anything of it. An absentee landlord. Hasn't been to the place in years, he says. No wonder you have never crossed paths with him at any social events in Bistritz. Of course, he's also older than you and I doubt you would have traveled in his circles anyway."

The waiter intervened with a silver platter of various cheeses and two tall glass flutes of champagne. With white gloves, a chilling bottle in ice was placed between them with a towel sporting the hotel's monogram draped over it. The waiter bowed and withdrew without a word.

"How would you know what circles I travel in, Istvan?"

"I wouldn't know for sure. I could only guess, but I suspect not. He did not say he knew you either, Julianna. I'm afraid this is probably a dead end.

More and more I think the evidence points to the Roma hetman, Nikolai. Yet both Kasza and Dr. Krafft say it would be almost impossible for him to have been a serial killer without the whole Sinti tribe knowing it. And why would they tolerate such a thing? Unless they were terrorized into silence, but Roma men are there who would not be afraid of Nikolai. No. It's a puzzle."

"I appreciate what you have done ... are doing, Istvan. You didn't have to do this. You could have left this to the higher authorities."

"Thank you, Julianna, but I'm glad to do this for you. In fact, I want to do this for you. I want to do this because it gives me an excuse to see you, Julianna. It's just that, these past few years, it's been so very lonely and I ..."

"You don't have to explain, Istvan," she said, reaching out with her gloved hand and closing it on Istvan's arm firmly. Then quietly, she continued in a low voice. "I know what you're saying. I thought that I would never ... could never be happy again after my husband died. Until I met you. Since then, I have felt ... alive again. Like a woman again, since I first saw you at the hotel. I began to feel there was something to look forward to ... something between us."

Istvan's heart was pounding as he heard her words. He felt an intense desire to pull her to him and wrap his arms around her. Her blue eyes and shy feminine smile. Her beautiful teeth and eyelashes. He wanted her. It was all he could think of as their conversation continued. Her sparkling eyes. They were both increasingly oblivious to the room and the world around them, as the evening and the champagne went on. Each was taking a last measure of the other one last time before plunging in. Each was savoring the slow, mutual seduction each knew was taking place and would end, perhaps not that night, but soon ... in a large, soft bed.

Chapter 25

Nikolai had gone over his woeful fate in his head a hundred times. A thousand times. There was no way out of it, that he could see, other than his own death. He was the abject slave of the Master now; he knew that. If Natália were still alive, he was her only hope. If she were dead, or worse, it didn't matter anyway. But there was the small matter of his leadership of the Sinti Estraxarja; his tribe. He knew there was a rebellion now. There was a faction out to get him. They would assassinate him, Nikolai thought, sooner or later. It was a matter of time. And then what? Who would care if he were dead?

Death seemed like a comfort to Nikolai anyway. His life had become unbearable, caught as he was between conflicting loyalties, fears and a deep self-loathing for his craven surrender to the Master. Handing over his neice. The Master had demanded it as the price for his life and in a moment of utter cowardice, craving life over his honor, he had done it. Now the shame of it seared his soul and burned as a never-ending guilty pain.

What was to be done? Should the Sinti flee or stay? If they fled, would the Master follow them and punish them? Kill them or worse? He had been over it a hundred times. What should he do? Try to rescue Natália? That was the only thing he could think of to atone for his humiliating, craven abandonment of her to the cruelty of the castle and the evil of evils that lived within it.

As he walked through the Roma village to his simple dwelling, Nikolai could feel the mistrust and seething anger of many of his tribe radiating toward him. Some averted their eyes. Conversations stopped in mid-sentence as he approached and passed, resuming in low, hushed tones behind his back. He knew. *They knew. It wouldn't be long before a knife was thrown, or something like it*, Nikolai thought.

He missed his brother. Béla had been pig-headed and impulsive, but no man ever had a more loyal brother or one he would more want in a fight to the death. Now he was gone. That black-hearted demon, the son of Lucifer if they were to be believed, had done it to him. Nikolai wanted revenge. He dreamed of revenge. He would kill this cursed nobleman. A vampire and a sorcerer he may be, but Nikolai knew the old ways. He knew how to kill them.

He had never had the courage to do it with Béla. They had thought about it and even talked about it more than once, but things had never been as bad as they were now. So they hadn't. Now he would have to do it alone. As the days went by, alone in his hut Nikolai occasionally sobbed suddenly and uncontrollably with despair. At other times, he raged at his weakness and fear but slowly, as the days went by, his heart hardened. He made up his mind to do something. To save Natália, to start with, or die in the attempt. It was better than a lifetime of despair and shame.

This morning, he quietly left his village at sunrise in the Forest of Tinovul Mohos and set out for the castle. The smell of the pines and the warming spring was in his nose as Nikolai's horse picked its way along the familiar path that brought him to the Coach Road. He turned left and began the slowly rising climb toward the Borgo Pass.

The sun had been up for a couple of hours and yet still had not crested the mountains to his right when he reached the crossroad with the small shrine marking the entrance to the private road to the Count's castle. He waited for a moment, gathering his courage. From his position he could see to the west a lowering range of mountains and hills, covered with dark pine trees under a milky, overcast sky. At this altitude, it was not out of the question that a snowstorm could still descend with little warning and cover the ground in white. He turned into the estate's road and began his approach. Within half an hour, he was in the courtyard in front of the castle, tying up his horse.

From his saddle bags, he removed the instruments he would need. A lantern. A mallet. Wooden stakes of hard oak sharpened to a lethal point. A large, butcher's knife. Long leather, suede gloves to wear while he did his work. Nikolai thought he knew where to begin. Beneath the chapel. He and Béla had explored it before. He knew the crypts were down there. He knew about the hidden door too. The one he believed would lead him to the inner sanctum. He took the tools and wrapped them in a cloth, tied them with twine and made his way to the entrance of the chapel.

A pair of ravens, perched atop of one of the gothic columns that had supported the roof of the chapel, peered down at him curiously. Their heads turned and tilted, as he made his way up the center aisle. Debris from the collapsed roof and stones from some of the columns and the tops of walls still littered the floor. The gothic windows that had once held stained glass gaped open and bare. A stone altar ahead marked the entrance to the crypt. Two spiral staircases began there, on either side of the altar, curving down behind it to a landing, where they joined and then a new set of stairs perpendicular to the upper flights led down into the dark. Nikolai lit the lantern and then slowly, cautiously, proceeded down.

The smell of earth, rot and mold was quickly noticeable as Nikolai reached the bottom of the stairs. The light from above, weak as it was on this overcast day, was almost entirely obliterated upon reaching the lower level. As his eyes adjusted to the darkness, he saw what he had seen before. Heavy stone columns, the base for those upstairs, and, interspersed among them, stone sarcophagi or wooden crates which could, and probably would, have been used as crude coffins. Rats scampered by in the shadows. He could hear their scurrying behind him, too. Other than these sounds, there was nothing.

Nikolai knew at the opposite end of the crypts was a concealed door. He and Béla had found it one day when they had summoned enough nerve to go down into the crypts together. Slowly, he made his way past the sarcophogi and crates, with the lantern in his hand. While the light was quite bright in a two meter circle around him, the lantern did little to illuminate the room generally, which appeared quite dim. Then he saw it; a dark, tarnished brass ring on the floor, close to the back wall. The door itself was covered with sand.

Nikolai put down his bag and set the lantern on the ground. Bending over, he grasped the ring and pulled. The door was immensely heavy. Béla had helped him with it the last time. He couldn't hold on and the ring slipped out of his hand. The door closed with a loud "boom" that reverberated off unseen walls and rooms, he imagined. If any living thing were on the grounds of the estate, it had heard that noise.

Nikolai swore under his breath. He waited and listened. Sure enough, he heard a sound. It was the howl of a wolf in the distance. Then another one. And another. In less than a minute, he heard dozens of them and the distance between them was closing. *Soon they would be coming down the stairs*, Nikolai knew. Now the dark abyss beyond the door was his only safe alternative.

Again he picked up the ring and again he dropped it after only raising it a meter or less off the floor. Again, the booming sound of its fall. Nikolai moved to the opposite side of the door. It was more strain to lift the door initially, but once he got it up, he could better leverage his arms and body and pull it all the way open. He raised it now to a perpendicular position, noting that a heavy chain was attached to the door that prevented it from toppling over on its hinges. Instead, it pulled the chain taut as the door tipped just over center, revealing another stairwell down into darkness.

Nikolai could now clearly hear the howling wolves above him in the chapel. It would only be a matter of seconds before they started coming down the stairs for him. He grabbed his instruments and the lantern and placed them on one of the steps. As he reached for the chain, he saw the red eyes and black fur of a very large wolf bolting down the stairs at the opposite end of the room. Hot on his heels were several more wolves, snarling and baying, their noise echoing off the stone walls as they dashed across the vast crypt toward him.

He yanked on the middle of the chain and the door hardly moved. He hung from the middle of the chain and succeeded in pulling the door over the top and then it smashed closed with a deafening blast, now that he was in the stairwell. In another moment, he could hear the wolves just above him howling in frustration and scratching with their paws at the door. He gathered his package and the lantern and headed down the stairs.

The masonry of the walls here was very crude. It was apparent this was a subterranean tunnel almost never seen by human eyes and so, Nikolai thought, any attempt at finishing work had been ignored. The floor was smooth and earthen. The ceiling was low. The tunnel clearly sloped downward and curved to the left until after walking a few moments, Nikolai could not have seen the door area from where he had just come, even had the light been better. He had no choice. *He had to press on, no matter what the outcome.*

The passage was quite long. In which direction he was going, Nikolai couldn't say. At times, there were other short stairwells that led further down; always down. There were no doors or other distinct markings along the way, as far as Nikolai could see. At last, Nikolai came to another door. It was locked. Nikolai smiled inwardly. *There wasn't a lock made by man that Nikolai couldn't pick.* From his pocket, he took his favorite instrument for the purpose, a half-diamond pick. His fingers felt with the pick for the pins to the lock. There they were. In a moment he separated them and turned the cylinder within the lock. He could hear the tumblers clicking as he turned it and yes, he felt the door give way. He pulled it open.

Nikolai was stunned by what he saw in the flickering light. He was at the threshhold of a large, octagonal room. Beautiful marble columns flecked with gold and silver veins reflected the light of his torch. There were three other doors, opposite and perpendicular to the one he was entering. The floor was smooth, polished marble in contrast to the crude, dirty flagstone of the crypt or the dirt floor of the tunnel. The room was empty except in the dead center of it, lying upon a marble plinth was a large, black coffin, inlaid with gold. On the plinth below, in carved, gold, letters was the single word: "DRACULA". At each corner of the massive black coffin were four smaller coffins on lower plinths, each one beautifully carved.

Nikolai set down his cloth sack and opened it quickly. He took out the large mallet and one of the oaken stakes, walked over to the coffin and set them down within arm's reach. With one hand, he held the torch. With the other, he felt for the groove that would mark the top of the coffin from the sides. He found it. He pushed his fingers under the cover to gain purchase and when he had gone as far as he could, began lifting.

As he had expected, the coffin had not been nailed or sealed shut, but opened rather easily. As he raised the cover, he could see that it was empty. He stared at it, letting the cover fall open fully. The moment the cover reached its full arc open, a startling sound of metal on metal reverberated around the room. At all four of the doors, heavy barred grating slammed down on concealed guides into grooves between the marble squares on the floor. By the sound of them, Nicholas knew that they were heavy. Very heavy.

Grabbing the lantern, hoping against hope, he ran to the door from which he had entered the chamber. He set down the lamp and grasped the grated metal. With all his might, he pushed up but to no avail. He could not budge it. The grating was either so heavy he did not have the strength to raise it, or there was a catch or lock that held it firmly in place once it had come down. Either way, Nikolai knew *it had been a trap*. An elaborate trap, prepared by the Master for hostile intruders like himself. Nickolai wondered to himself how many men had been trapped and killed in this room over the centuries? Now Nikolai would simply have to wait, he knew. His desperate gamble to kill the Master had failed, but the evidence of his intentions was on the floor. *No explanation would convince anyone otherwise*. No excuse would avail. He would come for Nikolai in time. After dark. Then he would arise and the wolves or the ravens or some supernatural power of nature would inform him of Nikolai's presence. And the lantern on the floor would soon run out of fuel. And eventually it would be completely dark and he would be alone. Waiting.

He sat down, slowly, as the wretched reality of his situation sank in, making him feel heavy and exhausted. He had failed. The life he had scratched out and propped up at such terrible cost was no more. He had watched it collapse to ashes in only a few days. First his brother. Then Natália. The tribe. Everything. Gone. He had been their leader. The older brother. The uncle. The one to whom everyone looked for leadership, wisdom and courage. He had failed all of them, and worse, had abetted this monster he had sworn to kill for most of his adult life. And this was the price he would now pay for his sins and mistakes.

His sadness at the futility of his own life girded him as he began to face his impending death. It was not such a great loss, Nikolai thought. He could play out the hand in wretched, craven fashion, begging for his life, groveling before the contempt of the undead. The Master and his whores might toy with him until they tired of him. Or they might torture him. He imagined hearing his own cries for mercy reverberating off the stone walls in some dank cell far below the earth. *He knew what the Master was capable of doing.* He had known all along. He had aided and abetted him.

Some things were worse than death. Someone had once told him that, Nikolai thought, as he rolled up the sleeves of his peasant blouse above the elbows. Maybe it had been his father? He thought about it. It sounded like something his father would have said, even if he hadn't been the one. Maybe it had been his grandfather. He talked like that, too. Damn, he hadn't thought of his father or his grandfather in a long time. Suddenly he felt a stab of sadness at their absence. They had been dead for years. Why now? Great tears rolled down his face.

Nikolai took the large knife he had brought from the cloth sack. It was sharp. Nikolai felt along the length of it. Sharp, as it would need to be. The torch was flickering wildly now. It would soon be out and then it would be completely black. And sometime, sooner or later, he would come. Shadows played on the floor. It was quiet. Deathly quiet. No, he thought. At least he would salvage one last speck of honor.

Nikolai took a deep breath. With the knife in his right hand, he slashed his left wrist to the bone in one cut. He could hear it. The blood gushing out. He couldn't look at it, though. He just let it happen. It didn't take long. He began to feel sleepy and faint. Little sparkling pieces of dust began to dance before his eyes. *He was going somewhere safe.* Somewhere light and green. Somewhere away from here, where they couldn't catch him and couldn't hurt him. The lantern's light seemed to be getting dimmer and dimmer until there was just the pool of light that circled the lantern itself. He closed his eyes and smiled. *Time to go.*

Chapter 26

Radu Popesu and his troopers arrived at the castle about an hour after sunrise. A heavy fog had shrouded their approach to the castle until they had nearly reached its gate. After passing through the portcullis, they immediately noticed a horse tied to a post in the courtyard, but no sign of its rider.

Radu knocked on the front door to the hall, but there was no answer. He and the other troopers called out for anyone who might be around, but again, there was no response. After several minutes, Radu and his men began inspecting the ruins of the complex, including the chapel. A search of nearly two hours ensued. The stairs down into the crypt were found, but after entry and a careful look into the gloom at the various sarcophogi, Radu shrugged and returned to the courtyard at the front of the castle. The only interesting thing he had noted was the multitiude of canine footprints in the dust and dirt of the floor of the vault. Wild dogs or wolves must visit or perhaps even inhabit the ruins, Radu concluded. It was clear that unless he wished to break and enter the premises, their visit had failed to reveal much of anything. It seemed clearly abandoned but the presence of the rider-less horse intrigued him greatly.

"Mount up, gentlemen," Radu commanded as he mounted his own horse. "One of you lead this horse with us back to the Monastery."

"Sir!" exclaimed one of the troopers. Radu looked at the man inquiringly. "I searched the saddlebags. There were some things in there that belonged to the rider."

"Anything interesting?" Radu asked.

"A canteen. Some rope. But then I found this." The trooper handed Radu a small figurine. It was large enough to fill his hand and was of a woman. A woman with blue skin and many arms. Eight arms he counted. She had some kind of a crown on her head with long dark hair. It was the Hindu goddess Kali, Radu realized. The individual who had left the horse was carrying around an idol of Kali.

"Very good," Radu nodded at the young trooper, who smiled and returned his nod, acknowledging the compliment.

"Thank you, sir."

"Mount up, gentlemen!" Radu kicked his horse into a slow ambling canter toward the steep, descending pathway that led down and away from the castle. He took one last look around. It was a ruined castle, Radu thought, but something was going on here. He could feel it. It might be just intuition, but something was wrong here. It would be a Roma horseman who had been here before them. Nobody else would have an idol of Kali in his saddlebag. Why had he ventured up to this isolated, abandoned place and left a horse with a saddlebag containing some talismanic idol? Why would he be here? And where was he now?

In a half hour, the company was back to the Coach Road. Radu had planned to return to Bistritz from the castle, but no. He would make a quick detour. They would return to the Sinti village and ask about the horse. It made sense to Radu the horse must belong to the Roma.

"Come!" Radu shouted to the startled troopers who had all assumed they would turn right and west to Bistritz. Many were anxious to get home. Instead, they turned to the left. Radu spurred his horse into a gallop now and with a thunderous beating of hooves, they headed for the forest of Tinovul Mohos. On the Coach Road, Radu Popescu's troop was intercepted by two of the troopers he had sent to Vatra Dornei after the hetman and his niece.

"There was no sign of them, Your Honor. Nobody had seen anyone matching their description. Then we stopped at the train station and interviewed the stationmaster. He recalled the crates delivered by the Roma.

He said there were about half a dozen of them. He has frequently seen shipments like this before from the Count's castle. Didn't know what's in them, but they're sent on down to Constanta or Varna on the Black Sea to be sent overseas."

What could be in those boxes, Radu wondered? What could possibly be shipped from a ruined castle like the one he had just seen that would be worth shipping overseas? Was there some buried treasure there? About halfway to the Roma village, they encountered the diligence that had left Vatra Dornei hours earlier, making its way to the Borgo Pass and on to Bistrtiz.

Chapter 27

The Budapest train steamed into Bistritz at 6 PM. Baron Krafft had left for Vienna from Budapest, wishing them the best of luck in unraveling the mystery of the serial killer and reminding them that he would be very interested in examining the criminal if and when they apprehended him.

Kasza and Istvan headed for the Golden Krone for dinner before turning in for the night. Count Dracula's overseer was to meet them in three day's time to escort them to the ruined castle. In the meantime, they would catch up on the news here. They did not have long to wait.

Oszkár and his wife were the owners of the Golden Krone. Istvan had met him his very first night in Bistritz when he had been greeted by the mayor and city alderman. He had lived at the hotel for a couple of weeks after he arrived and spent many evenings dining there. The Golden Krone was a place for Istvan to relax. In the months he had been in Bistritz, Istvan and Oszkár had become very friendly. After dinner, Istvan waved Oszkár to the table, inviting him to sit down with them for a few minutes. Slivovitz was poured all around, cigars lit and they began to talk about Budapest, Bistritz and a young Englishman who had stayed at the hotel while they were gone.

"What was his name?" asked Kasza.

"Harker Jonathan," Oszkár said, in the Magyar style, reversing names. "A solicitor. From London. Said he had been invited here by Count Dracula.

He took the diligence a few days ago. Said he was going to see the Count at the castle at the Borgo Pass."

"Really?" Istvan said, puffing on his pipe.

"I told him no one lives at that castle, but he showed me a letter. The letter was signed by Count Dracula, all right. It said that he should take the diligence to the Borgo Pass where his coach would meet him to drive him the rest of the way to the castle."

"A forgery," Kasza said.

"We were just with Count Dracula in Budapest. Did you see the date of the letter?" Istvan inquired.

"No, but it was delivered the day before he got here, after you had left for Budapest."

"Interesting," Istvan said.

"Have you seen him since?" Kasza asked.

"No, I haven't. If he comes back this way, shall I let you know?"

Chapter 28

Radu Popescu had ridden into Bistritz around midnight from the opposite direction Istvan and Kasza had arrived from Budapest, hours earlier. He was tired and saddle sore from riding. Exhausted, he had dismissed the troopers on arrival after putting their horses up for the night in the stable, gone home and collapsed into bed. It was very late the following morning before he arose from a deep, dreamless sleep. It was not until early afternoon when he appeared at the Bistritz Polizeipräsidium and made his report to Istvan and Kasza. He told them about the shipments that had been made by someone from the castle. He described in detail the scene at the castle, including the rider-less horse and the detailed search they made of the grounds and areas near the Borgo Pass.

"We went back to the gypsy village with the horse afterward. At first, they pretended ignorance, but after a while, one of them came forward. He confirmed the horse belonged to the hetman Nikolai. The figurine we found is of the goddess Kali, who they worship in their strange religion. Many of them have such charms and talismans on their persons or in their dwellings. In any event, Excellency, it seems that after the murder, the hetman Nikolai left the village with his niece on the horse we found at the castle. His whereabouts after that are unknown, but one would conclude that at some time, he visited this ruined castle and left his horse for some reason."

"Someone is impersonating the Count," Kasza ventured, lighting a cigarette. "Someone is using the estate to smuggle contraband of some kind from here into Romania and from there to Turkey or elsewhere. The Roma know about it. At least some of them do. I don't know what it is they're doing, but they want people to stay clear of their business there. So they make up these stories that it's haunted. Vampires. All that sort of stuff. They have the people up there spooked."

Istvan drew on his pipe and exhaled. The hetman Nikolai and his band of followers among the Roma were the obvious suspects. Perhaps he knew of some way to get into the castle. Perhaps there was something of value in there. The Roma had found something, no doubt. Perhaps treasure. Perhaps some archeological finding that was valuable. Something buried or hidden there from the time when the castle had been inhabited and used by the Dracula princes of Wallachia and Transylvania and their retainers. They were smuggling whatever it was from the castle. Stealing it from underneath the noses of the Dracula family and selling it overseas where the transaction would never be noticed. Smuggling was, of course, a habitual pastime of these people, Istvan thought.

"Well done, Radu. The post mortem, especially, was well done under these circumstances. Curious, as you say, about there being no blood despite the impaling wound. He was already dead when he was impaled, you think?"

"Yes indeed, Vezér."

"The method of impaling, Kasza ..." Istvan recalled Count Dracula's description of his ancient ancestor's methods.

"Yes, I thought about that, too," Kasza replied. "A throwback to a bygone age, one might say," he continued. "Curious that someone went to the trouble to resurrect this grisly practice from the days of the Turks. Surely, just as in those days, the cruelty and horror of it is meant to terrify and intimidate people who see it."

"I am more anxious than ever to inspect the interior of this castle," Istvan replied. "Radu, I want you to prepare the men to return to the Borgo Pass in two days' time. That will be when the Count's manager arrives who will unlock the doors and escort us into the castle to explore."

"Why not go now, Vezér?" asked Radu.

"We have no authority to crash through the doors of a nobleman's house, even if it isn't inhabited," Kasza replied. "We would have to get a warrant from

Chip Wagar

His Majesty to do that. This isn't Russia, Radu. We have laws. We have to wait. Besides, the owner has given us permission, if we just wait. These murders have been going on for a long time. Another couple of days will not matter."

"Yes, Vezér." Radu nodded his acceptance. For another hour or two the group discussed the situation, how the various clues fit together and what might be done to pull together a case against the Roma chiefs that Istvan increasingly felt must be the perpetrators of these criminal acts. Just after one of the orderlies brought a late afternoon Jause of tea, ham, cheese and biscuits, one of the functionaries in the postal section knocked on the door and entered the room.

"Excellency, you said to notify you immediately if you should receive a post from the Vatră Ciobănesc in Poiana Stampei. He held out a brass plate with a single letter on it, addressed to Istvan. Istvan took it and quickly opened the envelope. After glancing at it for a moment, he read it to the group aloud:

28 May 1896
Excellency —

This night I would report that a large caravan of leiter wagons and horses stopped at my tavern. They were Slovaks from the Bukovina. Their leader revealed to me in conversation that they were transporting some 50 crates bound for Varna by rail from Vatra Dornei. He informed me that the cargo had been received at Schloss Dracula from some Roma working there that evening after sunset. I did myself see this entourage while bidding the hetman good evening and safe passage. My Lord, there must have been nearly 100 mounted Slovak guards armed with rifles and drivers who dined at my establishment this evening and set out for Vatra Dornei.

Trusting that this letter finds your Excellency in good health and with all due respect and best wishes, I remain ...

Your humble servant
Dieter

The letter had come in that afternoon from the diligence that passed between Vatra Dornei and Bistritz through the Borgo Pass. Istvan calculated that nearly a day had passed since it was written.

"One hundred Slovak guards! Can you imagine? A bodyguard for a king!" Kasza exclaimed.

It would take a full day to get to the Borgo Pass and another half day to get from there to Vatra Dornei. There wasn't time. He turned to the postal clerk.

"Get a telegraph to the Stationmaster at Vatra Dornei. Instruct him that this is official police business. Tell him he is commanded on the authority of the District Police and the Royal Hungarian Gendarmerie to arrest and detain the cargo delivered into his hands by a certain entourage of Slovakians believed to consist of some fifty crates from Castle Dracula bound for Varna." Istvan looked at Radu and Kasza. "It seems as if we are always just behind events in this case. Tomorrow we ride."

Chapter 29

Although the Master slept somewhere in the vast maze of underground crypts beneath the castle during the day, he had demonstrated to Natália the futility of attempting to escape the castle while he was to be away, within a day or two of her arrival. Standing at the glassless window and balcony that overlooked the Courtyard, she watched as Dracula beckoned to unseen listeners in the darkness beyond in a strange and ancient tongue:

"Come hither, children of the forest. Thou hearest my voice in thine ears from far away, I know! I call thee to my door. Come to me! Come my children!"

Almost immediately a wild baying and howling could be heard from a pack of wolves in the distant forest. In the dark they could not be seen, but a hysterical outburst of yips and yowls answered the Count's call and could be heard approaching closer and closer. Within minutes, they began to pour into the Courtyard, looking up expectantly at their Master. More and more arrived until there appeared to be something like one hundred grey and black beasts below, their yellow eyes fixed on the window. The noise of their howling reverberated off the walls, making a deafening din.

"Come with me, my dear," the Count commanded. He led Natália down the stairs to the huge front doors in the Great Hall through which she had first entered the castle. To her horror and astonishment, he unbolted the doors and swung them open. The dogs fairly flew into the room, swirling around them in a large circle. Natália thought she would faint. The smell of their wet fur filled her nostrils as more and more of them crowded into the room. They were enormous wolves with huge heads and jaws that would snap her wrist or leg in one massive bite, she knew, but they did not harm her standing, as she was, next to the Count.

At last, a particularly huge, black wolf slowly entered the room; the last and greatest wolf of the pack, Natália somehow knew. He had a certain dignity as he padded up to the master. For a moment he stood expectantly, then stretched his forelegs in front of him and lowered his head and the entire front of his body, as if bowing in homage to the Count.

"Silence!" the Count said in a loud voice, and immediately the wolf pack was silent and sat down in place. It was an unimaginable sight to behold. Natália turned around in a complete circle once, taking it all in. A hundred sets of yellow eyes watched her, with the pervasive sound of panting but otherwise quiet. Then the Count bent down and stroked the head of the black wolf, as one would pet an ordinary dog. He mumbled something in its ear that Natália took as an affectionate greeting in a low voice. Then he turned to Natália.

"This is but one of my packs of children, but this is the greatest of their chiefs," Dracula said, motioning to the great black wolf before him. "You see how they come when I call them to me?" Natália dared not answer, only nodding. Then the Count turned back to the Chief wolf.

"Thou art my most noble and trusted servant, Cerberus, art thou not?" The wolf whined and nodded in agreement, obviously understanding the ancient tongue being spoken by the Count that Natália could barely understand. Then, speaking to all the wolves, he continued.

"Thou hounds of the Netherworld! And thee, warrior chieftain of the wolves of Tinovul Mohos! Hear my will and my command! Thou guardians of my ancient and sacred hearth! Thou shalt not let this maiden nor any man that enters these doors and partakes of my hospitality to depart these walls without my blessing! Wilt thou honor my trust? Wilt thou carry out my dread command, on pain of thy lives?"

With that, a howling broke out again as the wolves rose as one in the room. The black chief wolf fixed his eyes on Natália with a supremely

157

malevolent glare, allowing his long, red tongue to lick his chops. His meaning could not be any clearer.

"Begone! Thou Satans of the night! Begone! Feast on thy prey this night and all nights, my children!"

Dracula thrust his arms up into the air as his voice boomed out and as quickly as they had come, the vast pack of wolves bounded howling out of the room, into the courtyard and out of sight. Their obedience to the power of the sorcerer Count had been demonstrated beyond doubt. The wolves were as obedient to the Master as lapdogs. Any attempt to trek on foot to the Coach Road would mean gruesome death, torn to pieces by these fiendish guardians. A horse might outrun them, but no human could for long.

Chapter 30

The English solicitor, Jonathan Harker, had arrived at the Castle in the dead of night. The Master had gone to fetch him disguised as a coachman in the black calèche. He had summoned Lajos, the new Roma chieftain, to deliver it to him from an outlying barn in the forest where he kept it and his horses hidden. Dracula had instructed Natália to prepare a warm supper for the Englishman and to set it out for him at a table in another tower where he would stay. This tower was the rear-most from the Courtyard. It was a suite at the top of some stairs and the end of a hallway. It consisted of a fairly large salon with a fireplace, another small hallway, a small room with a toilet and dressing table and a bedroom in a circular room. The bedroom was not too different from the one in which she slept except the view from the windows faced away from the Courtyard, gazing out over miles of silent forest.

The master had also instructed Natália to stay out of sight and to have as little to do with the Englishman as possible. She was a servant. She would cook his meals, clean his room and give every appearance of normality in the castle during the daytime. It was late morning after he arrived that she first saw him. He had slept late due to his late arrival and the Count had kept him awake during a long interview that had lasted until nearly dawn. She brought him a breakfast tray of coffee and pastries, ham and cheese. He seemed relieved to see her and attempted to speak to her in German and English, but since Natália didn't understand the English tongue, they could only communicate crudely by gestures and facial expressions. She understood, for example, he was thanking her for the breakfast. He pointed at himself and said "Jonathan", so she reciprocated with her name for him and so on.

He was an exceedingly handsome young man, Natália thought. He was tall and slender and athletic in build with light brown or even dark blonde hair, blue eyes, a sparse but well-trimmed mustache. His hair was cut short which must be the style of an Englishman as compared to her own people who wore their hair much longer. He had a fair complexion and his clothes were quite beautiful and well tailored. When he smiled, she felt her heart skip a beat and her face flush with shyness. All in all, Natália concluded as she walked back to the kitchen, Jonathan Harker must be the strangest but most attractive man she had ever seen. She only wished she could understand him better and wondered how much he knew about the Count and his secrets and why he had come here.

The first few days Harker had wandered about the castle ruins, and she had met him from time to time exploring one area or another. He was very polite and pleasant, but the language barrier made it awkward. Nonetheless, his gentle personality she could still appreciate and his striking good looks only seemed to grow finer on each occasion to her eyes. She found herself fantasizing about him and the life she imagined he led in England, so far away.

On one occasion, however, he fell asleep in one of the rooms in a remote area of the castle and lay there after the sun set. Before the Count had returned, he was discovered by Anasztázia and the other wives. They had been overcome at the sight of him as well and the desire to taste him, but before they could do so, the Count had returned and had thrown them out of the room in a rage.

After that, Jonathan Harker was locked in his suite of rooms and the Master bade her to always keep the door locked. Then Jonathan's manner changed. He soon realized he was a prisoner, she knew. She could see the fear, anger and eventually, the sadness in his face. Her heart went out to him but she could not think what she could do for him that would not result in their dying, either by the wolves or by the dreadful methods of the Master. A bond had slowly developed between them, though.

On another morning, at nearly noon, she returned to her tower room after working in the kitchen to discover her uncle's horse was in the castle courtyard below. She raced down to the doors of the great hall and attempted to open them but although she could lift out the heavy boards that reinforced the doors, she realized she did not have the iron keys that would be needed to unlock the doors. She raced up the stairs to her room again but as she did so, she heard a loud booming sound, followed by another one. By the time she reached the window of her room, she saw in horror the arrival of the Count's wolf pack in the courtyard below. The black wolf paused and looked up at her for a moment, as his brethren continued on through the courtyard and beyond. Then he was gone too.

That evening, the Count appeared suddenly in the kitchen where she was preparing the Englishman's dinner.

"Thou knowest, dost thou not, that thine uncle came here?"

"No, my Lord! I did not!"

"Nay ... Thou playeth me false, child! Thou knowest! Hath thee forgotten Cerberus? Think thou that my dark prince of wolves would not warn me of thy treachery?"

With this, the Count advanced on her. The fury in his face was intensified by the sudden appearance of large canine fangs behind the red lips and burning eyes, glaring at her. His cold hands clenched her arms with the icy force of a steel trap closing on a deer.

"My Lord!" Natália cried in terror. "I saw my uncle's horse. That is all. I did not see my uncle. I never spoke to him. I thought you had summoned him, my Lord. My heart rejoiced, I must admit, but then your wolves came and ..."

The Count released her rudely and pushed her away.

"Thine uncle is no more. Ended is his treason, dost thou understand? He hath come to take thee, child. He could not wait for me to release thee again into his care and he came to take thee from here. Death to those who disobey me! Death! Hearest me now, Natália? If thou betray me, thou wilt die like thy father and now like thine uncle! Thou knowest my power!"

Nathalie felt sick with fear and grief. In an instant she comprehended the confirmation of her father's death and that it had somehow been delivered by the Count. And her uncle. Her family was utterly destroyed now. She was the only one left.

"Know this, my child. Know that the ravens in the sky watch for me. The wolves in the forest watch for me. The creatures of the forest and the night all watch for me and heed my command. They tell me everything. I know everything. More men will come. If thou speaketh to them … if thou let them see you … Thou wilt curse thy mother for bearing you into this world … Thine existence in this world and the next is known to me and to me alone. Mark my words, my child!" With this terrible threat, the Count turned on his heel and disappeared in a whirl of black dust.

Natália found herself on the floor, trembling uncontrollably and sobbing in fear. All was lost. She was alone in the world and helpless. A slave to the Lord of this God-forsaken castle and his minions.

It was only a day later when a troop of uniformed police clattered into the Courtyard and found her uncle's horse, still tied to a post. As the mounted police called out, Natália shrank back from the window, trembling but saying nothing. After a couple of hours, the troop clattered out and she watched them ride into the distance, into the embrace of the dark forest on the way back to the Coach Road. She was alone again in the castle, except for the Englishman.

Chapter 31

The following afternoon, Natália delivered Jonathan his lunch in his rooms. She was about to leave after setting down the tray when Harker motioned her to sit with him on a couch in the room. He looked desperately sad. For a long time, he searched her face and looked into her eyes as if considering what to say. She saw the frightened look on his face. She knew very well what he was feeling, even if she could not understand his tongue. As she sat with him for what seemed a minute or so, it seemed he made a decision. He took her hand in his and held it in his for a long moment. Then he pressed it to his chest, looking at her eyes all the while. She understood. For the first time in her life, she was being sought by a man she desired. A man in trouble. A man in grave danger, as was Natália. They shared a common danger and dread.

Jonathan leaned slowly toward her. As his face neared hers, she noticed how full and soft his lips were. He whispered something to her softly. He closed his eyes. She had not seen another living soul herself in the castle in many lonely weeks until this Englishman arrived and so she let him kiss her. It was a sweet, warm kiss and then there was another, and another, each one longer and more succulent than the last. She felt a heat rising within her. She put her arms over his shoulders and around his neck. Slowly he pulled her closer to him with his arms. He murmured something again in a low voice in her ear. Something tender, she knew.

She would probably be dead soon, Natália thought. Or worse. Her existence was so precarious that every day might be her last. This young

Englishman was her only hope of escape and salvation and Natália imagined that he must be thinking the same thing about her. If she were going to die, this moment might be the only one she would ever have to experience the love of a man and so she decided she would abandon herself to whatever came next with him.

It was an early spring afternoon and even high in the tower, with the windows open, the fragile warmth of the early afternoon could be felt. The smell of raw earth and fresh pine wafted into the room as they explored each other, minute after minute. Natália felt the constant anxiety and fears crowded out of her mind, replaced by sensual desire for his soft mouth, the feel and the smell of him, his muscles and bones, his hands, his hair and the sounds of his breath. She loosened the drawstrings of her peasant blouse as he watched her, saying nothing. There was nothing to say and neither of them could understand the other anyway. Except this day, they did understand each other. The coincidence of their dire situation in the ruins of this castle had brought them together in this unspoken alliance. An alliance they both knew would be consummated by the only means of communication available to them.

He watched as she let the blouse slip down her shoulders and arms, revealing herself to him. His eyes were fierce with longing and desire now, she saw, as they lingered over her breasts and then back to her eyes again. His hands lightly touched her breasts as he leaned forward to her again. Her breasts felt heavy and his soft, caressing touch sent a hot, electrifying pulse through her body. She could not repress a sigh of pleasure which encouraged him further.

She felt the warmth of his hand on her ankle and then on the inside of her leg, her knee, her thigh and then the feeling of his thumb slowly massaging her. She found she had become wet with desire. She quickly unbuttoned his shirt and felt his hard chest and muscled abdomen. He peeled it off with his other hand and it fell to the floor. He unbuttoned his breeches and she let her hand slide down into his depths until she felt him, throbbing and hard. It was the first time she had ever felt a man's organ and while she could not see it because he had by then gently nudged her to a supine position on the couch, she let her hand linger, feeling the length of it and exploring its thickening, pulsing largesse. Jonathan murmured something as she did so and the pace of their lovemaking quickened, becoming urgent and even fierce.

He roughly pulled off her skirt leaving her naked on the couch. Off came his trousers and boots. She saw for the first time, his erection and the sinewy muscles of his legs and arms. He tossed his clothes on a nearby chair and then turned her on her stomach. She felt his hands on the crests of her hips and his legs between hers. He pulled her toward him irresistibly and penetrated her in a few long thrusts.

The sensation of his being deep inside her filled her with pleasure. A growing warmth and shivering spread through her as his rhythmic strokes rocked her body. He was breathing deeply and loudly now as his motion became more urgent and intense, saying things she could not understand. Her mind was completely lost in the mounting tempo of his thrusts. Crowded out of her mind were all her worldly fears and sadness of the past days and weeks in the castle as she abandoned herself to him. She wished her escape would go on for hours and hours and never stop. A deep and quickening series of spasms arose from within her. She gripped the end of the couch with her hands as uncontrollable contractions and waves of ecstatic pleasure swept over her. They kept at it in this way for more than an hour and formed a bond that would last between them for the rest of their lives.

Chapter 32

Dimitru, the orderly from the Polizeipräsidium who had served Jause had just ridden home to his small farm on the road out of Bistritz to the nearby village of Sigmir. The weather had been exceedingly pleasant these past few days. He had enjoyed the ride home past the farms and fields being recently plowed and planted as the sun set. He unsaddled his horse and carried it to the tack room of the stable. He picked up a currycomb to groom the horse before entering his modest farmhouse where his wife and two daughters waited for him with his dinner. As soon as he returned to the stable he saw his horse had turned away from him and he heard murmuring in a low voice. The hair on the back of his neck stood on end as he saw that a man was standing on the opposite side of the horse. The silent visitor's high, shiny black boots and riding breeches were those of a gentleman and, with a shudder, the orderly guessed their owner.

"My Lord?" he inquired in a timorous voice.

The intruder moved around the horse now, his pale face and dark eyes seeming to float in the dim, flickering lantern light of the rickety stable. As he came closer, into the light, Dimitru saw that he looked many years younger than the last time he had seen him. His hair had grown longer and less gray.

Dimitru was not only afraid of the Master, but had been in the Master's pay for quite some time. The farm and stable had been well out of reach for this Wallachian peasant's son until the Count had made his acquaintance soon after Novotny Janos, the former police chief, had suddenly disappeared. The Count's gold had changed his life, but his service was a lifetime and increasingly doleful commitment, he had come to understand.

"Dimitru," the Count replied, smiling as he approached. The police orderly felt his heart pounding with anxiety over the purpose for this nocturnal visit. "Tell me, my loyal Dimitru, what hath transpired this day? What news from the Politzei in Bistritz?"

Chapter 33

Dieter Zeigler made it a habit to extinguish the fire at the hearth of the Vatră Ciobănesc every night rather than let it burn out. It was an example of his meticulous, Saxon nature. No chances of a stray cinder igniting a damaging fire were taken, no matter how low the fire might be. The tavern was the culmination of Dieter's ambition to break out of the farming life in which his ancestors had labored thanklessly for as long as anyone could remember. He stepped outside into the cool evening air, turned and locked the door. It was nearly midnight. The Coach Road had long emptied of its daily traffic of coaches, leiter wagons, passing riders and the occasional cavalry troop.

As Dieter placed the key in his pocket, he stopped short when he heard the snap of a twig nearby. Then it was silent again. He looked around in the dim moonlight, pausing to look carefully for any sign of movement. Then he felt something whiz by his face. Whatever it was, it bounced like a pebble a meter away from him. Then another. This one struck him in the side of the head. Where were they coming from?

"Dieter ... up here!" came a voice from high above his head. He looked up at the thatched roof of the tavern. Outlined in the light night sky was a dark black silhouette of a man. He was standing at the apex of the roof, looking down at him. Backlit by a slender, crescent moon, Dieter could not see his face, but he knew who it was. He had been expecting him.

No matter what assurances the police captain from Bistritz had given, Dieter had never really believed his correspondence with him would for certain escape the baleful eye of the Evil One. Dieter's house was only fifty meters away on the opposite side of the road. The yellow light beaming out of the windows might as well be on the moon, he knew.

"Where are your policeman now?" came the mocking voice from above. There it was. He knew, Dieter thought. He reached for the chain and the silver crucifix that hung from his neck, pulling it out in front of his chest. It snagged on his wool sweater for a moment. When he pulled it free and looked back up on the roof, the silhouette was gone. Now it was cat and mouse. Where was he? Should he break for his house? Or try to get back inside the tavern. He knew that if he could just get inside one or the other, the Undead could not enter without his consent.

He decided to make a break for his house where his wife was. He sprinted hard for it and had made the road when he looked back. Coming for him in full stride was a white wolf with blazing red eyes. Had he turned and faced him with the dangling crucifix in sight, it might have saved him but Dieter gave in to panic and ran through the gate toward the door to his house. The white wolf bounded over the low fence that ran parallel to the road and in an instant leaped on Dieter's back, sinking his teeth into his neck. The force and weight of the wolf flying into him knocked Dieter to the ground. The massive jaws of the wolf did their deadly work, crushing his throat, collapsing his windpipe and piercing the carotid artery. With no air Dieter could not cry out. In a few seconds, blood was pulsing out of his neck and Dieter's dreams and ambitions were over.

The door to Dieter's house opened cautiously, spilling light on the footpath from the road. Freda, his wife, in her dressing gown, gaped at the sight of the darkly clad man on one knee, bent over her husband who was lying still on the path in the darkness. The man turned to look at her with a worried look on his face.

"Madame," he said in good German. "Your husband? He is hurt. May I bring him inside?" He picked Dieter up in his arms.

"Yes, yes ... Please ... bring him inside ...." she cried.

Chapter 34

Kasza lived in the city center, not far from the Polizeipräsidium. It was rare that he arose from his bed once down for the night, but the pandemonium awakening him around four o'clock in the morning was from the clanging bells and pounding hooves of the fire brigade. They passed under his open window, which he had left that way for the fresh spring night air that had wafted into Bistritz for the past couple of days. In bare feet, he padded over to the window and looked in the direction the fire brigade had gone.

There certainly was a major commotion coming from the direction of his office and, the more he thought about it, the more uneasy he felt. The misty, cloudy night sky reflected the flickering yellow and red of the fire below. It was a big fire, wherever it was. Kasza decided he couldn't sleep anymore and that he might as well investigate. He threw on some slacks a shirt and a coat, pulled on his boots, quietly descended the stairs and stepped out into the night. The smell of burning wood and cinders wafted through the air, becoming stronger the closer he got to police headquarters.

When he finally turned the corner, he was appalled to see the Polizeipräsidium heavily enveloped in flames as two pumping engines shot water into the building, their steam powered, coal-fired engines fully engaged. Hours later, his office with all his files, all his research, all his notes, maps, photographs and evidence he had been collecting for months was a charred ruin. Istvan's office where they had just discussed their case had been completely consumed as well.

Chapter 35

Istvan was spending the night in the bed of the Baroness of Jelna, whose residence was on the outskirts of the city. The distance of the house from Istvan's office was not the main reason he noticed nothing amiss during the night.

They had both known almost from the beginning something could happen between them. That possibility had become a probability and then a certainty by leaps and bounds as the attraction both felt was exactly mirrored in the other and for largely the same reasons. Her physical beauty awakened in Istvan a passion he had thought dead, but her intellect and spirit had completely beguiled and eventually smitten him. For her, Istvan was a manly equal of her late husband; a military man, a warrior, and now a hunter of men. Intelligent, yet modest. Respectable, but not stiff or conventional. A man who, she had suspected from the beginning, genuinely loved and appreciated the company of a woman like herself.

"We will not be long in the mountains, I don't think," murmured Istvan in a low voice, looking from his pillow into Julianna's face, illuminated in the moonlight that seeped through a large window in the bedroom.

"What do you think you'll find?"

"I don't know. Evidence of criminal smuggling by the Roma from the castle, I suppose. It's the probable cause of all this business. Missing persons, usually women and perhaps sold into slavery in Turkey? Boxes full of artifacts or treasure found in the castle being transported and sold abroad. Murders. We're not there yet, but I suspect it will be something like that."

"Does this have anything to do with my daughter? What about her?"

"I'm not sure, Julianna. On the one hand, her disappearance seems to have no connection at all. Then again, there is something that tells me it is connected in some way. I just can't put my finger on it. Perhaps it was her marriage to Novotny Janos? Perhaps he was on to them and, in their cruel ambition, they thought they could take her and use her against him? I don't know, Julianna. We'll just have to see. I'm hoping your daughter is still alive, but you should prepare yourself for anything."

The bedroom became heavy with silence as Julianna thought about the terrible possibilities. Perhaps death was the least of them. She imagined her daughter submitting to the sadistic, erotic cruelties of a Turkish harem, or as a prisoner of some Balkan prince, desperate for her mother's aid which she could not give for ignorance of her whereabouts. It was enough to drive her insane. She drew herself closer to the naked warmth of Istvan, letting her hand caress the hard muscles of his hips and legs. For now, she just wouldn't let herself think about it. It would be there to face again soon enough in the morning. At least she had an ally now that would not leave her side. That was something, she thought.

After another hour of sleep, there was a knock on the door. Julianna placed a robe on as she spoke through the door to the butler.

"The police is asking for him, ma'am," said Grigore in Wallachian accented Magyar to the woman he served.

"Yes. All right. I'll be down in a couple of minutes. Make him comfortable in the salon."

"Said it was an emergency, it was …"

"Who is here?" Istvan said to Julianna. "Get the man's name. I'll get dressed, my love. Let me see what it's all about." She thrilled to his having called her his love. It was the first time and she felt her heart throb. He blew her a kiss from the bed as he swung his body around to get out of bed and dress.

"Oh, all right. I'll be down in a few minutes after you, then. Who could it be? Did anyone know you were going to be here?"

"No. Not really, but I think Kasza may have put two and two together. He saw us in Budapest, you remember. He might have guessed I might be here when he couldn't find me at home. So it must be important, if it's he or someone he sent to get me."

"Of course, my love ..." She pointedly repeated the phrase back to him and he smiled. He pulled her close to him and gave her a rough kiss and sensual squeeze and smiled again. Then he got dressed, pulled on his boots and hurried downstairs.

"Inspector Gábor sent me, my Lord," said one of the mounted police by the name of Antal, an exceptionally gifted horseman and rider; a handsome young Hungarian and the son of local gentry.

"What is it?"

"You'd better come with me, Sir. I have a horse outside for you. The watch commander must see you immediately. The Polizeipräsidium, sir. It burned early this morning. Your office ..."

"I see." Istvan steeled himself from betraying any emotion to the young officer when he heard the news, but he was alarmed. Could it be a coincidence that just as they were about to ride out to the Borgo Pass this had happened? Istvan was professionally and instinctively skeptical of coincidences. He sent the trooper back to Kasza and told him to tell Pulszky Imre, the night commander, that he would be there as soon as he could.

Julianna heard the door close and knew that the messenger was gone, so she came downstairs in her nightgown and robe. Istvan marveled at her aristocratic bearing and appearance compared to the uninhibited and frenetic lover she had been the night before. He could only describe it to himself as erotic. This was a woman who stirred his blood and he hated to leave. Nothing less than the disaster described by the young Antal would have roused him, but he had no choice.

"I have to go," he said mournfully, looking at her from the bottom of the stairs.

"I know." She glided down the rest of the way, coming to rest on the first step so she could look directly into his eyes. She rested her hand on his lightly and he reached for her, pulling her to him again.

"I'll be back as soon as I can, and then we'll take up where we left off this morning." Istvan smiled ruefully as he said this.

"I hope so," she replied. "Be careful, Istvan. Don't be too heroic, my love." She said it again and smiled. He smiled too. Then he was gone.

Chapter 36

In the Great Hall of the castle, Count Dracula, the man she had known since childhood as simply "the Master," summoned Natália from the kitchens where she was preparing dinner for Jonathan Harker. His reverse aging was also very pronounced now, Natália thought. His hair was almost uniformly black and of shoulder length. He looked like a rigorous nobleman in his 40s and getting younger every night.

"Child, I will be away for a while. Perhaps for years. Thou hath been a good and loyal servant to me, unlike thy treacherous father and uncle." He paused for a moment, gazing deeply into her terrified eyes, as if searching her soul for something. Any sign of guilt or betrayal. Apparently satisfied, he went on. "Thy beauty and thy youth are wasted here and our servant, Lajos, seeks thy company in our Tinovul Mohos. Knowest thou of whom we speak?"

Natália knew him well. Her father had despised him as if he were a jackal. His obvious glances of longing had frightened him when she was a girl and they had not lessened over the years. He had flirted with her in his clumsy way and sulked when she had not returned his overt interest. A simmering uneasiness had always troubled her relationship with Lajos, such as it was.

"Thou will go from here on the morrow, child. Thou wilt go to Lajos who will prepare a place for you. He is my most loyal servant now. Your father and his brother betrayed me, you see. Now it is Lajos who serves me. Thou art repayment for his quiet obedience to me. Dost thou understand me?" With that, his eyes grew wide and peered into hers, again searching for anything other than complete submission to his will. She felt his power and knew she dared not defy him. At least not openly.

"Yes, my Lord. But how will I get to the forest? The wolves ..."

"Thou shalt not fear them. They will let thee pass. No harm will come to thee. So pack thy belongings this night and on the morrow, thou shalt go to Lajos who awaits thee in thy village."

"What about the Englishman, my Lord? What about him?"

Again the piercing gaze, searching her face and mind. She struggled to maintain her calm composure, thinking of him in the tower and their secret affair. She knew if the Count were aware of their liaisons, he would have killed her and Jonathan as well. He knew they had no language in common and assumed they would never be able to communicate with each other. That and her fear of Dracula and his wrath if any aid were given to him to escape from the castle or defy the Count. In time, the Count replied.

"He hath become the object of the desires of my wives, and he shall pleasure them long before he leaves this place," Dracula smiled. "I have promised him to them and now I must let them have their way with him. But thou needst not fear that moment, child, when they acquaint themselves to him again. Thou wilt be gone by then to the forest." He paused. "Thou wilt quit thee from here in the morning light and thou wilt never hear his pleadings and cries when night falls." The Count was clearly amusing himself by telling her this. Natália was unable to hide her mortification at the thought of his fate.

"So, I bid thee farewell, my dear. Have many children with Lajos. Someday, perhaps, we will meet again. Adieu."

And with that, he turned on his heel. The heavy doors swung open on their own, without apparent human intervention. Outside, immediately beyond the doors, was a black *calèche*, with yellow spoke wheels and the letter "D" inscribed on the door. A coachman sitting on the bench above the horses clambered down to open the door for the Master. With a nod of his head and with a cheerful glint in his eye, Dracula climbed into the calèche and in a moment, the coachman skillfully turned it around in the courtyard and then clattered down the stone ramp to the road below. As he wheeled out of sight, the doors closed, locks turned and bolts slotted themselves leaving her standing alone in the Great Hall.

Natália calmly thought about the situation. She wondered if this might be a trick of the Count's to catch her betraying his orders but to what purpose? He had essentially commanded her to take up with Lajos and granted her safe passage across his wolf-infested lands. She couldn't stay here now. But the Englishman ... She felt her face flush as she thought of him locked away. She couldn't abandon him and she didn't want to. She would much rather be with Jonathan Harker, someone who couldn't even speak her language, than with Lajos.

It would be dawn in a few hours. She would visit Jonathan when it was safe. When they were gone and could not interrupt them. She knew the wives slept in the crypts under the chapel. Sometimes they slept there for many days and then she would catch sight of them wandering around in the moonlight, calling for their husband, Dracula Vlad. They were terrifying but sad. One of them had crossly expressed her resentment that Natália could spend time with the young English gentleman and she could not; forbidden, as she had been by Count Dracula, from having anything to do with him. Until he had finished with him. Now he had. Now they would come for him. She must save him.

She went to her room and lay in her bed, thinking, while waiting for the dawn. Dracula was leaving. For a long time. Maybe years is what he had said. Where was he going? She didn't know, but imagined it must be very far away. And he was going to stay there for a long time. If she never saw him again, she would count herself blessed, she thought. She might be able to get the Englishman out, she realized. If the wolves really were going to allow her to pass, it stood to reason they might let a human companion in her immediate company also pass. Perhaps not, but what choice did he have, she thought?

If they did get away, she considered, what then? She did not want to return to the Roma camp ever again. With her immediate kin dead and Lajos waiting, she wanted to escape with the Englishman to his far away land but would he take her? On the other hand, if she could just get him away from here with his life, he might help her, she knew. He would reward her. He would take her far away from here even if he could not take her to England. She drifted off to sleep without realizing it. When she woke up, the yellow rays of the sun were already dancing on the mountain tops in the distance. Natália hurried to get the key and visit the Count's prisoner.

Chapter 37

There was nothing to be done about the District headquarters Istvan realized once he and Kasza could see it. It was a shambles. What the flames had not consumed, the water had obliterated. By early afternoon, Istvan left Imre Pulszky in charge of salvaging what they could and locating new, temporary quarters. He would ride out to the Borgo Pass with a troop, all right. Police and Royal Cavalry. Lieutenant Sarkozy would accompany them with a troop of His Majesty's Light Cavalry. All in all, over fifty mounted police and cavalry would be under his joint command and serving his mission.

It was at the Abbey of Piatra Fantanele where they first heard of Dieter's death and that of his wife the night before. Their bodies had been found in the house. He appeared to have been mangled by an animal and died of shock and blood loss. She had two puncture wounds on the carotid, just like the ones found on the corpse of the Roma hetman, Radu remarked in his message. The vampire legacy again, Istvan thought.

"Who knew he was our agent?" Kasza inquired over dinner in the Abbey where he and Kasza had eaten breakfast a few weeks ago. Istvan thought about it. There was himself and there was Kasza, of course. Radu had been in the room when he had read aloud Dieter's urgent letter but his loyalty and discretion was without question. Who else? The orderly that delivered the letter? He had been in the room when he had read the letter, Istvan thought. And then there was the postal clerk who had sent the telegram to Vatra Dornei. As he thought about it, Istvan wished there was a telegraph nearby. He wanted to advise Imre to take precautions with those two. The telegrapher and the orderly. What was his name? Dimitru. Place them under surveillance as soon as possible, Istvan thought as he gratefully accepted a mug of steaming coffee from one of the nuns after dinner.

"I'm going to smoke," Istvan said, rising from the table. Radu and Kasza nodded to him as he left the room and they continued to talk.

The mounted police and cavalry were decamped in and around the abbey and the little village adjacent to it, settled down in barns or small tents in pastures or yards. Little campfires dotted the landscape as troopers in twos and threes sat together eating, smoking or drinking. Istvan walked outside and into an interior courtyard or cloister within the walls of the Abbey. The days were getting longer now, Istvan thought. There was a red glow in the western sky where the sun had been until just a half an hour ago.

The grassy area and garden in the middle of the enclosure were surrounded by crushed gravel and then trees and shrubbery around the perimeter that softened the stone walls of the cloister. It was a beautiful and peaceful place. Tulips and daisies had already shot up in the garden, Istvan noticed. Some of them had blooms already. The night was cool. There would be a heavy dew by morning, Istvan reckoned as he pulled on his pipe and savored the rich flavor. Then he noticed something out of the corner of his eye.

It was a movement from one corner of the cloister. The darkest corner. There were several large trees there. Between the trunks of the trees and the stone wall behind was a shadow of pitch blackness. Yet something had moved. Istvan was sure of it. He started approaching it carefully when he suddenly saw a pale face gazing intently back at him. Someone or something was watching him from there. Someone dressed in black. Istvan stopped in his tracks when the face became a man who then emerged to meet him.

Istvan saw a tall man with largely dark, long hair. He had on the livery of a bygone military figure, Istvan recognized. A black vest. A white blouse. Tight, black riding breeches and tall, black boots. A riding crop was in his hand. He made a striking but dangerous appearance. A long scabbard and sword also hung from his belt. Istvan uneasily realized he had no weapon on him.

"At long last, my Lord," said the figure who jauntily gave him a half bow before coming erect and smiling at him.

"I don't believe we've met," replied Istvan as calmly as he could. He could cry out, he considered, but if he did and the nobleman meant harm, he could slit his throat in a moment with that rapier if he knew how to use it. No, best to play along and give no sign of fear, Istvan thought.

"I am the one thou hath come seeking here," the Count said, continuing to advance. "Thou hath come to visit us at our ancient house, am I not right?"

"You are the Count Dracula, then?"

"Of course. Didst thou think I did not notice ye? Thy presence here hath become my greatest interest and preoccupation yea these past few months. It hath all been reported to me. I know everything ..."

The Count had come within a few meters of him and Istvan observed the details now. The wide pupils, like an opium addict might have. The bloodshot sclera. The full red lips. White teeth. His perfect confidence. He certainly made an intense and ominous impression.

"You are to be complimented, my Lord," Dracula continued. "Thy cleverness and persistence have much amused me, but, alas, I am afraid things have reached the point where I cannot indulge thee and thy colleagues anymore."

With that, the Count's face seemed to contort into a fury. Large fangs appeared in a mouth that gaped open in a horrifying leer, just as the legends described. Istvan was captured in wonder. He knew in a corner of his mind that he should be terrified, but he was so dazzled by the fascinating sight of this bizarre specter before him that he could not move. As if sinking into a trance, Istvan saw the Count raise one arm and a hand appeared with long, pointed and dark fingernails. Then another arm and then he felt himself fall into an embrace he could not resist. His arms were powerful.

Then there was a blaze of light in his dream trance. He felt himself being released and falling slowly, softly to the ground. There was a woman with a strong light. Istvan squinted into the light to see her but the light was so bright, he couldn't. It seemed to be coming from something she held in her hand. He heard a woman's voice saying something in Latin. He couldn't understand it. Lying on his back, on the soft, wet grass, Istvan turned his head to see the tall, dark form of the Count retreating. Back and back he went. Into the dark corner from whence he'd come. A black shadow and then the fluttering sound of wings. A dark bird of some kind flew over the wall and disappeared. It was too much for his mind to comprehend. He felt himself slipping away and then he was overcome by darkness.

Chapter 38

Radu was gently slapping the side of Istvan's face when he regained consciousness. Radu and Kasza had apparently been fetched by the Abbess who stood nearby, watching them.

"Bring him inside at once," the Abbess commanded. "Let me see him in the light."

Istvan allowed himself to be helped to his feet but declined further ministrations from his two deputies as they followed the Abbess inside, down a corridor and into the library. The room was ablaze with candles.

"Sit down, my Lord," the Abbess said as she pointed at a chair near a candelabra. Istvan was too shocked and confused to do anything but obey her. As he sat down, the Abbess came close to him for the first time. With her hand she raised his chin to examine his neck, turning his head first one way, then the other. Then she looked into his eyes.

"I know of no other living person other than myself that has seen what you have seen and is still alive," she remarked.

"It was you who drove him away?"

"Yes. For now. He has never dared to come here before tonight. He would have killed you, if he had been given another minute or two. He will kill you, if he can. All of you," she said, glancing at Radu and Kasza. He must believe that your return here is an intolerable threat to him and his cursed minions and, as he has always done, he seeks to kill."

"My Lord, what happened?" Kasza blurted out.

"I'm not sure," Istvan replied. "I was smoking when I saw a man. He just appeared from somewhere in the darkness. He said he was Count Dracula and that he knew everything we were doing. He said he could not allow me to live and attacked me."

"What did you do? How did you stop him?" Radu asked, turning to the Abbess.

The Abbess smiled a wan smile. "I summoned the one true God. The one even he cannot resist."

"Yes, but ..." Radu pressed.

"He cannot face the cross of our Savior in the presence of one who truly believes," the Abbess said as she raised the prominent, silver cross hanging from her neck by black rosary beads. Istvan realized that it must have been her silver cross that was the object he had seen emanating a hot, white light.

"You said something to him," Istvan continued. "It was in Latin and I couldn't understand it. What did you say to him?"

The Abbess looked off into the distance and then slowly repeated the incantation she had delivered just moments ago: *"Princeps gloriosissime caelestis militiae, sancte Michael Archangele. Protegat adversus mundi rectores tenebrarum harum contra spiritalia nequitiae in caelestibus."*

"What does it mean, Holy Mother?" Kasza asked. She translated.

"Most glorious Prince of the Heavenly Armies, Saint Michael the Archangel! Defend us against the rulers of this world of darkness, against the spirits of wickedness in high places." There was a dumbstruck silence in the room when she finished.

"And that drove him away?" Kasza finally said, skeptically.

"Yes, Kasza, it did," Istvan replied. There was another long silence as everyone considered what this meant. Then Kasza spoke again.

"Couldn't he be some demented Roma who stole into this Abbey to kill you?" Kasza asked. Radu remained silent.

"Past dozens and dozens of armed guards in and about the Abbey?" Istvan rejoined. "And what about his escape? Did you see him race past you on his way out?"

"Do you doubt what you have seen with your own eyes?" the Abbess asked looking directly at Istvan. Istvan considered the situation carefully, his mind going over and over the encounter in the cloister, looking for a logical, scientific explanation of what had happened, but he could not see one. There was no scientific explanation.

"I saw it too," the Abbess said, maintaining her steady, unsmiling gaze at Istvan, waiting for his reply. She came closer to Istvan, who had been seated in one of the chairs near a table in the library upon which stood a large candelabra, full of flickering candles. She placed her hand on his hand, in a comforting gesture.

"Do you believe in God, Istvan?"

"Yes."

"Do you believe in God even though you have never seen him?"

"Yes. I believe, but ..."

"What you and I have seen is not so hard to accept then, is it? Where there is great good, there is inevitably the opposite. Where there is God, there is also the Opposer. Did you know the Hebrew word for the Opposer is Satan?"

"No, Holy Mother. I did not."

She continued, quietly, gazing into his eyes intently.

"You have met a servant of Satan tonight. It is as simple as that. You have seen him. I have seen him. I have long known of him, but until tonight, I have never laid eyes upon this monster. He meant to extinguish your life and your colleagues using the great powers he has been given many centuries ago by his Master. Powers that go far behind what your rational, scientific mind could understand or accept before tonight. Now you have the evidence of your own eyes. You are all in mortal danger. If you do not accept and act upon what you have seen and what you know, you will surely die and many others will die as well. Be careful, Istvan. It is not just your own life that is in the balance now. Many lives depend upon you now."

Istvan had no answer for the Abbess. Now she looked at Kasza and Radu, and then back to him. She continued.

"They will not believe it because they have not seen it, and they are scientific men. But you have seen it. You must lead them now. They will believe you and you must believe your own senses or all is lost. This evil sorcerer has afflicted these lands for centuries. He has preyed upon the disbelief of the people in Bistritz and Budapest and Vienna for centuries. His guile and cunning know no bounds. You are now the one person in the world who can put an end to him once and for all. You must do it."

"He will not enter within the walls and doors of this building. He cannot enter any dwelling until he is first invited by his host. This is a holy place and full of believers. You and your companions are safe here. For now. Take with you what you have learned here tonight and rid us and the world of this vampire ... this cursed, inhuman predator."

Kasza and Radu had listened in silence and now looked at Istvan expectantly. She was right, Istvan thought. He could not deny what he had seen with his own eyes. The more he thought about the details, the more it confirmed to him that what he had seen was a supernatural being. It had known who he was. It had known that he had come to see the castle; his "house". It had responded to the name of Dracula. Its apparel was from a different time; a bygone era. Its silent arrival and inexplicable disappearance was consistent with his new, improbable and extraordinary thesis. If it were not a satanic being, why would it have retreated from a mere woman, unarmed but for a cross? It would have killed them both. Its appearance fit the legend that he had for so long dismissed as superstition. The fangs, bloodshot eyes and immense strength Istvan had felt of his embrace were inhuman.

It was fantastic, but until he could think of some other explanation, for the good of all of them, Istvan decided that the apparition he had just seen had haunted these environs for centuries was indeed a vampire and a sorcerer. He was also, apparently, the incarnation of Vlad Tepes of the House of Dracula described to Istvan by his distant kin, Dracula Radu, in his study in Budapest.

"Kasza. Radu. What do you know about vampires?"

It was Radu who replied. "I know a few things, my Lord."

Chapter 39

At dawn, the bugle sounded and the cavalry arose from its sleep. The nighttime air had been not too cold, most of the troopers agreed. They had seen a lot worse in Bohemia or Moravia or Tyrolea this time of year, some said. It was late May and were it not for the fact that they found themselves in the mountains, the night air would have been downright pleasant someone said while boiling coffee over a fire pit.

The cavalry had brilliant uniforms in these days, before the Great War. Their helmets, uniforms, epaulettes, boots and indeed their horses were eye catching. Their weapons, revolvers, sabers and lances, were intimidating. Most of the troopers were strong men who knew how to handle horses expertly. Their horses knew it too. They seemed like a continuing extension of their masters as they were mounted, briskly directed to go here and there or do something in a particular way.

The police troopers, not quite so impressive in their comparatively drab uniforms, were roused by the bugle call as well and made ready for the day's events. Many of them had been former cavalrymen themselves and knew how to handle horses. Before long, both troops were formed up in a field beneath the Abbey. Istvan, Radu, Kasza and Leutnant Sarkozy faced them on their steeds. With them was the Faktotum of Count Dracula Radu, of Budapest, with the keys to the castle doors, who had arrived that morning at the Abbey from Bistritz by the diligence.

Istvan had considered what he would tell the troopers in the early morning hours, as he lay restless and awake while waiting for the sun to rise. He had decided that he could not tell them of the supernatural possibilities that might await them. They were not ready for that. Indeed, Istvan himself was still having difficulty accepting what he had seen "with his own eyes", as the Abbess had said. No, he would not tell them that.

Radu had shared a surprising cache of information about vampire lore and legend before they had gone to bed that had raised the hair on the back of his neck. One thing became clear, and that was that any contact with the undead must take place after sunrise and before sunset when their nature compelled them to sleep in a dark place to avoid being burned to ashes by the rays of the sun. To confront Dracula after sunset would be a near suicidal task, Radu explained, as legend made clear.

Istvan recalled Dieter's warnings as well, waiting for dawn. No, he would have the troopers on alert for banditry and violence all night, and that would have to do for now.

"Gentlemen," Istvan called out to the police and cavalry troopers. "We ride now to the castle of Count Dracula, whose permission we have to search it for evidence of criminal activity. Once we have arrived and the doors are opened, you will each be given instruction on what to do. You will follow these instructions to the letter. It is the opinion of the Royal Hungarian Gendarmerie and the District Police of Bistritz that this ruined castle has been used for murder and concealment of these murders, perhaps in graves and crypts on the premises. Some of our work may entail opening of tombs and graves to identify and seize evidence. We also have information suggesting armed brigands in the area have been using the castle for their criminal activities and for this reason, we will remain armed and ready while we carry out our work. Understood, gentlemen? Any questions?"

There was no reaction to Istvan's statement other than the murmur and whinny of horses as they listened in the cool morning air.

"Cavalry! Form up into line ahead!" came the shouted command from Sarkozy and immediately the Light Cavalry responded, forming into a line two abreast. Sarkozy wheeled his horse in the direction of the Coach Road and the cavalry fell in behind him in perfect, parade-ground order.

"Troopers, ho!" shouted Radu and in slightly less orderly fashion, imitating the cavalry, they fell in as well. Istvan, Kasza and Nagy Lázár, the Count's servant, hurried forward to lead the contingent to the castle. It was a perfectly sunny day with no clouds and a dark blue sky overhead. They made good time to the Borgo Pass and turned into the road to the Castle about an hour after leaving the Abbey.

It wasn't more than a kilometer before they met a young Englishman and a Roma woman coming toward them in the opposite direction. Kasza saw them first, from a distance. They were running toward them. They waved their arms at them, as if in distress. Istvan spurred Balazs forward into a trot and in a few minutes, intercepted them. The girl was obviously a Roma and she spoke to Radu in the Wallachian tongue with wild-eyed excitement.

"She says that they have escaped from the castle this morning and have been fleeing Count Dracula since sunrise on foot," Radu translated to Magyar. The girl said some more. "She says we are in great danger. She says that there are vampires in the castle. They were going to kill her companion, an Englishman. She says she does not speak the Englishman's language, but she knows that he must get far away from here or he will be killed." The girl continued to speak rapidly to Radu, but Istvan was distracted by the Englishman who suddenly spoke up.

"Sir ... do you speak German?"

"Yes, I do," Istvan replied.

"Oh! Thank God! We are so grateful to have met you. Please help us. You will not believe what I have to tell you. The castle over there is haunted. It is haunted by a man. Count Dracula. A client of my firm in London. I was sent here to meet him and complete the purchase of some property in England ..."

"Are you Jonathan Harker?" Istvan inquired.

"Yes," he replied, startled.

"I know who you are. Your arrival in Bistritz was told to me by the innkeeper at *Die Golden Krone*. I am Kálváry Istvan, Chief of Police, Bistritz

District. These are my colleagues and there is Leutnant Sarkozy. We were just on our way to visit the castle."

"My God, Sir. It is an awful place. It is inhabited by undead monsters of the most diabolical nature. I know that sounds incredible, Sir. Unbelievable. But if you could know what I have seen in my time here …"

"Yes," Istvan replied, dismounting from his horse. "I have met Count Dracula myself."

"What?" Harker replied. He was clearly astonished.

"I do believe you, young man," Istvan said, placing his hand on Harker's shoulder comfortingly. Radu interrupted.

"The girl says that the Count left the castle in a calèche last night, my Lord. He said he was leaving for a long time. She says that there are three vampire women in the castle who were going to kill the young man who may still be there. She said the calèche departed the castle just after sunset."

Istvan thought about this for a moment. He had seen the Count at some time after nine o'clock in the evening; well before midnight in any event. After escaping from the Abbey, he must have rejoined the driver and his calèche in some way. He looked at his pocket watch. It was now nearly nine o'clock in the morning. Where was he now, Istvan wondered. Had he gone east into the Bukovina? Or west to Bistritz and Budapest? Or perhaps elsewhere. Then it hit him. London. What was it the Englishman had said?

"You say that the Count had purchased some property? In England?"

"Yes. There is a ruined abbey in Purfleet and another residence in Piccadilly."

"Where are these places in England?"

"I'm sorry, Sir. Piccadilly is in the heart of London. The abbey is known as Carfax and is in Purfleet, a short distance outside the city."

"I see. I know you cannot understand the girl. She says that Count Dracula told her he was leaving the castle for a long time …"

"I'm sure he is going to London, Sir. He spoke with me about it many times. He wanted me to help him with his English, although he spoke it fluently. He was very excited about the prospect of living in London. If he has left the castle for good, I would expect he must be headed for London now."

"Yes. Perhaps. But how? As you and I both know, he is not, shall we say, the normal traveler. He cannot be abroad during the day, as I think you know."

"Hardly normal indeed, Sir. He is a fiend. I have seen him climb down the side of that very castle, head down like a lizard. I have seen things you just wouldn't believe ..." Harker's eyes now reddened with tears as he fought to maintain his composure. Many hours and days of terror had he endured with the Count and now it overflowed. The girl, who had been talking to Radu, who was taking notes, looked at him and gently took his hand. He looked back at her gratefully, blinking back tears.

"Young man, you have been most helpful. I would like to speak with you further about all that you have seen. We must, however, push on and inspect this castle during the daylight hours, as you will no doubt understand. I must ask you to summon up the last measure of your courage and to accompany us back to this place and assist us ..."

"Oh God, Sir! Please! I couldn't. I just couldn't ... You don't understand."

Istvan spent the next twenty minutes assuring Jonathan Harker that he would be guarded by several troopers and himself at all times and that his help would be invaluable in putting an end to the dastardly terror that had afflicted this part of the Empire for hundreds of years. Eventually, with a trembling lip and watery eyes, the Englishman agreed. Radu had quickly persuaded the Roma woman, whose name was Natália, to do the same. An extra mount was saddled that had been brought along in case it was necessary to carry material evidence from the castle. Harker swung himself up into the saddle and the girl was helped up behind him by some admiring troopers.

In another twenty minutes, the castle was in sight and soon after, the entourage clattered into the Courtyard. After all the trouble and waiting to get permission to enter the castle and to obtain the keys, it was unnecessary. The doors were open, just as Harker and Natália had left them in their hasty departure at sunrise. The troopers dismounted and fell out, waiting for orders. Sarkozy, Kasza and Radu looked at Istvan expectantly as the Englishman and Natália watched. Istvan climbed the stairs to the door and entered. The others soon followed.

For the next hour, the investigators were shown first the tower in which Natália had lived and then the one where Harker had been imprisoned. They made their way down through dark stairwells, musty hallways and dusty rooms. Most of the hallways had heavy wooden doors that were invariably locked. Nagy had keys for some, others had to be forcibly opened. Most of the rooms were empty with narrow windows and nothing but dust or the remains of rotted timbers from furniture, crates, beams caved in from the ceiling or who knew what.

The overwhelming impression on Istvan was of a ruined medieval stronghold that had always been a Spartan habitation meant more for war than any comfort. The wind blew through openings in the walls and hallways. The gothic architecture allowed little light but made excellent slits for bowmen and archers to fire missiles down on attackers, Istvan thought as he watched the troopers' progress from room to room. Other than the kitchen and the two tower rooms inhabited by the Count's involuntary guests, there was little to suggest life in the ancient building. Finally, one of the troopers called out that he had found something.

Istvan entered yet another room but this one had a stairwell down into the depths of the castle that faded to black in the weak light. Torches were procured and Istvan led Kasza, Radu and Sarkozy along with a half dozen other troopers down the stairs that spiraled down and down. The air became cooler and musty smelling as they descended, downward, round and round. Eventually, they reached a landing with another door. It was not locked. Istvan turned the door handle and pushed it open with his foot. It was pitch black inside as the heavy door swung open and came to rest against an inner wall with a boom.

Istvan stepped into the room. His heart skipped a beat as he saw several coffins resting on the floor near the far wall of the room.

"Open them," Istvan commanded the troopers. They had brought with them crow bars and mauls and soon they set to work in the flickering torchlight prying and banging open the lids. As soon as the first one popped open, two of the troopers stood up, stepped back abruptly and looked over to Istvan. He approached and looked into the coffin. There were the decomposing remains of a woman. The stench was overpowering, now that the top was open. Istvan pulled out a handkerchief and covered his mouth and nose with it as he examined the body. Radu had moved close to look as well and was the first to speak.

"Dead perhaps a month or so, I would guess by the extent of the decomposition," Radu said. Istvan was quietly amazed at Radu's calm and professional demeanor. Istvan had seen hundreds of dead corpses in his career. Custoza had been littered with gruesome remains, some with limbs and heads hacked off or blown to bits by artillery, but this was repulsive and vile. Something told him that these women had been innocents and had spent the last hours or days of their lives in the dark embrace of a merciless fiend somewhere in the dank prison of this God-forsaken castle; their pleas and cries for mercy or aid unheeded and unheard.

Radu had also clenched a handkerchief to his face, but knelt down to examine the body more closely. Then another coffin lid was popped open. Another woman, but this one could not have been dead for more than a week or so, according to Radu's professional opinion. There were dark, purple marks on her neck that were still visible. Another coffin revealed another woman in advanced decomposition.

"My God," Kasza exclaimed. "These are not ancient remains! These women have only died recently!"

"Look at the neck of that one," Istvan gestured with a gloved hand toward the one with the puncture wounds. Kasza and Radu gazed into the coffin. There was no doubt. The other two corpses might also have been bitten in this way, Istvan thought, but the decay was too far advanced to be sure just looking at them in this dim light.

"Sir, what shall we do?" one of the cavalrymen asked, his eyes wide with horror.

"Put the lids back on for now," Istvan commanded. "Let's see what else is here."

With that, he stalked back to the heavy door where a trooper holding a torch nodded and preceded him out the door, lighting the way further down the stone stairwell. After a short while, Istvan calculated by now, they must be underground. They reached the bottom of the round stairwell finally and found themselves in a large round room with four heavy doors equidistant from one another around the circumference of the room. Three of them were locked, but one opposite the foot of the stairwell was not.

"Open it. We'll come back with a ram if need be to force the others," Istvan said. The lead trooper pushed hard on the unlocked door. It swung open with a squeak of rusty hinges, revealing another dark corridor. Cautiously they entered. Istvan noticed sconces in the wall and what appeared to be extinguished torches.

"Try one," Istvan said to the trooper, nodding at the sconce. The trooper touched his burning torch and sure enough, the torch burst into flame. Istvan was not surprised. Obviously, this castle had been in use by someone or some people all along he had concluded. This was just more proof. The trooper continued lighting sconces down the hallway, but Istvan had noticed that the doors in this corridor had bars over openings in the upper half of the doors. They were cells.

"Shhh!" Kasza said in a loud whisper that stopped everyone in their tracks. "Did you hear that?" The whole party stood stock still, hardly breathing. Yes, Istvan did hear something. It was a whimpering, faint, hushed sound but as they all listened, it became more and more clear that it was a human voice they were hearing. Where was it coming from? It was from one of the cells, Istvan suddenly realized. He snatched one of the torches out of the sconces and bolted down the corridor, stopping at each barred door, looking in.

"Here!" Istvan shouted. As the others caught up to him, Istvan held the torch as close as he could to the opening. Its flickering flames revealed a scene of utter despairing horror. There, huddled in the corner of a small cell, cowering in terror was a young woman, her eyes wide with terror and tears. The floor of the dungeon was covered with foul smelling straw, no doubt from human excrement. The woman was wearing the remains of some garment that was in tatters. Her face and skin was pale as she gazed back in amazement at Istvan. Then he saw the two puncture wounds on her neck. Enraged, he raised his boot and smashed it against the door, but it would not open.

"Get to work on this!" he roared at the troopers who had brought the mauls and crowbars down from the mortuary room above. Quickly they set to it and in a moment, with a groan and a jolt, the door was forced open as the others watched. Istvan entered the dark cell. The woman cowered in a corner, whimpering and squinting at what was, for her, the bright light of the torches. Istvan knelt down about a meter away and for a moment, just watched her. Then, slowly, gently, he extended his hand toward her. She looked at it for a moment, her face contorted in fear. In a low quiet voice that Istvan used when calming a horse, he spoke to her in the Magyar tongue.

"My child ... come to me. We are here to take you away from this place. Nobody will hurt you. You want to leave here with us, don't you?"

The woman's eyes seemed to have adjusted to the light. "Igen. Eljövök veled," she slowly replied. "Yes, I will come with you." She was Hungarian.

"What is your name, child?"

"Ema, Uram. Novotny Ema," she said in a whisper.

Chapter 40

For the next several days, the Castle of Dracula Vlad was searched meticulously by an army of police and cavalry troopers. On the second day, Török with the Transylvanian Constabulary arrived from Klausenberg to take over the investigation with militia. Methodically, subterranean room after room was discovered, catalogued and mapped. There was a vast underground labyrinth of rooms, vaults, corridors, stairwells and tombs beneath the main floor of the ruined castle. The castle had been occupied for quite a long time, after all, but below ground for the most part. Many of the rooms were roughly hewn of stone that seemed unfinished and were used as dungeons or crypts. Skeletal remains of at least a hundred human victims were found. Dozens and dozens of sarcophagi were also found with dusty, ossified remains of long dead members of the House of Dracul.

A curious discovery was made a couple of days into the excavations by a party being supervised by Radu. A treasure room with urns full of coins and jewelry. The value of the loot was incalculable, not only because of its quantity but its age. Some of the coins bore the image of Matthias Corvinius from the 15th century. Others, Habsburg coins with the images of Emperors Ferdinand I, Ferdinand II, Leopold and others from the 16th through the 18th centuries. Ottoman coins with their Arabic script and absence of imagery in contrast to the Europeans dated from the 17th and 18th centuries. Russian golden rubles with images of the Tsars and their Cyrillic script were also among the coins. Obviously, the master of this castle had been accumulating wealth from the Empires adjoining Transylvania for a long time.

Natália revealed the existence of the Count's three "wives". Harker had confirmed them as well. One by one, the tombs and sarcophagi were pried open and the remains within examined. Dozens and dozens of skeletal remains were exhumed, but nothing that resembled a sleeping vampire. Harker revealed that he had seen the Count shortly before his escape in a sarcophagus beneath the chapel, in daylight hours, seemingly asleep and insensate. He had hit the vampire with a shovel located nearby, but to no effect. It was as if he was freshly dead and immune to any earthly pain or trauma. Nothing like this was seen and, as the days turned into a week and then a second, the examination of the castle's nefarious towers, dungeons, tombs and sarcophagi were eventually, exhaustively finished. The Count and his wives, however, remained at large.

Istvan brought Ema with him back to the Abbey where he placed her in the care of the Abbess and her nuns. After Ema had been taken away to be bathed and doctored, Istvan spoke with the Abbess at length about what they had found at the castle and had learned from Natália and Jonathan Harker. She listened with rapt attention, but said nothing. Istvan could tell as he spoke to her that what he was saying merely confirmed what she had always known but doubted others would believe: the existence of a diabolical, satanic monster.

"And so, now what will you do?" the Abbess inquired when Istvan had finished.

"I will pursue him to the end," Istvan said grimly. "His or mine." The Abbess looked at him for a moment, then rose and walked slowly to the window where she gazed for a moment over the vast country below and beyond the monastery to the distant mountain ranges. She seemed deep in thought. Istvan waited, himself deep in thought. Then, as if from a great distance in a very low, solemn voice, the Abbess spoke again.

"Yes. You must. It is God's plan for you. He meant for you to come to us. You have done more in your short time here than has been done in centuries. Yes. He must be destroyed or he will spread Satan's power forever. He is a follower of Lucifer. You know that now, do you not?" The Abbess turned away from the window and was looking directly at Istvan. Istvan nodded. In his heart, he had seen enough.

"How do you catch and kill this vampire sorcerer who can change himself into different forms at will? How can we hope to find him, corner him and destroy him?" Istvan looked into her face, seeking her spiritual advice.

"He is not invincible. There are no invincible ones. He is very clever. Yes. He has no soul and no mercy; no hesitation in killing and even torture to provoke terror and obedience to his will. Yet he is weak in his own way. He cannot abide the light of the sun, which will destroy him utterly. He is completely helpless when he sleeps, but he conceals the secret of his resting place with the knowledge and fear that if it is ever discovered, he is doomed. I have thought about this many a day. He must have dozens and dozens of resting places, but it is said that he must sleep in the soil of his burial place to regain his strength and power each day. And, as a disciple of the anti-Christ, he shrinks in terror before the image of his own master's nemesis when displayed by a person of faith. She touched the large, silver crucifix hanging from her neck with the image of Jesus. You remember? It saved your life."

Istvan did remember. It was as if it had taken place in a dream. More like a nightmare. As he remembered, he saw in his mind's eye again the image of the Abbess with the cross in her hand, exorcising the demonic being about to kill him from her cloister. Dracula. The evil vampire murderer, shrank back in fury and disgust when the cross was wielded at him.

"We should place images of the cross everywhere in the old castle, to prevent him from ever coming back."

"The soil of the castle must never again be removed and taken abroad or overseas to hiding places far away. He must be deprived of any sanctuary or place of sleep and refuge. His hiding places must be found and destroyed until he has no more and must risk exposure to the sun or discovery while he is helpless and asleep. Chased from sleeping in his native soil, he will have to return here to regain his strength and then, you will be waiting. You will make an end to him once and for all."

The Abbess explained to him how to negate the ancient castle as a sanctuary for the vampire. She gave him holy wafers, holy water, simple wooden crosses and other Christian artifacts to place everywhere in the castle. Most importantly, the doors and windows to the castle were carefully adorned with garlic, crosses and images of saints and sealed with holy wax as tightly as possible.

Kasza and Radu rode into the Roma village with a large troop of cavalry to impress the tribe and forbade the Roma to come anywhere near the castle henceforth under any circumstances. An abandoned barn along the Coach Road was quickly repaired as a stable for Radu's detachment of troopers who would now be stationed here with Radu himself at a District substation that would be built in the next few months. The castle would be patrolled daily for signs of anything suspicious.

Chapter 41

Upon securing the castle and the hill country so long terrorized by the Count, Istvan determined he would take Ema back to her mother himself. She was now cleaned and dressed, but her mind was clearly disturbed. She was weak from so many months of meager rations and hunger, sickness and disease. Although seemingly free of disease at the moment, she could not weigh more than forty-five kilograms, Istvan thought. He decided to bring her to Bistritz in the diligence, which was hailed down as it neared the gates of the Abbey. Istvan rode his horse behind the coach all the way back to Bistritz. When they arrived, he arranged for his official landau to meet the diligence from Vatra Dornei and from there, he brought her home to her mother.

As he had expected, the scene at the Baroness' residence was one of high emotion and drama. Mother and daughter wept at the sight of each other and embraced for a long time without even speaking. There were no words anyway. Even Istvan was moved by the tender scene and, after a time, they all went inside.

"God bless you, Istvan," said Julianna softly as they entered the house, taking his hand in hers.

Chapter 42

"The 50 crates transported to Vatra Dornei seen by your informer were shipped to Varna in Bulgaria. They were then loaded as cargo aboard the Russian ship *Demeter* bound for Constantinople, Palermo, Cadiz and Southampton," Török Ferenc explained at the conference called in a salon in the Town Hall.

Istvan had received permission to take over a wing of the building while repairs were being made to the Polizeipräsidium. After the detailed search of the castle had been completed, Török had returned to Bistritz and pressed Kasza and Istvan to remain active in the continuing investigation before returning to Klausenberg.

The Count was nowhere to be found. He had vanished into thin air. The carriage that Natália had described seeing at the door was missing. Evidently, the Count had followed his cargo out of the Empire into Wallachia, probably in the direction of Bucharest. If so, the Count and his retainers were out of the jurisdiction of the Austro-Hungarian authorities and had disappeared into the wild, primitive mountains and forests south of Transylvania.

"The Englishman, Harker, felt sure that the Count was planning to embark to London. The *Demeter's* ultimate destination is England," Kasza offered.

"What can we do?" Török replied, shrugging his shoulders and shaking his head. "We could telegraph Scotland Yard, I suppose. Ask them to arrest him upon landing in Southampton ..."

"They will never see him," Istvan said quietly. "If he is aboard the ship, he will fly off. We don't even know if he is on the ship. He could have safe places anywhere in Europe. He may never go to London. He may not get there for years, or a century for that matter."

Török shot Istvan a wary look. After everything, Istvan knew Török simply did not believe the serial killer he had long suspected in these regions was a supernatural vampire. His beliefs would not permit him to accept Istvan' account of the Count's abortive attempt to murder him at the Abbey, witnessed only by the Abbess. Nor did the detailed statements given by Natália, Jonathan Harker nor Ema von Jelna. He remained convinced it was all an illusion; a façade perpetuated by a madman who cultivated the image of a supernatural to terrorize the peasants and locals while carrying on a ruthless serial slaughter for his own diabolical ends. In the end, that was Török's working hypothesis. A hypothesis Istvan would also have adopted had he not seen the Count's powers with his own eyes.

Indeed, that had been the hypothesis he, Kasza and Radu had pursued for many months leading up to his attempted murder at the convent. In the days following his return to Bistritz, Istvan contemplated his position and situation in depth, going over and over it in his mind, probing for some other rational, scientific explanation for everything he knew. He was visiting Julianna more and more, these days, preferring her company and her bed to the solitary life and lodgings of a widower.

Chapter 43

Julianna had accepted at once the conclusion both he and her still deranged daughter had drawn from their respective experiences with the Count. This early and firm endorsement of Istvan's viewpoint eased his mind which still, at times, balked at what he had come to believe. Julianna was an educated and intelligent woman. Istvan found himself confiding in her as he researched what knowledge there was on the existence of vampires. He and Julianna spent a week in Budapest at her villa so that Istvan could read and complete research at the Széchényi Library, the national library of the Kingdom.

"They can lie asleep for years; centuries, even," Istvan explained to Julianna one evening in July as they sipped tea on the balcony outside the doors of her bedroom on the second floor of her house. The villa had a hillside view of the city that was quite beautiful. "This one may have risen and slept many times over the past four hundred years. There are reports of local panics in various places from time to time, followed by long periods of quiet."

"Really? Where?" Julianna inquired.

"Prussia, for one place. In the early 18th century. It's well documented. And in the Empire as well. As our forces pushed back the Ottoman Turks and the lands in Transylvania, the Balkans and the Bukovina became part of the Empire, reports began to arise of vampire attacks as well. It became so terrible that in some villages where the vampires were recognized, the people dug up the bodies of the dead and exterminated them by decapitation of the corpse, driving stakes through their hearts and similar rituals."

"My God," Julianna exclaimed. "What about the government? If these were happening in crown lands, wouldn't the government do something?"

"Yes," Istvan replied. "Yesterday, I was reading a document by Gerard van Swieten called Discourse on the Existence of Ghosts. It seems that by 1755, the problem had become so pronounced that the Empress Maria Theresa looked into it. Van Swieten was her personal physician. She asked him to investigate. In this document, he explains away the appearance of these undead as hysterical, superstitious nonsense and with that, the Empress forbade people continuing to desecrate the bodies of the dead, as she called it. She forbade any further staking or decapitation of corpses by the people and with the censorship of those days, all reporting of these appearances stopped."

"What do you think happened?"

"I don't know. When you look at the map and see where these reports of vampire attacks and reprisals occurred in the last century, you see that communities as far north as Prussia were involved, all the way down through the Carpathians to Serbia and the Balkans."

"What do you make of that?" Julianna asked.

"Well, Bistritz and Transylvania are in the dead center of this arc of terror," Istvan replied. By the late 1700s, we see nothing more for nearly a century and a half. It may be due to censorship. Or perhaps Count Dracula went to sleep for all this time."

"Or perhaps he left for someplace else?" Juliana wondered out loud. "Perhaps when the Turks retreated deeper into the Balkans, he followed them?"

"Perhaps," Istvan replied. He began to pack his pipe with tobacco as he considered her point. "If he is the ghost of Vlad III, he would have no love for the Turks or the Hungarians."

"Why?"

"I've done some reading about this man who was so hated and feared in his day. His descendent, Dracula Radu, explained some of it to us when we visited him here in Budapest months ago. When his father died, Vlad succeeded to his titles and estates as Prince of Wallachia, but his brother fell out of favor and fled to Turkey where he became a vassal of the Sultan. Radu betrayed his brother. He made war on his brother with Turkish money and soldiers in Wallachia and then in Transylvania, seeking to replace his brother as Prince."

"Did he succeed?"

"Yes. Eventually. Overwhelmed by Turkish hordes, Vlad nonetheless inflicted some stinging defeats on them, particularly in Transylvania where the mountains gave him the ability to swoop down and surprise the Ottomans, inflict casualties and then disappear into the mists and the mountains. It was during these times that Vlad attempted to make up for a lack of soldiers by terrorizing the invader. After one battle, he and his men impaled thousands of Turkish soldiers on spears and left them for the Sultan to find. Vlad became "the Impaler" then and for all time in Europe. News of this exploit alone reached into Germany and Russia, but in the end, the merciless brutality he cultivated was not enough.

"And then?"

"He began to run out of money and soldiers. So he asked the king of neighboring Hungary for support. Matthias Corvinius was the king. At first he gave Vlad aid due to his fear of the Turks, but then there was a truce between the king and the Sultan. The Sultan wanted Vlad to be arrested and turned over to him so that he could put Radu on the throne of Wallachia as his puppet. The king summoned Vlad to Budapest and he had no choice but to go if he wanted more money. When he arrived, Matthias Corvinius betrayed him. Arrested him and placed him in jail. Vlad lost everything. His brother took it all. Just to make sure Radu remained peaceful, however, the king never actually turned Vlad over to the Turks. He kept him alive, locked in his castle under house arrest for ten years guarded by the Hungarians and close to Radu's capital in Bucharest. If Radu took up arms against the king, the king would release Vlad as the "legitimate" ruler of Wallachia and Transylvania.

"My God. So Vlad was betrayed by everyone?"

"Right. His own brother. The Turks. And then the Hungarians. And he had ten years to think about it. Brood on it. His hatred and contempt for all of them steeped and bubbled for years and years in that castle we saw until they say he went mad. Eventually, the king released him when war broke out again with the Turks.

"And then?"

"Radu had died in the meantime. It is then that his whereabouts were lost for a time to history. Legend says in his madness, Vlad of the Dracul had made his way to Scholomance, the school of black magic and sorcery high in the mountains south of Hermannstadt, supposedly taught by the Devil himself. There he learned the black arts, sorcery and alchemy. Sometime after that, he emerged from the forests, now a legendary figure among the people and gentry of the mountains. He gathered a fierce Roma bodyguard, and aroused a small army of Székelys from the Eastern Mountains and the Bukovina near his home. He raised a rebellion against the Turkish overlords of Transylvania and Wallachia in 1475. In the middle of that war, he disappeared again.

"Supposedly he was assassinated by his own men in a forest near Bucharest while on his way to capture the city from an Ottoman garrison. It seems a great effort was made to convince the Sultan he was dead. The Sultan was ostentatiously presented with the head of a man in a barrel of honey that the leader of his Roma guard claimed was Vlad who had been killed. Of course the Sultan had never seen Vlad, nor had anyone in his Court so it could never be verified. A bit of Gypsy cunning and trickery there," Istvan said.

"Some say his body was burned. Others say it was buried at a monastery near Snagov in Wallachia or at another one at Comana. The fact is, Vlad died under vague and obscure circumstances that were never properly, forensically confirmed, as we would do today. Especially given his high nobility and his knighthood in the Order of the Dragon. It was after that when the vampire "superstition" first arose in Europe. A coincidence? I think not." Istvan slowly shook his head. Then he turned seriously to her.

"Julianna, I think he is the one. I think he is the father of all vampires. I think he has plagued the Ottoman lands and Transylvania for centuries, wreaking his vengeance on the people and these lands. Giving vent to his deep hate and madness by murder, torture and worse. Possessed by the devil's own magic. He is now a monster. A sadist with no soul."

"What can you do now?" Julianna asked in a soft voice, placing her hand on his arm.

"I've been thinking about that question," Istvan replied softly now, looking into her eyes. "For centuries it seems people have allowed this monster to escape as long as he does not plague them or their people. I imagine at other times in the past four centuries, there have been other Kálváry Istvans who got close to destroying him, but were too late. And I imagine at other times, he has disappeared into the night to settle in other lands where his murders continue for decades or even centuries at a time until he is discovered again. By then, his castle ... his mountain stronghold and prison are where he returns. To the soil of his true burial place where the Roma and the Székelys still remember him, shelter him, hide him and help him in return for some devil's bargain that we don't know and will never find out.

"After awhile, rejuvenated and having calculated in his diabolical mind the next part of the world he will curse with his presence, he gathers his servants and talismans, his sacred soil in boxes and bags are transported with military cunning and a new nest of terror and despair will be created.

"If what you are saying is true, then London is where the preparations seem to have been made. Why don't you go there?" the Baroness asked.

"First, because they will think I'm a lunatic, just as Török does. Kasza and Radu believe me but they have never seen him. They would not be the modern detectives I hope them to be if there weren't some doubt in the corner of their minds. I know this.

"Second, because any mind so clever and evil would have made safe places elsewhere in Europe to rest in the light of day that afflicts and endangers him. He could be creating a place now that he will not use for a hundred years. His existence in time is so vast that our minds would not think on the scale of this Beast as he gazes out into the future.

"But this begs the question, my dear," Istvan said.

"What do you mean?"

"Other Kálváry Istvans in time, if they existed, gave up the chase and he is still here. The question is should I do the same? Or shall I give chase? It is up to me, I think, whether Count Dracula is found and extinguished for all time. I could do nothing and if I did, we will probably never see him again in our lifetimes, but we will have to live with the knowledge, as did my predecessors, that he is still murdering and tormenting mankind. Just not us."

"Or?"

"Or I give chase to him with all the power at my disposal. Wherever it may lead. Until I find him and destroy him utterly."

"And what have you decided?"

"I haven't. I thought I would discuss it with you first." Istvan replied, smiling faintly now. Julianna smiled back at him. It was the first flush of pleasure between them during the entire conversation.

Chapter 44

Natália and Jonathan had soon reunited once their presence in Bistritz was no longer needed for the police investigation and their passion, rekindled by the sight of one another with no social restraints soon burst into an obsession in hotel rooms in Budapest, Vienna, Munich and across Europe to Amsterdam. She soon realized her dark beauty, so unlike how she imagined pale English women would appear, mesmerized him. She learned how to arouse his desire for her. Her willingness, even eagerness to engage in every form and sort of sexual deviance Jonathan taught her was in part due to her own lust for him. Sometimes they spent most of a day naked in their rooms, abetting their lust for each other and falling back into deep sleeps only to resume again and again. Like a camel consuming vast quantities of water before going into the desert, she could not get enough of him to sustain herself for a lifetime nor, did it seem, could he.

In the weeks they took to cross the continent, Natália bent her mind and energies to learning English. Jonathan helped her and slowly they began to be able to communicate with one another. By the time they reached Amsterdam, Natália could tell Jonathan was struggling with something; trying to solve an insoluble problem, it seemed. Finally, he began to explain to her about his engagement to Mina Murray in England. She felt her heart sink as the meaning of his words cut into her like a knife.

"I will provide for you, Natália. I will. I want to help you and I do care about you. I really do. After all we have been through together …" She cried bitterly as he went on and so did he. She knew he cared for her and his physical affection for her had transcended any language barrier. In some ways, it had made their lovemaking urgent and dramatic, especially at the beginning, because they could make their desires known to each other only in this simple way. She could not deny that she would miss that about him most of all.

They walked the streets of Amsterdam together, looking for a flat for her to stay. The architecture of the strange city was at once bizarre to a Roma from Transylvania, but beautiful as well. In the days after their arrival, they explored the city, supping in small restaurants by the canals, sipping espresso coffee at the cafés. Jonathan bought her a chest and then a wardrobe full of clothing, shoes and accessories which she gladly modeled for him in the Lindengracht flat he rented for her. A year's lease was paid in advance and he opened a bank account for her at the Bank of Amsterdam with £800 for her to live on. He clearly intended to keep her as his mistress, she understood, and she was not against it.

Yet Natália could not ignore the effect she had on the Dutch men who saw her in Amsterdam. Her dark skin and striking features turned heads as she walked along the canals and cobblestoned streets of the city for her shopping, but her worldly clothing gave her an unusually appealing, exotic appearance. The Dutch seemed to care little about her Roma heritage, if they realized it. By the time Jonathan finally left for England, Natália had learned English well enough and was beginning to understand and speak the Dutch tongue as well. Her apartment looked over a quiet inner courtyard where she could sit and enjoy the peace and quiet of the gardens. She had a flower box made and installed on the tiny balcony outside her window and before long, her world was quite cozy and felt safe. There was nothing to do but live and await Jonathan's return, whenever that might be.

Chapter 45

Kasza remained in Bistritz with the RHG during the summer of 1896 as their agent in the district and also Acting Chef der Politzei. He remained assigned to the case, although it was now considered inactive due to the absence of the suspected serial killer. Kasza was now increasingly involved in security measures in and around Bistritz for the army maneuvers that would be attended by Kaiser Franz Joseph himself in August.

Istvan and Radu had received permission from the RHG and the Hungarian government to pursue the serial killer, Vlad Dracul, and had been given passports and letters of introduction commending them to the royal Romanian government. Letters requested the assistance of police and judicial authorities in finding the whereabouts of the criminal, Vlad Dracul, portraying himself as the Count Dracula of Transylvania.

Progress had been very slow at first, questioning local farmers and estate owners on the roads leading out of the Empire into Wallachia in the kingdom of Romania. Eventually, though, they had a response from a tavern owner in Brezoi, a small town in a mountain valley. He had seen the Count's black calèche at around the last time it had been seen in the Borgo Pass. He recalled it had been left for a day at a local farmer's barn. He could not remember seeing the owner of the calèche, but it had left immediately after sundown the following day.

There was only one road into and out of Brezoi, and so Istvan and Radu continued on the road southward, ever deeper into Romania. Careful, painstaking questioning and investigating turned up a clue here and there, a sighting now and again. The Count had stayed at this inn or that hotel, always during the day, while his manservant guarded the carriage and his property. By nightfall, he was gone. It was always the same story. Down into Bulgaria they went and finally to Varna on the Black Sea. There the *Demeter* had stopped in port for a day when the calèche had been placed in storage at a warehouse near the pier where the *Demeter* had briefly docked.

Istvan reviewed the paperwork with the assistance of a Bulgarian clerk. The *Demeter* had originated in Odessa and was of Russian registry. It had stopped in Constanta, to the north, in Wallachia and picked up cargo. The *Demeter* was basically a "tramp" ship that opportunistically picked up passengers and cargo in a coastal port and then went on to the next. The *Demeter* would stop in Constantinople, Piraeus in Greece, Sicily, Marseille, Barcelona, Cadiz and reach Southampton in late June. By the time Istvan came into this information, the *Demeter* had reached England and was probably on its way back.

In Constantinople, Istvan and Radu carefully interviewed the Turkish clerks who had received and serviced the *Demeter* when it docked there. There was no cargo dropped off; only shipped. Interestingly, however, one Turkish official recalled the name Dracula. He had seen shipments of furniture, crates of valuables and even carriages had been delivered to several residences in the city in the past. They checked and confirmed that indeed, the Count owned several pieces of property in the Ottoman capital, but here things became more difficult. Attempts to obtain official permission to enter the houses were repeatedly rebuffed and denied. Even official requests procured from authorities from Budapest and Vienna would not move the Turkish bureaucracy.

"It doesn't seem as though he got off the vessel here," Radu ventured.

"No, but if he had wanted to do so secretly, nobody would have seen him anyway," Istvan replied. "It's going to be just guesswork." They were sipping Turkish coffee at the Sark Kahvesi café just outside the Bazaar. Smoke from hookahs and cigarettes floated in the air and mingled with the smells of roasted coffee to produce a distinctly Balkan atmosphere.

"Nonetheless, I would like to contaminate his return to these residences that we know he uses," Istvan continued.

"Contaminate?"

"Yes. I want to get access to these places. Scatter the dirt. Put crucifixes, holy wafers and holy water in the boxes, crates, coffins or sarcophagi he has placed there for his need. Deny him sanctuary here in Constantinople and then go to the next."

"I see."

"Either we see this through as thoroughly as possible or we don't."

"How will we get entry?"

"*Baksheesh.*"

"Ah, yes. There is always that," Radu nodded as he pulled on a very pungent Turkish cigarette, thinking how deserved was the reputation of the Turks for tobacco. "But where will we get the money to ease the consciences of our Turkish hosts in letting us into his hiding places?"

"Leave it to me," Istvan replied. He thought he would get the money from Budapest or he would use his own.

Chapter 46

The Roma are, above all, ubiquitous people. They have no permanent attachment to land or any country in which they reside. From their migration from the Indian subcontinent more than a millennium ago, the descendants of the Roma spread across the continent of Europe. Some countries had more than others, but every country in Europe had some. Often, they formed their own tribes and groups, but they themselves recognized their uniqueness no matter where they went, and so did their hosts.

It wasn't very long after Jonathan left that Natália encountered her own people in Amsterdam. No amount of fancy clothing or perfume could hide her from another Roma, who immediately recognized her as one of their own. One summer evening, walking along one of the canals that demark the city in concentric rings, she saw some men working on what looked like a barge tied up to the quay, but one that had been made into a houseboat. They were dark and as she approached, she knew that they were Roma. She stopped short, considering whether to turn away and avoid them, but it was too late. Her exotic beauty had already elicited a glance and then a stare from one of the men who said something to the others. In a moment, all of them were staring at her. She decided she could not appear afraid of them, and so continued walking. Shortly, she was alongside the barge. The men had not taken their eyes off her.

One of the younger men said something to her in a language she did not understand, smiling as he did so. She guessed it might be Spanish.

Hoping to walk by without further conversation, she shook her head and said in Magyar she did not understand him. He blinked back at her incomprehensibly, but an older man now stood up on the deck and spoke to her.

"Young lady, you are far from home, are you not?"

Startled, Natália hesitated for a moment considering how to respond or what to do next. The man looked at her expectantly, as did his three colleagues.

"Perhaps," she eventually replied, noncommittally.

"What is your name?" By this, the man meant the name she would use to strangers since the Roma never told anyone but other members of their tribe and family their real name and to nobody their secret name. Natália knew this and told him her name. The man nodded, now hopping down off the deck of the barge and on to the quay, approaching her. She thought he was in his 30s. He had a handsome face with a dark mustache but no beard. He wore a white tunic and blue overalls with sandals on his feet. She felt uneasy at his approach.

"I am called Carlos here," the man said, in perfect Magyar. His eyes searched her face without any compunction, clearly puzzled by her fashionable clothes and bearing and inexplicable presence. His dark eyes flashed when they met hers, drinking her in. She felt his boldness and confidence as he now stood in her path. She could walk around him and he would not harm her, she thought, but he wanted to know her and was demonstrating it in the way a Roma male would to a Roma woman. Dominating and demanding. She would permit it, she thought to herself, but only for a few moments to see what he would say. She did not have to, as she would have back at home in Transylvania.

Carlos had now given her his name. The name he used with the Roma here in Amsterdam and wherever else he had been lately. This seemed to include Spain, given the sound of the others with him.

"How came you to Amsterdam from Hungary?" he asked. He began rolling a cigarette with some papers he carried in a pocket.

"With another man," Natália replied coolly. Carlos glanced at her and nodded, nonchalantly.

"Where is he? No man should let a woman like you walk the streets alone." Again, the dark eyes flashed with energy. Natália noticed the two other Roma watching quietly from the boat, lighting cigarettes as they talked, then sitting down on the deck to smoke and see what happened next.

"He's abroad for awhile. In England," Natália replied, and then instantly regretted it.

Chapter 47

Kasza had been holding down the two jobs of Acting District Chief and District Inspector for the Royal Hungarian Gendarmerie for a couple of months when he discovered the clue that led him to Dimitru. He had by then deduced the murder of Dieter Zeigler at the Vatră Ciobănesc could only have been from an informer inside the police force in the pay of Count Dracula. Kasza burned with a quiet rage that a traitor in their midst had betrayed them all and made it a top priority to find him.

Only a very few individuals had access to the telegraph information that would have tipped off the Count that Zeigler was a police spy, which narrowed things down a bit. Dmitri's apparent affluence distinguished him from the others right away. It could not be squared with his pay. The bartender at a particular Bistritz pub, *Die Löwen Höhle*, was a police informer. He visited Kasza and reported Dimitru's heavy drinking and frequent, dark ravings about vampires muttered from his bar stool. Kasza decided to arrest and interrogate him, springing the trap one morning when Dimitru unsuspectingly arrived for work.

Kasza used the technique that he already had hard evidence that Dimitru was guilty and was merely affording him the formality of confessing, which might spare his life. Details were all he was after he assured Dimitru as he lit a cigarette for him in the dungeon-like interrogation room, the heavy door guarded by two militiamen. It worked.

Dimitru was also a believer in vampires, and this one in particular. He was terrified of him.

"It wasn't the money, Vezér," Dimitru argued. "He would kill me. He will kill me now," he continued in despair. "He will kill everyone. He will kill you too, Kasza."

"Tell me everything," Kasza insisted. "Tell me how it happened." Dimitru told him how he had first been recruited by Dracula and how he had betrayed them that night in his stable. He seemed not to mind his revelations were incriminating him because he doubted he would live long enough to reach the gallows.

"His voice is milk and honey but his eyes blaze with the fires of hell. No man can withstand his power for long. He knows about you, Kasza. He knows about the Chief from Budapest. He will come for you and all who we love. He is especially cruel about that. He has no soul and no remorse. No mercy and no forgiveness is in him. You will see."

Kasza could not repress a shudder as Dimitru went on about their fiendish enemy. How would they ever defeat him, he wondered? His superhuman strength and centuries of preparation and cunning could hardly be imagined. Over the succeeding days, his interrogation of Dimitru continued, probing for more details about the Count, his personality and characteristics, noting them in his daily work diary. There were other informers and spies, he learned, but Dimitru didn't know who they were. The Count's eyes and ears were everywhere reporting everything of interest to their Master. Kasza wondered how many details the Count must have known of Kasza's months-long investigation before Istvan had arrived.

A note arrived one day just after Kasza finished reading a brief telegram from Istvan and Radu from Athens. It was from the Baroness Ribanszky Julianna. She asked him to come quickly to her house. It had to do with her daughter. Kasza asked one of the orderlies to fetch his horse, quickly gathered up his valise in which he carried some basic investigative tools, pens and paper, and within an hour was at the door of the Baroness' residence. He was shown in to the conservatory where the Baroness of Jelna waited for him.

"Thank you for coming so quickly," she began. She had her hands clasped in front of her and her face showed signs of fatigue, Kasza noted.

"What is it, my Lady?" Kasza replied, bowing slightly.

"It's Ema. Something is happening to her. I don't know what to do. Istvan is so far away and I don't want to bother him, but I thought you might have a look."

"Of course. I'm at your service, my Lady. But what exactly is it?"

"When she first returned to us, she was deeply disturbed from her ordeal. That goes without saying. Give her rest, the doctor said. Make her rest, he told me. So we did. After a few days of rest and good food, I saw she was improving but she was still in a most fragile, emotional condition."

"Yes, I'm sure of it," Kasza said.

"Please! Sit down, Kasza," the Baroness said, suddenly realizing that in her anxiety she had not sat down and Kasza was still on his feet. He smiled and sat down in a large chair where she had motioned him. He placed his case on the floor at his feet. The Baroness sat down in another chair facing him.

"Yes. Most fragile," the Baroness resumed. "She seemed to be reasonably well during the day, but she has been experiencing the most violent and terrifying nightmares. They began a few days after Istvan left for the Balkans. I heard her from down the hall. It was after midnight and I thought I heard voices down the hall, coming from her room. I went to investigate. As I drew closer to the door, there was only my daughter's voice or rather, a sort of moaning sound.

"I opened the door and lit a candle. Ema was in a very agitated state, convulsed in the bed, twitching and turning, grasping the bed sheets and moaning. I sat down on the bed and gently shook her. She awoke with a terrible start and screamed, waking up some of the servants who came running. At first she didn't recognize me and shrank back, away from me as if trying to escape. I called her name and tried to calm her, but for nearly a minute she continued whimpering and crying, staring at me in the most horrified way. Then, slowly, as if finally awakening, she suddenly became calm and recognized me. . .

Ema, darling ..." I said to her. "It's me. It's your mother. Don't you recognize me?

'Oh," she replied with a deep sigh, as if catching her breath from her hysteria. It's you! What are you doing here?'

The poor girl was clearly confused. She didn't know where she was for a minute or so. By now several servants in their nightclothes were in the room with candles, gawking at her. I asked her what she had been dreaming, but she couldn't remember. I slept with her the rest of the night after dismissing the servants, but nothing else happened. Then it happened again a few nights later. Another terrible nightmare. And another a couple of nights after that."

"Her mind must have been terribly disturbed by her imprisonment in the castle," Kasza ventured as she paused. "It's probably not surprising ..."

"Exactly what I thought," Julianna interrupted. "I thought it was something she will just have to endure. I called the doctor back to see if there was anything he could do. He gave her laudanum, instructing her to take it before she went to bed to help her sleep. It did no good. In fact, it made it worse. It was harder to arouse her from her sleep as she was experiencing these terrible dreams. When she did, she was soaked with sweat and it took me hours to calm her down."

"Did she ever tell you what her dreams were about?"

"Not really. I asked her, of course. And you might think as terrifying as they seemed to be they would be fixed in her mind, but that's another strange part of it. She can't remember much of anything."

"Much? What can she remember?"

"Red, blood-shot eyes," said Ema, who had now entered the room. Kasza stood up again and kissed her outstretched hand. She was drawn and haggard. The white summer gown she was wearing accentuated her bloodless, pale face. Her eyes darted between him and her mother as she languidly walked to another nearby chair and sat down.

"His eyes," she continued. "I can see his eyes in my dreams. It's him. He is calling to me, I know, but I don't remember what he says." There was a moment's silence in the room. Kasza opened his case and took out a pen and notepad. He scribbled down a few notes and then looked up at the two ladies.

"That's not all," Julianna continued. A few nights ago, I woke up listening for Ema, but there was no sound. I decided I would check on her. I put on my dressing gown and slippers, lit a candle and went down the hall to her room. I opened the door and my heart stopped. Ema wasn't there. I called for the servants and we searched the house. I discovered the door in the conservatory was ajar and thinking Ema might have gone out into the gardens this way, I went out but I saw nothing.

"It was dark and my candle blew out. I called my butler and we quickly got some lanterns and torches. We resumed the search outside, calling Ema's name with no success. We split up into small groups of two and three, moving out away from the house. After another fifteen minutes or so, I was about a hundred meters from the house. In one corner of the grounds, we have a maze made of tall shrubs. It was built by my husband as an amusement to our children and guests at garden parties many years ago. In the dim light I thought I saw something at the entrance to the maze.

"At first, I thought it was an illusion. It was cloudy and the moon had briefly shown and then become obscured again by another passing cloud. We stopped and I pointed toward the maze. There were two or three figures, I thought. As we approached, it seemed that there were two, and then just one. It was Ema. She was standing there in her nightgown, I could see. I started running toward her, calling her name. As I got close, I am sure I heard the sound of a low voice. A woman's voice, I think. It came from within the maze, but I couldn't see anything.

"After that, I was consumed with attention for my daughter and in any event, in the darkness, with the maze, there would have been no way for us to have caught whoever was in there."

"Of course," Kasza said, quickly making notes. "Do you remember anything of it?" Kasza asked, to Ema.

"No," Ema replied. "I just remember waking up shivering cold in my mother's arms in the garden with servants staring at me and blazing torches."

"Show him your neck," the Baroness commanded in a low voice. Ema reluctantly turned down the white collar and there Kasza saw two, distinct purplish scabs circled with white skin. A shudder coursed involuntarily up his spine. There were more of them here, Kasza concluded. For some reason, they wanted Ema still.

Chapter 48

As June rolled into July, Istvan and Radu continued their investigation to Athens and other Balkan cities in a slow, wide circle that would take them back to Budapest and Bistritz. They found nothing in Athens. If Count Dracula had property there, it was hidden and in other names. In Tirana and Dubrovnik there was nothing either, but in Belgrade, there was a quiet mansion on the outskirts of town. Again, it was difficult to gain entry on police business but in Serbia, the insistent requests of the neighboring Empire were more persuasive than in Constantinople. Eventually, the doors were opened, coffins and Transylvanian soil from the Borgo Castle found and contaminated with holy wafers, crucifixes, and other Christian symbology. Agram and Laibach, the capitals of Croatia and Slavonia respectively, proved barren ground.

"I wrote to Harker Jonathan," Istvan said to Radu as they waited for a waiter to bring them each an espresso at the Hotel Danielli on the Grand Canal in Venice, a few paces from the Doge's palace and the entrance to the Piazza San Marco. There were staying at the Hotel while they awaited delays from the Italian bureaucracy to allow them into a villa their research discovered belong to *la Famiglia Dracula* since 1672. A dinner had been consumed and they had been watching the passing boats and pedestrians along the Grand Canal in the early summer evening.

"Did you hear anything back?" Radu inquired.

"Not yet. I told him about the *Demeter*," Istvan continued. "I asked him to find out for me where the crates of dirt and other cargo sent by Count

Dracula had been deposited in England. Addresses. Thing like that. This vampire has been busy over these 400 years. Who knows how many more lairs he may have and in England, he will build more. You see, Radu, this evil genius has built his own empire over the centuries. His tentacles reach out in all directions. I want to find him while we can. Maybe others have tried in centuries past, but failed. Maybe they didn't have our resources. For what he has done, I want him dead."

Radu nodded and lit a cigarette. The waiter arrived with two espressos and set them on the table. The heat and humidity of the summer weather in Venice was not to his liking, Istvan knew, having lived most of his life in the cold climate of Transylvania where summer meant thawing of the mountain passes and flower boxes in the windows of the stucco and brick houses of Bistritz. A cool evening breeze rippled past, causing the candle in the wine bottle on their table to flutter.

"I'm with you, Vezér," Radu replied.

Istvan watched him as he sipped the demitasse and thought how far his young adjutant had come in the brief time he had known him. A Wallachian he might be, but the young man was intelligent, ambitious and loyal to him and to the crown. Whatever doubts Radu might have had about the existence of a supernatural vampire, he betrayed no evidence of it in his daily interaction with Istvan. He had seen the coffins and the evidence of a sinister mind who had prepared multiple safe houses and havens whence to escape if he were chased out of one venue. Yet he hadn't seen what Istvan had seen.

A messenger was shown to the table. He produced a paper with a seal from the Magistrate to enter the house of one conte Dracula who maintained a residence in the Santa Croce Quarter of Venice, near a church known as San Giacomo dell'Orio. They would be met there by a detective, Vittorio Marucci at 7 o'clock, the note that accompanied the document said. Istvan looked at his pocket watch. It was 6:15.

"We had better be going," Radu said, hastily swallowing the remains of his espresso. "Who knows how long it will take to arrange another entry if we miss this one?"

As they boarded a vaporetto and headed toward the residence, Istvan had misgivings as he looked at the white water churning at the stern of the vessel. The sun would set by 8 o'clock. He now carried a small leather bag with holy wafers, water, crucifixes and, in the bottom of the bag, a mallet and wooden stakes. Istvan looked at the other passengers on the vaporetto. A couple of old women, dressed in black from head to foot. Old men, smoking cigarettes with weathered faces. A gentleman looking at his pocket watch. Before long, the boat came to the stop closest to San Giacomo and they got off.

Already, shadows were beginning to dim the small streets and footbridges that honeycombed this section of the city. Lamplights were being lit. The smell of cooking wafted in the air and there were occasional voices, echoing off the facades of ancient buildings that had blankly stared across the tiny canals for centuries. Istvan wondered when the last time Count Dracula had stalked the very same pavement on which he was now walking? What foul deeds had been done in this neighborhood, he wondered?

"There they are," Radu said quietly, pointing ahead where Istvan could see a short, dark haired man standing with a Carabinieri next to him. These military police could easily be identified with their military style uniform and the distinctive Napoleonic hats. Istvan felt his instinctive dread and dislike of official Italians welling up in him. He had resented them ever since the War of 1866 but now, he knew he would have to summon up his best diplomatic skills to accomplish his mission.

"*Bona sera*," Istvan said as they arrived. He received a perfunctory nod from the Carabinieri and a wary acknowledgment from Signor Marucci. He showed the paper to the detective who took his time looking it over, then nodded and handed it back to Istvan. Radu remained silent.

"*Entrare*," the detective said in Italian, motioning toward the door with his head. Radu had procured a key from a locksmith after having made a wax impression of the lock a couple of days earlier. He stepped forward and pushed the key into the hole and turned it. The tumblers of the lock turned and the handle now moved the bolt in the door. Radu swung open the door. The interior was dark and smelled moldy, as if nobody had been inside the place in a long time. The Carabinieri had a lantern. He lit it and the interior of what seemed to be a large salon was dimly illuminated.

Istvan could see heavy curtains that draped the windows completely, allowing no light into the room as the detective shut the outside door. On a table there was a candelabra. Istvan motioned the Carabinieri to light it, and he obliged. Gradually, more light filled the room. A heavy, Persian style rug covered a wood floor. There was a piano. A table. A heavy red velvet couch with matching chairs. A long table of polished wood with two more candelabra; these of crystal. All told, this was the richest and most impressive residence of all of the ones Istvan had seen so far, he thought.

"*Un momento, per favore,*" Istvan said to the two men, who nodded. Istvan walked to the table and took two candles out of one of the crystal candelabra and lit them from the candelabra on the other table. He gave one to Radu and, together, they walked into the next room which was a hallway, leading back into the house. Normally, they had found coffins and sarcophagi in basements, but here in Venice, that would not happen. Basements were virtually unheard of in Venice due to the high water table. Istvan heard the bells of San Giacomo. It was 8 o'clock. He could hear the murmurs of voices from the other room as the detective and the Carabinieri spoke in rapid but low Italian.

Radu and Istvan lit more candles on tables and wall sconces as they made their way along the hallway into a study, a bedroom, the kitchen and then a staircase. It was a dark winding staircase that led upward to the second floor, no doubt. Radu looked at Istvan. Istvan set his bag on a table and pulled out a heavy crucifix and gave it to Radu. He nodded and put the necklace around his neck. Istvan snapped shut the bag. Whatever they might find upstairs, they would be ready for it. Radu made for the stairwell, but Istvan grabbed his shoulder, gently holding him back. Istvan would go first.

The stairs creaked under his weight as Istvan slowly ascended, candle in hand. He could barely see more than a meter or two ahead of himself in the darkness but up they went. In a minute, they reached the top of the stairs and another hallway. There were closed doors every few paces, suggesting a

The Carpathian Assignment

number of bedrooms on the second floor. The hallway was wide and tables and other furniture were interspersed with oil paintings and more sconces in the passage. Again, Radu and Istvan lit the sconces and candles in the hallway and in the rooms as they carefully made their way along. Room by room, they went but there was nothing. The dust and musty smell of the place was beginning to convince Istvan that this particular hide-away may not have been used for a very long time.

They reached the last room. Radu placed his hand on the door knob and, with a nod from Istvan, pushed it open. They peered into the darkness, holding their candles slightly above their heads. There was a bed, chair, dresser and a desk. A large, heavily draped window was on the wall opposite. Nothing. There had been no other stairwell encountered and, indeed, the building was only two stories tall.

"Can it be that this was not a safe house?" Radu asked in a loud whisper. Istvan was about to answer when he noticed in the water closet, on the ceiling, a discreet trap door. He pointed up at it. Radu was just about to say something when there was a loud pop, followed by two more in rapid succession. Shouting downstairs. The two men looked at each other for just a moment and then they both sprinted for the hallway and the stairs. In a moment, they were down the stairs and running toward the front parlor. Ominously, things had fallen silent. They rushed into the room.

There, standing in the room, back to them, was a woman dressed in a black velvet cape and hood. The Carabinieri and the detective were both lying on the floor at her feet. She raised her hand to her head, as if wiping something off her face. Then she turned slowly to face them.

"*E voi chi siete?*" the woman said to them. She had a pale and hard face with long white teeth. There was blood on the back of her hand.

"I don't speak Italian," Istvan replied warily in Magyar.

"Ah. You speak my mother tongue," the woman replied, also in Magyar without a trace of accent. Istvan was not surprised, but a feeling of dread came over him as he looked into her blood-shot eyes. Radu was speechless. "I said, who are you?" the woman continued. She was now advancing on them using tiny, almost imperceptible steps under her long cape that swept the floor. Istvan had no doubt that he was regarding the second vampire he had ever seen in his life.

"We have come a long way looking for the Count Dracula Vlad. Do you know him?" Istvan inquired, fingering the crucifix and rosary beads in his pocket.

A tittering laugh came from the woman. "Of course. He's my husband. What do you want with him?"

"A few questions about a number of murders and missing persons on his estate at the Borgo Pass in Transylvania," Istvan continued in as calm a voice as he could manage. "Where is he?"

"Not here, my Lord," the vampire replied. She had now reached a point only a few meters away. He could see her well, even in the candlelight. Her skin was very pale, like that of a corpse, Istvan thought. Yet her lips were red and her sharp, canine teeth were very pronounced at close range. Glassy eyes, dominated by large, black pupils, darted between him and Radu, seemingly sizing up which one of them would be best to attack first in a sudden burst of frenzied aggression. It was now or never, Istvan thought. He pulled out the crucifix and raised it in the air between them. The vampire hissed in disgust, but started backing away.

"How dare you enter our house," she said in a low, menacing voice. "I will kill you for this. He will kill you."

"No you won't. I am here to kill you, my Lady, and that is exactly what we will do. I will drive a stake through your heart and you will be dead by the morning's light," Istvan replied with more courage than he really felt. He now stepped toward her with the crucifix in his hand. As he did, she stepped back with a look of hate and fear. Radu stepped forward too, crucifix in hand.

Chapter 49

Natália thought about Carlos long after she had left him standing at the side of the barge. She had feigned disinterest and coldness when the bold Roma *vezér* continued plying her with questions about herself, where she lived, what she did in Amsterdam and abruptly turned on her heel and left. She had heard his soft laugh as she left.

"I'm sure we will meet again," he called after her, mockingly. His supercilious and patronizing tone toward her was at once attractive and a little frightening. It stirred something in her. An ancient memory? Passed down through generations of how the Roma were? A conditioned reflex from her upbringing in the forest, perhaps?

His manner reminded her a little of her father's enveloping, overwhelming, masculine aura that had dominated her young life. Carlos was a man like him. She smiled to herself. A younger and handsome version she allowed. His eyes; slightly wild and intense. He locked on her with a concentration that made her feel alone with him and the center of his attention on a city sidewalk.

Natália reached her apartment. She climbed the stairs and reached the locked door to her flat. It was a simple lock she thought as she closed the door. For a Sinti lock-pick, it posed little more of a barrier than the knob on the door itself. She really should get a better one, she thought. She put her groceries away and readied a small dinner of Dutch *stamppot* and pea soup. She uncorked the bottle of *Müller-Thurga* white wine she had opened the previous day and poured herself a glass. The window to the flat was open and a summer's breeze of warm night air gently cosseted the room. It was sunset. And within a few minutes, there was a knock at the door.

It was a soft knock. Not the impersonal rat-a-tat-tat knock of a stranger, but the more knowing cha-cha-chah of a friend or acquaintance.

"Who is it?"

"Carlos."

She felt her heart skip a beat. How did he know she lived here? Had he followed her? He must have.

"What do you want?"

"I have something for you."

"I don't want anything. Go away!"

"You will want this."

"What is it?"

"Open the door and I'll show you."

"Go away!"

"I'll leave it at the door for you."

Natália heard the sound of some object being put on the threshold of her door. Then, after a moment, his voice again.

"Good night, Natália."

She said nothing. Then there were sounds of his sandals on the wooden stairs, going down and out. She waited, wondering what Carlos had left at her doorstep. She did not hear the sound of his bare feet silently climbing the stairs, so when she opened the door she started when she saw him there. A bottle of *Anís del Mono* with its bald monkey on the label stood at her bare feet and his just outside her door. He had his sandals in one hand and deftly scooped up the bottle by the neck with the other.

"May I come in?" he asked as he walked into her apartment, smiling.

His raw boldness had flabbergasted her. To her own surprise, she closed the door behind him. She felt her heart beating hard in her chest, like the feelings she experienced when she saw Harker Jonathan. The anticipation.

"What do you want?" she said in as calm a voice as she could manage as he pulled a corkscrew from his pocket and began opening the bottle of anisette.

"Cold water. Bring me two glasses and cold water. It's not as good if you pour the liquor into a glass of water first. They have to be poured at the same time."

"What are you talking about?" Natália asked, but made for the kitchen and a bottle of water she kept in a cupboard.

"*Palomina*. That's what they called it in Spain. It's a drink. You'll like it."

"You have a lot of nerve coming here like this. Do you often go where you are not invited?"

Natália placed two glasses on the table. Carlos picked up the bottle of water and the anisette, one in each hand, and simultaneously poured them into one of the glasses. The liquid turned very white. Then the next glass, the same thing. He put the bottles down and moved one of the glasses toward her.

"*Egészségedre*," Carlos said to her as he raised his glass. A Magyar toast to her health. Natália raised the glass to her lips, as he did. She watched him watching her. He tossed his head and the drink back, swallowing it in a couple of quick gulps. Then she did the same. She felt the sweet liquid turn to fire as it made its way down her throat into her belly. The warmth of the alcohol surged out to the tips of her tingling fingers. She gently wiped her mouth with the back of her hand. His black eyes flashed in the flickering candlelight of her flat. His eyes had roamed appreciatively over her figure that afternoon, and he was doing so again, she noticed. But first, he poured another two glasses.

"Another?" He set the glass down on the table next to her with a sharp clack. Then his own. She had only been with one man her whole life, but instinctively she knew she was going to be with another one. Again she raised the glass to her lips and again she drank the sweet anisette and water as he watched. He pushed his glass toward her.

"Again?"

"No. It's too much."

She was already feeling a flush of color in her face from the second shot and saw he was pouring another for himself and drank another. He had shockingly straight white teeth under his black, close cropped mustache, she noticed. It was rare for a Roma. Many had lost teeth or had been born with crooked ones, but his were different and contrasted with his purplish, dark lips and dark skin. He was watching her watch him.

"Why did you come here?" she asked him.

"I thought you would be missing your man," he replied, glaring at her now with just a little edge to his voice. "As I have been missing my woman."

"You have a woman?"

"Yes, of course. Home."

"And where is home, Carlos?"

"It was Spain, but before that, near Hermanstadt and Sholomance. I grew up there. My tribe is from there. My woman is in Spain. I am here."

"I see."

"And your man is in England?"

"Yes."

"So. You see? We have something in common. Would you like another?"

Carlos gestured to the bottle of *Anís del Mono*. Natália, shook her head no. He stood up, looking at her. Swaying as he stood in front of her with hard wanting. It was as if waves of heat emanated from him toward her. She could feel his desire.

She considered he could rape her right then and there if she resisted, but in truth she wanted him too. It had been more than a month since she had last seen Jonathan and the daily, hot release of her tensions with him. Her mind was cautious and even a little fearful. Her body was not. It longed for him. The warmth of the anisette reached her thighs and the wet warmth she had felt before Jonathan as she contemplated the prospect of Carlos.

He must have known the effect he had on her. Maybe he had this power over most of the women he met. Maybe that accounted for his cocky confidence. His powers of persuasion, tinged with a hint of violence. She knew it would be violent and rough with him, and it was, but he knew how the Roma were. How she was. And his brutal lovemaking that night was just what she had needed.

Chapter 50

It was in Venice when Istvan got a telegram from Kasza about the attacks on Ema. He and Radu had their hands full with the judicial inquiry into the deaths of the Italian police while at the same time contaminating the resting place of the vampire they had encountered in the palazzo where the murders had taken place. Her coffin was found in the dark attic, as Istvan had expected. She had fled somewhere else in the city, however, after their encounter. Somewhere dark and hidden. Here in Venice it would not be a subterranean cellar, that was for sure. Istvan and Radu were puzzling over a map of Venice considering the possibilities where she might be when Kasza's message arrived.

"It's a miracle that he didn't murder her," Radu remarked as Istvan put the telegram on the table between them.

"Perhaps not a miracle," Istvan replied. "He has a reason, I'm sure, for playing with her like this."

"Do you think he is back home?"

"Who knows? There were the others. The wives, Radu." Radu nodded. They were also unaccounted for. "They may have remained behind, doing his bidding, but what would they want with Ema?" They talked about it for a while but if there were some diabolical motive for Ema's continued interest to the vampire family of Count Dracula, it eluded them for now.

"Her safety is the most important thing," Radu said after awhile.

"Yes. I'm sure Kasza is seeing to that."

Chapter 51

Richard, Baron von Krafft-Ebing found a telegram waiting for him inside the mail slot of his rather spacious mansion in Hüttling, only a short distance from the splendid residence of Otto Wagner, the Viennese architect who was taking the city by storm with his radical Sezession style. He opened the envelope and read the contents, dropping his case on the floor as he did so:

ROYAL HUNGARIAN GENDARMARIE REQUESTS AGAIN YOUR ASSISTANCE IN BISTRITZ DISTRICT STOP RENEWED ACTIVITY REQUIRES YOUR SPECIAL TALENTS AND EXPERIENCE STOP PLEASE COME IMMEDIATELY STOP ALL WILL BE EXPLAINED UPON YOUR ARRIVAL HERE STOP GÁBOR KASZA

Krafft felt a surge of excitement as he read the telegram again. Since leaving Budapest after the interview with Count Dracula Radu, he had been given only the most sporadic news, culminating in the eventual revelation that the Hungarian detectives, as he thought of them, had discovered the lair of a serial killer in and under the ruins of Count Dracula's castle in Transylvania. And yet, the killer was himself still at large. He wondered what new evidence had been uncovered.

The next morning, he cabled back to Herr Gábor his acknowledgement and his agreement to rendezvous with him again in Budapest the following day. It was at the Hotel Gellert where he renewed his acquaintance with Gábor Kasza and was now formally introduced to the beautiful Baroness von Jelna and her daughter, Ema. He recalled having seen the Baroness from across the room the last time he was there with Kálváry Istvan and Kasza.

"A pleasure, Your Highness," said Krafft, bending to kiss her hand after the introduction by Kasza.

"The pleasure is ours, I am sure," replied the Baroness as she curtseyed and bowed her head gently acknowledging his noble rank. "My daughter Ema," she said, introducing her as she also curtseyed.

Krafft noted a wan, pale slip of a girl. Quite attractive, like her mother, but appearing as though she was suffering from some disease. She did not smile, nor did she say much of anything in the ensuing hour or so that the trio spoke in the sumptuous lobby of the hotel where Krafft would be staying the night.

Kasza brought him news of the latest investigation and manhunt underway for the killer who, to Krafft's astonishment, Kasza asserted must be a vampire.

"Surely you don't really think ..." Krafft started to say as Kasza paused for a moment to let the words sink in.

"I'm afraid we do," replied the Baroness. "My daughter is the proof of it. Ema. Show him."

The girl silently lowered the high collar of her dress. At first, the Baron could see nothing, but as the collar slowly fell open, he became aware of two pink marks, perhaps three or four centimeters apart. He leaned closer to examine them. He let his finger pass over the marks. There were indentations. They had been wounds. She smiled, shyly, when he had touched her neck and he noticed the small, sharp canine teeth as well and the bluish hue to her gums and dry, cracked lips.

"Well, well, well," Krafft said. "I can see why you might think ..."

Again the Baroness interrupted. "Think, nothing my dear Baron. Istvan has seen one. I believe I have seen one myself."

Krafft sat down, silently considering the situation. As a rational man, he could not bring himself to believe in this Balkan superstition. There had to be another explanation. And yet, he assumed the marks on the young woman's neck had come from something, and the teeth? What about that? She couldn't have been born that way, could she? His distracted thoughts were interrupted again, this time by Kasza.

"Baron Krafft? I was reading one of your works and I believe you are a practitioner of the art of mesmerism, is that correct?"

"Hypnosis? Yes, we use it in therapy sometimes. We believe it can sometimes release thoughts that my colleague, Sigmund Freud, would call the subconscious. The id as opposed to the ego ..."

"Yes, exactly," Kasza continued. "Ema here has been troubled by nocturnal dreams. Powerful dreams that even drive her to sleepwalking and wandering out of her house in the night."

"I see ..."

"She has no memory of these dreams. Very little memory."

"Yes. Yes. And you would like me to hypnotize her? And see if we could get at her repressed dreams? Find out what they are?"

"Do you think you could?" Julianna asked. Her motherly concern for her daughter was evident in her quavering voice and watery eyes.

"Well, we can try. Are you willing my dear?" Krafft asked Ema. She nodded in reply.

After dinner in the main salon the four of them retired to Krafft's room upstairs. It was a large room, thankfully, with a balcony overlooking the city of Budapest. Night had fallen. Krafft lit a single candle and placed it on a small, round table. Ema was seated in a chair by the table. Krafft sat opposite her while Kasza and the Baroness were seated on a sofa by the wall in the dimness of the candlelit room, out of Ema's line of sight.

"Now, my dear. I want you to look at the candle." Ema turned and looked at it. "I want you to concentrate on the flame. Look at the flame. Look into the flame deeply. I want you to think about nothing but the flame. See the colors in the flame. See its shapes. I know you are seeing the flame now and the room is dark. Very dark. You cannot see anything but the flame now. It is beautiful. You can see how beautiful it is and its colors. And as you watch it you are starting to feel a warm feeling inside you. You are feeling very sleepy now. You are falling asleep now. In a moment, I am going to click my fingers and you will be completely asleep, but you will still hear my voice. Do you understand, Ema?"

"Yes."

"Now I am going to count to three, Ema. And when I get to the number three, I am going to snap my fingers and you will be completely relaxed and asleep. Are you ready?"

"Yes," she replied in a languid voice.

"All right, Ema. One. Two. Three," and with that, he clicked his fingers. Ema sank back in her chair now, her body going limp. Her head bowed, chin to her chest. Her eyes were closed and she began breathing heavily. Krafft had seen this many times before. So far, so good. She was a good subject. For a moment, he let her rest in the trance into which he had placed her. The room was heavy in silence. Then Krafft spoke again in a soft, low voice.

"Ema? Can you hear me?"

"Yes."

"You are very relaxed now, yes? Very peaceful. You feel very calm."

"Yes."

"You are safe here with us, Ema. Completely safe. Nothing can happen to you and you know this, don't you?"

With this, her eyes fluttered and she began to shift in her chair. Krafft was surprised, but kept his voice calm.

"What is it, Ema? You are safe with us."

She did not answer him at first. Her head started to roll first this way and then that, as if a struggle were taking place in her mind.

"Ema. I want you to think about your home in Bistritz. Your mother's home. I want you to let your mind go back to the night where your mother found you in the garden. Do you remember that, Ema?"

"Yes. I remember it."

"I want you to tell me, Ema, why you were in the garden? Why did you go from your bed into the garden?" There was a long hesitation. Then she spoke in a soft voice.

237

"Because the master came to me. He made me do it. He called to me. He is my master and I cannot disobey."

Krafft was stunned.

"Who is the master? Who?" With that, Ema opened her eyes. They were bloodshot and filled with hate. A low rumble like the growl of a dog came from her and then, in a deep masculine voice came the reply.

"I am her master, thou fool. Thy days are numbered, Baron Krafft, if thou meddle with me and this my servant!" Now Ema stood up and turned on her mother and Kasza. "Leave her to me!" the voice bellowed. "Thou cannot evade my power! I know that thee doth search for me, Gábor Kasza! Thou and thy knavish companions. Verily thou art a fool to play with me. Forsake thy mission now. Recall thy companions from their folly and I will spare thee and them an agony that will leave thee begging for death. Do not mock me. Thou art so close to death. My servants watch thee and tell me everything. Look to thy safety and abandon thy quest this night. I send thee my greetings even now!" With that, Ema began a hideous laughing and pointed at the balcony window.

With the hair on the back of his neck standing straight up, Baron Krafft turned to look in the direction Ema pointed. There, standing on the balcony silhouetted in the dim light were the unmistakable figures of three women, outside the glass French doors. Ema raised her arms in front of her, as if reaching for them, and began to take a step toward them. The Baroness leapt from the sofa and tackled her daughter. They both tumbled to the floor as Kraft watched. Ema's face was contorted in fury and deep guttural noises emanated from her as she struggled with her mother on the floor.

"Ema!" Krafft exclaimed. "You are dreaming! When I count three, you will awaken! One. Two. Three!"

And with that, Ema went limp on the floor with her eyes closed. The Baroness was still holding her arms tightly when her eyes fluttered open and a look of surprise overtook her.

"Mama?"

"Yes, darling. I'm here."

"What has happened? Why am I here?"

Krafft bent down to help the Baroness and her daughter stand. He looked again at the balcony, but the figures were gone. Kasza rushed to the doors and opened them. Krafft watched him as he helped the two women into their chairs. Kasza looked to the left and right, then approached the railing and looked down for a moment. The Baron's rooms were on the fourth floor of the hotel. He walked out on the balcony with Kasza. There was no trace of the three women.

"Gone!" said Kasza, looking Baron Krafft in the face.

Krafft also looked over the balcony. There was a sheer drop of perhaps 20-25 meters to the ground. No human being could have leapt to the ground uninjured. The nearest balcony was far to their right; well out of any reach.

"You see?" Kasza asked. "You see now what we are dealing with?"

Krafft had to admit he could not explain it. The strange voice that came from the girl, speaking in an antique form of German. The sudden appearance of human figures on the balcony and just as suddenly, their disappearance. His mind insisted there must be a rational explanation, but damned if he could think of one.

"It is perplexing, I must admit," the Baron eventually replied. He found himself looking around the vacant balcony and the grounds of the hotel as if trying to figure out a magician's trick. If it was an illusion, it was a very good one. No, he thought to himself. It couldn't be.

Chapter 52

Kálváry Istvan and Radu had returned to Bistritz on the express train from Budapest after having eventually given up on their search for the hidden lair of the female vampire they had encountered in Venice. It had been a botched encounter, Istvan knew, and he blamed the bungling Venetian authorities that had delayed their arrival at the vampire's residence until after nightfall. He would not make that mistake again, he swore. It was August 4, and a warm breeze swept through the city as Istvan visited the newly restored Polizeipräsidium for the first time since the fire.

His office was largely bare. It had not been occupied since its reconstruction, but there were a pile of unopened papers on the desk. He ordered an espresso from the orderly and sat down to see what was there. A telegram from England immediately sparked his interest and he opened it.

```
DRACULA SEEN HERE AT WHITBY STOP CLOSE FRIEND
OF WIFE MURDERED MADE UNDEAD AND THEN STAKED
STOP FLED AFTER MANHUNT HERE STOP BELIEVED
TO BE ON VESSEL MOROS BOUND FOR VARNA STOP
IN PURSUIT BY HORSE AND TRAIN STOP WILL AT-
TEMPT INTERCEPTION IN VARNA STOP SEEK YOUR
HELP IF D ESCAPES BOUND FOR BORGO STOP AR-
RIVE VIENNA 2 AUGUST AND WILL CABLE FROM
THERE STOP HARKER
```

The telegram had been sent a week earlier and there was another telegram further down in the stack from two days earlier:

```
VIENNA. ON ORIENT EXPRESS STOP ARRIVE BU-
CHAREST 3 AUGUST STOP BY HORSE TO VARNA ON
4 AUGUST STOP STAND BY STOP HARKER
```

So the Englishmen were in Varna by now, Istvan thought. They would have to time it perfectly to capture him. The ship must arrive during the day, for one thing. Otherwise, he would be impossible to catch and kill. The Count would know that as well and would surely take precautions. Perhaps he would transform himself into a giant bat and fly from the ship to a nearby shore on the Black or Aegean sea and the English would board the ship only to find their quarry had vanished. There was nothing to do but wait.

Chapter 53

Oszkár at the Golden Krone had sent a young boy as a messenger to summon Istvan to the hotel. A Dutch physician and a young woman had arrived by carriage that morning from the train station, the boy told him breathlessly. Oszkár thought Istvan should come and see him. It was something about Dracula.

Istvan put on his official coat and the high cap with the polished brass double headed eagle of a Habsburg official. He took a pair of white gloves from the nearly empty drawer. His ceremonial sabre and scabbard were buckled to his waist. He would look every inch the high, official of His Majesty, Franz Joseph, Istvan thought. It would impart just the right degree of trust and security that might be needed in his conversation with these foreigners.

He slid the sword out of the scabbard easily, as he examined himself in the mirror. It gleamed. He examined the inscription on a small flat section of the blade, just below the hilt. In Magyar, it said: *Presented to Sir Kálváry Istvan, 17th Regiment, Hungarian Hussars, for Exceptional Bravery by H.M. Franz Joseph, King of Hungary at Custozza, 1866.* Embedded in the gilded handle in red, white and green enamel was the cross of St. Stephan, his namesake. He did not often look carefully at this gift anymore but now, for a fleeting moment, he felt a small glow of pride and satisfaction at this material possession that symbolized his life-long service to king and country.

As he stepped briskly down the marble stairs to the doors and out into the dusky glow of the town just after the sun set, a red blaze of color was just now starting to change to a more purple hue which Istvan noticed as he walked the cobbled street to Oszkár's place. Empty carts and draw horses being taken back to their barns clattered by. A woman watering a flower box from her second floor window shot a glance at him as he walked by. A dog barked in the distance.

The Dutchman was seated with a pale English woman at a table across the room but facing the door into the hotel's dining room. The same room where Istvan had eaten his first meal upon arrival in Bistritz as the new district chief of police months ago. They were talking as they ate. The gentleman was speaking in a low voice to the woman between mouthfuls and occasional swigs of what looked to be the inn's finest local ale. The woman picked at her food.

"An hour they've been here," Oszkár said, nodding in their direction from behind the bar at the near end of the room. "Odd pair, I thought. Wanted to know how far it was from here to the Borgo Pass and where they could rent a landeau and horses. 'Borgo Pass', says I? 'What would you want to go there for?' I asked him. Then he pretended he couldn't understand me. Never got a straight answer from him. A lot of mumbling and all that. I says to myself, the Chief might be interested in that, what with all the going's on of this past year and all."

"No," Istvan said quietly. "You were quite right. You did the right thing."

He continued to gaze discreetly at the couple. The Dutchman had long grey hair swept back away from his forehead. His eyes were deep set. He could see the ribbon leading to the lapel pocket that probably held a pince nez. An academic, he looked like, Istvan thought. The woman was quite young and beautiful in that delicate, English way but pale, Istvan thought, even by English standards. She had dark hair and dark eyes. She wore a rather modest, plain dress with a high collar up to her chin. She was listening intently to the man who had finished his dinner and was drawing a pipe out of his trousers pocket. Now was the moment.

Istvan slowly approached the table, drawing his own pipe out of his pocket, watching to see the moment when he caught the man's eye. It was about halfway across the room when he was noticed. Istvan smiled, genially, as he continued his approach. He would cut an impressive figure to the Dutchman, he knew, in his official uniform. So typical, he imagined the Dutchman thinking. So Central European, he would be thinking.

"*Mein Herr*," Istvan ventured in a soft voice to the couple seated at their table as he arrived. "*Wilkommen in Bistritz.*" The Dutchman rose from the table and extended his hand.

"*Danke, mein Herr*," he began as they shook hands and continued in accented German. "Van Helsing is my name. This is my young associate, Mrs. Mina Harker."

"And I am Kálváry Istvan," he replied, nodding now to the young lady who remained seated. Her fragile beauty was even more striking now that he was near it. The dark irises of her eyes floated in a network of tiny red capillaries that criss crossed the sclera. Mrs. Harker's polite smile in greeting ominously displayed the same sharp, canine teeth that Ema also possessed and probably for the same reason, Istvan thought as he politely nodded to her in return.

"This may surprise you, Madam, but I am acquainted with your husband and his visit here some months ago," Istvan said in a low voice.

"I am sorry, Sir. I do not speak German." Van Helsing intervened at that moment, translating into English. Then she replied.

"Is that so?"

"Yes, and it is my understanding that he is, at this moment, attempting to intercept a member of our local gentry in Varna, is he not?" Mina Harker and Van Helsing looked at one another for a moment.

"Won't you sit down and join us?" Van Helsing said, motioning to the chair across from them. Istvan did so and placed his cap on the table. He pulled out a bag of fresh Virginia tobacco which he had acquired in Budapest before returning from his expedition to the Balkans and Italy. Van Helsing, pipe still in hand and empty, looked appreciatively at the bag.

"Please …" Istvan murmured as he gently opened the bag and then set it down in front of Van Helsing. The Dutch doctor lifted the bag to his nose and breathed in the dank, organic lushness of the blend.

"The best in the world nowadays, I think," said Van Helsing, scooping out a bowlful gratefully and handing the bag back to Istvan who did the same. In a few minutes, their corner of the inn's dining room exuded the fragrance of the tobacco while the two men continued making small talk, each sizing up the other. Mina Harker sat silently but attentively. Eventually, the talk rounded to the business at hand.

"And so, *mein Gnädiger Herr*, I suspect that our encounter here is not by chance." Van Helsing began.

"No. The case of our Lord, Count Dracula, has consumed me practically since my arrival in this town many months ago." Istvan briefly recounted his involvement in the case culminating in the discovery of the foul vaults of the ruined castle and the manhunt that then ensued in which he was involved.

"You see, we are searching for a needle in the haystack, *Herr Doktor*, and your colleague's telegram advising us that the Count has been actually seen and chased to a specific place is excellent news for us. We must be very careful not to lose track of his whereabouts now."

Van Helsing had been quietly smoking during Istvan's explanation, but his intense gaze had never left Istvan's face.

"Unfortunately, as we have crossed Europe, we have not been able to ensure that the progress of our friends with Mr. Harker has been as we had planned it in London, before disembarking. This is also wonderful news, of a kind, that you bring to us, Herr Kálváry. We separated from them at Budapest."

"And what is this plan you spoke of?" Istvan inquired.

"We are to place ourselves at the Borgo Pass to intercept Count Dracula and his party should he evade capture and death by our colleagues in Varna and attempt to return to his castle, as he must to recapture the earth of his burial place to seed new hellish sanctuaries for him and his kind."

With that, Istvan sat bolt upright in his chair with surprise.

"But surely ... you and this woman alone do not imagine that you could seriously hope to stop this villain should he come your way"? Istvan imagined the man and this pale sickly woman arrayed against a band of armed Roma carrying or, if it were night, led by the most powerful vampire in the world. It was preposterous. They would be cut down in a moment, or worse.

"I am not afraid to give my life to this cause," Van Helsing exclaimed. Istvan carefully regarded the man. Perhaps a little eccentric, he thought. Perhaps he was not in his right mind?

"It is not just your life, Herr Van Helsing," Istvan replied. "There are fates worse than death and the monster we are confronting is the embodiment of transcendental evil unknown to most of mankind."

"I know very well what we are confronting." Van Helsing was becoming strident now in his defense of the plan this group of Englishmen had concocted some 2,000 kilometers away, apparently with this Dutch doctor's concurrence. Istvan had not met many Englishmen or Dutchmen in his life, but from what little he knew about them, this crackpot scheme seemed typical.

"Why did you not contact us?"

"We didn't think anyone here would believe what we were describing," Van Helsing replied earnestly.

"Here? In Bistritz? Of all places on earth ..."

"Yes, yes," Van Helsing replied, "but we imagined educated officials here would scoff at the idea of vampires."

"Didn't Jonathan Harker tell you about us?"

"No, he didn't."

Istvan was stunned. "What did he tell you about his escape?"

"He said he had escaped the castle through a window and taken refuge in a monastery where he was stricken with a brain fever that lasted for many weeks. He never mentioned anything about you."

Istvan eyed the young lady to Van Helsing's right, calmly sipping water from a glass and watching him. He wondered if she were possessed by Dracula, as Ema was, and whether whatever he said to Van Helsing within her hearing would be reported directly to the Count, even if she did not understand German. Deciding discretion was the best path, he decided to invite the good doctor outdoors for a private chat.

"I say, Herr Doktor, I think the air is getting a bit thick with our smoke in here. Why don't we take it outside? What are you smoking these days, if I may ask?" Istvan rose from the table and, after a moment's awkward hesitation, Van Helsing rose as well, took his leave from Mrs. Harker and ambled out the door into the night air.

◎ ◎ ◎

"A Turkish blend is my choice these days," Van Helsing said once they reached the cobblestone street. He passed the pouch of tobacco to Istvan who examined it carefully. He knew the brand. Laferme. Dresden. They sold it in Budapest, but he had not seen the Turkish brand in Bistritz since he had moved here. He plunged his pipe into the bag with a grunt of approval. One of two great tobaccos from that city, the other being Patras whose cigarettes were widely sold as far away as Paris.

Out in the street it was an August, summer's evening with a lingering twilight dusk. Lamps were being lit out in the street where they were standing. A heavy leiterwagen rolled by as they watched, followed by some young boys on foot; probably the driver's sons. Yet long dark shadows cast themselves across the cobblestones as they slowly walked in the most ancient quarter of the city. There was a sound of a dog barking. Meat was cooking somewhere from up above them in the kitchen of a pension, or was it from a courtyard?

"I want to tell you something, Herr Doktor," Istvan began. "This monster you and your lady plan to intercept at the Borgo Pass will require much reinforcement. Together we can have the chance to end almost 400 years of oppression and death. Death in the most hideous of circumstances. In dank cellars, chained to a wall. In cages of death. Ravished for weeks and months by bloodsucking undead until their victims die or worse. Every century or so, the arch-vampire who lives here will make another. Usually a woman. A beautiful woman, like your Mrs. Harker. Another companion to amuse him in another city in Europe or the East.

"Three of them live on here, in Transylvania, and they have been active since their Master has been gone. They do their Master's bidding, somehow hearing from him in their minds. Knowing what he wants them to do. They are connected with him in some supernatural, un-dead way. If you and Mrs. Harker are out in the wild, in that place alone, without help, you will die. They will kill you long before the wheels of the Master's calèche will be thundering up the road to the Borgo Pass. You cannot be out there after sunset and there is nowhere nearby to stay except a monastery a few kilometers away. It is suicide. Believe me, mein Herr, I have been there."

"I am not so arrogant as you may think," Van Helsing said quietly as they turned the corner on to a broad boulevard with many street lamps lit. "I had no way in England to imagine the kind of country where this Borgo Pass would be found. We were not given to understand, by Mr. Harker, that there would be the possibility of some assistance from the local authorities, such as yourself."

"Yes, a curious omission to me as well," Istvan replied. "May I rely upon your discretion as a gentleman about what I will reveal to you? Something that occurs to me now that is best left unsaid within the hearing of Mrs. Harker?"

"Yes, of course."

"When he was here, of course, Mr. Harker was not yet married to your companion, Mina Murray. That was her name before, wasn't it?"

"Indeed it was. I met her in Whitby before the death of her best friend, Lucy Westenra and she was not yet married to Mr. Harker. What of it?"

"Let me just say while he was imprisoned at the castle of Lord Dracula, he came into contact with a certain Gypsy girl who served the Count out of terror, who was also, essentially, a prisoner. Their departure from the castle came about when forces under my command and, with the permission of the actual present-day owner of the ruins, were going to search it. The fiend who we now seek to destroy fled this ruin before we could capture him and, for reasons not known to us, before killing Mr. Harker, the girl and another prisoner he held in the dungeons below the castle." Van Helsing listened with interest as they walked the now darkened streets of Bistritz, nodding and occasionally acknowledging the points made by Istvan with small grunts of understanding.

"It became apparent to us in questioning the girl, whose Roma name was Natália, that there was a bond between her and Mr. Harker, which was not surprising given the common horrors they had both endured. Nonetheless, in the days and weeks following their release, we became aware of the fact that their attachment was not merely a spiritual bond, but, to put it delicately, a physical one as well. Mr. Harker did not escape the castle out of some window and walking along some precarious ledge. Had he been able to do so, I can assure you, given the conditions he was under, he would have done so long before he did. He did not have brain fever. He did not lay in a monastery under the care of the sisters. You see?"

Van Helsing took a match from his pocket and poked around the bowl of his pipe with the distal end, re-lit the bowl and took another few pulls of smoke before replying.

"And so, what you are saying is that Mr. Harker's affair with this Roma woman while engaged to Miss Murray in England was a source of embarrassment to him that he has obscured with us, thinking that there would be no means by which we would ever discover the truth?"

"I suppose that, yes. In this country, a relationship between a gentleman and a colored woman of this type is not unknown, but never public."

"Yes, in England too. I see what you mean. Where is this woman now?" Van Helsing asked.

"She left Bistritz with him, actually, and we have heard nothing of her since then. Frankly, we were more concerned with capturing Count Dracula and lost track of her after we completed our inquiries with her and Mr. Harker. Perhaps she is in England?"

At that moment, they passed a dark side street in the circular progress they were making back to the Golden Krone. As he glanced into the gloom, Istvan thought he detected something moving. A dark shape. Two red dots reflected the gaslight back to him. He stopped and gazed more intently down the lane. After taking a couple of steps, Van Helsing turned and looked at Istvan in surprise. There were more dark shapes and more red flashes of what Istvan now took to be the retinas of some animals in the darkness who were now moving and coming at them with great speed.

Three of them. There was a deep rumbling, growling sound as these canine beasts came into sight, their hair standing on end of their necks, fangs bared and at full gallop.

In an instant, they were upon them. One lunged for Istvan's throat, while a second knocked Van Helsing to the ground. Istvan fought off the black and grey wolf but his arm was bitten as the jaws of the beast clamped shut. He felt a pain in his calf as another one bit him and began to shake his head to tear the flesh. With a supreme effort, he reached for his saber and wrenched it out of the scabbard. The pain in his leg was excruciating but he managed to keep his balance while he brought the blade down with force against the neck of the beast. With one heavy swing, he severed the head while the teeth of the animal were still embedded. The second wolf, sensing the danger, now backed off and in cowardly fashion retreated back down the dark street. The third released Van Helsing's arm, and likewise quickly fled as Istvan advanced, saber in hand.

It had all transpired in less than a minute and the commotion had roused the inhabitants of the neighborhood. As Van Helsing rose to his feet, bleeding profusely from the wound in his arm, Istvan became aware of a mocking laughter from above. He looked up and there, on the roof of one of the ancient townhouses, was the figure of a woman, swaying in the darkness, a hand covering her mouth and the other arm pointing at them below. She was clearly one of them, Istvan knew in an instant. Laughing at their brush with death below. She had summoned these wolves from the forests near the city and set them on him and Van Helsing. The doctor looked up and saw her too. The noise of approaching townsfolk evidently prompted her to turn and walk down the sloping roof on the opposite side so that she quickly disappeared into the night.

Chapter 54

Carlos was a traditional Roma in some ways. In others, he was quite exceptional, Nathalie thought. Practical. An improviser. Adaptable to his circumstances and surroundings in an almost supernatural way. A man who could blend into any society. He learned foreign languages with speed and perfection and knew four of them besides the tribal tongue from Transylvania where he had been born and his own tribal *Caló* from Spain where he had grown up with his father. What were the odds that she would cross paths with another one of her kind from the dreadful country of their shared birth. His mother was a Sinti and lived in the Forest of Tinovul Mohos and was dying.

Then there was the fact he was an even better lover than Jonathan Harker had been. He was rougher and brazen, sometimes delighting in ambushing her and demanding her compliance. Of course, in the end, she complied and served him completely. He could be a dominating and domineering lover at times, but increasingly saw that she was pleasured to her heart's content. So his demand that she come with him back to Transylvania and the Forest to help him with his mother's death and funeral was something she had to accept, to her dismay.

"It will only be for a little while. I don't like it there either, my love. It's my mother. I have to be there for her at the end of her life. And you are my woman now. You must be my woman and be with me at this moment. I will need you. Then, we will go and probably never return again. My mother is the only one left in my family there." He was sitting on the end of the bed, his brown naked body wrapped only in a white bed-sheet and only slightly. His sinewy, brown, hairy legs stuck out with his broad, strong feet. He had a hard, almost Slavic physique. She was nearly as tall as he was, but packed into his frame was all muscle and bone.

Natália ran a pearl handled comb through her dark hair as she sat naked with a silk robe wrapped around her before a mirror. This was her world that she had created for herself. A colorful room with a few feminine luxuries she would never do without again. A full sized mirror. A vanity bench. The combs and brushes. Her firm youthful breasts arose and fell through the opening in her robe as she combed, knowing she risked igniting an irresistible desire in him.

"You cannot understand what that place means to me. Dislike is not the world I would use for the Forest. And that's not the worst of it. That castle. The road to that castle. The Borgo Pass. I would rather walk into Hell itself than go back there."

He watched her from the end of the bed with sympathetic, wide brown eyes, saying nothing. Hearing her out. He had by now heard the story. They had talked about it. The tribe in the Forest was not his tribe. It was his mother's tribe. His tribe was the Calé from the Basque country of Spain.

He had heard the legends before, of course. His own people believed in vampires as a matter of course, along with the Goddess Kali. And his mother's tribe, the Sinti, had learned after a century of depredations, that there was one nearby. They assumed, however, that it was like this all over the world. They assumed everybody had a sort of regional vampire that the living would have to beware. The Sinti and to some extent the Calé thought that vampires were part of the natural order of things, to be taken for granted.

"You will be with me now, my Love. Back there, in that mess, you had no one you could trust. No man to rely on. This time I will be there with you and it will be very different from the last. I will protect you."

"Protect me? From what? The wives of the disciple of Satan? That's what he is, you know. Yes. I learned this from the detectives later. He is said to have gone to a mystical school of black magic, taught by Satan himself.

Sholomance. This one is as wicked as Lucifer. You cannot protect me from him. He will know me. He will find me. I am afraid of him, Carlos. Do not ask me to go with you."

It went on like this for days, but gradually he broke down her resistance. She had fallen for him hard. If anything happened to him, if he should disappear she would never forgive herself. And besides, Dracula had been driven out of Transylvania, hadn't he? She had been there when he fled and the police had swarmed over the castle. No, they had fled. All of them, surely. They would be there a few days, a week or two at the most, and then never return. She could bear it, she decided. She would bear it. For him. She saw the glint of pride and love in his eye when she finally gave in. Gave in to his will and to his desires. And so they went.

They had horses. Carlos saddled two. They were Roma horses, chestnut brown with their distinctive black and white manes, their feathering and flowing tails. These beautiful animals were the result of centuries of breeding by the Roma. A combination of strength and beauty was in these two, as in all Romani horses. The saddles were a showpiece of Romani leathercraft, with elegant carvings, pockets, pouches, pommels and other pieces that were secret, as so often smuggling was required. Carlos looked like a highwayman, Natália thought as he sat his horse, watching her swing up into the saddle.

It was high summer and the days were long at this latitude. They set off on the old highway from Amsterdam to Cologne, then down the Rhine highway to Freiburg and Nuremburg. After that, they would return to Austria-Hungary through Linz, Vienna, Budapest and then Bistritz. It would take them almost two weeks to get to the Forest. They would live by their wits in the meantime, as the Roma always did.

Chapter 55

Kasza was sitting with Baron Krafft in the hotel lobby of the Gellert when a bellman brought a telegram for him on a silver plate. It was mid-morning, and they were drinking tea and eating some pastry. He opened the envelope and read the telegraph. It was from Istvan.

WORD FROM ENGLAND. STOP. COUNT SAID TO BE IN FLIGHT. STOP. HARKER AND OTHERS PURSUING. STOP. SEEK TO INTERCEPT HIS ARRIVAL IN VARNA BY SHIP. STOP. NEED YOU TO RETURN TO CONFRONT HIM IF NEED BE AT BORGO. STOP. KÁLVÁRY ISTVAN.

Kasza handed it to Krafft. Krafft read the lines, then handed it back in silence. Kasza spoke first.

"Come with me," Kasza said. "You know this case. You're a scientific man. A medical doctor. You know what we're dealing with. No other man of your learning would believe me if I told them what we have both seen and know to be the truth."

Kasza watched as Krafft thought about it. What good would it do his research and his practice of psychiatry, he was probably wondering? Nothing that he could imagine. What they were dealing with was off the medical and scientific charts. It was by definition supernatural. One of a kind or, at least, a very rare psyche Krafft would most certainly never encounter again in his entire career. No, it would be sheer curiosity that decided him, Kasza thought. Men like him were preternaturally curious. They couldn't help themselves. To his quiet delight, Krafft didn't disappoint him and endorsed Kasza's ever more sensitive detective's intuition.

"All right. If I wouldn't be in the way."

"Don't give it a thought, my Lord," Kasza replied, sipping the last of his tea as he rose. The massive, fluted, marble columns surrounded the vast open area where they had been sitting. The high ceilings and plush carpets, antique furniture, soft chairs and couches, chandeliers and high windows gave the opulent hotel its popularity among both foreign and domestic guests.

"The train we want leaves for Bistritz at 13:50. I will meet you back here in an hour, if that will be convenient?" Kasza said softly to the Viennese doctor, then turned to return to his room up the wide staircase.

Chapter 56

"That was not the boldest attempt on my life, Herr Doktor," said Istvan when they were back at the Golden Krone. "The monster once almost killed me at an Abbey not far from here. The Holy Mother at the Abbey saved me. She showed him a cross she wears around her neck. A silver relic, she told me later." Istvan took a snifter of cognac at the bar. His leg throbbed from the savage bite of one of the wolves and his chest burned with pain where another one of the vicious dogs had smashed into him with its paws.

Oszkár came out from the kitchen where he had been supervising the closure and clean up. The bartender who had served the two men had quietly passed the word to his master, who now arrived with a worried look at his friend, Istvan.

"What was it?" Oszkár asked in a hushed voice.

"Wolves. Three of them."

"Here? In Bistritz?" Oszkár was astonished, then worried again.

"How bad did they get you?"

Istvan seemed a bit embarrassed. He hadn't actually taken a good look at the wounds. Oszkár came round the bar and squatted down at Istvan's knee and rolled up the trousers of his uniform which were stained red with blood. Then he got to the wounds. Istvan winced as he touched first one wound, then another.

"It's getting all black and blue and you've got some puncture wounds here, my Lord. You don't want them to get infected. Bloody bastards. Come with me!" Istvan knocked back the cognac and turned to Van Helsing.

"What about you?"

"I'm fine, exept my arm." There were puncture marks and red stain on Van Helsing's tweed jacket.

"The both of you, then ..." Oszkár said with barely a glance at the Dutchman.

Oszkár was one of those people whose life was spent in hospitality. He was an improviser. Always prepared for almost anything that could go wrong, he was once again the master of the moment. Before long, he had Istvan sitting on a long, wooden table used during the day as a work space to cut meat, vegetables, and generally spread out instruments and foods. His wife, Nadia, was immediately enlisted to do the necessary. There seemed to be no reason to call for the surgeon in town and after that, what the innkeeper was doing was about all you could ask for in Bistritz for wounds like this. In another hour, both Istvan and Van Helsing were once again sitting at the bar in the pub off the dining room with bandages on their cleaned wounds.

"Where is Mrs. Harker?" Istvan wondered aloud. Her seat at the table where he had first met her was empty.

"Probably upstairs," Van Helsing replied. Istvan instantly felt a deep unease. This semi-possessed woman who had ventured into the land of the most ancient and powerful vampires in the world had no chance against the charms of the one he had just seen in the streets. She was present. In the city. And she had just been seen nearby. By him.

"Let's find her. She should not be left alone," Istvan said with some urgency. Van Helsing's face went immediately taut when he sensed Istvan's anxiety and the ominous tone of his voice.

"Follow me," Van Helsing said as started toward the lobby stairs. In a few moments, they were in the narrow hallway of the second foor. There were doors on both sides of the hallway to about a half dozen rooms on this floor. Dull, glowing gaslights dimly lit the hallway, with its dark red carpet. The noise from the inn downstairs became muffled as they padded along. The room on the left was silent. Now they came upon the next door, on the right.

"This is mine. The next one is hers," Van Helsing whispered. He pointed across the hall. On the left side. As they approached, at first Istvan heard nothing. Then he saw Van Helsing's face freeze and his finger moved to his lips, signaling to be very quiet. What he heard made his heart stop. There were two female voices speaking in the room. He listened intently to be sure. Intuitively, he knew who would be inside. He took out a large silver cross that he now carried at all times in his pocket.

"Go get Oszkár. Have him bring an extra key to this room," Istvan whispered quietly in Van Helsing's ear. Van Helsing nodded and then darted off quickly down the hall and out of sight, down the stairs.

Istvan returned his concentration to the talking going on inside the room. He couldn't make out what they were saying, or even what language they were saying it in. Their voices began to fall off. Istvan quietly pressed his ear against the door. Nothing. Then there was a very loud noise in his ear like a bolt being shot and the door flew open. He was face to face with the vampire Anastázia and in his shock, he dropped the silver cross on the floor.

Her long, dark hair with hazel, green eyes blood shot and menacing surveyed him for a just moment. Then her gaze went to the cross on the floor at his feet. A mocking look of hurt and disgust flickered across her face. She looked away from it and back at Istvan. Her eyes were hypnotic and her beauty, but for the pale face splashed with blood and the prominent, white fangs was arresting in every way.

"So. You?"

Her left arm and hand shot out to his neck and he felt her sharp, strong fingernails dig into his flesh. She muscled him backwards like a child in the hands of an angry mother until his back slammed up against the wall, knocking the wind out of him with the force. Her mouth was open now and he could see the teeth and red, pointed tongue, but there were noises now, coming up the stairs. It was Oszkár and Abraham Van Helsing. They were shouting something at them.

In a deep voice and perfect Magyar, Anastázia spoke to him. "I could kill you now, Kálváry Istvan." She glanced at the figures coming down the hall. She seemed to decide something and then her gaze was upon him again and the world slowed down. She said nothing, but he could hear her voice in his mind.

You are known to our kind now. In all the world your name is known to us. You will die by our hand, Istvan. If not mine, one of us. I am his oldest bride and lover. We have walked for centuries together. Do you think you can defeat us? Give up this quest. You alone can stop this. Call your men off and you will be left alone, even now, as a sign of respect from all of us for what you have done. We will make you rich beyond your wildest dreams. Your loved ones will be left in peace. And I will love you like you have never known.

With this, she pulled him to her. He gazed into her eyes. The thoughts and emotions of this ancient queen welled up in his head irresistibly. She held his head in her two powerful hands and then she kissed him. He felt her soft, thick lips as they pressed against his. Her soft body and pendulant breasts were against him. He could not help himself. He felt his eyes close and for a moment, all he could see in his mind's eye was her enormous, hazel eyes.

Then he was with her in a dark bedroom somewhere. There was an enormous bed and candelabras with candles were placed around the dimly lit room. Heavy, dark red tapestries hung over windows. He lay naked on his back and she was climbing on him like a predatory leopard. Her sensual beauty consumed him with lust, but he was bound to the bed, hand and foot. Her hands kneaded the muscles in his aching calves and thighs as she neared him. He felt himself aroused and saw that he was. She opened her mouth and slowly engulfed him. He felt a shudder of helpless desire watching her. Her dark hair now spread over his belly and hips as she worked him to a peak and then relented again and again. She seemed to know just the moment when his desire was about to burst, retreating and advancing and retreating again.

A film of perspiration covered his body. He writhed and pulled against the restraints, but he was held fast and helpless against her ministrations.

He felt ashamed at his now uncontrollable desire for her. His mind screamed with greedy thoughts of consummation and realized he was screaming out loud. His voice was bellowing when suddenly, he was in the hallway with her, fully clothed, standing up.

She released him and whirled into the room in a rustle of black. Istvan could see from the dark hallway through the open door another woman, pale and forlorn, standing transfixed in the dark. There was a large open window at the far end of the room. In an instant, the vampire began to transform into a mass of floating blackness while her altered form spilled out of the window, formed into a large black bat and was then lost in the outer darkness before Istvan's very eyes.

Oszkár barrelled into the room at that moment, having missed the vampire's exit out the window. Van Helsing moved to help Istvan to his feet from where he had fallen when she let him go. They looked at each other for a moment and then both of them said the same word at once:

"Mina."

Oszkár was closing the windows and Mina Harker was now sitting on the edge of the bed, calmly. Two blood holes punctuated her slender neck with a smear of blood. She seemed weak and almost sick, in a daze of confusion and anxiety. She caught a look at Van Helsing's face.

"What is it?" she asked.

Like a child with a face smeared with ice cream, unable to understand how an adult knew what she had just eaten, Mina seemed confused. Istvan was sure he knew what had been happening in this room only moments before they arrived. He sat down heavily in a chair in the room as Van Helsing tended to her, dabbing her neck with his handkerchief. Every bone in his body now ached.

They were losing, Istvan mused. They were still losing the game to this diabolical spirit who possessed these women and so many others. He was still alive. They all were. Despite everything they had done, it had been futile. Istvan knew now that these Satanical beasts had not survived the centuries with faint hearts and half-measures. How could they defeat such a quartet of monsters as these, he wondered?

They would have to find where they slept if they wanted to kill them all. How in the world would they do it? In this mountainous, rugged province of a vast Empire, they could be anywhere. And yet, perhaps there was a key. He decided to consult Van Helsing about it.

Chapter 57

Carlos and Natália had been riding for a week when they came to Freiburg, in the heart of the Schwarzwald in the Duchy of Baden in Germany. The Black Forest was Roma territory and, indeed, there were Roma in camps near the outskirts of Freiburg and at various twists and turns in the road through the Black Forest. Most were from other tribes, but deep in the woods when they pulled into a camp for the evening, they came across one of their own. It was Lajos from the Sinti tribe in the Forest.

Lajos had always wanted her, Natália knew. When she had been a village girl, keeping her father's house, he had stopped to talk with her and flirted with her in his cocksure, Roma way. He was handsome and young, like her, but with a bold personality. Now he recognized her. His pleasure at seeing her was quickly staunched when he realized she was with Carlos. Carlos made a mental note to ask Natália about the attitude of the young Lajos.

"What news from the Forest?" Carlos asked him. Lajos turned to face him with a cool look, neither provocative nor passive.

"Who wants to know?" Lajos replied calmly. Carlos thought the man was insolent but immediately decided to let it pass. They were not on familiar ground. They were guests here and who knew what kind of relationship Lajos might have with this local tribe; their hosts.

"Carlos", he said as he extended his hand. After the briefest of awkward moments, Lajos took the hand. As they eyed each other with a slight wariness, Carlos now inquired.

"And you?"

"Lajos. I knew her before," he replied, nodding in Natália's direction. Carlos looked at Natália who nodded, confirming what he said.

"I see."

"Where are you bound?" Lajos asked.

"To the Forest. I have some business there."

"The village was deserted for a while after the Master left, but now the Sinti have come back to the Forest. I'm on my way back. Would you mind if I joined you tomorrow?"

The young man's brashness and spirit appealed to Carlos. He was beginning to remind him of himself about ten years ago and anyway, it would be rude to say no. He looked over at Natália who betrayed no inclination one way or the other.

"All right." Carlos said. "Why not? Now, what news?"

"Like I said, our people are coming back. The smuggling trade is better than ever. The castle is deserted again. The police and the army were bivouacked there for awhile, but nobody liked it. Nothing happened and they became bored and scared. Wolves. Things moving around at night that they couldn't see. Some troopers went missing. You know how it goes," Lajos was smiling as he said the last of it. He knew why people went missing in that area of the world, at least most of the time.

"So one day, they just cleared out and left a token guard, but they always cleared out at sunset. Spooked. The wolves would have overwhelmed them at night and anyway, they were afraid. Before you know it, nobody was guarding it anymore. Just like it was. Just like it will always be. The lady Narcisa was the first of them to visit us in the village again. She said the Master was coming back and we must be ready."

"What did she mean, ready? Ready for what?"

"Ready to help the Master in whatever he wants. Like we always have done for him."

"You would help him?" Carlos asked.

"Why not? We have a choice, we Sinti. We can help the townspeople and farmers or we can side with our Lord and Master. The townspeople and farmers hate us. They cheat us, murder us, rape our women and drive us away with guns and police. The Master welcomes us. He protects us from them. He gives us land and all he asks is that we serve him every so often when he asks. Which would you choose?"

"He murdered my father! He murdered my uncle! He kept me a prisoner and I had to serve him and his wives for months," Natália answered with some vehemence. Lajos regarded her silently for a moment.

"Your father and your uncle betrayed the Master. Your father would have murdered me. Lord Dracula has never molested the Sinti, except for those two. Yes, I can imagine how you feel, but they were disloyal."

In the next few minutes, Lajos explained what had happened on the road to Vatra Dornei and the exposure of one of the undead to the light of day. He told them about the cover-up her father and her uncle had contrived and the near mutiny of the other Sinti when they attempted to coerce them into the betrayal. Carlos and Natália listened in silence.

"Yes, our Lord can be brutal in his ways but you know what he is. He needs us and we need him. Why do we camp here in the Schwarzwald with our kith and kin? Because no inn or hotel in Europe would let our dark skin touch their pillows. Because no tavern would allow our tongues to touch their silverware. They act as if we were diseased and carry the plague. We are shunned everywhere we go. In Hungary, we have been slaves for centuries. We have been massacred, burned, spit upon and chased, all because of our dark skin. They make us wander and then blame us for our shiftlessness. How brutal are these white men? What do we care if Dracula and his women prey on them? They prey on us.

Natália could see Carlos nodding his head as they listened. It was the truth. The Roma had only themselves and precious little else. When they came across a village or town that tolerated their camps, they made a little money sharpening tools or blacksmithing or cooking or picking orchards. All too soon, though, some of the townsfolk aroused others to hatred and the tribe would have to move on. Down the road they would go in their colored wagons with their beautiful horses. This was their way of life. Always moving with no place of their own. Lord Dracula changed that. The Sinti had a place now. One tribe out of all the tribes had a place they could call their own where their children could play and where they could live in peace. Where they could hunt and fish. Even the wolves left them alone.

"The word has been passed. He is coming back. He has sent word to us and summoned us. We must help him now as he has helped us in the past. He will be grateful."

This was the dreadful world Natália had left. The choices were always filled with misgivings and danger. It seemed to her, as she sat and listened to Carlos and Lajos talk by the campfire, that they were trading one slavery for another. She had liked Amsterdam where she had been free and easy. She was colored but the Dutch didn't seem to mind too much.

Lajos had given her disturbing news about her father that she hadn't known but always suspected. He had been murdered for reasons she had never understood. Now she did. Her father and her uncle had dared to disobey the Master and had suffered his retribution. Her own slavery had resulted from their treason. As she curled up with Carlos under his blankets under the stars, she wondered why the Master had not killed her, as he had killed her father and her uncle. It was a confusing world. A dark world. All she knew was that she dreaded going back there and would be glad to leave it all behind. Forever.

Chapter 58

It was breakfast. Oszkár himself served them black Hungarian bread and jam with Oszkár's strong tea at a table in the inner courtyard of the inn he reserved for his special guests and friends. It was quiet and sun drenched. Window boxes of flowers on the upper floors bloomed. A Wallachian peasant girl who worked there as a housekeeper opened a balcony door on an upper floor to shake out a carpet. Another elderly servant was sweeping the granite tiles at the far end of the garden.

Istvan had collapsed into a deep sleep in one of the spare bedrooms Oszkár saved for him after the ordeal they had been through. The Golden Krone had now become a sort of de facto headquarters for the resistance to the vampires that Oszkár knew had plagued the region from time immemorial.

Now it was time to be rid of them, Oszkár had concluded. There would never be a chance like this again. The windows of the inn were now festooned with garlic without exception. Crucifixes and images of the Virgin Mary were nailed to windows and doors, not merely on the outside, but inside as well. In hallways, stairwells, the public rooms and lobbys, the image of Christ and icons were placed to dispel the Undead who might seek to visit again. And Oszkár had put the word out through his staff and the patrons of the restaurant and pub. Where did these ladies of the night sleep? Who was giving them aid and comfort?

This very subject was at the heart of a discussion Istvan was having with Van Helsing that morning in the courtyard of Oszkár's inn.

"There are hundreds of farms and hamlets in these mountains," Istvan was saying as one of the servant girls poured orange juice into crystal goblets. It was the time of year when this delicacy from Greece and Palestine was available. Van Helsing sipped it appreciatively and then replied.

"Yes, but you must remember. The vampires must always rest in the soil of the ground in which they were interred to regain their powers. Otherwise, they become weak and helpless in time. Their retreat to darkness merely saves them from extinction."

Istvan thought about this for a while in silence. His detective's mind began to work. The Gypsies, as he thought of them. Those treacherous rascals. All their digging and boxes and lieter-wagens. Of course. They were always making new havens for these fiends. They were his accomplices, enabling this monster and his hellish wives to prey upon the innocents who lived in terror and dread. Damn them. Just then, Oszkár entered the courtyard, wiping his hands on a towel, his white apron stained with food.

"Look who's here, my Lord," he exclaimed, sweeping one of his arms in the direction of Kasza and Baron Krafft who were coming through the archway into the courtyard. Van Helsing rose from the table, dabbing at his mouth with a napkin. Istvan likewise arose.

"Kasza! My Lord!" Istvan exclaimed, smiling broadly at the Baron whom he had not expected. "I'm delighted! You have come in the nick of time. Let me introduce you to Herr Doktor Abraham Van Helsing, from Amsterdam." Kasza stepped forward and shook hands. Krafft, however, was visibly excited, gripping his hand with both of his own.

"Doktor Van Helsing? An honor! I have read your works on anemia, leukemia and diseases of the blood. Fascinating studies. My congratulations to you, sir."

"No, the honor is mine," Van Helsing replied, visibly pleased to be reminded of happier times and to receive the compliments of another member of the medical profession. "Your works on psychiatry and sexuality are widely read in The Netherlands and, I'm sure, in all Europe. I have a copy of your book in my study. A pleasure, indeed, to meet you, sir." While the two scholars continued to exchange pleasantries, Istvan took Kasza aside.

"Go to Radu. Have him muster a squadron of our men. Twenty or twenty-five should do it. We ride for the Forest of Mohos Tinovul tomorrow. You muster another squadron. You will ride with us and then make camp at the Borgo Pass." He explained quickly what had transpired yesterday evening upon the arrival of Van Helsing and the Englishwoman to Kasza's mounting interest.

"Damn it that there is no telegraph up there. Have a couple of mounted men wait at the telegraph office in Bistritz for any communication from Harker to me. Tell them to fly with any information at all the moment it comes in. Without fail, understand? Have several of them, if need be, in case another telegram comes in after the first rider has left. I want every telegram sent by Harker brought to me immediately."

"Yes, vezér," Kasza replied.

"Good. And when we go, you will take Van Helsing and the Englishwoman with you. Radu and I will go on to the camp and make some inquiries there. We must find out where these three wives are hiding and kill them once and for all, but we must be ready for their master too."

By the time Istvan arrived at the Polizeipräsidium, there was a telegram awaiting him already:

VESSEL MOROS LATE ARRIVING IN VARNA STOP SUSPECT MISCHIEF BUT CANNOT BE CERTAIN YET STOP BEWARE ARRIVAL BY COUNT SEEKING REFUGE AT CASTLE AND THEREABOUTS STOP WIFE AND DUTCH COLLEAGUE VAN HELSING ARRIVING BISTRITZ WILL NEED YOUR HELP STOP HARKER.

The game was indeed afoot. All signs pointed to a return of the Count to his old homeland where century after century he had hidden and menaced the Turks, the Hungarians, the Wallachians, Saxons and everyone else. *Everyone except the Gypsies*, Istvan thought. *The Gypsies never seemed to run from him. Well, we will see about them.*

Chapter 59

Natália, Carlos and Lajos rode into the Forest and the Sinti village at dusk and were met with unconcealed enthusiasm by the Sinti tribe, especially Lajos. A new hetman was a particularly brutal looking elder by the name of Ilje. He had shoulder length black hair and dark eyes. His face was pock-marked with acne scars and a long scar that slanted across his left cheek, probably from a knife fight. A long black mustache snaked around the corners of his mouth and down to his chin. He was a heavy man with a large belly and an insolent swagger as he approached them in greeting, a gold tooth glinting in the evening sun as he smiled.

Natália remembered Ilje. He had been an accomplished smuggler, never working in the trades the Roma peddled to the villagers and farmers. Instead, he guided wagon trains of illicit cargo, usually from Turkish merchants in Constantinople, over the borders between Hungary and Wallachia, taking a cut of the goods for himself but saving his clients the taxes they would have had to pay for legal goods. But he also smuggled opium into the Empire as well, which was even more lucrative. Ilje was often away from the village with his men, whom he kept busy in "the trade" as it was known amongst the tribe. Formerly, he had been required to share some of his booty with Natália's uncle when he had been alive and hetman. Now, she learned, he kept it all to himself.

"So? You are coming home, eh, Natália?" the hetman began amiably, but in a mildly mocking tone. "We thought we would never see you again when your uncle took you away. By the way, where is he? Your uncle? Is he coming back too?"

"I don't know," Natália replied. "I don't know what happened to him after he took me to the castle."

"Is that what he did, now, is it?" the hetman replied, with some interest. "We had all wondered what became of him. He returned for a couple of days, and then he just disappeared. Never heard of him since. We figured he must have fled for some other part of Europe."

Natália observed Lajos shifting on his feet uncomfortably. He looked away from her when she caught his eye. He knew something about this, Natália concluded. He hadn't told her everything. Carlos asked about his mother, only to find out that she had died a week earlier and had been cremated in the Roma way. Her ashes had been duly collected in a clay urn, which the hetman presented to Carlos with his sympathies.

"She had some things that I have for you," said Ilje. He brought them to his house. It was one of the few wooden constructions in the village, a sign of his relative wealth from the trade. Inside were brightly painted furnishings, a low couch, a table and chairs. They could smell meat cooking with onions and garlic in the kitchen in the rear of the house. "Sit down, sit down …" the hetman beckoned, motioning them to the couch. In a moment, he disappeared and then returned with a medium sized chest. It had carvings on it and was painted many colors. It was locked and it was heavy.

"We found this," said Ilje, handing Carlos a key. Carlos looked at it for a moment.

"Open it!" Natália exclaimed. Ilje held up a hand.

"I will leave you in private," he said and then left the room.

Carlos fit the key into the lock and turned it. He felt the tumblers unlatch the cover. He removed the key and opened the box. Lying on top of the contents of the box was what appeared to be a jeweled dagger resting on a black scarf of some kind. Carlos picked it up and felt the blade. It was razor sharp and came to a needle sharp point. The handle was of some kind of polished, white ivory, probably from an elephant or a whale. It was carved with grips for fingers and the hilt and the top of the handle had colored stones embedded. It was a beautiful knife and there was a leather scabbard that went with it that could be attached to a belt, concealing its twinkling beauty from a casual observer. Carlos handed it to Natália.

"My God, it's beautiful. But where did she get it?"

Carlos dug deeper and took out what appeared to be a costume of some sort. A military uniform. There was a helmet and breast plate. Silver spurs. It looked like nothing she had seen before. Then, at the bottom was a leather bag with drawstrings. He opened it and spilled out the contents. There were golden coins. Dozens of them. Thick, heavy gold coins. Natália looked at them and saw that there was scribbling in what looked like Arabic.

"What is it?" Natália asked, as Carlos sat back on the couch and regarded the whole thing. It was worth a fortune, Natália thought. The jeweled dagger alone was priceless. What was an old woman doing with such a fortune and why had she never used it?

"I think it's from my father," Carlos said quietly. "He has been dead for many years. He was an officer in the Janissaries. This is his uniform. I think this was a dagger he took from a captured Bulgarian prince. These coins are plunder from some siege or campaign, no doubt."

"A Janissary?"

"Yes. They were the Sultan's elite military force. Christian boys taken as tribute from the Christian lands who served as slaves and personal guards of the Sultan himself for life. My father was an orphan and he was given up by his tribe to the Turkish pasha when he was young. I barely knew him when he died. My mother said he was sent to Egypt to crush a revolt there and died in the fighting. This is what he left behind, I suppose. I had no idea ..."

There was no reason to stay now, Natália thought as she comforted him. With this fortune in hand, they would start a new life somewhere else. Anywhere else but here. They would leave this cursed place of strange mysteries and death and go to someplace where the sun shone all the time, where it was warm and where their color made no difference. They would leave the next day, she thought.

Chapter 60

Istvan, Radu, Kasza and their entourage had arrived at the Monastery of Piatra Fantanele where they left Van Helsing, Mina Harker and Dr. Krafft in the safekeeping of the Abbess before the entire two squadrons of mounted police resumed their progress to the Roma village in the Forest. They arrived shortly after noon, making no attempt to conceal their approach. Some forty horsemen thundered into the village, quickly surrounding it and herding the inhabitants toward the central clearing in the village. There were to be no exceptions, Istvan had made clear. All of them, man, woman and child were to be present.

As he sat atop Balzacs he waited for the hetman to make himself known to him, and soon he did. It was Ilje who came up to his horse.

"My Lord, what is the meaning of this?"

"By whose authority do you squat in this forest?" Istvan thundered down to him. He was actually angry, even though he didn't know this man. He was angry at these people who had collaborated with the enemy for years and by doing so had caused so much death and misery, in his opinion. If it weren't for them, this would all have ended years ago. He loathed Gypsies anyway, as he called them and thought of them. Nothing he had seen in the past six months or so in this corner of the world had changed his opinion of them in the slightest. In fact, he felt his convictions had been confirmed in every respect and had no intention of sparing them the harshest of penalties now for what they had done. He had had enough of their Gypsy ways. Their clever lies and dodges.

"My Lord, we have lived here in peace and quiet for many years ..."

"I asked you a question!" Istvan said and brought down his riding crop across the man's face, slashing him and drawing blood. A murmur of anger rippled through the crowd as Ilje drew the back of his hand across his face. In an instant, there was a shout from Radu and a shiver of metal sound as sabers were pulled out of their scabbards and held at the ready by the troopers. The message was not lost on the Roma. Carlos and Natália were among the two or three hundred assembled now in the clearing. They watched with shocked horror as the invasion of their sanctuary went on.

"Now I am going to ask you one more time," Istvan said in a quiet, grave tone. "By whose authority do you occupy this land?" He leaned forward in the saddle and cupped a hand to his ear to hear the response. The hetman hesitated, then spoke.

"By the grace of our Lord, Count Dracula. It is by his leave that we live here."

"And where is he now?" Istvan asked. Again a pause, and then an answer.

"I do not know, my Lord. He has left these parts as far as I know."

"Has he? And his women, have you seen them?"

"No, my Lord."

"You are lying."

"No, my Lord. I have not seen them."

"Where do they lay? And do not tell me you do not know. You have served them. You and your den of thieves. Where did you take their dirt in which they lay?"

"My Lord, I don't know ..."

Istvan brought the riding crop crashing down on the man again. He reflexively cowered this time and the leather crop hit the back of his neck and shoulder, ripping the fabric of his tunic and raising a red welt where it struck.

"Don't pretend with me, hetman. I have no time for your tricks and your games." He nodded at Radu who immediately dismounted and took a large coil of rope from his saddle. The crowd watched as he threw it up over a low branch of a nearby sycamore tree. They all saw that it had a noose on one end that was left dangling. Sweat now poured from the hetman's face in terror.

"But my Lord, please. I cannot ..."

"You there! Seize him!" Istvan commanded, pointing his riding crop at a young Gypsy in the crowd. Natália saw that it was Lajos. Two troopers walked over to him and grabbed him by the arms. He did not resist. It would have been pointless. "Strip him down and bind him. The troopers immediately pulled off all his clothes until he stood naked in front of the dangling rope which they placed over his head and tightened on his neck. His hands and feet were quickly bound as well. Radu pulled on the rope until Lajos was barely touching the ground, on his tip toes.

Istvan knew the next part would be the grimmest work of all, and he had decided to do it himself for this reason. He dismounted his horse and removed a long, leather whip and walked now to where Lajos was hanging. He collared the hetman as he did so, bringing him within a few feet of Lajos, facing him so he could see his face and hear his cries.

"Now, Sir, I ask you one last time. Spare this man the pain and tell me where they lie. Tell me now and we will leave you in peace, taking only a hostage to ensure the truth of what you tell me. Speak!"

The hetman was clearly terrified now. Natália wondered if he really knew the answer or not. She hoped he did. She hoped he would tell Istvan the deadly secret. She would have no regrets if they found the three of them and put them down for all eternity. Evidently, the hetman was equally terrified of the revenge that the Master would take if he betrayed him and hesitated.

There was a loud whoosh as the whip flew through the air and then snapped as it cracked across the helpless Lajos' back and buttocks. He shouted as the red stripe mark instantly appeared. Then another crack and another. Lajos shouted out with pain at each stroke, but then manfully stifled his cries before the next one fell. A wail went up among the women in the crowd and angry shouts could be heard from the men.

"We love you, Lajos!" screamed a woman's voice in the crowd.

"You are our hetman now!" cried out another. Shouts of encouragement and defiance roared out from the crowd.

Natália watched in panic as Carlos cupped his hands to his mouth and shouted: "We are with you, Lajos!"

Several troopers wheeled their horses into knots of Roma where the shouts emanated and struck them with the flat side of their sabers, but it did no good. The crowd was enraged as the punishment continued. It was a dangerous situation. Natália realized that the crowd would have murdered Istvan and his whole entourage if they could and only the certainty that they would be butchered kept them at bay. At last the hetman relented.

"Stop! Stop it! I will tell you!" the hetman shouted.

In an instant, Istvan whirled around walked to the hetman and punched him full in the face, knocking him to the ground.

"You stubborn fool! You idiot! Why did you make me do this?" He spit on the man, grabbed his hair and stood him up, cracking him across the face again with the back of his hand, furious. Natália was appalled at his cruelty, but she did not dare say a word. Carlos, next to her, was clenching his teeth in hate and, if there were not so many armed troopers and the possibility that Natália could be wounded or killed, she knew he might have instigated a revolt, but instead, he stood there like the rest.

"Now, listen to me and listen to me well. I have no time for Gypsy tricks and lies anymore. I came to you people once in peace and asked for your help. You lied to me. You all know what this vampire has done. You have helped him for the last time. I say to you now that if you lie to me once more, if you waste my time, I will hang him and all the rest of the men in this village, by God! We will be back here and burn your village to the ground, do you understand me?"

The hetman, his face bloodied and swollen nodded.

"Well? Where are they?"

As the troopers let Lajos down, the hetman told him about a shipment of boxes they had made a few years ago. It was to a farmhouse just outside Bistritz. As he described the house and its location, Radu interrupted.

"Dimitru" he said, simply. It was the farmhouse and stables of the orderly who had betrayed Dieter Zeigler to the Count that Kasza had arrested and interrogated months ago. He was still sitting in a cell in Bistritz awaiting trial. Radu offered a few more details about the farmhouse, just to confirm it. Ilje agreed and it was settled.

Istvan looked up at the sky. It was early afternoon. Radu could not get to the farmhouse before nightfall.

"Take half the men. Take this one with you," Istvan said, pointing at the hetman. "Go back to Bistritz and wait until dawn tomorrow. Go out to the farmhouse and find their tombs. Look for cellars, basements, hidden doors. They will have hidden their places well. Take your time and find them. If they are there, stake them all and cut off their heads. Put their heads in a bag. I want to see them myself."

"Yes, vezér!" Radu responded. With that, he turned on his heel and began shouting out commands. About twenty of the horsemen thundered out of the village. Istvan mounted his horse. He noticed that Lajos had walked away, still naked, in the company of some Gypsy women who would, no doubt, apply some medicines to his wounds. Before he disappeared into the crowd, the man turned toward him and raising his arm, pointed two fingers at him, glaring at him in hate. Silently, a few in the crowd did the same. Then more and more until in sullen hatred, the entire crowd was cursing him in the Gypsy way, Istvan noted.

He didn't care. He didn't believe in their superstitions anyway. Their false Gods. Their enmity meant nothing to him now. Balzacs stomped around wildly for a moment after Istvan gained his saddle. It was as if he sensed his master's contempt for them all. He ambled menacingly toward part of the crowd, who drew back for fear of being trampled. The other troopers closed ranks behind Istvan, their sabers still unsheathed and glittering in the afternoon sun. Suddenly, Istvan decided that a final warning should be given.

"Listen to me! All of you! I will not come back here except to drive you out once and for all if you ever again give aid or comfort to Count Dracula. He is declared an outlaw! An enemy of the Crown! He will be arrested and executed on the spot whenever and wherever he can be found. Anyone who has helped him to escape or to hide from the Crown's justice will also be punished and this village will be burned to the ground. Cooperate with us, and you will all be spared. It's just that simple. Decide carefully and Good Day to you!" With that, the second contingent of troopers spurred out of the village.

Chapter 61

"Oh no. This must be answered," Lajos said as his mother touched his wounds with an herbal anesthetic. She had begged him to leave again, but he refused. His ordeal that day had made him a hero to the tribe and hardened his own long-held beliefs about the white men. The Roma had lived too long, cowering in the shady outskirts of civilization, Lajos thought. Their servility and cowardice had disgusted Kali who would not protect them against the white man's hatred until they rose up. Kali had sent them a messiah, Lajos had come to believe, and that was Lord Dracula.

When his wounds were plastered and he was able to rise off the straw cot where his mother had doctored him, he went to the little shrine to Kali and lit the incense sticks around her carved, black ivory statue. He sat and crossed his legs. His elbows resting on his knees, his hands out to the side, palms up in prayer, he began the ancient incantations. He continued in this way, summoning the Goddess. One of the women who kept the little temple quietly entered, bringing with her a pipe of opium which he smoked. More men came into the temple to share in the meditation. As they entered, each of them came to Lajos and kissed him gently on his cheek and bowed low to him, as a sign of respect. For now, he was their leader. Ilje was simply a rich thief. Lajos was a warrior.

Lajos' prayers did not take long to answer. At dusk, Narcisa appeared out of the forest, and she was brought to the temple. Her long blonde hair cascaded in ringlets and her blue eyes blazed with interest as the day's events were recounted to her. When the tribesmen finished, she came to Lajos and took his face in her hands.

"You have made a great sacrifice for us, Lajos," she said. "We will not forget what you have done. You will be rewarded beyond your wildest dreams when the Master arrives. He summons you now, Lajos. Gather your men-folk and when all is done, you will wreak such a vengeance on these men. I promise you."

Chapter 62

When Istvan returned to the Monastery, Kasza sought him out at once. There was another message that had been brought up from Bistritz:

MOROS BYPASSED VARNA STOP DOCKED IN CONSTANTA THIS EVENING STOP COUNT DRACULA DEPARTED AT DUSK WITH SLOVAKS AND SEVERAL LIETERWAGEN PER SHIP'S CREW STOP GOING TO GIVE CHASE BUT NOT CERTAIN ROUTE TAKEN STOP BELIEVE HE WILL ARRIVE BORGO PASS IN DAYS UNLESS WE OVERTAKE HIM IN DAYLIGHT STOP HARKER

So, the devil was on his way home, Istvan thought. With any luck, he was down to his last few boxes of cursed soil and had no choice but to come back to where they would be waiting for him. With Harker and his Englishmen on his heels and Istvan and his men lying in wait, it would be a matter of time. He considered how the final drama might well take place.

The worst would be if they arrived at night. Then, the Count and his wives would be at their most powerful and well-nigh invincible. It was crucial that he not arrive at night.

"Get me a map, Kasza," Istvan commanded. In a few minutes, in the library, they had a map of the whole Balkans spread out on a large table. The Abbess watched as Istvan carefully examined the various possible routes to the castle. Given the escort of Slovaks and the presence of several liter-wagon, the possibilities really narrowed down to two routes through the Carpathians from Wallachia into Transylvania. A liter-wagon with a pair of horses or even a quartet would probably only make 25 or 30 kilometers a day, but the Count would drive them day and night. Especially at night. The horses would have to be rested, though, Istvan thought. It would be four or five days, Istvan figured. There was just no way to be sure that he would not arrive at night.

Van Helsing interrupted Istvan's ruminations.

"There is something I need to share with you. I have been able to bring Mrs. Harker to a state of hypnosis and then, in that state, she is in communication with Dracula. She can see and hear what he sees and hears, to a limited extent. Perhaps that will help?"

"The same thing with Ema, the daughter of the Baroness!" Krafft exclaimed. He then described what to Istvan, Kasza and Van Helsing what had happened at the Hotel Gellert a week earlier. "Only with her, the Count could also see and know us. Perhaps it would be a little dangerous?" Istvan considered the situation carefully. It seemed they had no choice. Dracula was powerful enough to murder and kill all of them, if he had the time and the opportunity.

"Bring her in. Let's see what she says. We will tell her nothing of our plans, so she cannot reveal them to the enemy." Van Helsing left to get her. Meanwhile, Istvan and Kasza pored over the map.

"If he landed in Constanta yesterday at dusk, then he could be either here or here," Istvan said, pointing at the two alternatives. "If he took the more northern route, he would be in these forests here. If he took the more western route, he would be in the mountains by now, coming into Transylvania here, near Hermanstadt." In fact, he might even be in Hermanstadt already if he flew ahead of his convoy and had a safe house there."

"He probably does have one there, my Lord. As many centuries as he has had to prepare, one would think …"

"Yes, yes. I agree. And plenty of people to lose himself in and feed upon."

Van Helsing now arrived with Mrs. Harker. She looked paler still than the last time he had seen her and her eyes were wild. Van Helsing said something to her in English that Istvan couldn't understand, but shortly she was seated, the lamps and candelabra in the room were extinguished until the room was very dim indeed and the hypnosis began.

Istvan knew that there would be some preliminaries before she settled into a trance, but after a short time, Van Helsing turned to him.

"Now, what would you like to know from her?"

"Ask her what she sees or hears at this moment from him." Van Helsing said something in English to her, in a low voice. At first nothing happened. Her eyes were closed and then she began to speak in a very low voice. Van Helsing translated.

"She says she is very high in the air ... she can see the lights of a town, below her. There are people walking in streets far below. It is a bell tower of a church where she is ... resting on the edge of a steeple ... a roof. There is a statue near her of a saint, looking down at the people ..."

"Ask her if she sees other steeples and other churches? How many churches does she see?" Van Helsing translated again.

"There are many. They are dark against the horizon ... she counts five or six that she can see. There may be more on the other side. It is a big city ... there are carts and carriages she can see in the streets."

"Ask her if she can see the sea?" Van Helsing did so. No, there was just a river with some bridges."

"That's enough, Van Helsing," Istvan said. "Let's not be too greedy. Before he realizes we're here." Van Helsing nodded and with a few words and a snap of his fingers, he brought her quickly out of her trance.

"Thank you," Istvan said to Mrs. Harker. It was one of the few phrases he knew in English. She smiled and nodded and Van Helsing then escorted her back to her room.

Kasza and Istvan looked at one another and both of them said the same word at the same time: "Hermanstadt." The Count had already made it to Transylvania. He would be here in no more than two days time.

Chapter 63

Narcisa had told Lajos where to find the Master. In the clearing in the middle of the village, Lajos spoke to the Sinti men. He reminded them how much their fate was bound up with their loyalty to Dracula. He exhorted them to vengeance against the Europeans who oppressed them and who had invaded their village today. In the torchlight, his face flickered with emotion and his youthful passion aroused ancient hatreds in the older men. Natália watched Carlos and knew that he would join this revolt that Lajos was stirring up. She knew she could not stop him and cursed the day she had agreed to come back here with them.

Of course she sympathized with them. All of them. She was a Roma. How could she not? But unlike these ignorant men and women, she had seen the world beyond the Forest and the mountains of Transylvania. She knew how great their world was and the Europeans' power. Carlos, with his pride, could not help himself even though he should know better. Perhaps he thought, if the worst happened, they could run and lose themselves in the vastness of the continent of Europe.

"Who will come with me? Who will help me take vengeance? When our Lord returns, he will strike them down without mercy. He will once again rout an enemy that thinks it is invincible. As he did to the Ottomans. And the Magyars. The Saxons and Wallachians. They have all been beaten in time by the Master. He will beat these invaders as well. We will be his instrument! We will be at his command and rise again, as our ancestors did. Come, Sinti warriors! Remember who you are! Let us ride!"

An enormous roar went up as he finished. Men jumped up on their horses, rifles on their backs and dark cloaks over their bodies, shouting vengeance. The women shouted too, shrieking curses on the Europeans and blessings of Kali on their husbands and sons as they rode out of the village, into the forest, their torches blazing in the night.

It was an impressive exit, Natália thought, as she watched Carlos and the others flicker and fade into the woods and darkness. They were taking the road to Hermanstadt. Perhaps fifty or sixty Roma horsemen would ride until they met their Master who would lead them to annihilate their oppressors in a massacre. That's what they thought, Natália knew.

"And you?" came a silky voice from behind her. She turned and was face to face with Narcisa. Her blonde hair was flowing in the night breeze. "You will come with me …"

Chapter 64

The next morning, two messages arrived at the Monastery. The first was from Radu.

My Lord —

We are pleased to report to your Lordship that the farm of the traitor Dimitru was located and thoroughly searched as your Lordship directed and in the manner instructed. As your Lordship suspected, a secret trap door was indeed located in the stables which revealed three wooden caskets that appeared to be the resting places of the three women in question. Alas, we failed to find them resting there, but thoroughly contaminated the site in the usual manner, as was done on our late excursion to the Balkans.

We are now required in Bistritz by His Excellency, the Lord Mayor, who begs me to remind you of the arrival of his Majesty tomorrow and of your need to be present.

- Popescu Radu

The second was from Harker:

OVERTOOK CARAVAN OF SLOVAKS IN CARPATHIANS BUT COUNT NOT WITH THEM STOP SECOND GROUP

BELIEVED PASSED THROUGH HERMANNSTADT YESTERDAY STOP BEWARE APPROACH OF COUNT AT ANY TIME STOP RUMORS AMONG SLOVAKS OF LARGE GYPSY CONTINGENT TO MEET UP AND ESCORT PARTY TO BORGO PASS STOP BELIEVE WE WILL OVERTAKE SLOVAKS TOMORROW STOP HARKER

"I'll be damned," thought Istvan. It would be an extreme act of *lèse majesté* to be absent from the official party greeting the King at the rail station, but he would just have to explain it later. There was nothing that could be done about Radu and his troopers, however. His absence cut in half the force at his disposal. They would check the Roma village first.

In a couple of hours, Kasza and Istvan along with the remaining troopers rode into the village. It did not take long for them to discover most of the men were gone, as were the horses. Now it was war, Istvan thought. It was no different than when he had been in Denmark or Italy back in the 60's.

"Burn it!" he shouted to Kasza. Kasza hesitated. "Burn it!"

"But sir ..."

"They can have no refuge here, Kasza," Istvan said, regretting that he did not have his old cavalry regiment with him. They would have set fire to the place without a moment's regret. These civilians did not understand the necessities of war. After a long moment, Kasza nodded to the other troopers. They lit their torches and began setting fire to the thatched roofs, wooden huts, dry straw and anything else that would burn.

The shrieking of the women was terrible but soon the place was a blazing inferno with flames leaping many meters into the air and jumping from one house to another. A good deal of the forest would be scorched too, Istvan reflected, but it couldn't be helped.

They had brought it on themselves. They had aided and abetted the monsters that had preyed on the good folk hereabouts for generations. Now it would stop. Desperate times required desperate measures. Radu had eliminated Dimitru's refuge. The Roma village could well be another.

He could take no chances. The scourge needed to be rooted out wherever it could be found. No half-measures could be allowed anymore.

As the troopers returned to the main road, Istvan decided to return to the Monastery. There was no point in trying to follow the Roma on horseback. They had a half day's ride on them. It would be better to try and intercept them when they returned to within range of the castle, Istvan reckoned. When he arrived at the Monastery, he found to his horror that Van Helsing and Mina Harker were gone and sunset had arrived again, all too soon. There was nothing to do but wait.

Chapter 65

The three wives were once again in the ruins of the castle with Natália where Narcisa had brought her. It was maddening. Somehow, she found herself recaptured in the Castle and plunged deeply into her personal nightmare. How could she have allowed herself to return here, she wondered bitterly. Anastázia spoke to her.

"You will wait here for the Master and your Carlos. Isn't he your love?" Anastázia asked. "We will both be re-united with our lovers soon. It may be daylight when they arrive and you will show them where to bring the Master. You will show them where to carry the box, down into the tombs, won't you dear?"

"But I thought that all the graves and tombs had been filled with crosses and holy water?" Natália asked. Sophia laughed.

"Yes. They were. But after awhile, the guards left, you know. And then Ilje and his men began to undo what the soldiers and the Gendarmerie had done. It didn't take them long. Now it's back to where it was."

"It's all a matter of time, Natália, and we have all the time in the world. A century from now, nobody will remember any of this and nobody will care. Or perhaps there will be another brave soul who seeks to exterminate us. Maybe he will or maybe he won't. We have been through this before. We have seen these men come and go. Now, I'm going to have to turn my attention to Mrs. Harker. ." Anasztázia said.

"Mrs. Harker? The wife of Jonathan Harker?"

"Would you like to meet her, my dear? As I recall, you had quite a crush on her husband when he visited us, didn't you? She is nearing the castle right now. Look!"

They guided her over to a balcony. Across the darkened fields a tiny light could be seen bobbing along. It was someone coming to the castle. Suicide, thought Natália.

"I have summoned her," Anastázia said, with a mocking laugh. "We will bring her here and she will be the Master's first blood slave when he arrives. A delightful present, wouldn't you agree? And then, you will have Jonathan to yourself!" The other two wives tittered their agreement with the diabolical plan.

Natália continued to watch as the little bobbing light came closer and closer. After about a quarter hour, she could see it was coming up the final approach to the castle itself. In the darkness, she could see that there were two horses. A woman was riding one. It would be Mrs. Harker, no doubt. Then there was a man. He was holding a torch and seemed to be shouting at her but it was in a language Natália could not understand.

All at once, the three women joined hands and slowly began to circle round and round until they were going so fast that they merged into a single, spinning black cone and then three great black bats. They flew out and off the balcony and Natália had no doubt where they were going. She went to the edge of the balcony to watch.

The woman dismounted her horse which then cantered off in the darkness as she continued walking toward the courtyard below. The man did the same thing, now shouting at her as she approached the archway to the courtyard in the front of the great doors.

Natália concluded it must be English he was speaking. He overtook the woman and grabbed her arm. She tried to shake him off but he held her fast. She struck him. He dropped the torch and slapped her hard several times. It seemed to stun her to her senses, but just then, the three wives whirled into being, forming a triangle around them.

The man picked up the torch and thrust it at them as Natália watched. They retreated as he did so, but continued to circle around them. He held fast to the woman who seemed to want to join the vampires, but was held back by the man. He stuck the torch in the dirt and its light illuminated a little circle around the two of them. The vampires remained at the edge, taunting him and the woman. Then the man pulled out a large silver cross, thrusting it at each of them in turn and began shouting at them in another language. It was Latin, she thought.

Each time one of the vampires came into the circle the man thrust the cross at her. One time he touched the silver cross to the forehead of Narcisa, making a flash of light. She shrieked with pain and retreated into the darkness. He pulled something out of his pocket. As Natália watched, she could see that he had little white wafers that he sprinkled around the entire circumference of the circle made at the edge of the light. Whatever it was, the vampires could not break the circle but remained outside, calling to the woman Natália knew must be Mina Harker.

This went on for quite awhile until it became apparent that it was a stand-off. The woman had crumpled to the ground after awhile, sobbing and then silent. The man continued to hold his ground with the torch in one hand, the cross in the other, continuing to recite whatever it was in Latin that held them at bay. Then the two remaining vampires transformed themselves into bats again and flew away, defeated. Where they all went from there, she did not know. Eventually, Natália curled up on the balcony floor and went to sleep.

Chapter 66

Before leaving the Monastery on the road to Hermanstadt, Istvan sent one of his troopers back to Bistritz with a message for Radu. He instructed him to warn the military authorities there was a Roma uprising underway and a large number of them were located between Hermanstadt and the Borgo Pass. Radu was to request cavalry attached to the summer maneuvers be dispatched immediately and, in the meantime, he would attempt to block their passage.

At dawn, Istvan and Kasza set off on the road to Hermanstadt with their troop of twenty mounted police. Before heading out, he warned the men what they would be facing and at all costs, they were looking for the cargo that the Gypsies would be escorting and, if he were cut down, to open the boxes in the daylight. Most of the troopers shared Istvan's contempt for the Roma, who they had seen in the village a couple of days earlier.

It was a beautiful summer day as they rode south. Blue skies and puffy white clouds on the horizon gave no hint of the grim business that was their mission. Istvan marveled once again at the drama of the Transylvanian landscape, as the hours went by. Rough, stony hills and mountains cut through by steep gorges that gave out onto thick, pine forests through which the little troupe rode, largely in silence. The clink of metal on metal, spurs and stirrups punctuated the drumming horses' hooves on the cart path they were riding toward Hermanstadt. A white marker with the number of kilometers to the city counted down the distance. They had gone about 25 kilometers south when they reached a small river, over which there was a sturdy wooden bridge.

"Let's stop here for lunch, Kasza," Istvan said, breaking a silence that had lasted for several hours now. "Let the horses drink. We'll start up again in half an hour." Kasza nodded and turned to the men, conveying the order. In a few minutes, the men had all dismounted and many had let their horses come up to the edge of the river which, like most Transylvanian rivers, fairly flew past with white water swirling around large rocks in the middle of the stream.

Istvan sat down on a blanket and took out a small loaf of bread and some cheese and began eating. Kasza sat down near him, but instead rolled himself a cigarette which he lit and exhaled the blue smoke. The silence was beginning to bother Istvan.

"What is it, Kasza? What are you thinking? You haven't said a word in hours." Kasza looked at him without expression for a moment, contemplating his response. Clearly, something was bothering him.

"I can't help thinking about the Roma in the Forest."

So that was it, Istvan thought. Kasza was an intellectual, Istvan reminded himself. He read a lot and thought a lot. He was a man of books, learning and science. The trouble with Kasza was he spent too much time thinking and reading and not enough out in the real world, Istvan thought.

"You think I was cruel?"

"There were innocents. Women and children," Kasza ventured.

"They were not. They were collaborators. They are accomplices to murder and torture. Kidnapping. What about the victims of their Master? What about their innocence?"

"They did none of those things, Sir."

"They might as well have done them, Kasza. The law makes no distinction between a criminal and those who collaborate with them in committing a crime or helping them escape. Am I right? Those who aid and abet are as guilty of a crime as if they had done it themselves. That has always been the law, since Roman times. Am I not right, Kasza?"

There was a long pause as Kasza stared at the ground, thinking. Istvan continued.

"It was a brutal thing. I admit that, Kasza. It is a brutal thing, but it had to be done. Sometimes one must be harsh and make difficult decisions to save the ones we love from far greater disasters. Let me tell you a story, Kasza, to make my point....

"In 1859, I was a young lad in the Army at Solferino. We were fighting the French in torrid heat and under terrible conditions. French artillery had been pounding our positions on the slopes of a hill for hours, killing hundreds of soldiers every hour. Then the attack came. Up the slopes the French infantry came and we mowed them down, rank after rank, but they kept coming and their artillery kept pounding us. A terrible thunderstorm broke out in the middle of the afternoon that was so bad all fighting stopped for almost an hour, and then it started again. Finally, the slaughter had reached a point where the Kaiser himself decided we should withdraw to reorganize and find a better position to defend, out of range of the artillery.

"There was a pause in the fighting while the French gathered themselves for one final lunge that would take the top of the hill and cut off our lines of retreat. We couldn't just leave. French cavalry would have chased us and cut us down if we had. And so a decision was made. A regiment of Croats and a battery of artillery would stay behind to delay the French while the rest of the army escaped. Now, you see, the officers and even the Kaiser himself knew this rear-guard would eventually be overwhelmed and slaughtered, but it had to be done. It was a necessity. And it was done. It saved our army that retreated into the famous Quadrilateral fortresses, an impregnable position of safety. After that, a truce was agreed between the Austrians and the French and then peace.

"Now these gypsies have made it possible for this vampire and his concubines to survive in this region for centuries. Even now, they collaborate with him to allow him to re-establish his murderous presence here once again. They know this, and yet they continue. They would not lift a finger for you, Kasza, if Count Dracula wanted your blood, now would they?

No. They would kidnap you and turn you over to him if that was what he wanted."

Kasza listened in silence to Istvan's explanation, at times nodding his understanding but still dubious of Istvan's methods.

"It is like putting down a horse to end its suffering. Harsh but a mercy in the long run, do you see?"

"Yes," Kasza replied at last. "I see it. I suppose that is why I am a detective and not a hangman. Some people are better suited to some things than others. That's all I can say. I don't know if that makes me a better person or worse, but I don't think I could have done it."

The sky had become cloudy as the troopers were eating their lunches and while Istvan and Kasza talked. At first Istvan had not noticed the darkening clouds that were coming over the tops of a nearby range of low mountains, but now he felt the cold breeze that signaled the momentary start of a thunderstorm.

"It looks like rain, my Lord," Kasza said.

It was then Istvan noticed an odd thing. As the clouds continued to build and a low crackling of distant thunder was heard, a flock of blackbirds flew up from the branches of the nearby trees. There must have been dozens of them, Istvan thought. No, hundreds of them. A number of the birds flew up into the sky and simply circled above them. Others alighted on the branches of other trees and watched. Dozens of yellow eyes peered down at them, heads cocking and swiveling to watch their every move and those of the other troopers. Black clouds now blew across the sky at an unimaginable speed, as if someone were pulling them like a blanket over their heads. Then the storm broke.

Immense blasts of thunder and streaks of lightening pierced the sky. One bolt shattered a huge oak tree near where the horses were congregated. A massive branch fell on two of the horses, breaking their backs and sending the others bolting into the woods in terror. Pelting rain drenched the men.

Istvan could not see a meter in front of him as he and Kasza made for the wooden bridge. Several of the men had gone off to chase the horses in the woods, leaving the others to find what shelter they could. At that moment, dozens of horses galloped on to the bridge from the far side, their cloaked riders bent over their mounts with rifles in their hands. For some reason, these horses seemed immune to the arcs of lightning flashing over their heads.

The Roma cavalry quickly spotted the troopers and immediately began riding them down. Into the woods the men scampered with the Roma horsemen in hot pursuit. Some of them were gunned down before they reached the tree line, while others made it that far, only to be ridden down and hacked to pieces. Kasza and Istvan had by then made it underneath the bridge and were standing knee deep in the rushing water, watching the scene as best they could between squalls of rain the slaughter being meted out by the vengeful dark riders.

The pursuit by the Roma left the area around the bridge deserted for a few minutes, but neither Kasza nor Istvan dared to move from under the bridge. Then they heard it. The low rumble of a wagon and more horses. From across the river, the sound was distinct as horses banged across the wooden planks. Then the sound of wheels. Heavy wheels of a laden wagon, rumbling right over their heads and then on to the cart path on the shoreline behind them. More horses followed the wagon, which was moving along very quickly.

Istvan and Kasza knew what had just passed over their heads, bound for the north and the Borgo Pass. Wet and exhausted from the terrors of the sudden attack, without their mounts or weapons, they were just two helpless men under a bridge in the middle of a forest with nothing to do but walk back in the direction from which they had come. Just as suddenly as it had come, the clouds rolled away over the mountaintops, the sky became blue again and the sun came out. The only thing that marred the scene as they clambered out from under the bridge were the dead bodies of the troopers scattered about the clearing, churned up with the prints of horses hooves everywhere.

Chapter 67

That same morning, Natália awoke to bright sunshine on the balcony of the castle. Her heart sank as she realized where she was and then the thoughts of what had transpired last night raced into her mind. She sat up and then jumped to her feet. Down below she saw the man who had fended off the wives and the woman who had come with him sitting on the ground and talking. She called down to them and waved. At first, their faces evinced stunned disbelief that any mortal person could possibly inhabit the castle.

"I will come down to you. Wait there for me!" Natália called out to them, but they couldn't understand her. They shouted something up to her in their language, but likewise, she could not understand them either.

Natália hurried into the castle and down the stairs to the great hall and then to the entrance doors. The castle doors were barred with heavy planks that rested on massive iron brackets across the double doors, but there were no locks. With tremendous effort she pushed up but could only manage to lift a plank halfway before the weight of it was too much for her and it fell back into place.

Natália felt panic rising in her. What if she were trapped again? She could hear some muffled sounds from outside the door, no doubt coming from the man who was calling to her, but she couldn't understand what he was saying. She pounded on the door with her fists to let him know she was there, but it didn't help. She looked around the great hall for a way out. There was a huge fireplace across the room. Evidently, the soldiers who had

The Carpathian Assignment

been here had used it to keep warm because there was wood piled up near the hearth that had not been burned. There were also some long tongs and pokers next to the stone face of the fireplace. In an instant, she knew what to do.

The pokers were made of black cast iron. She took one from the fireplace and brought it to one end of the wooden plank in the wall bracket. Wedging the poker underneath and behind the plank, she slowly worked it up. It was still heavy and a couple of times, she misjudged her position and it fell back into the bracket, but after a few minutes she managed to get it all the way up to the top of the bracket and let it fall with a loud clatter. She grasped the fallen end and, with all her might, slowly pulled the other end toward her until it too fell out of the bracket to the stone floor with a crash.

With all her strength, she grasped the massive door handle and pushed it down. She heard the tumblers in the lock click and then she pulled. The door opened and there, blinking in wonderment were the man and the woman she had seen from the balcony high above. The man said something in English to her she could not understand. Then German. Natália tried Magyar to no avail and then the only other language she knew, Dutch.

"Can you understand Dutch, sir?"

"My God," the man replied. "It is my native tongue. How in the world do you know Dutch and who are you?"

"My name is Natália and I am from these parts," she replied. "I have lived in Amsterdam for awhile and learned to speak Dutch there."

"Amsterdam? That is where I am from! What are you doing in this place? How are you alive with those devil women about?"

"Them? I know them. They have been living here in this castle for centuries. I watched you last night. You are very brave. They would have killed you if they could. And you, Madame. I know you are Mrs. Jonathan Harker. It is Mina, isn't it?"

Van Helsing was dumbfounded. He translated and then the woman responded.

"Yes. That is my name. How could you possibly …"

"The three women told me. They knew who you are. They were told by the Master of this Castle, Count Dracula. He is coming here soon, perhaps tonight. We must get away from here."

"My dear Natália. We have come all the way from England to kill this vampire. He has been in England and murdered a young woman who was a friend of Mrs. Harker. Her name was Lucy Westenra. He probably killed quite a few other victims while he was there but we found his lair, thanks to Mrs. Harker's husband, in an ancient Abbey near London. We could not catch him or kill him there, however. Dracula escaped before we could find his last lair and we found he had left England on a ship called the *Moros*. We found that this ship landed in Constanta a few days ago. We believe that Count Dracula and an escort are on their way back to this castle to escape from us and to restore their supply of hiding places using the soil from the burial grounds here. We mean to destroy him here, once and for all."

Natália could not understand every word of what Van Helsing said. Her Dutch was not that good. She did understand the gist of it, though.

"But you cannot possibly hope to defeat him here. Alone. He is much too powerful and all around these parts, he has many allies and friends who will warn him and help him. The birds in the trees. The wolves in the forests. All of them will warn him you're here. I am sure they have already warned him. He will kill you for sure and he will enslave Mrs. Harker as he did me."

"We must do what we can. Do you know where his women lie during the day?" Van Helsing asked.

"Not really. They are probably lying somewhere in the crypts of the castle, but I do not know exactly where."

"Show me," Van Helsing commanded, and so she did. They quietly entered the ancient burial chamber, full of tombs and sarcophagi. Van Helsing picked up some wooden debris and withdrew a large pocket knife from his pocket. After a little while, he had whittled three sharp stakes, closed the knife and put it in his pocket. "Now we are ready," he said grimly.

For several hours they explored the tombs below the ancient chapel and then the catacombs beneath the castle. Even though it was daylight above,

The Carpathian Assignment

the darkness and bleak interior of subterranean passageways and rooms depressed and terrified Natália as the hunt progressed. What if they weren't in the castle at all, she wondered.

"To regain their powers, they must sleep in the dirt where they were buried or entombed when they became a vampire," Van Helsing said as if thinking aloud. "So we search where the dirt is. But if they want to just survive, they could be anywhere the light of day will not penetrate. Maybe that is where they are. What about the rooms up above the Great Hall?" Since they had explored all of the rooms and passages they could find below, they went back upstairs to the Great Hall and then to the next floor above.

Since the castle was in ruins, there were not that many rooms and places to search and, as it was light and air from the outside filled the rooms, the work of searching was not as dire as it had been. A few hours more passed as doors were forced and rooms explored, but to no avail. At last, they reached the last room in at the end of a hallway only to find it empty and deserted, like most of the other rooms. It was now late afternoon, Natália realized. In only a few more hours, the summer light would be gone and if, God forbid, the Count should return in the night, with all his powers intact, he would destroy them all as his wives had failed to do.

"We must go!" Natália said. "It's hopeless. There is no more time." Mina Harker said something to Van Helsing in English, seeming to agree with her, but Van Helsing did not answer. He was thinking.

"We must have missed something. Let us go back to the crypts once more," he said. Despite Natália's protests, Van Helsing would not be dissuaded and soon she found herself walking down the stairs below the ruined chapel to the underground crypts. Van Helsing had lit a torch. The sarcophagi of innumerable departed, their tops off exposing their interiors to the musty air of the vaults were everywhere. There must be a lower level somewhere. This is exactly where the inhabitants of this castle were buried and entombed for centuries. It would be exactly where the soil these vampires need is located. Come, we must find it. A door. A trap door disguised in some way. They lit more torches and carefully began to examine the stones and dirt of the floor. Van Helsing organized them systematically and they worked the room from one end to the other.

It was Mina Harker who found the door in the floor. It was covered with dirt, but there was no mistaking it. Van Helsing kicked the dirt off the door to reveal the huge ring. He struggled to lift the door but, with the help of the two women, he eventually lifted it to reveal the stairs leading down.

"This is what we were looking for," Van Helsing said in Dutch and then, to Mina, in English. They took the torches and the stakes in hand, and went down into the vault below.

Chapter 68

Kasza and Istvan had been walking for less than twenty minutes from the bridge when they heard the sound of horses' hooves behind them. They were still in the forest and, after what they had been through, fearful that it could be the Roma horde again, they quickly stepped into the thick woods to watch. In a minute, a band of four men went galloping by. Istvan recognized one of them. It was Jonathan Harker. Istvan sprang up and called out his name, but the little group was so intent on their pursuit or the pounding of their horses so noisy that none of the men heard or saw him. By the time Istvan and Kasza reached the road again, the four men were already out of sight.

"My God, do you think they'll catch him?" Istvan took out his pocket watch. It was mid-afternoon already. There was about four and a half hours of daylight left, he calculated. It would take about that long to reach the Borgo Pass from here.

"It'll be a close thing," Istvan replied. There was nothing to be done but to keep on going. Before long, they came to a clearing where there was some pasture land and cows grazing on the land. Istvan had barely noticed it on the way south that morning, but now he noticed there was a small farmhouse and a barn about half a kilometer from the road.

"Come on," Istvan said. In a couple of minutes, they were at the door of the farmhouse. Kasza banged on the door loudly, but there was no answer. They shouted and called aloud but again, there was no answer. The barn invited them and, under the circumstances, the two policemen wasted no time in opening the doors which revealed a tack room off to the side and several horses who watched them curiously. Kasza went to the door again and called out again, but the only sound was a brief reply from one or two of the cows in the distance.

"Let's go!" Istvan said. "We'll bring them back later and explain."

In a few minutes, they had the horses saddled and without further delay, they were ready to ride when there was another sound. A low rumbling of horses. Kasza, at the barn door, put his finger to his lips and then pointed, as if the approaching riders could have heard them. Nonetheless, Istvan warily approached the door, which was half open.

Sure enough, it was the Roma, Istvan could see, their black cloaks whipping out from behind them, their butchery complete, he thought. They strung out for a kilometer or more, in bunches of twos and threes. Very inappropriately done by military standards, Istvan thought. Cavalry was most effective when closely and tightly bunched together in a compact mass. For many hours, Istvan had participated in maneuvers to instill military discipline that would become instinctive in the heat of battle where thinking and calculation were impossible. Despite their ambush and defeat earlier, Istvan felt contempt for their rag tag tactics as he watched the last of them pass.

"Sixty-six," Istvan said.

Istvan had counted them. It was an old habit from scouting days and for lack of anything better to do. After about ten minutes, the last of them seemed to have passed. They did not dare leave the barn for another ten minutes, until the sound of them had faded to nothing. As they waited, Istvan felt his heart sink in despair. The odds of success had lengthened. As he mounted and spurred on his horse to follow the Gypsy band, he realized that several things would have to go just right if they were to kill Dracula rather than him killing most or all of his pursuers.

"Do you think the Gypsies will catch the Englishmen?" Kasza wondered out loud.

"It's not just that. Will they catch them before sunset? With Dracula able to join the battle, their strength rises one hundred fold. And what can four Englishmen in a foreign country do against all that? Our only hope is that they catch Dracula before sunset, that they overpower the Slovaks and kill him before the Gypsies arrive. My God, what are the odds of that?"

Nonetheless, there was nothing to do but press on. It occurred to Istvan that his own time might be coming to an end. It would probably be near sunset when they reached the highway between Bistritz and the Bukovina, let alone the Borgo Pass. If the Englishmen didn't succeed, all hell would break loose over the countryside for sure. Literally. All hell.

Chapter 69

Natália and Mina followed Van Helsing along the dank passageways of rough-hewn rock where rats and insects scurried in the unaccustomed light of their torches. For several minutes, they followed the passageway this way and that until they came to an open door. There was a large room behind it, Natália could tell as the dim light from Van Helsing's torch illuminated what seemed like, incredibly, a polished stone floor. She felt her heart pounding as first Van Helsing, then Mina Harker and finally herself passed over the threshold into a magnificent underground chamber. Immediately her eye was drawn in the gloom to a plinth and coffin in the middle of the room with four smaller coffins pointing each corner of it.

"This must be it", Van Helsing whispered to the two women. Quickly he looked about for someplace to lay his torch when they all noticed that the walls of the room were punctuated by wall sconces with torches protruding. Van Helsing walked over to one and touched his torch to the tip of the sconce's torch. It lit. He did the same half a dozen more times until the room was fairly well, if unevenly lighted. They extinguished their torches and lay them on the floor.

"Now our work begins, my dear," Van Helsing said to her in Dutch and then repeated to Mina Harker in English. "These old coffins are heavy. I will raise the lids. Mina will push a stake into the chest and then you will smash this down on it and drive it through the heart."

Van Helsing handed Natália a heavy fragment of one of the stones that had fallen out of the wall in the passageway. Natália nodded her head, terrified. She listened as Van Helsing said the same thing to Mina in English. Her eyes were also wide with terror but she nodded as well at the end of it.

Van Helsing approached one of the coffins by the end, opposite the hinges. He grunted and nodded his head for the women to stand on either side of him. Then, the muscles in his face grimacing and with all his strength, he raised the lid. There lay Anastázia in her flowing robes, eyes wide open but yet unseeing and dead. Her skin was as pale as wax.

"Do it!" Van Helsing commanded Mina in a loud voice. Shaken from her morbid fascination, Mina slammed the stake down on the vampire's chest. She did not move or betray the slightest notice until Natália brought the stone down, driving the stake through the sternum and into the chest. As if awakened from sleep a bloodcurdling shriek reverberated off the stone walls of the chamber. A deafening scream that was unbearable but now Van Helsing brought the knife down on the vampire's throat, piercing the larynx and cutting the scream to a choking, gurgling sound.

"Again!" Van Helsing shouted and again, Natália brought the stone down on the stake, driving it deeper while Van Helsing cut the vampire's neck to the spine and then stabbing through the gap in the vertebra to completely sever its head. The body meanwhile was writhing in an uncontrollable frenzy of desperation until Van Helsing finished his work and raised the head out of the coffin by the hair. His face and clothes were spattered with blood, as were Mina and Natália, but his eyes glinted in triumph as the ghastly Medusa-like head swung from his grip.

"Two more, Ladies! Two More!" And with that, Van Helsing bellowed with a laugh that also echoed off the walls of the death chamber.

In twenty minutes time, their work complete, The little party departed the underground tomb without disturbing the giant black coffin in the middle.

"Nay, we leave that one alone," said Van Helsing. If the devil escapes Lord Istvan and his troopers, he will come here. It will be his last place to hide, I hope. So we leave it as a trap for him, in case we need it." With that, they hurried out into the passageway and up, out of the crypts to the ruined chapel. The fresh air smelled wonderful, but alas, Natália realized there were only a couple of hours of light remaining.

"Come, let us leave this cursed place," Van Helsing exclaimed. He walked over to the edge of the castle wall and threw each of the heads of the vampires out into the void. Natália noticed it was Narcissa's head that was last to fly, her blonde hair streaming in the wind as Natália watched it fall hundreds of meters to a pile of rocks below where it ricocheted and bounced further down the rocky slope into a gorge below; a black pin point that eventually she could not make out any more.

The two horses were still in the courtyard in front of the castle and the three of them wasted no time mounting and riding away. Mina and Natália shared one mount while Van Helsing took the other. As they road toward the Borgo Pass, Natália could not help but think of the irony that she had been saved and was sharing the saddle with the wife of her first lover, Jonathan Harker. She hugged Mina's body close, hanging on to her on the back of the horse, without stirrups, and smiled to herself.

After reaching the junction with the main highway at the Borgo Pass, the three of them began the descent to the Monastery of Pietra Fontanelle. The winding road emerged around a bend about ten minutes later where they could see across a deep ravine a sight that made Natália's heart run cold. It was a large liter-wagon with a team of six Gypsy horses pulling it along at a rapid pace. On the wagon was a large canopy and under the canopy was a large wooden box. There were four riders ahead of the wagon, a teamster driving the wagon and two more bringing up the rear.

"My God," Van Helsing exclaimed. Here he is. Here he is!" There was no doubting that it was the Count and in less than a half hour, he would be entering the courtyard of his castle. Natália imagined that the wagon would reach them in about ten minutes as it climbed and curled its way around the treacherous mountain road.

"Come, we must hide!" Natália said. "We can't possibly defeat him here! These are Slovaks. I can see from their clothes. They will be armed and will kill us. It's hopeless. We're the only ones who know where his final coffin is hidden. We have to live! Come!"

The Carpathian Assignment

Van Helsing seemed to consider the situation for a few more seconds and then concluded she was right. They began riding back toward the Borgo Pass until they came to a straight-away where the woods were deep by the roadside and the mountain slope shallow enough to provide cover for them. They dismounted their horses and hurriedly led them into the woods to where they were hidden but could still see the road.

The minutes went by slowly but soon, they could hear the faint rumbling sound and horses. Many horses. It became distinctly louder and then, down to their right, they saw the Slovak guards in front of the wagon. Something was amiss, however, They kept looking back over their shoulders. There were shots, now. Cracks of the sound of rifle fire. Natália could not see from where the shots were coming, but, looking at the Slovak guards, she realized they were hesitating. The wagon kept rolling, however, and the guards made up their mind to keep going. More rifle fire and then she saw four horsemen overtaking the wagon, just as it came even in front of them.

"Jonathan!" Mina Harker exclaimed. On an impulse, she spurred her horse forward and Natália, still mounted on the back, gripped Mina as they bounced forward through the thicket and trees. Natália realized Van Helsing had belatedly started up behind them as well and was shouting something in English she couldn't understand.

One of the men with Jonathan Harker had clambered on to the back of the wagon and was making his way forward to the teamster who was madly whipping the horses forward, apparently unaware of the intruder. The man was hunched over and unsteady as he approached the driver from the rear. Natália could see he had a huge, silvery knife in his hand.

"Quincey!" Mina exclaimed, as they broke the tree line near the road, now behind the fray. There was a flash from behind the box as a hand holding the knife raised it and plunged it into the driver several times. The team of horses was slowed to a halt by the man who grabbed the reins from the teamster who was slumped over. More shots were fired as the Slovaks rounded on the ambushers, guns blazing. The man with the big knife that Mina called Quincey crumpled under fire but the other three, now on foot and steady at the back of the wagon picked off the guards one by one until they were all dead.

"Open the box!" Van Helsing's voice boomed out as he emerged from the woods. "Open it now!" The sun was indeed on the horizon and there was not a moment to lose. Jonathan Harker leaped up on the wagon and with a crow bar he picked up from the floor of the wagon, began to pry open the top. Another Englishmen was up on the wagon in a moment with him, madly pulling the top until it came off and fell to the side of the box with a clatter. What happened next, Natália would never forget.

With a deafening roar, a well of fire erupted from the box. Up into the sky a column of black smoke ascended, twisting and swirling like a dark tornado. The force of the blast knocked Jonathan and the other Englishman off the wagon to the ground, where they watched in amazement as the column reached up into the reddened sunset clouds high in the sky. And then it stopped and there was no sound except the blowing of a gust of mountain air through the Carpathians.

Mina was the first to react. "Jonathan" she cried as she ran to his side. He was stunned to see her there and hugged her tightly to him. Over her shoulder, though, he caught sight of Natália. His eyes went wide with even greater surprise.

"Oh no!" called out the other Englishman, "Dr. Seward! Come quickly!" Another Englishman rushed to where Quincy lay and put his fingers to the side of his neck and then bent his head to listen for breath sounds at Quincey's mouth. After a minute, Dr. Seward raised his head and then shook it from side to side.

"He's gone, I'm afraid," Dr. Steward said.

"Oh, Quincy," Jonathan said, choking back tears.

It turned out the man with the big knife was an American and a friend of Jonathan's as well as the other two, Arthur Holmwood and John Seward. Yet the sadness of the death of the young man could not diminish the joy Natália felt at the extinction of the monster who had been resting in the box. His cursed reign had come to an end. She climbed on to the wagon and looked into the box. Nothing remained of the Master except a pile of charred ashes and a few inches of dirt at the bottom of the box.

Chapter 70

About an hour after sunset, in the twilight, at the junction of the road to Bistritz, Kasza and Istvan arrived to a scene of fearful carnage. Dead horses and black clad Roma lay scattered about along with their weapons. It wasn't long before Istvan spotted Radu along with several officers of His Majesty's 123rd Regiment of Hungarian Hussars. Radu spurred his horse up to greet Istvan.

"What happened?" Istvan asked.

"We got your message and shortly after His Majesty arrived, I advised General Beck there was a Gypsy revolt in the mountains and you had requested help. He dispatched this squadron of cavalry and, no sooner did we reach the road here than we came across a bunch of them riding hell for leather toward the Bukovina. We hailed them but they refused to stop, so we gave chase. More of them kept coming up the road but as soon as they saw us, they started to race into the woods. The lieutenant, here, gave the order to fire and you can see that we hit quite a few of them. The rest of the squadron rounded up the others.

"Well done, Radu, but did you see another party come through? Some Slovaks with a leiterwagen and then a group of Englishmen giving chase? Headed up the road to the Borgo Pass?"

"No, my Lord," Radu responded. "They must have passed by before we got here. What happened to you?" Istvan spent the next five minutes describing the debacle by the river, their fortuitous discovery of the farm and horses and their chase up to this point. Radu was horrified to hear about the slaughter of the troopers.

"Serves them right, then," Radu said, waving his arm toward the scattered bodies of the Roma about the road. "I'll send a detachment back there to look for the men."

Istvan nodded. Just then, Istvan spotted a group of horses approaching from the direction of the Borgo Pass. As they came closer, Istvan recognized the lead rider was Van Helsing. Then Jonathan Harker with his wife and then a few more he did not recognize but assumed they were the other Englishmen he had seen from a distance from the woods. Then the Roma girl. What was she doing here? She led another horse with a blanket obviously covering a dead body that was laid across the back of the last horse. Van Helsing rode straight up to Istvan.

"He's dead! The murderous bastard is gone!" A number of officers from the cavalry ambled their horses over to listen to Van Helsing as he described the hunt for the three wives and then the slaying of Dracula himself, with the spectacular shaft of smoke.

"That's the most fantastic story I've ever heard," one of the Hungarian officers muttered in Magyar, while lighting a cigarette.

"Is he English?" another one said. "I can't place the accent."

"English for sure. Superstitious people, I hear. Believe in ghosts and all that sort of thing ..." the second one rejoined. Istvan's practiced ear detected their accents to be from Budapest. City boys, Istvan thought. He thought about reproving them but decided against it. It wasn't worth the effort.

A trio of hussars came next up the road. Some others lit torches as the twilight deepened as they stood guard over about a dozen Roma whose arms were tied behind their backs and were sitting in a circle on the ground. Three more prisoners with their hands bound behind their backs sat on the horses behind the cavalrymen. Istvan heard a woman's voice call out.

"Carlos!"

It was the young Roma woman he had met fleeing the castle months ago with Jonathan Harker. He watched as she ran up to the prisoner who dismounted one of the horses in the custody of one of the cavalrymen. She ran up to him but the rider would not let her come too close. Istvan watched as they spoke to one another.

"Good evening, Herr Kálváry," he heard from behind him. It was Jonathan Harker. Istvan was glad to see him and smiled broadly. They shook hands.

"I would like to introduce you to my wife, Mina," Jonathan said.

"Yes. We have met before. Mrs. Harker... I am so glad you're safe and...."

At that moment, Natália interrupted them.

"My Lord. I beg you a favor. This man, Carlos, is my husband," Natália began. It was a slight exaggeration, but she could think of no other way to put it. "He is not one of those in the Sinti tribe. We came here to bury his mother who died just a week ago. We were there when you and your men came into the village and Carlos was pressed to go with them. He could not refuse. He is not one of them ... one of us ..."

Istvan listened to her plea for her husband's life, considering what to do.

"You remember me, don't you?"

"Of course I remember ..."

"I helped you when you first came to the Borgo Pass, didn't I? I saved the life of Harker Jonathan, didn't I?" Natália shot Jonathan a look and he spoke up.

"Yes. You did. If it weren't for her, I would have died in that castle," Jonathan said.

"I beg you, my Lord," Natália continued. "Let me take Carlos away from here." She knelt down and kissed his hand, then looked up imploring him. Istvan remained silent for a moment. Then Van Helsing joined in.

"She helped us find the three wives, my Lord," Van Helsing volunteered. "She was indispensible in finding the lair of those three fiends. She has done as much as anyone to rid us of this vampire and his harem. She deserves to have one wish granted."

One less Gypsy would not be missed, Istvan considered. The girl had been one of the most valuable sources of information in bringing Dracula's curse to an end.

"All right, young lady," Istvan replied. Take him with you and leave this place. I give him into your custody on the condition that you leave Transylvania and never, ever come back here. Do you understand?"

"Yes, vezér," Natália responded with a smile, jumping to her feet. "Thank you, vezér. *Vislat*. And with that, Natália disappeared into the night with Carlos and was never seen again in Transylvania.

◉ ◉ ◉

"Well, Kasza, I think you have completed another successful case of serial murder," Istvan said as he, Kasza and Radu headed back to the Monastery. They would stay the night there and head back to Bistritz in the morning.

"Not exactly, Vezér," Kasza replied. "It was you who really closed the case."

"Nonsense," Istvan replied. "I intend to write a report to the RHG and your friend, Török Ferenc, and give you the credit. What do I need with honors at this point? I'm at the end of my career. You are at the beginning. Anyway, it really was you who got this investigation going and in the right direction, I might add."

"Thank you, my Lord. You are very generous."

"And you, Radu. I don't know how my predecessors did not notice you, but now you are second in command of Bistritz District and I am going to write the king and suggest you should be knighted for your work."

Radu was speechless.

As they approached the Monastery of Piatra Fantanele, darkness had descended. The few farmhouses they passed were cooking and smoke rose out of their chimneys, mixing with the smell of pines. He couldn't see it, but he knew that next to the doors of these farmhouses would be crosses or Madonnas nailed to the frames to ward off the evil spirits.

These peasant folk and their ancestors, who had been oppressed by the Count for four hundred years, were now free. They didn't know it yet but it didn't matter. Istvan knew it and that filled him with pride as the three of them ambled on down the road together. They could see the glow of lights from the many windows of the Monastery off in the distance. Beyond, the jagged darkness of the Carpathians, above which was a dark sky full of stars. A full moon was rising on the horizon, over the mountains and off in the distance, softly but distinctly, they heard the baying of a pack of wolves from somewhere in the forested mountains. Now they were just wolves, Istvan thought. And even they were free.

Epilogue

Kálváry Istvan, my grandfather, married Julianna, Baroness of Jelna, in the Spring of 1898 and remained Chef der Politzei in Bistritz until he retired in 1905. He and Julianna lived mainly in Budapest after his retirement until his death in 1913. Julianna's daughter, Ema, never recovered her sanity in the years following the death of Dracula and his wives. Tormented by nightmares and intrusive thoughts of her horrific confinement and torture in the cellars of the nightmare castle, she consulted Baron Krafft in Vienna for a time, but sadly committed suicide in 1919, after the Great War.

Gábor Kasza became the head of the Transylvanian Constabulary after his mentor, Török Ferenc, became the Director of the Royal Hungarian Gendarmerie. In the aftermath of the disastrous collapse of the Empire in 1918 and the Communist revolution in Budapest under Béla Kun, Kasza left Hungary for the United States. He settled in Pittsburgh where he learned the English language and eventually married an American woman. He is now an executive with US Steel and has two children.

Radu Popescu was knighted by His Apostolic Majesty, Franz Joseph, in 1898 at a glittering ceremony attended by his entire family and my grandfather at the Royal Palace in Budapest. He succeeded Kálváry Istvan as Chef der Politzei in Bistritz and then in 1911 became Inspector General of Transylvania until the end of the Great War in 1918. His keen intellect, patience and undeniable talent had allowed him to overcome his Wallachian (now Romanian) nationality in his career, which was no small feat in Royal

Hungary. When Transylvania was annexed to Romania after the War in 1919, his nationality became a virtue. His network of police connections proved invaluable to the new Romanian government. It has retained him in his position in Transyvania to this day. He remained personally loyal to my grandfather and was a pallbearer at his funeral in Budapest.

Carlos and Natália never returned to Bistritz or Transylvania. They settled in Amsterdam, where they had first met and where they had three children together. They found The Netherlands to be largely free of the hateful prejudice against the Roma that pervades most of the rest of Europe even to the present time. Nonetheless, when the opportunity arose to acquire a substantial plantation with the inheritance Carlos' mother left him, they emigrated to the Dutch West Indies and settled on the island of Sint Maarten in 1901 where, to my knowledge, they live to this day.

Jonathan Harker and his wife Mina returned to England where they had a son they named Quincy in 1898, in honor of their deceased American friend with the big Bowie knife. Tragically, Jonathan was killed in a Zeppelin raid in London during the War in 1916. Mina Harker and her son Quincy returned to Whitby where she had formerly lived before her marriage and became a schoolteacher.

In the late summer of 1897, Count Dracula Radu of Budapest ordered the complete destruction of the ruins of his family's castle at the Borgo Pass after hearing of the events there in the late summer of the previous year. He died childless in 1909 and with his death, after nearly 500 years, the house of Dracula became extinct in all respects.

Printed in Great Britain
by Amazon